THE COWBOY

and

THE COSSACK

THE COWBOY

and

THE COSSACK

by

Clair Huffaker

Thorndike Press • Thorndike, Maine

TBC

Library of Congress Cataloging in Publication Data:

Huffaker, Clair.
  The cowboy and the cossack.

  Originally published: New York, N.Y.:
Pocket Books, 1974, c1973.
  Published in large print.
  1. Large type books. I. Title.
[PS3558.U325C6 1982]   813'.54   82-10540
ISBN 0-89621-385-4

Large Print edition available through arrangement with Clair
Huffaker Company.

Cover design by Karen Trittipo.

FOR SAMANTHA CLAIR,
  WHO IS A COSSACK IN LOS ANGELES.
FOR IVAN IGOROVITCH,
  WHO IS A COWBOY IN LENINGRAD.
AND FOR A LADY NAMED BIG RED,
  WHO IS EVERYTHING, EVERYWHERE.

Oh, East is East, and West is West,
and never the twain shall meet,
Till Earth and Sky stand presently at
God's great Judgment Seat;
But there is neither East nor West,
border, nor breed, nor birth,
When two strong men stand face to face,
though they come from the ends
of the earth!
—RUDYARD KIPLING, "The Ballad of East and West," 1889

FROM THE DIARY
OF
LEVI DOUGHERTY
BORN 1861. DIED 1905.

R.I.P.

HERE LIES A GOOD FRIEND

Part One

HARD TIMES AT VLADIVOSTOK

Diary Notes

It's the spring of '80 on the coast of Siberia when our greasy-sack outfit first runs up against those cossacks. We establish instant hate for those fancy foreigners, which is reciprocated.

Various and sundry unlikely things come to pass, like getting our bunch of Montana longhorns drunk on Russian vodka, which I will try to honestly and faithfully relate, as much as is humanly possible.

1

I'd managed to limp up to the main deck of the *Great Eastern Queen* to stare off, squinting hard over her swaying wooden railing against the black horizon, hoping to see those first lights along the coastline of the far Siberian Gulf of Peter the Great. I was limping because a big yellow cow had stepped heavily on my foot where I was sleeping near the cattle down in the hold. And that's enough to make a fella wake up quickly, and maybe even mutter a few choice words of resentment.

Still in some agony, leaning over the rail looking off, my eyes were starting to be tearful from the foot hurting and from the cold, howling wind tearing at my face. Hundreds of handfuls of stars were tossed and scattered at random all over the sky, and some of the big ones were hanging so far down on the horizon you'd have sworn they were getting wet, way off over there, from the surging ocean spray.

"There," a low, strong voice said from behind me.

Shad had silently come up, and now he

hunched his broad shoulders on the railing beside me, shifted his tobacco, slowly chewing, and nodded so that his deeply creased black hat somehow pointed exactly where to look. I followed his steady gaze, frowning against the wind-made tears in my eyes, and finally made out that a couple of those low-lying stars were dim, distant, man-made lights.

"Yeah!"

And then Shad said one more word, very tightly and very hard.

"Russia."

The way he said it, I got a chilly feeling in my backbone that was more than the cold sea wind could account for. I looked at the lights again, and then back at him. "Well – hell, boss. After all this time at sea, any solid land ought t' look pretty damn good."

Old Keats came up then and joined us. "Look *pretty* good?" He pulled the collar of his sheepskin coat higher around his neck with his good hand and grinned, his teeth chattering briefly. "Me and five hundred cows and bulls have been seasick longer than any of us would care to remember. Anything without waves on it has to appear to be pure heaven right now."

Somebody had once pointed out that Old Keats's name was also the name of some English poet, and he tended to talk in fancy terms, so he'd gotten the part-time nickname of "The Poet." Maybe his bad left hand had something to do with that too. Old Keats could do wonders with that hand, except he couldn't lift it higher than his chest. And sometimes, when he got serious and was talking fancy, and went to waving that hand at chest level, it looked like he really was talking poetry, or even making a speech.

"There sure is somethin' out there!" I told him. "Shad just now spotted it!"

Old Keats stared ahead, his smile-crinkled eyes nearly closed. "Yes. That'll be the growing metropolis of Vladivostok."

Shad's voice still kept its tough edge. "All ten buildings of it — counting outhouses."

The lights were coming clearer and I said, "It looks t' me a little bit bigger than that."

Shad glanced down at my boot. "That yellow cow hurt your foot much?"

"No." I flexed my ankle to make sure. "It's okay."

Old Keats said, "We ought to be there in an hour or so, boss."

"Want me t' roust out the men?" I asked.

Shad looked off once more toward the lights that were now getting a feeling of inky black land hovering around them. He pulled his hat down against a gust of bitter wind. "Give them a few more minutes' sleep first. Then wake 'em."

He went across the swaying deck and up the ladder toward the captain's cabin, walking surely, with a cougar's instinctive movements and grace.

"That Shad" – Old Keats shook his head thoughtfully – "never gets thrown off balance. Never clumsy, never even gets seasick. I personally think that he believes this ship is nothing more than a big wooden horse, swaying and bucking and jumping all over the place. And he rides it just like one. Never misses a beat."

"Yeah," I said. "He don't never miss nothin'." I was the only one who could know about a cow stompin' on my foot in the dark down there. But he not only knew it happened, he even knew it was the old yella who done it! Seems t' me he's got eyes in the back a' that hard head of his, even when he's asleep."

"He's got a good eye." Old Keats held his sheepskin collar close around his neck. "But I think you'll see this country better than he does, Levi."

I turned and looked and still couldn't see much more than the few lights that were just vaguely beginning to separate themselves and the shadowed earth from the stars and the sky.

"You're crazy, Keats."

Old Keats leaned closer, seeming to gain warmth from my shoulder, or wanting perhaps to give warmth to me. He said very seriously, "A gigantic new land is ahead of us."

I shivered in the cold and dark. "That's for damn sure."

"We've a long way from Montana, with a far way yet to go." Old Keats hesitated. "For whatever reasons, Shad is going in there hostile, and therefore blind. And he will never see Russia, or Siberia, anymore than we can see it now. A few dim lights fighting in the distance against the dark."

"Well, now, if Shad can see my foot accidentally stomped on in a pitch-black hold, with a bunch of beeves jumpin' all around, and even know the stomper was that old yellow cow, that keen-eyed bastard can see anything."

"Not necessarily," Old Keats said. "There are many ways you can see things, aside from your eyes."

"I'd sure be interested t' know just how."

He touched me on the shoulder, swaying a little with the boat. "You know how else, Levi. A man can see with his mind, his spirit, his heart."

I grinned at him a little. "Ah, c'mon, Keats. You don't have t' live up t' that nickname."

17

"The Poet?" He stretched his bad hand just high enough to rub his lowered chin with the back of it. Then he looked back at the approaching lights of Vladivostok. "I'll prophesy you something, Levi." His gray eyes were level with the horizon and deadly serious. "We do have a long way to go." He hesitated. "And if we don't learn to see with lots more than our eyes, none of us will come out of that big country right-side up or alive."

2

Crab Smith was the first man I woke up when I got down to the dark forward hold. He was one of the few lucky cases who had a bunk. The others, like I'd been, were wrapped in their bedrolls on the floor, most of them using saddles for pillows. I scratched a match and lighted the kerosene lamp on the wall only a few inches from Crab's face, then turned it up bright.

"Jesus!" he muttered, blinking hard at the light. "Just what the hell d' you think you're doin'?"

"Time t' get up. We'll be there pretty soon."

"Good God. Don't this goddamn boat never get no place except in the goddamn middle a' the goddamn night?"

"C'mon, Crab. T'night's somethin' really special."

Slim was now awake in the bunk beneath Crab. "Hell, Levi, Russia ain't about t' disappear on us. It's been there a hundred years."

Some of the others were beginning to wake up now. Slim started to pull on his boots and said loudly, "Bust out, fellas! Your pleasant ocean voyage is comin' to an end!"

Slim, who was really a little on the heavy-set side, was sort of an assistant ramrod to Shad, and made ten bucks a month more than the rest of us. Like Shad, he could give an unpleasant order in such a way that it didn't sound too bad, and the men would do it without hardly thinking twice. Come to think of it, if a younger, kind of green kid like me had just gone down there and lighted the lamp and yelled "Get up!" I'd have more than likely been bruised and battered somewhat severely during the process.

Rufus Hooker stood up groggy and mad, his stomach hanging out over his belt. He rubbed his small dark eyes between his mass of matted black hair and scrubby beard.

"Damn hell!" he grumbled. "I just barely got

19

m'self t' sleep!"

"No one could ever guess it, Rufe," Slim said. "You wakin' up just now is a vision a' rare beauty."

But some of the others had the same kind of excitement jumping in them that I had. Sammy the Kid sat up near where I'd been sleeping beside the rope barrier separating us from the cattle starting to stir around in the main hold, where the yellow cow had stepped through the ropes onto my foot. "Hey!" he said. "Russia?"

"Unless the captain's made one hell of a mistake." Slim was now up and shrugging into his Mackinaw jacket.

Shiny Joe Jackson sat up and whacked his brother, Link, on the butt to rouse him. "Heard me, one time, that them Rooskies are all coal-black, an' got themselves horns."

Mushy Callahan was sitting up near Shiny, buttoning his shirt. "Just grow some horns an' you'll be right at home."

Shiny and a couple of the others grinned, and then Dixie Claybourne said, "That's bullshit, a' course. But I really damn well did hear that they skin their enemies an' tan their hides an' make tents out of 'em!"

"Hell," Link yawned, half awake now. "In that case me an' Shiny Joe oughta be worth a fortune betwixt us. If they like black tents."

Mushy grinned, now standing up and buttoning his pants. "The two of you'd look a lot better as a tent than you ever did in real life."

"Get your gear packed an' then come on up topside," Slim said. "It's about time you lazy seagoin' bastards started workin' as cowboys again, an' at least halfway earnin' your keep."

I went back on up with Slim, thinking of the men getting ready below. Thinking of the whole actually pretty fair outfit. What Old Keats had said about being right-side up, or maybe dead or alive and all, was still kind of on my mind.

The boss, Shad Northshield, always came to my mind first and most.

Maybe that was because after my parents died in the big blizzard of '65, he'd kind of naturally become like an older brother to me.

I was just four that hard wintertime in '65, and my Ma and Pa had frozen to death in the little cabin they'd built, both of them hugging each other in bed one night to fight off the awful, persistent cold. The reason I'd lived is that they were hugging each other with me in between them, to give me that last little bit of warmth they had in their lives.

Shad had found us, and pried their arms apart from around me. He'd put his head on my chest. And Old Keats, who was with him, described it one time to me later by telling me my heart "sounded like the hopeless, tiny wingbeats of an exhausted baby sparrow inside me trying to fly."

Shad sent Old Keats on to check the blizzard-stranded cows they'd been looking for. Then he ripped up some of the inner planks from the floor of the cabin. That was the only wood in miles that wasn't too frozen to burn. He built a fire, and not getting too close, he wrapped me in a blanket and hand-rubbed me for maybe twenty-four hours.

Then, finally, when my heart and breathing were stronger, he left me in the blanket by the fire and went out to dig graves for my Ma and Pa with a pick in the ice-hard ground.

Shad buried them there, and built fires over the newly loose ground to thaw it down. That way, with the earth melted, it would freeze over solid again, and wild animals couldn't get to them.

Old Keats came back late the next day to find him standing, kind of bent over, near the dying fires on the graves.

"The boy?" he said.

Shad looked up at him. "He'll be okay." And then, "The cows?"

"Froze."

Shad nodded slowly. "Everything out here'd

be dead if they hadn't kept that kid between 'em."

I guess it was then that Old Keats noticed Shad was standing there over those graves in that bitter gray, freezing late afternoon in his shirt sleeves.

Along with the blanket he'd wrapped me up in, he'd also put his coat on me.

When I came around, they'd brought me back to the nearest line shack on Joe Diamond's ranch, and Shad was forcing luke-warm water between my teeth with a beat-up tin spoon. Old Keats was standing quietly just off to one side near him.

I gagged a little on the water, and kind of looked around, and then first thing asked where my Ma and Pa was.

The answer was clear, but gently so, on Shad's face. And, somehow, he did a strange thing. To the best of my memory, he never really quite said they were dead, but instead he talked onward, toward the future. And because of that gentle way he had, they've never ever been truly dead in my mind, even to this day.

He told me to try a little more water because it was good for me. And then he said that, me being a young man already, he'd get me a job milking cows and chopping firewood and such at the main ranch house. And since he'd told me, in just that certain way that he did, that I was now a "young man," I could only cry a little bit about my folks. But they were good tears.

And then I worked a lot and grew up some, and that was the way it was.

Right now Shad was pushing close to forty, or maybe he was even over the hill there. In any case Slim and Old Keats were the only ones among the fifteen of us who were older than him. Shad had shoulders that were about an ax handle wide and he stood over six foot high, with no gut at all and a minimum of butt, which is about as good a way for a man to be built as any. As far as his face was concerned, he had more than his share of nicks and scars from run-ins with men, beasts and violent acts of God. But you had to look close to see those marks because a lot of rain and wind and snow and sun had covered them over into one tough, not too ugly looking, but damn well used face. He had light-blue eyes that could nail you like twin iron spikes if he was mad about something, which was fairly common. Shad never grew a beard, like a lot of the older fellas used to do, but favored the sloping longhorn mustache, which drooped slightly down around the edges of his mouth toward his rocklike jaw.

But the main thing about Shad was a rare

kind of a strong inner quality that stuck out like a sore thumb. He was a natural-born man and also a natural-born boss. I guarantee that if Shad had been a new private in Napoleon's army, and Napoleon was figuring out his next attack and happened to see Shad standing there, he'd have just naturally had to go over to Shad and say, "What do you think?" And I double guarantee that whatever Shad told him would have been smart enough to get him put on Napoleon's general staff. And if that staff didn't happen to go along with him, he'd have had those poor bastards shaking in their boots in no time. He was purely tougher than a spike. And yet, hard as he was, Shad never asked anything from any man that he wasn't willing to give twice back.

Funny thing too that was part of Shad's quality. He was as good or better than any of the rest of us at the things we were best at. Like Old Keats, hands down, was the wisest and best-read man in the outfit. For example, with an eye toward coming here, he'd even managed to teach himself a little of the language from a pocket-size book on Russian he carried. But Shad generally had a wisdom that matched Old Keats's. Chakko, an Indian gone white, was the best tracker and runner and reader of signs, but Shad was just as good.

Among men raised on horses, Natcho was probably the best rider, but Shad could move any horse any direction on a dime and give you change. I was the only one who'd finished McGuffey's Reader, but Shad could read and write and add and subtract as well as me. Maybe even better, because he had one hell of a head for learning. And Big Yawn, born somewhere in Poland, was far and away the strongest of us. But the one time he and Shad went to Indian rassling it lasted for nearly twenty sweating, muscle-crushing minutes, and finally turned out to be a Mexican standoff.

If there was one bad thing about Shad, it was that once he got his head set on something, that tended to be it. You might say he was a little stubborn. Or, as Old Keats once said, "If Shad made up his mind and him and a giant longhorn bull ran head on to each other, the bull'd get knocked ass over teakettle."

I know I'm going on a long time about Shad. But there's a joyful, and sad, and good reason. And you'll understand why. In time.

Right now, Slim and I got to the main deck, where the *Great Eastern Queen* was pitching around worse than before in the tossing, white-capped seas. Vladivostok was getting closer and by now you could make out a couple of long wooden wharfs set up on pilings that jutted out into the Gulf of Saint Peter with big, dark waves crashing angrily against them. Beyond the wharfs, on the land, clusters of small buildings could be seen, lights glinting dimly through their windows. At the end of the closer wharf, a man was waving some message with a couple of lamps, and up near the bow of the *Queen* a signalman with lamps was answering him back.

"C'mere!" Old Keats yelled from the railing, and when we got to him he pointed at a small boat approaching the side of the ship through the waves, four men pulling strongly on the oars and a fifth, who seemed to be in charge, holding the tiller.

"Russia's reception committee," Old Keats murmured quietly, holding on to the railing for his balance. "Just on general principle, I sure hope they're friendly."

"Hell, Keats, why shouldn't they be?" Slim grinned. "We're bringin' 'em the only good cattle this godforsaken place ever had!"

Three crewmen broke open a nearby gate in the railing and rolled a rope ladder out so that its far end fell down to the waves below. Our other cowhands were coming up onto the main deck now, some of them struggling with their gear. Shad and the captain of the *Queen*, a short heavy-set Scotsman named Barum, came down from the bridge at about the same time.

The man holding the tiller in the small boat got a grip on the rope ladder and started climbing, a couple of the others behind him. When he got to the top, Captain Barum gave him a hand up onto the deck and he stood there for a minute, looking us over in a not too friendly fashion and catching his breath as the other two came up behind him. He was middle-sized, with a lot more fat than muscle on him, and most of his forehead seemed to be a mass of thick brown eyebrows. He was wearing a heavy, long brown coat and a little brown cap that had a little shiny gold medal on it. I guess it was some kind of a naval uniform.

"I'm Captain Barum," the captain said. "And this is Mr. Shad Northshield. He'll be disembarking here tonight with his fourteen men and five hundred and thirty-six animals. And their baggage, of course."

Shad said curtly, "Tell him, we're in a hurry to get docked so we can get unloaded."

The Russian frowned at Shad and he spoke to the captain in a guttural, harsh voice, with an accent you could have cut with a dull ax. "I am Harbor Master Yakolev. I know nothing of all these men and animals."

"That's what we're telling you about now," Shad said, an ominously hard edge to his voice.

Yakolev glared at him. "What travel permission is it you have? Letters from immigration authority, passports?"

"Goddamn," Slim whispered grimly to me and Old Keats, "I knew we'd forget somethin'. Ain't one a' all them five hundred longhorns got no passport."

But Shad was already handing the Harbor Master a thick envelope. "Our Sea Papers," he said levelly. "From Seattle through the port of Vladivostok. Okayed by the U.S.A. and by your Russian Consulate." Then, as the man opened the envelope, he added flatly, "If you can read it, Yakolev."

In terms of establishing a long-time friendship, Shad wasn't making, or trying too hard to make, a whole lot of points. Yakolev glowered at him and then started to read the Sea Papers by the light of a lamp hanging from a roughly paneled bulkhead near him.

At last he said, "What's this?" Which the way he talked sounded more like "Wawssis?" but it was getting so I could pretty much tell what he meant.

"What's what?" Shad said.

"This — this Slash-Diamond?"

"That's the brand on our cattle and horses. Just in case some of you Russians should get a mind t' try t' steal some of 'em."

29

"Mr. Northshield doesn't mean to say —" Captain Barum started uneasily.

But Yakolev silenced him with a raised hand and spoke to Shad in a high, angry voice. "I know the reason there is of branding! Under our most gracious Tzar, my friend, when a man does not behave just properly, here, that man himself is sometimes branded." He smiled, but his smile looked more like he was about to bite something. "Your nation does not put you, or your men, outside our — our sometimes very strict laws."

"We didn't think t' bring a lawyer," Shad said. "Just check our papers."

Yakolev, his face tight, studied them for a long, silent time, finally flipping them back and forth aimlessly.

"All right, Yakolev," Shad said impatiently, "you can't find one damn thing wrong with those papers, so stop wasting our time and let's get this ship docked."

But Yakolev, more hostile than ever, was now going to take all the time he could. "Levi Dougherty!" he suddenly said loudly, reading the name off the Sea Papers.

"Yeah?" I stepped forward curiously.

"Is not Levi, it's a Jewish name?"

"I don't know."

"Where did it come from?"

"Well" — this was getting to be kind of em-

30

barrassing because it wasn't a generally known fact — "I was named after a pair of pants."

There were snickers from a couple of the men behind me, and without turning I said quietly, "Anybody who don't like those pants ain't a real American."

Yakolev scratched one of his hugely bushy eyebrows. "Tell more," he said suspiciously.

"The pants're called Levi-Strauss. Ma wanted Levi an' Pa wanted Strauss. Ma won." Somebody, I think it was Dixie, chuckled from behind again, and I was starting to get mad anyway. "I like the name whether it's Jewish or a pair a' britches or anything else!"

Yakolev wasn't about to let it go at that. "There are certain areas of Imperial Russia," he said coldly, "where Jews are not welcome, or safe."

"For Christ's sake," Slim said, starting to be as impatient as Shad. "How can anybody hold anything against a pair a' Levi's?"

"This is going to take much time," Yakolev said. "Captain, you will bring a table and chair."

Shad stepped forward. "Those papers clear me and my men into Russia. What is all this bullshit?"

"Bullshit? What's this?" Yakolev said, making it sound like "Vullssit? Vawsis?"

Captain Barum said anxiously. "My sailing schedule and the tides don't allow me more than a few hours here."

Yakolev suddenly turned viciously ugly. *"I am Harbor Master! I say a table and a chair!"*

"Drop anchor!" Captain Barum bellowed to the men up forward. Then, resentfully, "Get a table and chair for the − Harbor Master."

A couple of crewmen went to get them, and Old Keats said quietly, "Our Russian friend's decided to try any way he can not to let us go ashore."

Crab nodded. "He was out of joint in the first place, and then Shad's bullheadedness really got to 'im."

"What I think," Slim said, "the sonofabitch is looking for some kind of a handout."

I went over to where Shad and Captain Barum were and said to Shad in a low voice, "Maybe the sonofabitch is lookin' for some kind of a handout."

"That's helped before when I've put in here." The captain rubbed his nose thoughtfully. "All these goddamn Russian officials think they're little tzars."

"No," Shad said.

"We've come clear out here to the end of the world, Shad." I took a deep breath, knowing how he felt. "Don't you think we oughtta go by

32

whatever their rules are just this once?"

He spit some tobacco over the railing. "Goes against the grain."

For at least an hour now everything went against the grain. Yakolev, with maddening slowness, asked all the men endless and stupid questions. Shad was tensely ready to bite a nail in half, and Captain Barum was getting more and more edgy, taking his pocket watch out every little while to see how many minutes had gone by.

The only good thing I can remember about that time was that we learned a few things about each other's names that wouldn't normally come up in any cowhand's conversation. They had told us when we got on the *Queen* in Seattle to be careful to put our real names down or we could be sent back. And it turned out, for example, as Yakolev read the Sea Papers, that old Purse Mayhew was actually named Percival.

After Yakolev got through talking to him, and we'd made a few casual remarks, he told us with some small resentment, "The name Percival is perfectly normal in England!"

Rufus said, "Sure, Percival."

Link put his hand on Purse's shoulder. "No need for explainin'. We think Percival's real sweet, Percival."

The next name that Yakolev called out was "Lincoln Washington Jefferson Jackson!"

"My God," Purse got back at Link, saying, "you're the only nigger ever elected President four times."

But under the circumstances we weren't really in too funny a mood, so nothing we said was overly hilarious.

Big Yawn's name was Jan Oblensky, but his first name happened to be pronounced the same as yawn. Dixie Claybourne was really Dick C. Claybourne. Chakko had a hard time until Shad stepped in and explained through gritted teeth that he was an Ogallala Sioux and he only had one name, which meant "The Silent One," and he didn't like to talk to strangers. Old Keats's first name was William, which nobody had ever known. Mushy Callahan was really Mushy. Natcho was just a normal Mexican nickname for Ignacio Rodriguez. Slim's actual first names were Leroy Eugene Cecil, which were so bad it would have been almost criminal to take advantage of them. And Crab Smith could have been a honey to kid, because his first name, which was a subject of grouchy, secret concern to him, was Jehovah. But by the time Crab's name came up we were all too mad at Yakolev to pretend any kind of a sense of humor.

And then Yakolev called a name that sure as hell threw me.

"Marvin Samuel Shapiro!"

A bunch of us looked at each other, kind of puzzled, and then Sammy the Kid stepped forward.

"That's me," he said.

"This name is Jewish," Yakolev said, saying it so it sounded like "Ziss name's Hooish." But I don't even want to bother about the way he talked anymore.

"You're damn right it's Jewish," Sammy said. "And so am I."

"Then you admit it!" Yakolev seemed pleased at finally finding a name he could, in his own mind, legitimately find some fault with. He repeated it, shaking his head. "Marvin Samuel Shapiro. For your own safety, I cannot allow you into Russia."

Shad had been just about ready to fight for some time, and now he leaned forward, knuckles down, on the table where Yakolev was sitting. His voice was low. "These men have all been given clearance by my country and by your consulate. With these papers, you cannot refuse us entrance."

Yakolev raised his hands up in mock concern. "But I cannot, in my small authority, guarantee this man's safety."

"I'll take my chances with my friends," Sam my said.

"You can't guarantee *any safety* for *any* of us!" Shad stood back from the table, his jaw muscles tight and hard. "We're taking our cattle over a thousand miles into Russia, and your 'small authority' won't last half a mile out of Vladivostok."

"But I do rule here." Yakolev smiled his smile that looked like he was ready to bite something. "Perhaps if we talked about it privately."

Shad leaned on the table again. Now his voice was not only low, but deadly. "I will not pay you one goddamn penny, mister!"

Yakolev said quickly, "I did not suggest that!"

Shad tensed forward, like a mountain lion about to spring. "Those Sea Papers *are* in order."

"Yes." Yakolev stood nervously, moving away from the table to where his two men were waiting near the railing. "The papers are in order. Your men and animals can enter the port of Vladivostok and go into Russia."

"Good," Captain Barum said relieved. "We'll arrange to dock immediately."

Yakolev started toward the rope ladder, then turned back before he answered. "I'm afraid that's impossible." He looked at Shad, his eyes malicious under those two thick eyebrows. "As Harbor Master, you have my permission to enter — sometime." Then he looked at the captain. "In my judgment, the bad seas are too heavy for you to put in tonight. Serious damage could happen in docking, to your ship and my wharf. Perhaps tomorrow — or the next day."

"I can't wait until tomorrow!" Captain Barum protested.

"It may be many days, or weeks." Yakolev rubbed a thick eyebrow.

"You know I can't wait here indefinitely!"

Yakolev raised his shoulders helplessly. "That is your decision, Captain." Then he turned quickly and hurried down the ladder, his two men following.

There was a long silence as Yakolev's men rowed away from the *Great Eastern Queen*. Finally Shad said, "Could you dock your ship in there all right, Captain?"

Barum nodded, his face grim. "Certainly I could. But not without his permission."

"What the hell we gonna do now, boss?" Slim asked.

"There's only one thing you can do," Captain Barum said. "I'll take you back to Japan on the *Queen* — no extra tariff. And you can make whatever plans about your cattle and getting back to America from there."

"Our outfit's been paid t' deliver a herd a' longhorns a thousand miles into Siberia," Shad said quietly, "and we're gonna deliver 'em."

"I tell you I can't put ashore!" Captain Barum's voice showed how bad he felt about the whole thing.

"I know you can't put the *Queen* ashore," Shad said. Then one side of his mouth muscled very slightly in the half grin, half frown he showed sometimes when he was thinking. "But we can get our longhorns onto the beach just outside town."

"How?" I asked. "Us and five hundred head gonna fly?"

"No." He turned to me. "But if any of our men or cattle haven't learned how t' swim, they damn well better learn fast when they hit that water."

3

Personally, I wasn't all too keen about getting into that black surging water in the middle of the night and swimming to a shore you couldn't even see from where we were. But when Shad called the men on deck together and told them about jumping off the ship, I seemed overjoyed compared to some of the others.

"Water is only to drink," Big Yawn said with heavy finality, "not t' get in."

"Ain't never swam a stroke in m' life," Rufus Hooker muttered. "Wouldn't be much good t' anybody if I wuz drowned an' dead."

"This is the way it's gonna be," Shad said. "Barum's men'll row our supplies ashore in small boats. Any man afraid of the water can go with 'em. But we'll need about every hand we can get t' drive those cattle t' land through the dark."

"But Christ, boss," Rufus complained, "if a fella can't swim – "

"You'll be on horseback, Rufe, and your horse can swim," Shad told him. "Just don't let

Bobtail's nose or eyes go under water, and don't let him turn belly-up under you. Either way he'll panic and likely kick your head off. And if you do get unseated, grab ahold of his tail and he'll pull you to shore."

Rufus thought about this, frowning sadly.

Crab Smith took off his hat and scratched his head. "We'd follow you most damn anywhere, Shad, but I doubt if more'n half of us can swim more'n a doggy paddle. The water's ice-cold an' black as hell, and the idea of goin' into it just plain scares me shitless! Maybe you ain't scared of it, but — " His voice trailed off.

"I know it's spooky." There was a quiet understanding in Shad's voice. "So take a boat, Crab."

Sammy the Kid said flatly, "I don't know about him, but I'm damn well takin' a boat, and that's that."

Shad nodded slightly. "No fault taken, Kid. So be it."

I had a sneaking hunch that Slim already knew the answer to the question he asked Shad now. "Can you swim, boss?"

Shad shook his head just once. "No."

"Well, that's sure good enough for me," Slim said. "I ain't about t' take no boat then if you ain't." He turned to Crab. "Hell, we're both at least a year past due for a bath anyhow."

Crab put his hat back on. "Okay, Shad," he said unhappily, "I'll go. But I still don't like it."

Sammy the Kid turned and went over to the railing, his back to the rest of us.

Shiny Joe called out, "Link an' me can swim like catfish. We can keep an eye out f'r Crab an' some a' them who can't."

Natcho was sitting in the chair that Yakolev had been using. He looked up now and smiled, his gleaming white teeth brilliant in contrast to his deeply tanned face and blue-black hair. "In Tampico I learned to swim before I could walk. And Chakko here is a strong swimmer too."

Chakko nodded.

"With luck maybe we can make shore," Old Keats said. "The thing I'm worried about is the cold. There's still chunks of ice in that water. And it's a good three-hundred-yard haul. A man could freeze."

"I'll be the first one in, and I'll let you know if it can be stood," Shad said. "Doubt it'll kill us. But my guess is it'll be invigoratin' as hell."

"Now that you got us humans convinced about how much sheer fun this swim is gonna be," Slim said, "What I'm wonderin' is, just how're we gonna convince them longhorns t' join along with us too?"

"After bein' cooped up so long, a lot of

them'll likely dive for the first openin' they get a chance at."

"An' the ones that don't make that choice?" Old Keats asked.

"We'll use gentle persuasion — and fire."

Forty minutes later we were down in the main hold about ready to go.

Following Shad's orders, half a dozen of Captain Barum's crew were now forcing open an old, unused sea door on this lower deck where we could drive the cattle out from where they were milling and bawling in the big hold. It was only about a five-foot drop from this sea door to the pitching waterline below, so they wouldn't bang each other up too much jumping out. That is, if Shad was right about us getting them to jump in the first place.

We'd lighted enough lamps to be able to see a little bit in this big, swaying place and with the cattle now getting nervous, grumbling throatily and bumping each other around restlessly on the heavy plank floor, there were all kinds of funny, deep noises and wild, flickering shadows wherever you looked. Our thirty-horse remuda and the pack mules had made the trip at one end of the hold, separated from the longhorns by a rough partition of nailed-up two-by-fours. All of us, except for Sammy the Kid, who had stood pat about taking a boat, had saddled our best horses and led them through the cattle up to near the sea door. Even Big Yawn had decided to ride ashore. It was the first time I'd ever known him to change his mind. He still looked pretty grim, but I guess most everyone else deciding to go had kind of shamed him into it.

Crab Smith, wetting his own lips uneasily, said to Big Yawn, "You look as edgy as a whore in church."

Upon occasion Big Yawn did manage to have a way with words. On this occasion he said shortly, "Fuck you and the horse you rode up on."

The sailors, working with sledges and crowbars, and swearing a lot, now got the rusted sea door sliding with an agonizing sound, and it slid all the way it would go, making an opening about twelve feet wide.

And, as the door grated open, looking out at that black, surging ocean just below gave a man one damn fearful feeling. I'd once swam across a twenty-foot-wide pond. But those ugly, dark waters pitching around in that inky night looked like their only use was for men to drown in.

Big Yawn swallowed hard. "How – how deep ya' think it is?"

"Hell," Slim said, trying without too much

success to be cheerful, "maybe a mile. Maybe only half a mile. Who knows?"

"There's one thing for sure," Old Keats said gloomily, "it's too damn deep t' wade across."

A couple of lights farther out from the town could be dimly seen on the shore, but right now they looked about a hundred miles away.

"Bring up Old Fooler," Shad said.

Old Fooler was one of the great lead steers ever born. If those longhorns would follow anything it would be that huge black ox with one four-foot-long horn raised up normally and the other dipped down. There seemed to be something irresistible about that gigantic butt of his that usually made the others just plain follow it regardless of wherever he went.

Mushy and Rufe put a lead halter on Old Fooler and he came up to the sea door easy enough. But once he took his first look out, Old Fooler decided that was as far as he was going.

Shad was looking across the water. The first of the *Queen's* small boats carrying our supplies was already being rowed toward the shore, about two hundred feet from the ship. There was a lantern raised on the boat that gave us a closer light to steer by.

"Get ready t' push 'im overboard," Shad said. Then he swung up aboard Red, his big strawberry-roan stallion. After two months at sea, Red shied under the unfamiliar weight on the shifting deck, but finally got all his legs under him. Shad put the noose of his lariat around Old Fooler's neck, leaving plenty of slack in the rope. Then he spurred Red forward. But Red wasn't at all interested in going either, and he did a little bucking dance instead, rearing back away from the sea door. Shad, who knew horses better than they knew themselves, let Red get away with this. He not only let him back off, but turned Red around as though they were in agreement and were now going to ride in the other direction. Then, still holding the reins in his left hand, he put his right hand over Red's eyes so the big stallion couldn't see, and he kept turning Red until they were again aimed at the sea door. Then Shad spurred the turned-around stallion fiercely and let go with a deafening cowboy yell that must have rocked the buildings in Vladivostok.

"Ahhhhhhh-hawwwwww-YIGH!" he bellowed, and Red flew forward. That big roan must have sailed twenty feet out of the sea door before gravity took its natural course and Red realized he'd been double-crossed. But by then it was too late. They both damnere went under in a spray of white foam against the black water, and then they were bobbing up, Red

swimming frantically and the rope around spraddle-legged, defiant Old Fooler's neck tight as a bowstring.

But tight as the rope was, not one ounce of Old Fooler's two thousand pounds was planning on going anyplace.

"Push the bastard!" Slim yelled, and seven or eight of us crowded around Old Fooler, heaving with all our weight. I think what turned the tables was Slim's pocketknife. Along with pushing, Slim stabbed Old Fooler in the rear. Not where it would do him permanent damage, but it still must have hurt like hell. The big black bull let out a bellow that damnere matched Shad's cowboy yell and leaped high into the air in the general direction Slim wanted him to go. And when he came down, he was in the Gulf of Peter the Great, complaining loudly and splashing all over the place.

And, as Shad had thought it would, that kind of broke the ice with the others.

"Look out!" Slim yelled, and we jumped back from the sea door as probably the only stampede of longhorns on a ship ever recorded in naval history began. There must have been three hundred cows and bulls that suddenly realized, after two months of imprisonment, that there was a way out. Once Old Fooler had unintentionally led the way, they couldn't have cared less if they were jumping off Pikes Peak, as long as they were getting out of that hold.

We were lucky not to get crushed in the wild mass exit.

And then suddenly, like a snap of the fingers, the stampede stopped in midstream. Longhorns are sort of like people, I guess. They don't know what the hell they're doing either most of the time. A big spotted cow with a yearling calf gave a terrified bawl and skidded to a halt at the sea door.

Evidently taking her word about something being wrong up front, the two hundred or so head behind her slammed on their brakes and now wouldn't be budged.

So this is when we used Shad's "fire."

"Levi!" Slim yelled. "Link, Rufe! Crab! Stay with me and light those torches. The rest of you hit the water!" Old Keats and Mushy were the first two mounted and out. The horses didn't really like the idea, but so many cattle had dived out by then that it must have started to seem like the natural thing to do. Natcho's big black didn't argue at all. Chakko, Dixie and Purse went next. And finally Shiny Joe and Big Yawn. Big Yawn was so scared his hands were shaking even before he got aboard his horse.

"Shiny," Slim said, "stick close t' Big Yawn!"

And then they were both gone, in almost one gigantic splash.

I'd already lighted a torch, and we were now lighting others from it. When we all had one or two torches apiece, we ran to the far side of the hold and started yelling our lungs out and scaring the hell out of the cattle with the flaming torches. Slim was up by the spotted cow who'd stopped the first stampede. He picked up her calf and threw it overboard. She must have been mad about it, but this was no time to argue. Bawling wildly, she went after her baby like a shot. And, terrified by our yells and waving torches, the others started to follow. One mean-looking dun bull lowered his head five feet away to charge right at me, so without thinking about it I burned him a quick, good one on the nose with the torch and, luckily, he changed his mind and charged the other direction instead.

I guess that ocean water must have cooled his nose off pretty fast.

I know damn well that about two minutes later it cooled me off fast. The rest of the remuda and the pack mules followed the longhorns, and when the last big balky mule got to the sea door, Slim whacked him on the tail with his torch and yelled, "Abandon ship, goddammit!" And an instant later they were all gone.

"We're bringin' up the rear, so carry your torches!" Slim said, swinging up onto Charlie, his calico stud. He went over and when he came up, still holding his torch, he yelled in a strange, choked voice, "Come on in! The water's fine!"

I got aboard Buck, who was, naturally, a buckskin, and who was as nervous as I was. But when I pushed him toward the edge, he went right on over, out and down without even looking back.

And great, holy *God* was it cold! It was already kind of cold because we'd all sent our warm jackets on the small boats. But now ten thousand wet, tiny icicles plunged paralyzingly into every pore of every part of my skin, through shirt and pants and even boots. It was colder right then than any time I can remember, even including the time Ma and Pa froze to death around me. Just the shock of it alone was so much I couldn't even try to get my breathing going for a while.

Slim was a few yards to my right, waving his torch and yelling, steering the cattle in front of us toward the shore. Looking at me he called, "Yell out, Levi! Holler! It'll start your breath goin'!"

"*Yowwwwwwww!*" I put all my lungs into it. "Shad was right about it bein' refreshin'!"

Slim called.

I could yell back by now. "Sure takes your mind off drownin'!"

Crab was on my left, holding his torch high. All he could manage through clenched teeth was a loud, chattering *"Jesus!"*

"Steer 'em!" Slim bellowed. "Keep pushin' 'em in!"

And then, in those freezing, heaving black seas, we lost one of the herd. A mud-colored cow with only one horn was about twenty feet ahead of me. For no understandable reason, she suddenly turned around toward me and started swimming back in the other direction. It sounds silly, but for a minute I had the awful feeling that she thought she'd left something behind on the ship. *"Hey!"* I yelled, waving the torch toward her. *"Back!"*

Her eyes were glazed over, and I don't think she was even aware of the torch or my shouts. She started to go under, but then swimming frantically she raised her nose up among the rough waves for one last pathetic half of a wheezing breath. And then she sank like a rock.

I dropped my torch and grabbed for her, which was pretty ridiculous, but didn't seem like it at the time. As the torch sputtered out in the water beside me, I caught one of her soft, water-soaked ears for a brief moment, and then it slipped out of my hand as the cow went down below into the dark, icy sea.

"Let go!" Slim was already bellowing. "You're pullin' your horse off balance!"

Somehow, cold and frozen and scared as I was, I was damnere ready to cry. And maybe even did, a little.

That poor damn cow!

I couldn't quite get all of my broken feelings for her in place. But it was just so sad for her to die alone and helpless out here in this black, terrifying water. So damn sad for her to die like that, way off at the end of the world where she'd sure as hell never asked to come. To die stunned and frozen, and not understanding it at all, in this unknown place, while she was trying blindly and so desperately to somehow struggle back home.

We were probably not in the water much more than half an hour, but it seemed closer to a hundred years of Sundays. Toward the end, up ahead, Purse lost his seat on Vixen somehow. But he managed to grab the saddle, and then the mare's tail as she went by, and she pulled him in all right. Along the way, Purse didn't have much chance that night to help a speckled bull. It got its horns caught in a huge bunch of seaweed. And the seaweed came up afterward but the bull didn't. Natcho's black Diablo turned over under him and started kicking and thrashing like hell. Natcho just got out of the way and the two of them swam along onto the beach together.

Finally, with both my hands almost frozen stiff around his reins, Buck's feet touched ground, and he just walked up through the water to the shore as calmly as if this kind of a cattle drive was an everyday, or every night, experience for him.

We were a little ways away from town here, and Sammy, who had been in the first boat, had already got a giant bonfire started on the beach. There'd been key gear on that first boat to hopefully keep us from freezing solid, including kerosene, and Sammy had poured a lot of that over a big pile of driftwood he'd gathered and struck a match to it.

"My God!" Rufe stuttered, almost falling off Bobtail. "That fire looks like the pot a' gold at the end a' the rainbow!"

As we came ashore we all headed straight for it.

Except for the sailors bringing more of our supplies from the boats up onto the beach, Sammy the Kid was the only dry one there. He'd already pounded stakes into the ground near the fire and strung a lariat between them to fix a handy rope hitch for our horses. And now he was keeping himself busy handing out dry shirts and britches and socks to us from our gear so we could change into them, and then passing out our jackets as soon as he could find them. But while he was doing it, he wasn't looking any of us in the eye too much, and wasn't saying anything.

He handed Dixie Claybourne's rawhide jacket to him and Dixie was just barely thawed out enough to say, "How was that boat trip Sammy?" Dixie had a way of saying things, sometimes, so that you didn't know if they were as mean as they sounded or not. But Sammy looked like he'd been slapped, and pretty hard at that.

"Well," Dixie kept on, "was it tough?"

"In case you didn't know it, Dixie," Shad said quietly, "we needed one man to take the first boat. And, all things equal, I elected the Kid."

"Sure." Dixie shrugged. "If you say so, boss."

"I wanted someone here t' start settin' things up for the rest of us. If not him, somebody else." Shad's tone hardened a little. "Maybe you." When Shad spoke this way, Dixie was smart enough not to answer too fast. He was thinking for some kind of an answer when Slim grinned, buttoning up his dry shirt with still-shaking hands.

"Hell, I wish it'd been me, boss. Right now my ass is froze damnere completely off!"

Shad turned to Sammy. "Break out the bourbon ya' got over there. If Slim froze his ass off, it'd be the biggest loss our outfit ever suffered."

There was some easy laughter from all around now, but everybody knew just exactly what had actually happened. It's kind of complicated, but it's honest-to-God true. Dixie had insulted Sammy the Kid, who was sure as hell feeling bad enough already. Shad, knowing the way the youngster felt, had protectively taken his side. Dixie had tried to back down, but his own pride had got in his way and wouldn't let him really back off altogether, or in an easygoing fashion. That kind of pride Dixie had, starting out with needlessly hurting the Kid, was a false pride, and Shad nailed him for it on the spot. Dixie was caught in a bind, and Slim came to the rescue of the situation by saying something for everyone's benefit that was kind of funny. Shad picked up on that and decided to let it go by saying something back to Slim even funnier, and at the same time getting us the bourbon he'd had brought in on the first boat.

I can guarantee the above is almost exactly accurate, because Old Keats brought it up to me a few minutes later, while we were all drinking tin cups of bourbon, the two of us standing a little apart from the others. "Strange thing, Levi," he said, raising his cup to drink with his good right hand. "There is no parliament, no congress, where the men can know each other so completely and well as men know each other who do hard daily work, sometimes dangerous work, together. No, not even the classic ancient Greek or Roman Senates."

"Well, I guess that's fair enough." The drink was starting to warm and help my gut the way the fire was helping my right side, at the angle I was standing to it.

"Like what just happened before." Keats sipped from his cup again. "Poor old Dixie lost."

"Well, he shouldn't have pushed Sammy."

"But don't you see, we all knew he was weaker, for having picked on Sammy's weaknesses?"

"Sure. Sort of."

"Give me a little more." Keats put out his cup and I poured from a bottle that was near us on a rock near the fire. "That's damn good," he said, tasting thoughtfully. "Jack Daniel's, Distillery No. 1, 1866. Great bourbon."

I looked at the bottle in the light of the fire and said, "Goddamn! You're right. You're a damn good guesser!"

"That wasn't such a good guess. It was a truth based on knowledge, which in turn was based on many years of happy and often heavy drinking."

"Oh, t' hell with you, that's really somethin'!" Despite still being chilled by the cold, I couldn't hold back a kind of genuine enthusiasm. "T' even guess the *year* you gotta be smarter'n hell!"

He raised his shoulders slightly, dismissing this. "I was talking to you about weakness before. And the strongest man I was thinking about has the greatest weakness."

"Who?"

He said quietly, "Shad."

"You shouldn't talk about Shad an' bein' weak in the same breath!" I said angrily.

He gestured with his left hand, raising it as high as he could, to about chest level. "I love the sonofabitch as much as you do, Levi, and I've even got a few more years of seniority there than you. But his great strength is what makes his greatest damn weakness. He's too strong to change his mind. Too strong to see something from someone else's point of view."

I had flared up before, but one thing both Shad and Old Keats had taught me was to always try to calm down, and I did my level best now. I took a deep breath. "Old Keats, sir, Shad can do anything!"

Keats took another drink, a long one, and looked at me with eyes as sober as two iron spikes driven into a railroad tie. "This deals with what I told you before about seein' or not seein' this giant land." His bad left hand came up and pointed at me again, in a tough but still friendly gesture. "Sometimes it's hard t' know, or to ever properly establish, Levi. But all of us, always and always, find in this world exactly what we set out t' give to it."

I started hard back at him, trying to make my eyes like iron spikes too. "Well, what the hell, then! Shad always gives everything!" My own iron spikes were starting to melt already, because there was no way for me to stay mad for long at Old Keats.

Keats now lowered his eyes for a moment, then nodded. "He always has – up – until comin' here t' this damn Russia. But he's got a hate for it that he may get back times ten." He put his cup down and started rubbing his hands together. "By God, the blood's startin' to flow again. We just may live for a while longer, after all."

"Hey, boss!" Sammy the Kid yelled from off on the other side of the fire where he'd been helping the sailors finish unloading our supplies. "Everything's ashore!"

The man from the *Queen* started rowing back in the last small boat as Shad came into the firelight from the side near where the cattle were huddled.

"Good luck!" one of the crewmen shouted, and some of us yelled "So long!" or whatever back. Then, after a silence, another sailor called with a certain warmth in his voice, "Cap'n Barum speaks for all of us! He thinks you're all daft!"

Since it wasn't really a tough line, some of us yelled back in a friendly way, "Get a horse!" and "Too bad for you!" and things like that.

And then the man's voice came across the water again, fading in the distance. "He speaks for us! An' he said if he wasn't born a sailor, he'd rather be a cowboy!"

It was too late to holler anything back by then, and what he'd yelled was kind of touching anyway, so we just waved by the light of the fire, and then stood around the flaming driftwood, kind of quiet.

And then Shad said thoughtfully, "Been takin' stock of the cattle, an' a lot of 'em are too cold from that water t' make it through the night."

The way he said that grim thing you could tell he was worried, but that he more than likely already had thought of the problem and had some kind of an answer to it.

"Them as made it'd be sicker'n hell," Slim agreed. "What you got in mind, boss?"

"Fire an' bourbon brought us around okay," Shad said, kind of musing. "We can't build enough fires to warm them, but we can get some booze into 'em. So we're gonna break out all the grain we brought ashore and make that herd the most potent mash they ever ate in their widely traveled lives."

"Ya' mean get 'em drunk?" Mushy asked.

"Just pleasantly," Slim told him with a small grin. "Not enough t' make any shameful scenes or nothin."

"Hell," Mushy went on, "we ain't got nowheres near that much bourbon."

"They've got booze in Vladivostok," Shad said. "We'll roust 'em out and if need be buy every bottle in town." Then he started telling us what to do.

4

A bunch of curious Russians who lived on the outskirts of Vladivostok had begun to gather just outside the light of the fire to look us over. While the other hands, working under Slim, started hauling gunny sacks of grain up closer to the fire, four of us went over to talk to them. There was Shad and Old Keats and Shiny Joe and me, and we were leading two pack mules to take on into town.

These Russians were mostly short and stocky, and all of them were timid, shying away as we came closer to them. But Keats called out a word that sounded like *"Tuhva-ritch"* a couple of times and that sort of settled them back down.

Old Keats was carrying a lantern in one hand and his book on Russian in the other. Shiny and I brought up the rear, leading the mules.

"Ask them if they talk American," Shad said.

Old Keats thought hard and then said, *"Gah-vereet Amerikansky?"*

Those in front stared at him like he was crazy, and a couple of them toward the back snickered slightly.

"Stupid bastards," Shad grumbled. "Not one of 'em talks American!"

But then one broad-shouldered young man near Keats answered something in a low voice.

Old Keats was as excited as a kid. He almost yelled, "I understood him! He says he speaks Russian!"

"That's a godsend," Shad said dryly. "We found a Russian who speaks Russian. Tell 'im what we want, an' that we'll pay for it."

It was an uphill job for Keats, but he finally managed to explain to them, mostly through the young man, that we wanted all the tubs or big pots or kettles we could get. He used his hands a lot to describe the biggest size possible.

When this was done and all of them were finally nodding and saying *"Dah,"* the four of us started on into Vladivostok.

It was a dumpy, dark, deserted town, with narrow dirt streets going up and down and curving around every which way. The houses and small buildings were made of plain unfinished wood planks, most of which seemed to have been nailed up by carpenters who had failing eyesight. Once inside the town, you got the feeling there wasn't a straight line left in the world. But still and all the houses must have been built securely, because once in a while high winds would come shrieking in off the ocean that would have knocked anything flat that wasn't pretty sturdy.

About our only greeting was from some occasional unfriendly dogs, who barked from a distance and slunk away growling if we passed by up close.

And then we saw a few lights from windows in a small building down closer to the water. There were three sleepy little horses that looked like undersized mustangs tied up outside, and there was a small hand-painted sign hanging over the door.

"What's it say?" Shiny asked Keats, staring at the strange, meaningless lettering.

"Hell," Keats muttered, "could be Chinese for all I know. But I think it's a bar."

We tied the mules to the hitching rail near the horses and went into the small building.

Old Keats looked around and said hesitantly, "I guess this is one a' those bars without a bar."

We were in a plain, poorly lighted room with nothing more than six or eight wobbly tables and some rickety chairs in it. Sitting at a table near the corner were three men in flea-bitten fur hats and thick brown homespun coats that came down to their ankles. They were all dressed enough alike to maybe be in some sort of uniform. They were drinking something that looked like water, and all three of them stared up at us with just barely controlled shock, paying particular attention to Shiny and his jet-black skin.

Then a fat man came out of a back door and we saw our first familiar sight in Russia because he was wearing a filthy grease-stained apron that had probably been white some years back.

"Thank God," Keats murmured. "A bartender."

Seeing us, he stopped short. Then overcoming his surprise, he started slowly toward us, asking some kind of question in a deep, rasping voice. Like the others, he seemed particularly fascinated by Shiny.

Keats said just one word, so I remember it all right. The way things turned out later I'd sure as hell have remembered it anyway. He said, *"Vautkee."* Then he added to us, "That's their name for whiskey."

The bartender waved us to a table and went back out the rear door. As we were sitting down he came back quickly with a bottle full of colorless liquid like the Russians in the corner were drinking and four glasses. He put it on the table and Shad poured a glassful. "Hope this stuff ain't as weak as it looks." There was a silence in the room as he lifted the glass, looked at it, sniffed it, and then shrugged. "Sure don't smell like much." The bartender and the three men in the corner were frowning at him with close, curious interest.

"Well," Keats said, "try it."

Shad raised the glass to his lips and downed it in two or maybe three, gulps. I couldn't tell exactly because at one point his throat seemed to become briefly paralyzed. He finished it all and put the glass down without a word. I could tell by his dead-set face he was either awful thoughtful or suffering something fierce. As Shiny pointed out later, Shad "looked like an iron man who'd just swallowed a large cannon ball."

"I think," Shad said finally, in an unusually husky voice, "this may serve our purpose."

"How 'bout us tryin' it?" I asked.

Shad just nodded, and I poured for Keats, Shiny and myself.

"Well, here's how," I said to them, raising my glass.

But the way I did it wasn't how at all.

I took one gulp and thought I'd die right there on the spot for sure. Pure, burning fire started scorching and searing down my throat at the same time that a massive flood of salty tears surged up around my eyes.

Gagging as slightly as possible and forcing

the nearly blinding tears back with fast, hard blinks, I put the drink down. Shiny was putting his nearly full glass back down too, not hardly breathing at all.

"Embarrassin'," I gasped.

Shiny just nodded, not yet able to speak.

Between short, mercifully cooling gulps of air, and trying to joke away my own failure as a drinker, I at last managed to tell him, "You almost went white there, Shiny — or at least gray — if I can make light of the subject."

Shiny swallowed slowly and then said, "Any — any color's better'n pale green, like you."

Old Keats had finished his entire glass, and without any noticeable side effects at all he shook his head admiringly. "Now that, by God, is one hell of a drink!"

"Tell him that we want t' buy a lot of it," Shad said.

"*Vautkee, ochen horosho!*" Keats said to the bartender, pulling up a chair and gesturing for the man to join us.

The fat man sat down, but he was suspicious and uncomfortable.

With the help of a newly poured drink and his language book, Old Keats went into an earnest conversation with him, using his hands and checking back and forth in his book from time to time. The bartender stayed unsmiling, just short of being hostile.

Finally Keats turned to Shad. "He and a couple of friends make it themselves for the whole town. I think he's got about fifty bottles here, and a keg of it at his house, I think. Which is about another forty bottles, I guess."

"Tell 'im we'll take it all."

"I already did, I think. But I think what he's curious about now is how much're we gonna pay him. And what kind of money."

Shad took a silver dollar out of his pocket and tossed it on the table. "In American dollars like this."

The fat man picked up the dollar and examined it closely on both side, frowning. Finally he pointed at a part of the coin and said something to Keats, who started looking through his book.

At last he said, "He wants t' know what that thing in the lady's hair is, with those spikes above it."

"It's a headband that says 'Liberty.'" Shad leaned forward impatiently. "Tell him what it means and tell him that's a word no goddamned Russian could ever understand in the first place!"

"The hell with all that, Shad," Keats told him. "I'm havin' a hard enough time already!"

After another few minutes of searching the

book and talking, Keats said, "He'll sell his *vautkee*. I think. But I think he thinks we're tryin' to cheat him."

Shad stood up, angrily shoving the chair away behind him. "How the hell can we be cheating him? We haven't talked money!"

Keats, equally angry, said, "Cool off! I think he thinks we're tryin' to buy his whole supply for that one dollar!"

Shad hesitated, taking this in, and then said, "Oh. Well, tell him we'll give him one dollar for every one bottle."

Keats explained, pointing at the dollar and the bottle on the table, and for the first time the fat bartender began to nod eagerly and say *"Dah"* in such a way that you couldn't help but know it meant "Yes."

About half an hour later Shad and I got back to the camp with one of the mules packing forty bottles. The Russians Keats had talked to on the beach had brought maybe fifty big containers. There were washtubs, large earthenware pots and even wooden and iron barrels that were cut into half sideways, probably to catch rain water or to feed stock. But by the time we got back, there wasn't a Russian in sight any longer.

Slim and the others had brought our ton or more of oats and barley and corn up from the beach and piled the gunny sacks near the fire.

"Hey, them Ruskies ain't half bad," Slim said. "Look at all these barrels and such they brang."

"We told 'em we'd pay 'em," Shad said flatly. Then he walked off toward the herd.

"Where the hell'd they all go?" I asked Slim.

"They just brang these things an' then took off. Maybe they have t' git up pretty quick. They're mostly fishermen, an' some farmers."

"How d' you know what they are?" I started unloading the bottles from the pack sacks. "Your Russian's not too fluent."

"I dunno. I just know that somehow ya' know if you're a' talkin' t' somebody an' ya' both know it's friendly." Slim started helping me with the bottles. "Some a' them fishermen've made purty good hauls in the last two, three weeks. They tell me fish've been runnin' real good out there."

Shad now came striding back into the light of the fire. He said tersely, "Some of those cows're lyin' down t' die."

"They ain't in real good shape, boss," Slim agreed. "Their leg muscles're startin' t' stiffen up."

"All right!" Shad's powerful voice carried to all of us over the sound of the fire and the wind. "We got some more of this white

68

whiskey comin', but we're gonna start now! We'll fill these containers with grain and wet it down with that whiskey! Fast!"

"How much whiskey for how much grain?" Crab asked.

"A little bit goes a long way!" Shad said. "Taste it and pretend you're a cow!" He wasn't fooling, for that was about as accurate a way to judge as any. Then he added, "Let's go!" and we all jumped to it.

The rest of the night was kind of funny, in a way.

Old Keats and Shiny showed up half an hour later with the rest of the "white whiskey," just at about the time we were running short. All in all, we fed nearly a hundred bottles mixed with more than a ton of grain to our five-hundred-odd head of cattle. As we figured it, that was roughly half a bottle to every ten pounds of feed. Depending on how you looked at it, that was either a pretty dry mash or awful wet.

Some of the stronger bulls started at the Russian white-whiskey mash first, as we all started lugging it out to feed them. On my third trip out, carrying a washtub with Mushy, I noticed Old Fooler sniff the air like a deeply damaged cowboy on Saturday night. He raised his right foreleg like he was waving an uncertain hello to no one in particular and headed vaguely but enthusiastically for the next refreshments he could find.

And what with all the mooing and calling and bellowing and snorting of the first ones to try this new recipe, it brought the sick and the lame, the halt and the mostly damnere frozen to their feet, even if it was just out of pure curiosity. On my fourth trip out, hauling half a big barrel with Big Yawn and Natcho, I saw that spotted cow with the yearling calf who'd stopped the stampede aboard ship. She'd had a bit out of a washtub herself and was insistently nudging her bawling youngster toward it.

Along toward daylight, they were the drunkest, healthiest, most relaxed bunch of longhorns anyone could ever hope to see. Most of them were out there on the frozen ground sleeping, but it was a deep, comfortable sleep, with easy, regular breathing and relaxed leg muscles.

"Them cows could all be takin' their forty winks on a block a' ice an' not know any different," Slim said as the first glimmer of sun began to break dimly in the east.

Shad looked off toward the dim gray dawn. "The herd'll be ready t' move in about four hours. I'll take two volunteers t' stay up with me an' watch 'em. The rest of ya' get a little sleep before we burst outta here."

Thank God Slim and Big Yawn volunteered because by that time I was too tired to hardly raise my arm or even speak. Along with the others I laid out my bedroll by the fire and almost died in it.

And when I woke up, a bright sun was shining and burning in my eyes. It was like a clear, brisk spring day anywhere in the world, except somebody was yelling that some goddamned cossacks were riding down the hill toward us.

5

I staggered up into a sitting position and started pulling on my boots, looking off up the far rise, the corners of my eyes still sand-filled with sleep.

Chakko, who never said anything, muttered, "Jumpin' Jesus Christ, Goddamn hell!" It was the longest sentence I'd ever heard him say.

And then, as my eyes focused better, I began to see why Chakko had made up such a long sentence.

Old Keats told me one time there was a fictitious thing called a centaur. Half man and half horse. Those men coming down the hill surely

71

looked like a group of those fictitious characters. There were about fifteen or twenty of them loping swiftly down, and you just knew that if any one of those horses flicked its tail at a fly biting its ass, its rider would have known all about it and, without looking, reached back and down and grabbed that fly and thrown it away onto the ground, all in stride.

Those men and their horses were that much together.

But on top of that they were an even more spooky bunch because there was, somehow, an invincibility about them that scared the hell out of you from a mile away. It was like nothing on earth could stop them from getting where they were going.

They wore uniforms no one ever heard of since the Napoleonic Wars. They had on trim black-fur hats and black capes that flowed behind them as they rode. But the inside of their capes and their thick laced vests were bright scarlet. They wore roomy black trousers tucked into very high, shiny black boots. They all carried handsome swords at their sides and had rifles strapped across their shoulders. Their leader, a black-bearded giant of a man, wore a huge sword that glinted silver and gold in the distance. Big Yawn, with his occasional grasp of description, muttered,

"Damn. Are they fancy!"

"I hope t' hell they're not after us," Slim said. And then he added grimly, "But they sure seem t' be headed this way."

"Both sides," Natcho said quietly, and Shad, who already knew about it, nodded.

I looked in the other direction and saw Yakolev barreling up along the beach on a little pony that looked too small to carry him, the bottom of his long brown coat flapping clear back and down against the hocks of the over-worked pony's back legs. Riding behind him, on equally miserable mounts, were thirty or forty men in long coats and scrubby fur hats like the three men we'd seen in the bar.

"Looks like Yakolev's mad about somethin' an' he's called out all the marines in the whole damn country," Slim said.

"I want every man to have a gun in easy reach." Shad slowly took out his pack of Bull Durham.

Most of the men who were up already had re-volvers on. I stood and quickly buckled on my old Navy Remington .44. A couple of others just moved closer to their saddles and the rifles they now had near at hand in their scabbards.

Yakolev jerked his undersized pony to a halt and swung down, slightly tripping in his fury, and stalked toward Shad. The men behind him dismounted and followed, looking ready for trouble.

"You came here ashore!" Yakolev snarled in his thick, muddy accent.

Shad was now pouring tobacco into the cigarette paper, but he knew exactly how much to put in, so he was looking right at Yakolev while he did it. "Want t' check our Sea Papers again?"

"I have brought these many soldiers to enforce our port laws! There are large import duties, many taxes that I must have to collect!"

Shad rolled the paper around the tobacco and licked it, then started to gently and slowly firm it together with his fingers. "We're all paid up front, mister. And you know it."

It was then that the cossacks rode up from the other side. Scared as I was, I couldn't help noticing the great difference between the two bunches of men. Yakolev and his soldiers were grubby hunks of dirt compared to the cossacks. Even their shabby little horses couldn't begin to compare with the cossacks' handsome, finely groomed mounts. The cossacks came up twice as fast, and with half as much noise, and when they dismounted, swiftly and surely, every man's foot seemed to touch the ground within the same split second.

The big, bearded man leading them strode

toward Yakolev and Shad. It struck me as strange that he walked with that same cougar's grace and controlled strength that was in all of Shad's movements.

"Christ!" Slim muttered. "It looks like we're gonna have t' swim back to Seattle!"

The big cossack said something to Yakolev in a voice that sounded like a bear growling when he hasn't decided whether he's mad or not. They started talking, with the cossack asking short questions and Yakolev answering a little uncertainly. A couple of us looked at Old Keats, wondering what they were talking about, but he wasn't able to keep up with them and just shrugged his shoulders.

As they spoke, Shad reached over to a box of cooking matches on a pile of gear and took one, striking it on his thumbnail to light his now-built cigarette. Yakolev was startled by the sudden spurt of flame from Shad's hand and stopped halfway through some answer or another.

"Whatever you two fellas are talkin' about," Shad told Yakolev, lighting up his smoke and tossing away the match, "tell your fancy friend that come hell or high water, we're movin' out right after breakfast."

"You're moving out before breakfast," the big cossack said.

Shad's reaction was a difficult thing to paint. The rest of us damnere fell down. But Shad looked, for a moment, like he had the night before when he drank the glass of white whiskey. In both cases he'd bitten off quite a bit, but he sure as hell was going to chew it.

He frowned slightly. "You talk American."

"Probably better than you do," the big cossack growled.

Shad's voice got harder. "In that case, you know what 'fuck you' means."

There was a silence as the two men stared at each other, both of them looking like something over six feet of solid granite.

"Now wait," Yakolev finally said with nervous anger. "I am Harbor Master here! First there are matters of import duties, taxes and other expenses!"

The cossack glared at Yakolev. "You have been paid."

Some of us glanced at each other, wondering who was on whose side.

"No!" Yakolev struggled to take a small brown cigar from one of his pockets. "And remember, I have forty soldiers here who represent the Tzar!"

"Ah?" the cossack growled thoughtfully. "Forty soldiers? And we are only sixteen cossacks?" He smiled, his powerful white teeth flashing briefly. "Perhaps, then — you have really not been paid in full."

Yakolev nodded, gaining courage from these words, and put the cigar in his mouth so that it jutted out arrogantly. The cossack reached for the box of cooking matches, obviously intending to light the cigar, and Yakolev now said confidently, "I must to have three dollars per each one of the beasts."

"Like hell," Shad said in a dangerous tone.

The cossack lifted the box of matches and struck one of them on the side of the box. With the box in one hand and the flaming match in the other, he extended his hands toward Yakolev's cigar. He lighted the cigar as Yakolev puffed contentedly, and then he touched the still-burning match into the box, which was just under Yakolev's chin.

That one burning match suddenly ignited all the others and searing flames hissed up against and around his face as Yakolev screamed and dropped to his knees, frantically slapping whatever beard he'd had and his thick, burning eyebrows and hair.

Then, as Yakolev was crouched down with shaking hands clasped over his singed face, the big cossack growled, "Now you have been paid in full."

Then he turned and thundered something in

Russian to his men and they roared with laughter as they whipped out their swords and started forward.

But by that time Yakolev's forty men weren't taking anything too funny. Every one of them suddenly looked even more scared than I felt. Two of them came up in a big hurry and grabbed the whimpering Yakolev and boosted him onto his horse. Then they all rode away, making a lot better time going than when they'd come.

"All them soldiers runnin' away from them few cossacks?" Sammy the Kid said in disbelief.

"They was scared shitless!" Slim glanced at Old Keats. "What the hell did he say?"

"I – I think him and his cossacks were gonna burn all the hair off any survivors, includin' the hair around their balls."

"Jesus," Big Yawn rumbled. "That even hurts t' think about."

We all started to drift closer in to where Shad and the big cossack were watching Yakolev and his men disappear down the beach toward Vladivostok in the distance. The other cossacks, every one of them some kind of a tough-looking man, were gathering around too, so that we wound up facing each other in a rough circle around Shad and the cossack boss.

Without thinking, I said to Shad, "That was pretty slick, what he did. Really drove those bastards off."

Shad gave me a look so stern it would have stripped the bark off an oak tree. "Hate t' waste good matches."

The big cossack turned from looking off at the distant, retreating soldiers and gave an order to his men in a brusque, low voice.

He'd obviously told them it was okay to put back their swords. And they obeyed his order.

But the way they did it was, in its own silent way, truly spectacular to us cowboys.

Every single one of them, hardly thinking about it and just out of sheer habit, drew his razor-sharp four-foot sword blade across his other arm enough to draw blood. Some of them just got a few drops, and some of them got a couple of lines of dripping red clear down into their hands.

And then they shoved their swords back into their sheaths, each one making a tiny, sliding, hissing sound.

You didn't have to be too bright, right then, to pretty much figure out their point of view. It looked like they never pulled those swords without drawing blood, and it was getting more and more apparent why those forty soldiers were long gone by now.

And, for whatever reasons, we were facing those cossacks in much the same situation.

The rest of the hands, at least counting me, had mixed emotions, but Shad looked quietly at the big cossack and spoke in a flat voice. "My men and me are moving out like I said, right after breakfast."

The big cossack's jaw went tight and Slim spoke quickly. "We thought you was here t' give us a hard time along with them others. In a outta-the-way place like this, it's nice t' meet some friends."

"We are not your friends." The cossack's hard, penetrating eyes briefly studied each of us, one after the other. "I am Captain Mikhail Ivanovitch Rostov of the Kuban-Siberian Cossacks. My men and I are here under orders. We're to protect you and the cattle on your trip."

This brought all of us up a little short, since nothing had ever been said about anything like that. Shad couldn't believe what he'd heard. With mixed irritation and amusement he said, "To *what?*"

"You're Northshield, I presume." There was iron in his voice. "As I said, to *protect* you."

And there was now iron times ten in Shad's voice. "This outfit don't hardly need any help, mister."

As the two big men looked hard at each other, there was a grim, hollow stillness in the air, like the feeling in a thunderstorm just before lightning cracks.

Old Keats, God bless him, broke in and said quietly, "After all, Shad, they have their orders. And they know the country, and what to expect."

Captain Rostov glanced briefly, piercingly at Old Keats. "Your man has common sense."

"He ain't my man," Shad said flatly, meaning something stronger than what his words were saying. "Every man with me is his own man."

"Well, what the hell" — Slim shrugged in a peaceful way — "these fellas oughtn't t' get in the way too goddamned much, Shad."

His two top men had in their own way, put in their votes, but Shad took another long, slow drag on his smoke, still hard put to agree with them.

"After all," I added hesitantly, repeating the earlier point that had impressed me so much, "they sure did pull those soldiers off our backs awful fast."

Shad took another thoughtful haul on his smoke. "We'll see," he said finally. Then he dropped the butt and slowly ground it out with his boot. "We'll decide it after breakfast."

By saying that, he'd backed off about half the

81

width of a gray hair, and Rostov, in a low, hard voice, backed away roughly the same distance. "When there's only one decision, that decision is always right."

There was still the feeling of intense, swift trouble hovering deadly and invisible between the two men.

"Well!" Slim clapped his hands together, making a kind of period in the conversation. "Now that's settled, what's for breakfast? You an' them cossacks a' yours like t' try some cowboy beans?"

Rostov ignored Slim's question. He turned curtly on his heel and walked back toward the cossack horses, his men following.

"Boy," Slim said, frowning. "He sure is kind of an abrupt fella."

Shad looked off toward the cattle. About half of them were up by now, others staggering to their feet and shaking their heads as if to clear them. Then he looked toward the hill where some of the curious Russians from the night before had begun to gather again. "Crab, you and Mushy cook up some bacon and beans. Natcho, you and Link and Chakko see t' the horses. Keats, go and tell those people they can have their pots and stuff back. And pay 'em whatever you think is fair."

As the others started away to their jobs,

Keats said, "I think those people mostly just wanted t' be helpful."

"Pay 'em. I don't care what, but *pay* 'em."

"I'll work somethin' out."

"The rest of you come with me. We may have t' punch a few a' those cows back t' life."

He was right. About forty head were lying down in a drunken or chilled stupor. We pounded on them to get their attention, and sometimes a few of us more or less hauled them up onto their feet.

All except one. A young coyote-dun bull had frozen to death, the poor darn animal's four legs stretched out straight and stiff and hard as rocks. Christ, how you hate to lose an animal!

We'd lost two cows on the sea voyage, and now three head in one night, and it hit Shad pretty hard.

"More'n likely a heart attack," Slim said, "and then he froze in the night."

Keats came up to where we were standing around the frozen bull. "Those people won't take anything at all," he told Shad. "They loaned us those things last night just t' be friendly, an' so I thanked 'em."

"You thanked 'em?" Shad looked at Keats with eyes still cold and grim from looking at the dead bull. "I told you t' pay them!"

"Well how the hell can I pay them if they

won't take any pay?"

Shad's hard words had the finality of a nail being driven strongly into an oak plank. "I don't want t' be beholden to any man in this country!"

"But there's no way t' pay those people! What they did for us was a free and open gift!"

Shad took a deep breath and looked down at the frozen bull for a long, frowning moment. "Then tell 'em we're giving them a free and open gift back! Fourteen hundred pounds of beef!"

That was one hell of a decision. Every man there knew that meat would have seen our whole outfit through more than two good months of steaks and stew.

"That whole beef for half a night's loan a' some beaten-up pots?" Dixie asked.

But Old Keats, who somehow looked kind of pleased about what Shad had said, was already on his way. And it surely worked out.

Those Russians didn't have much in the way of beef, according to Keats. And while they were too proud to take anything in terms of pay, they were really deeply moved about the gift they'd been given in return. While we were eating breakfast beans some of the white-shawled women got over their shyness enough to come down and get their pots and barrels, and they even nodded and smiled at us a little. In the meantime some of the men had started skinning and dressing the coyote-dun bull.

A short distance away, the cossacks were waiting, but it seemed like there was always an air of being ready to go, of impatience about them. Some of them were tending their horses, while a few were eating something cold, for they hadn't built a fire. We noticed one of them who had a thick funny-looking plate.

"What kind of plate's he eatin' off?" Purse Mayhew asked.

"That ain't no real plate," Slim said. "That there's a hardened pumpkin rind. Indians used t' use 'em. Works good."

Chakko nodded and grunted in agreement, which was one of his normal sentences.

"Pumpkin rind?" Crab scraped his spoon over his tin plate for some final beans. "Sounds heathen t' me. Ain't they never invented metals?"

"Pumpkin rind's kind a' handy for eatin'," Slim said. "If you're low on water, ya' just scrape off a thousandth of an inch from the top with your knife an' you've washed your dishes."

"They've damn well invented metals," Mushy said to Crab. "Those swords a' theirs prove that beyond a whole lot a' question."

"Do they have t' cut themselves every time they take those things out?" Sammy the Kid asked. "That was kind of horrifyin'."

"Either that or cut someone else a lot deeper," Link said. We all knew he was guessing, but it sure sounded accurate.

"Forgettin' them swords," Slim muttered, "in case we ever get in an argument with 'em, I hope you fellas have took note a' the large amount of artillery they're packin'." He chewed slowly, glancing off toward them. "Every man's got some kind of a side arm and a rifle, along with that oversized Mexican toothpick."

Natcho was too entranced to even bother about or notice Slim's words. "By the dear Lord," he said, "they certainly know about horses. Look at those animals! And their saddles and spurs and bits! Beautiful!"

Mushy chewed his last piece of bacon slowly and grudgingly. "Yeah. They're a hasty an' heavy-lookin' outfit."

Captain Rostov came toward us and stopped a few feet from the fire. "You've finished breakfast." He looked at Shad levelly. "Now I hope we can have a brief, intelligent conversation."

Shad stood up. "It'll be brief."

Rostov's face grew hard for a moment, but he

forced himself to control his anger and took out some papers. "If there is any question of our identity this is a copy of the bill of sale between your ranch and our ataman in the city of Blagoveshchensk."

At a nod from Shad, Old Keats took the papers and started looking them over.

Rostov continued, saying, "Your duty is to deliver that herd to its destination."

"I'll do it."

"*My* duty is to make certain you get there." Rostov was getting close to fighting mad. "And *I'll* goddamn well do *that*, too."

That was the first time Rostov had sworn in English, and it made his statement kind of impressive, almost as though you weren't necessarily talking to a foreigner. Maybe that's why Shad eased off enough to explain something, which he didn't often do. "I've got maps t' show where I'm goin'. And I've got fifteen men armed with sideguns an' repeating rifles, and they know how to use 'em. Plus some other various and sundry weaponry in our packs. This country's no rougher than the country we're used to. So there just ain't no way we won't get there. And we don't need any unwanted company or help. Is that clear, mister?"

Rostov breathed deeply, impatiently. "I'm pleased that you're well equipped, *mister*. But one thing you don't know is that those cattle are immeasurably more important to me and my people than they are to you. Another thing is that you haven't any idea how deep or swift the Ussuri and Amur rivers are at this time of year. You don't even know exactly where they or their tributaries are. Thirdly, you probably never heard of a Tartar warrior. And most important, you certainly never heard of a man named Genghis Kharlagawl, who has an entire army of Tartar warriors somewhere between here and our destination."

There was a long moment of silence, because we sure as hell did not know any of those things he was talking about.

Finally Old Keats handed the papers back to Rostov. "That's a legitimate copy, Shad. Listen, there's just no doubt in my mind we'll be able to use any help we can get along the way."

Slim nodded. "I don't like the idea a' outside help anymore'n you do, Shad, but I second that motion. But a' course whatever you say goes, boss."

Shad thought about their opinions for a moment, then he grunted. "Okay. We'll try it a while. But if you Russians cause any trouble the arrangement'll come to a screeching halt."

Rostov ignored this. "We'll ride ahead of you

and around you to scout the way. I want one of your men to ride with me."

I expected Shad, in his tough frame of mind, to refuse, or maybe to volunteer Old Keats. But instead he looked at me. "You go, Levi."

"Me?"

"You."

So while the rest of the hands were working at packing and breaking up camp, I saddled Buck up with shaking hands and started ahead with the cossacks.

I didn't know quite what to think as I rode up to the cossacks. It came out kind of a nervousness and fear and excitement and even fascination, all mingled together. For the first part of the ride I knew they were just waiting for me to fall off old Buck or do something else stupid. But I managed to keep up with their swift pace and not look too silly, I think.

At the top of a hill, after moving like bats out of hell, Rostov suddenly stopped us and we looked far back down at the beach. Most of the Slash-D men were asaddle by now, and yelling and twirling lariats to start the herd moving up toward us. Old Fooler, who always seemed to know the right way to go anyway, was following Shad riding point on Red, leading the cattle off in our direction. The Russians on the beach, who'd skinned the coyote-dun bull, were still busy dressing the meat, and a couple of them waved as cowboys rode by.

Beyond them, the blue gray waters of the sea stretched forever.

Rostov glanced down at the scene and then at me, with hard eyes that seemed to go right through me and out the back of my head. "You gave them that entire bull."

Remembering what he'd said about how important the herd was to him and his people, I hesitated a little bit before I answered. "Yeah."

"Good."

He turned and rode on north, and I spurred after him.

6

If I'd had any suspicion that getting out of riding herd was going to make life easier for me, that first day with the cossacks changed my mind.

Keeping up with Rostov was like trying to race full tilt with a deer, outguessing what direction it was going to veer off to at any instant. When Rostov said he was going to scout ahead, he surely meant just that. The cossacks leading the spare mounts and pack-horses didn't have it too bad. They just walked their mounts at an easy pace in the lowlands, usually staying about half a mile ahead of the first longhorns. But the others, and especially me and Rostov, had been all over every foot of every mountain in sight long before Old Fooler and the first cattle ever stuck their noses into a valley below. Yet with all his hard riding, Rostov always somehow saw to it that his horse never got winded or tired, and I never once saw a drop of lather on that big black stallion.

A couple of times, when Rostov and I were alone near the top of a ridge, the ride got downright terrifying, too. Rostov, without hesitation, went barreling over a narrow, broken ledge that would have made a mountain goat stop and consider. Even though he hadn't said a word since morning, and never even seemed to look at me, I still had the impression he was testing me every minute. So with the reputation of the good old Slash-Diamond at stake, I barreled along right after him. I was still trying to get my heart back in place a minute later, when we came to the second ledge, which was even higher and trickier to cross. He galloped over it as smooth as though his horse was a big, black bird, and thinking fatal thoughts I stuck right behind him. Mostly the path was the width of a skinny ironing board, and if we'd gone over the side it was at least two hundred feet to jagged rocks below.

And after maybe a minute, and aging ten years, I made it.

Rostov still didn't look back or say anything.

But a while later, when we'd stopped and dismounted, he took a little meat out of his fancy, soft leather saddlebags and wordlessly offered me a bite of it. All in all, that wordless gesture of his seemed to be one hell of a compliment. I honestly didn't know quite what to do. So I shook my head. But I compromised the refusal by giving him a very slight, brief grin.

Finally, around sunset, when my butt and the saddle under it felt like they were both about to shove themselves right up through the top of my head, Rostov pulled up on a bluff overlooking a beautiful and wide green flat with a creek running through it.

"I would suggest this as our camping place."

Not wanting to agree with him too much, I said, "It's not bad."

"Ride back and tell Northshield."

"Well, I'll say it like you said first — about 'suggestin' it."

He gave me a brief, piercing look in which there just might have been a glint of humor and then put his horse down the steep slope

92

before us at breakneck speed.

Well, at least I'd found out why he wanted me with him, and why Shad had agreed. I patted Buck on the shoulder and told him, "You should be proud of me, old horse. At last I've come to my great calling in the world — I'm a goddamn messenger boy."

Then I turned Buck and we headed back for the herd.

Shad was still riding point, and when I told him about Rostov's suggestion, all he said was "Place look okay t' you?"

"God never invented a nicer one. We just veer left up ahead, around that buffalo-backed hill."

While we were camping down, Mushy and Crab tried to make some sport of the fact that I'd been off "sight-seein'" while the others had been doing an honest day's work. But I was too dead beat-up to bother trying to explain the error of their ways. I was asleep, literally, before my head ever came close to the saddle. All I remembered was sitting on my bedroll and starting to take off my boots.

The next morning I decided to take it easy on Buck and left him with the remuda, saddling Blackeye instead. Blackeye was a sturdy, feisty little pinto with an all-white face except for that one eye.

The cossacks were camped about five hundred feet away on the flat, and I rode over to them as Rostov was mounting up.

He looked at me and Blackeye and said, "You're sparing the other horse because of yesterday."

"Yeah."

I got the feeling he approved of that. "You yourself managed to ride along with me fairly well."

I shrugged. "Hell, I'm the worst horseman in the outfit."

He called some orders in Russian to his men, and then we took off again.

After a few more miles of rough mountains, the terrain gradually started getting a little easier, which was a blessing even though it was still another hard-riding, wordless day.

When the sun was finally getting low in the west a young cossack about my age wound up riding with Rostov, too. He was tall and husky, with sandy hair and clear, constantly frowning blue eyes. His scraggly beard looked sort of new, unlike Rostov's thick, trim, jet-black beard that looked like it'd probably been on him when he was born.

The three of us rode to the top of a low hill, the two of them, as always, searching to both sides and as far ahead as they could see.

I'd gone along quietly all day before and most of this day, and still hadn't intended to break the silence, but curiosity finally got the best of me. Somewhat mad at myself for speaking, I must have sounded angry. "Would ya' mind tellin' me what you're lookin' for, so I can look for it too, for Christ's sake?"

Rostov glanced back at me, that tiny bit of humor lurking somewhere in those hard, dark eyes. "The puppy barks."

I don't know if the hair on the nape of your neck really stands up, but mine felt like it did right then. "*Puppy!*" Somewhere in the rear part of my mind I knew I was going out on a suicidal limb, but the front part was boiling over. "Just one a' two things! Take that back or fight!"

I meant it flat out and couldn't and wouldn't back down, but once I'd said it that anti-suicide part of my head was banging away something fierce trying to find me some way, any way, out of this fix.

Rostov's look didn't change, and he didn't move a hair. After an eternal few seconds he said, "The puppy barks — and the wolf bites." Then, "Perhaps you are a young wolf."

Thank *God!* He's given me my way out. He hadn't exactly taken back what he'd said, but he'd allowed me a fair escape route which that panicky rear area of my mind was grateful to accept.

Trying to keep up what I hoped was a fearless look I said, "I ain't all that young, and you'd have t' try me as a wolf. But I'd still like t' know just what we're scoutin' for."

He let the whole thing go, and answered me. "Primarily Tartar raiding parties. From across the Ussuri right now."

"What's a Tartar look like?"

"Just let us know if you see anyone we don't see, on foot or horseback." He added quietly, almost warmly, "Your eyes will be much appreciated," and I knew he meant what he said. Then he turned back to search the horizon ahead.

"Uhh, Captain Rostov?" I said uncomfortably.

He looked around at me, questioning.

"That's kind a' nice — appreciatin' the offer a' my eyes like that. My name's Levi Dougherty. Just Levi'll do, though."

He indicated the sandy-haired young cossack near him. "This is Corporal Igor Zarutski."

I nodded at the corporal and said the only thing I could think of to say, which was "Igor."

Igor stared at me, concentrated hard and said in a very slow, studied, funny kind of a one-noted way, "I-am-very-pleased-to-have-the-honor-of-making-your-acquaintance-Mister-Levi."

That line of his hit me like a sledge hammer.

If anything, I was even more stunned than Shad had been when the same kind of thing happened to him before. My expression must have been odd, because Rostov laughed for the first time since he'd singed off Yakolev's beard and eyebrows, and Igor grinned over at him in a proud, pleased way.

I never did think of anything to come up with, and Rostov finally slowed down his laughter enough to say, "Believe me, not all cossacks speak English. I've taught three of my men to speak reasonably well, and the others know a few words."

I finally just barely managed "I'll be damned." And then a sort of resentment of my own shortcomings must have welled up in me because I said, "An' I don't speak *one word* a' Russian except *'Daughhh,'* which sounds like some idiot tryin' to start off a sentence!"

Rostov said, "A language takes time. And we've been planning on getting these cattle for more than two years. I wanted someone else to be able to communicate with you Americans in case I should happen to be killed along the way."

He didn't say that grimly, but somehow the

words had an ominous ring to them. And then he rode quickly down the hill before us, looking as impossible to kill as any man I ever saw.

Igor frowned in concentration again and said, "Let-us-go," and we galloped down after him.

We made a fine, sweet-water camp again that night, with enough grass to feed ten thousand head. Purse, Mushy, Rufe and Link had the first watch, and the rest of us were feeling pretty good about how the drive was going so far, sitting around the fire after supper. Sammy got out his guitar and started fooling around softly with the strings, and we got into one of those easygoing bullshit talks when nobody's got a whole lot to say and yet nobody's quite ready to go to bed as long as there's some hot coffee left.

The cossack campfire was burning about five hundred feet away, and you could faintly make out the shadowy flickers of men moving around it.

Natcho leaned comfortably back against a tree, stretching his shoulder muscles. "Not a bad day." He smiled. "Everything considered, my only regret is that we didn't have that one night in Vladivostock, so as to better judge that white Russian whiskey and the ladies there."

"Didn't miss much." Shiny Joe grinned. "That white whiskey's poison an' there wasn't no ladies. Not even women."

"Christ," Dixie said. "After all that time on the boat, even them cows're startin' t' have a strange effect on me."

"Only the good-lookin' ones, I hope," said Slim.

"Well, there'll be other towns." Big Yawn moved his huge shoulders in a philosophic way. Then he said, "Hey! I heard a couple a' them cossacks hollerin' back and forth t'day, and I kinda understood a couple words!"

"That makes you about even," Dixie said, "since ya' only know a couple words of American too."

"Screw you." Big Yawn scratched his ear. "Sounded kinda like some a' the words Ma an' Pa used t' use when I was a kid."

"Speakin' of that," I said, "Rostov ain't the only one of 'em who knows American."

"Who else does?" Shad asked.

I told him about Igor. "An' there're two others. Don't know which ones yet."

"Underhanded of 'em." Shad glanced at the distant fire suspiciously. "Not lettin' us know."

"They're not tryin' to keep it a secret. But we haven't exactly encouraged a whole lot a' friendly talk back an' forth."

"You stickin' up for them?" Dixie asked.

"Hell, no!"

Slim looked up at me curiously, from where he was idly whittling on a stick. "After two days now, what do ya' think of 'em?"

I hesitated, then said, "All in all, they ain't too bad."

"Huh." Crab grunted. "Sounds like you're soft on 'em."

"I am not! But they've been all right with me. An' they're damn good t' their horses. One time t'day, when it was hotter'n hell, one of 'em went t' take a drink and his water bag was almost empty. So he gave his last water to his horse instead."

Natcho shrugged. "Any real horseman would do the same."

"Well, that's sort of what I mean. They really care for their mounts, like us."

"Difference is, I'd hope in this rich country none of us would be stupid enough t' run out of water in the first place," Shad said flatly.

"Boss's right." Crab grinned. "Dumb heathen didn't deserve a drink."

"C'mon." Old Keats sounded slightly irritated. "Levi's basically got the right of it. We can't go over a thousand miles with them fellas without ever talkin'. I ain't sayin' we oughtta be friends, but we should try to have some kind

100

of halfway decent relation with them."

I was surprised that almost none of the men thought Old Keats was right. With looks and a few words his idea was generally voted down. Crab said, "Farther off they are the better," and Dixie threw in at about the same time, "It'll be a lukewarm day in hell b'fore I kiss no cossack's ass."

Even Sammy the Kid now hit a hard note on his guitar. "I still ain't figured out just what they think they're doin', anyhow." He hit a second harsh note, disgusted. "Tartars!"

"Well, since I'm the one's been with 'em," I volunteered, "I think what they're doin' is this. I think they think we're just supposed t' herd the cattle. An' if we run into any trouble, I think they think they're goin' to do all the fightin'."

Natcho laughed, Shiny Joe said "Shit," and even Chakko grinned slightly. Crab shook his head. "If they think we're gonna do all the work and they're gonna have all the fun, they're crazy!"

For some reason, maybe just knowing Rostov the little I did, my back got up. "I have a strong hunch, Crab, you'd not find fightin' Tartars all that much fun."

Crab frowned at me. "You are sidin' with them foreigners! Maybe you'd rather bunk down over at *their* fire!"

I stood up angrily. And damned if I didn't accidentally come out with exactly the same thing I'd said earlier. "Take that back or fight!" But I felt a lot safer with Crab than I'd felt with Rostov.

Crab started up and I moved toward him but Shad said quietly. "Hold it." He didn't have to raise his voice to stop us. He got up and walked slowly between us and threw the little bit of coffee he had left onto the fire, where it made a brief, sizzling sound. "Levi?"

"Yeah?"

"That Igor, who knows our language."

"Yeah?"

"Tell Rostov I want him ridin' with me startin' tomorrow."

"Couldn't I just suggest it to him?"

"Tell him any way you want."

Crab and I were still standing there, sort of facing each other down. At Shad's order to hold it, we'd held it, but we were both still feeling pretty unfriendly. Shad looked at us mildly and said, "It's sure a hardship, havin' two such grouchy sonsabitches on your hands."

He wasn't making fun of us, yet something about the way he said it made us both want to laugh somehow.

"He's grouchier than I am," Crab finally said.

"That's impossible," I told him.

"Well" — Shad shrugged — "you two go ahead and fight all night, if you really want to. But just don't make one damn sound doin' it because the rest of us sensible fellas are goin' to sleep."

He'd left no way for a fight. He'd given us both room to back off gracefully from a fight neither one of us actually wanted. And it crossed my mind that he'd stopped that potential battle with the same kind of instinctive, tough humor that Rostov had used with me earlier that day, when he'd gotten me out of the "puppy and wolf" situation.

Crab grimaced in a half grin and hit me on the shoulder just hard enough to let me know he was pretty strong but not mad anymore. I hit him back in the same way, and that was the end of that.

And we all went to sleep.

Until those giant lobo wolves showed up just before sunrise.

7

There was a sudden, wild bellowing from a cow that sounded like it was being murdered, and three or four gunshots banged on top of each other.

That greasy-sack outfit came to life like lightning. I'd jumped up and was jerking on my second boot when a voice yelled out from the other side of the herd, *"Wolves! A million of 'em!"* The watch had changed and it was Slim's voice.

"Don't shoot into the herd!" Shad roared. He'd gotten up early and was already dressed and saddled. He jumped aboard Red and tore off toward where there was now more scattered firing, and that section of the herd was starting to mill around in wild panic, the other cows quickly picking up the feeling of fear.

From the cossack camp I heard Rostov give a loud, brief order in Russian.

And then the rest of us were getting aboard horses, and if it hadn't been so serious it would have been kind of funny. Most of us were in various states of undress, and about half of the hands were still in red or white long johns, a couple with the rear-end flaps still flopping open. I always slept with my shirt and pants on, so that was no problem for me. But in the whole group there were only three things every man had on without exception — his boots, his gun and his hat.

I threw a bridle on Buck and jumped on his back, not taking the time to saddle him, and galloped off at about the same time Natcho and Chakko did.

There was enough gray morning light to see fairly well as we forced our way through the milling herd toward the center of trouble.

The first Siberian wolf I saw scared me and Buck so much we almost went down in a heap together. It was bigger than any timber wolf I'd ever seen, with a mottled gray body and a black stripe running all the way down its back, from the top of its huge head to the tip of its tail. It flashed across our path almost under Buck's front legs and Buck reared up, nearly over backward.

"Jesus Christ!" Slim was yelling. "*These* crazy wolves are outta their *minds!*"

By any of our standards he was certainly right. Those first shots should have sent any normal pack hightailing it. But these fierce bastards weren't afraid of the gunfire or of our loud shouting. Come to think of it, they didn't seem to be afraid of anything. Unlike our wolves they didn't make, and hadn't made a sound, no howling or growling or snarling. They also hadn't bided their time to sooner or later pick off a stray, but had boldly hit the whole herd, probably to cut one cow and kill it. And while any normal wolf will retreat in an instant once the pack is broken up, these didn't feel that way. With yelling, sometimes shooting cowboys on their tails, and badly split up within the wildly milling cattle, every damned wolf seemed to be making his own individual fight of it. Shad charged Red a few feet up a hill out of the herd and a big gray monster lunged for Red's hind legs. Shad swung around in the saddle and shot him through the head so that he went sprawling away down the hill. "Look t' your *horses!*" Shad roared. "They're goin' after *them too!*"

It was a chaotic, deafening, rough situation. In those close, swirling quarters a shot might hit a beef, a horse or even another rider.

And if one wolf bit through the hock tendon of any animal's back leg, that animal would be gone.

It was about then that the cossacks, who'd had a little longer way to come, charged into the melee. They were mostly bareback, and mostly half-dressed too, though even their underwear was fancier than our long johns, a lot of it shiny and colorful cloth.

But they had something we sure as hell didn't have, and I suddenly knew what command Rostov had yelled to them in their camp before. He'd heard what Shad had called out, about not shooting into the herd, and so he and every man with him had his sword out and held up high.

And, in that massive, churning whirlpool of men and animals, the way they used their swords was plain and simple awe-inspiring. With us and our guns it'd just been a confusing mess. Now, with them, it was still a confusing mess but it was a battleground too. Leaning half off their saddleless horses with some of their blindingly swift, incredibly accurate swings, they sliced and cut at the wolves they came upon as they slashed their way among the bawling, desperate cattle.

One cossack and his more or less pinto suddenly went down not far from me, and I slammed Buck through the bellowing longhorns toward him. A wolf had severed his horse's rear left tendon. As I closed on him, the wolf, with hooves thudding all around them, leaped toward the man's throat. The cossack, one elbow on the ground, swung with his sword and cut the wolf's entire head completely off, where it lay still snapping blindly at the air.

I reached down, realizing for the first time that it was Igor. Understanding instantly, he reached up from where he was lying with one leg still under his horse. A big, bewildered bull leaped partially over his downed horse, one forehoof landing with crushing force on Igor's other leg before the bull swung off. I knew how much that hoof hurt, because it'd happened to me in gentler circumstances on the boat a few nights before. But Igor acted like it was nothing, and a second later we'd gotten him behind me aboard Buck.

By now there wasn't much left of the wolf pack. The four or five of them that were still alive sped away behind their leader, a giant who'd lost about half of his tail somewhere, and who was almost completely black.

Slim and some others took a few pot shots at them as they raced toward cover in the forest. They knocked down a couple more, but then the black giant and the others were out of sight among the trees.

Old Keats has always claimed that cows are sometimes among the great philosophers of the world, and I guess he's right because the herd calmed down almost instantly once those last few wolves were gone.

I dropped Igor off Buck near where Rostov and most of his men had dismounted. The other cossacks were making a count of dead wolves, which was getting easier because the cattle didn't like the scent of blood and were gradually moving away toward the more pleasing smell of simple, fresh grass.

Igor looked up at me and nodded slightly, but he didn't say anything. He seemed embarrassed because I'd helped him out of a jam, and I could understand that. But there was something else that seemed to be bothering him even more. And I should have understood that — even more.

Igor said something to Rostov in a very quiet voice. And Rostov, who was wearing a revolver, took it out and handed it to him.

Igor then walked over to his horse, who was still alive. It was only a hundred feet or so, but it was a long, long walk for him.

I felt like I shouldn't be there, but I didn't quite know what to do, and just riding off would have seemed sacrilegious.

Igor stroked the helpless animal's muzzle and face, scratched the horse's forehead a little and then rubbed his neck. He was still rubbing his neck when he shot him. The horse didn't make a sound. He just stretched his legs out so they quivered gently for a moment, and then he died.

Igor walked back and handed Rostov the gun. Then he turned and started walking back toward the cossack camp. Rostov looked at me, his dark eyes searching mine even though I wasn't looking right back at him. I didn't feel like looking at anybody just then.

That poor darned horse could have just as well been old Buck.

So without looking at anybody or saying anything, I turned Buck around and rode back to camp.

Shad and the others were already there. One of the wolves had bitten Crab's right forearm to the bone, and Shad and Old Keats were working on it to clean it and stop the bleeding.

Shad noticed me come up and dismount, and he spoke with quiet warmth to Crab, who was in considerable pain and held a bottle of bourbon in his other hand. "Don't know what t' do with you, Crab. Keep ya' outta one fight with Levi an' ya' go right out an' get in another fight with a wolf."

It was a vicious, double-fang wound, the torn-out kind that it hurts to even look at. I had the sinking feeling that Crab could lose the arm. "One thing I'll guarantee ya'," I told Crab as lightly as I could. "In a fair fight, I'd never bitten ya' quite that hard."

Crab took a long drink and then forced a small grin, though his hurt arm was beginning to involuntarily shake. "That damned wolf was really mixed up. Leaped up on me like he was gonna throw me outta the saddle an' ride m' horse."

At this point Rostov rode into camp and got down from his big black. "I heard one of your men was hurt."

Shad said, "We're takin' care of it."

"I'm sure you are." Rostov walked over to them and looked at the wound. "This could be serious, and I've had some experience with wolf bites."

"So have I," Shad said curtly.

"I'd take it as a personal favor, Captain Rostov," Old Keats said quietly, "if you'll stay here and give us any advice you might happen t' have."

Shad gave Keats a critical glance, and then he gave me an even tougher one when I poured a cup of coffee from the pot on the fire and handed it to Rostov.

Slim said, "We're in pretty good supplies right now. Ya' like any sugar, or maybe whiskey, t' lace that coffee, Captain?"

"No. It's fine," Rostov said easily.

It sort of looked like, up to a point, the way

any one of us talked to him was the way he was going to give it back.

Sammy the Kid, more curious than friendly, asked, "How many wolves get killed back there, all together?"

"Twenty-three." Rostov's answer was in kind, crisp and to the point, with no trace of friendship in his voice. "Four by your guns. Three by the longhorns themselves."

"Them longhorns ain't too bright," Slim said, "but they're tougher'n nails when they git mad."

"Jeez!" Mushy frowned deeply, thinking. "You got sixteen of 'em with them old-fashioned swords!"

"Sabers."

There was a silence as we all took in that different word, and grimly watched Shad and Keats working tensely on Crab's arm.

Finally Shad said, "It's gonna take stitches."

Old Keats, only half thinking about it, looked at Rostov, who nodded just once.

"Who's got needle an' thread handy?" Keats asked.

Mushy said, "I have. Been fixin' my chaps."

"Jesus Christ, no!" Crab groaned. "That leather-workin' needle's big as a railroad spike!"

Purse said, "I got one not so big right here,

for shirt buttons and the like."

"Heat it in the fire," Shad said. Crab wet his lips and Shad went on. "Hit that bourbon hard as you want." As the hurt man drank deeply, Purse heated the long, narrow needle until its end was glowing yellow. Then, threading the needle, Shad said, "As long as I've got t' do all this work anyway, ya' want me t' sew a couple of buttons on your arm?"

"Not particularly." Crab took another long drink and put the bottle down.

"It'd be damned interestin', and might even possibly make ya' more attractive."

But now in dead silence, Shad concentrating intently, the hot needle was already going quickly, efficiently and terribly painfully through Crab's flesh, drawing the muscles and skin closer together. Crab was gritting his teeth and in a cold sweat, both from the pain and from the repulsive idea of his arm being sewed together. "Goddamn it!" he said weakly, and yet angry at the same time. "Somebody say somethin' so I can listen to it!"

Sammy, grasping for something, said loudly, "What I want t' know is why that herd didn't stampede t'night!"

"They'd a' stampeded except they couldn't make up their mind which direction t' go," Slim answered equally loudly.

"Huh!" Chakko grunted abruptly. "Natcho! Old Fooler!"

"What he means," Natcho said strongly, watching Crab's pain-stricken face, "is that I rode by Old Fooler and was smart enough to jump off of Diablo onto him instead! My shirt was only halfway on anyway so I took it off and held it over Old Fooler's eyes so he couldn't see! Most of those cows are so used to followin' him that when he went in circles they must have thought that was the right thing to do! It seemed like a lot better thing for me to do than go off and get my arm half chewed off by an unfriendly wolf!"

"And also," Slim's voice boomed, "without Old Fooler them cows didn't know whether they was comin' or goin' anyhow! If they run off from one wolf, they was runnin' right smack t'ward another one! Them dumb damn wolves is the only ones ever made a whole stampede take place all in the same place!"

"Which just goes to prove a simple fact!" I said loudly. "Those dumb wolves must be about the same level a' cowhand as this here old fella Crab Smith! Equally dumb and grouchy! No wonder one of 'em tried t' take over his horse an' ride it! Probably wanted his job!"

Mushy picked it up and half yelled, "Hell,

yes! That goddamn wolf no doubt rides better! And sure as hell'd be worth more salary at the end a' the month!"

And now with his quick, powerful and yet at the moment very delicate hands, Shad had finished sewing the gaping flesh of Crab's arm back into place. He knotted the thread in place and bit it off and leaned back to take a deep breath.

I'd thought Crab had passed out two or three times, but he managed to raise his head slightly, knowing that it was over. "That wolf might a' killed me," he said weakly. "But with you fellas, an' the jokes ya' come up with, I'll damn well never have t' worry about laughin' m'self t' death!" And then he laid his head back down and closed his eyes.

Shad looked at us with grim, hard approval. "He's right about your humor not bein' too vital of a danger." Then he took the bottle of bourbon and poured it on the sewed up wound, gently squeezing as much of it as possible into the places where the closed flesh had been torn open. "He'll be okay now."

"No he won't." Rostov's voice was very quiet and dead on the level. "The arm has already been infected."

Crab's arm did seem a little bigger.

Old Keats stood up. "We've done all we

115

can for him, Captain."

Rostov shook his head and said very simply, "No."

Shad turned slowly and faced him, and as always there was the feeling between them of an earthquake about to hit the whole area. "The sewin' was good, and bourbon's a good outside cure."

None of us, except maybe Shad, could get mad at what Rostov said, and the way he said it. "Those wolves don't have the cleanest fangs in the world. Infection has set in."

Shad nodded. "That's always possible."

"Whatever poisons are in there must be drawn off."

They both meant every word they said, and for the first time this was a quiet, thoughtful duel between the men, backed up by the things that each man knew.

"If his arms swells any more," Shad said, "we'll make a poultice outta cowshit. That'll draw everything but a man's bones out."

"You need a simple, swift thing, *now.*" Rostov stepped to Crab, kneeled down and put his hand on his forehead, then his hurt arm. "Otherwise he'll lose this arm, or die."

I loved Shad for saying what he said then.

He said, "This man means more to me than any fifty men you'll ever know." Then as

Rostov looked up at him with those damned, dark, piercing eyes, he said, "He's only twenty-three years old, and he hasn't had as much trouble and fun as he ought to, and if you got anything constructive, I'll listen to it."

"What medicines do you have?" Rostov asked.

"Just two. Quinine, for the fever, and whiskey."

Rostov was already working with Crab, rubbing his wrists hard between his powerful hands, and then putting his right hand very softly and lightly over Crab's heart and on his forehead. With all his obvious concern for Crab he suddenly said a thing that shocked and almost stunned me. He said bitterly, "I'd have expected more from the modern, up-to-date United States of America!"

Rostov was leaning down over Crab, and Shad now leaned down over him again, one of them on each side of the hurt man. "All right," Shad said, his jaw hard, "I told you this man means somethin' to me! You and your god-damn Russians come up with somethin' that'll help him more than me and cowshit and bourbon can help him!"

Rostov put his hand on Crab's face and worked with it softly. "Come awake. Be aware. I need one thing from you. Saliva."

Crab kind of woke up but didn't quite understand what was going on. He mumbled something, but nobody knew what it was.

"I can use my own, or others', but it's best from you," Rostov said.

"This dumb bastard says he needs your spit!" Shad told him.

Chakko, Indian-like, nodded and grinned at this.

"Hell, I ain't got any left," Crab whispered.

"Then make some!" Rostov lifted him, cradling him in his arm.

"You *make* some!" Old Keats leaned down near Crab. "It may have t' do with havin' one arm or two — or bein' dead!"

In just a little while I was really proud I hadn't fought with Crab last night, because with no spit left in him, and too tired to hardly breath anyway, he spit a handful of spit into Rostov's hand. Part of it was natural and part of it was choking, but it worked either way, I guess.

And Rostov just mixed that spit with a little dirt he picked up from the ground in his other hand. And finally Rostov had a little handful of sort of wet spit and earth, and he said in a very soft voice to Crab that it was okay for him to go to sleep again.

And that American spit and Russian ground was the poultice.

Shad didn't complain and he didn't cooperate either. He stood back while Rostov and Old Keats bound the poultice around Crab's arm with a piece of fairly clean cloth.

When that was done Rostov said, "If the swelling goes down within three hours, his arm will cure itself and he'll live."

It seemed a hundred years longer, but the top edge of the sun was just coming up over eastern hills now.

"Get ready to move when all of that sun's in sight," Shad said.

Rostov swung up onto his horse before replying. "No."

"Why not? My men'll be ready!"

Rostov took the time to swing his big black around. "My men have to attend a burial."

"Burial?" For a moment Shad was really concerned. "One of your men —"

"No. One of our horses."

"One of your *horses!*"

I somehow knew Rostov was talking about Igor's horse, and I couldn't help but agree with him, though I said nothing.

Rostov said patiently. "A warrior's burial. He died bravely, and with honor. We'll dig a grave for him and bury him with the honor he has earned. And after those things are taken care of, we'll be ready to leave, about noon."

He turned and rode away.

8

That was some kind of funeral.

Those cossacks always looked pretty shiny, but that morning they turned out with more gleam on their boots and their saddles and sabers than ever before.

Some of them had dug a grave, which was quite a job in itself, since it was big enough for the horse. It was more than six feet deep and about four by eight in top size.

Midmorning they were all on horseback, gathered around the grave and the dead animal. Us cowboys, not used to such a ceremony and mostly not putting a whole lot of stock in it, hadn't fancied ourselves up at all, naturally. We just rode over partly out of curiosity and courtesy, and partly killing time until we'd get the herd moving.

But like I said, all those cossacks were scrubbed and polished up fit for the burial of a king. They were circled around the grave, so

Shad and the rest of us just sat on our horses a little distance away, watching and listening.

Igor had ridden up on a kind of scrubby-looking little splay-foot pony that was obviously second-string and had probably been a packhorse up until this morning. Slowly, with a ceremonious feeling about it, he and Rostov dismounted to stand at the head of that big grave.

Rostov started to speak. And somehow on that lonely Siberian plain, even with his tough voice, it sounded like Rostov was speaking in church. His voice was deep, resonant, and filled with emotion.

"What's he sayin'?" Slim quietly asked Old Keats.

"Well —" Old Keats hesitated.

Mushy whispered, "He's sure serious!"

"He's *prayin'* for that damn horse!" Dixie muttered. "He's lookin' at the sky an'—"

"Shut up!" Keats said. "If you dumb bastards all talk at once, I can't make heads or tails out of it!"

And then he began translating haltingly, in a low voice, as best he could. "Captain Rostov says — that horse was — part of everything living. — Man, horse, or beast. — Or anything. — Like everything else, it's got its own feelin's — it's got its own courage." He hesitated, frowning. "I ain't sure, but I think he just said that that horse probably had its own sense of humor. — Which Rostov claims is almost always the better part of courage." He waited for a while, listening carefully as Rostov spoke. "And he says he consigns that beautiful warrior horse to the place where all brave spirits go."

Rostov stopped talking then, and Igor moved up beside him to speak one short, quiet line, his voice a little unsteady.

"He says because of its funny coloring, his horse's name was 'Spotted' or 'Spot,' or something like that," Keats said.

"Hell," Dixie grunted. "Rotten name for a horse."

But nobody paid much attention to him.

Igor was taking something out of a little leather bag, and it glinted in the rising sun. As he moved toward the dead horse it chimed with a crystal sweetness in his hands.

It was a silver bell.

Saying a few words, his voice still shaky, he started to tie the bell around the horse's neck.

Old Keats was genuinely moved, and he said, "I think — he said — that the sound of that silver bell will help him to find his horse — in whatever land there is — beyond death."

Then Igor, with the bell tied in place, whispered one last thing that none of us could hear, so Old Keats couldn't translate it. He slowly drew his saber and touched its blade softly on the shoulder of his dead horse. And after that gentle touch he slowly drew the sharp edge across his wrist so that blood began dripping down from it. Finally, he put his saber back in its sheath and stepped back to watch the final part of the burial, his damp eyes now, slowly, becoming stone dry, and his jaw firm.

"Christ," Dixie said in a low voice. "Why don't he just marry his goddamn horse and get it over with?"

Nobody laughed and Slim turned to Dixie. "How'd you like t' get your head handed to ya' on a tin plate?"

We were silent for a long moment as the cossacks very gently put ropes beneath the animal and, with men holding them at each side, started lowering him slowly into the grave.

It was quiet while the cossacks filled the grave in over that good horse, Spotted or Spot, or whatever his name was.

Shad hadn't spoken all that time. As they were finishing filling the grave he said to me, "Go tell Rostov I want Igor riding with me in front of our bunch." He called to the rest of the outfit, "Get ready to move out!"

I rode Buck the little ways over to where

Rostov had just mounted. "Captain Rostov? Mr. Northshield, Shad, suggests that Igor ride with him. That way you'll both have somebody you can send messages back and forth with."

Rostov glanced at me with those hard, dark eyes. "He suggests?"

"Something like that."

"Tell him I think it's an excellent idea. I'll send Igor over."

I rode back to Shad. The other hands had left, and I told him that Igor riding with him was okay with Rostov. And then I said, "Listen, boss. There's one more thing."

"Yeah?"

"Well —" I couldn't quite find the words. "Blackeye kinda' belongs t' me. Right?"

"He's your second-string pony in the remuda."

"But I mean —" It was hard to say.

"Yeah? What d' ya' mean?"

"I mean — I want t' give Blackeye t' Igor. That's what I mean."

Shad looked at me with those tough eyes of his for a long, hard moment, and I couldn't help wonder whether it was rougher being looked at firmly by him or Rostov. He said, "Blackeye belongs to Joe Diamond and the Slash-Diamond outfit."

After that burial, I was somehow rough-out

determined. "Then take Blackeye outta my pay! It's a gift I wanta give!"

Right about then Igor came trotting up to us on his little pack pony, so I couldn't say any more about the subject. He pulled up and said to Shad in that funny one-note way of speaking American that he had, "I am to report to you, sir."

"That's right!" Shad spoke so harshly, almost snarling, that it scared the hell out of both me and Igor. "And you don't call me sir, you call me Shad!"

All in all, Igor had had enough hard time already. And now this sudden attack of Shad's made his language go away. Struggling the best he could, he stammered, "I — I am — to report to you — Sir Shad."

"You're goin' t' ride with me." There was no mercy in the iron voice.

"Yes!" Igor was plainly trying to do the best he could, and yet it was clear at the same time that he was getting about ready to fight if nothing reasonable worked out. "Yes! Sir Shad."

Shad looked at me with his eyebrows pulled down tight. "I hate bein' called 'Sir Shad' even if it's by accident."

"You're bein' awful hard on Igor!" I said. "He's just tryin' t' be polite!"

"An' I'm gonna be even harder." Shad glanced at Igor's scruffy little pony. "Nobody can keep up with me or this outfit without a fair horse. Levi?"

"Yeah?"

"Go break out Blackeye." Shad was sure a surpriser from time to time.

"Huh? Ya' mean —"

"An' bring 'im back for this cossack t' ride. If he can."

He was saying quite a bit, and I knew it, though he wouldn't let on.

I welled up a lot more than I wanted to, so I didn't say anything, but just rode over and roped Blackeye and brought him back.

Igor sort of got the idea when I came back with that feisty pinto on a rope. He still wasn't too sure, but as we switched the saddle and harness from his raunchy pack-horse to Blackeye, he began to realize what Shad was doing and it hit him kind of hard. With his black eye, Blackeye looked fairly ridiculous, but otherwise he resembled Igor's dead horse in looks, fire and spirit more than any other pony in our whole string.

We switched the saddle and gear, and Shad swatted the packhorse on the ass, sending it back in the direction of the cossack remuda.

Igor swung up onto Blackeye and just sat

there for a minute, feeling the pinto's muscle between his legs. Then he said, "I will take good care of this horse."

"You better," Shad said. And then he nailed it. "Because he's yours."

"He is mine?"

"That's what I said."

Igor couldn't decide whether to laugh or cry. Holding any possible emotion back, he rode Blackeye away a little bit, just sort of taking the top of him, and Shad and I were alone.

"I think, if you're not careful, you just may make a friend," I said.

Shad swung up onto his big Red. "He lost a damn good horse protecting our cattle. And this outfit always pays its own way."

"Shad," I reminded him, "I wanted t' just give him that horse, before. And I wasn't tryin' to pay nobody's way for nothin'."

"Then it's done both ways." Red reared a little under him. "You outta friendship, and me because it just seemed like the fair thing t' do. It's his horse."

"Okay." I swung up on Buck. "Does Blackeye come outta my salary or the Slash-Diamond?"

Shad turned Red and looked back at me. "It was my decision and it comes outta my salary."

Igor was riding back, and Shad called,

"Come on with me, you goddamn Russian!"
He spurred Red away.

Igor pulled up beside me briefly. "What is a 'goddamn' Russian?" he asked, toying with Blackeye's reins and patting the horse.

"One of the best kind a' Russians," I said.

And then I rode toward the cossacks far ahead, as Igor joined Shad and the cowboys started whooping and hollering to move the head.

In the next couple of weeks we went through some of the most beautiful country I ever saw. It was mountainous, some of it pretty rough, covered by vast but never crowded forests. And there was damnere every kind of tree you could think of, from oaks to birches and maples, from aspens to poplars and elms. And everywhere you looked, there was a green blanket of high grass. And just about every time you were thirsty, you came upon clear, sweet water, a lake or stream or creek. Those cows never had it better, nor probably as good, in Montana and they were getting fat and sassy and contented, even making about twelve miles a day. And some of the big bulls were getting rambunctious as hell. I could double guarantee, for example, that we had a whole lot more pregnant cows after those two weeks than we'd had at Vladivostok. And all too often, singly or in groups, those longhorns would up and decide that they just wanted to go their own way and the hell with the rest of the world. When that happened, it took some artistic, persuasive cussing and hard whacks on their asses with lariats to finally get them back to following the main herd and Old Fooler.

But those were the problems of the average, dumb cowhand. As an average, dumb messenger boy, I was spending all my time trying to keep up with Rostov. Whenever he stopped long enough to talk, he talked pretty freely now. One time, when we were riding far ahead of all the others, he spotted two big deer, far off. By the time I'd seen them, now bounding away, he'd pulled up, jerked out his rifle and fired twice. They both went down, and at that distance that was some kind of shooting.

"One of them is for the Slash-Diamond outfit." He lowered his rifle.

"I don't know how Shad'll take that. He likes t' make do on his own."

"Tell him it's a gift. In partial repayment for the pinto he gave to Igor, after you made him do it."

"How'd you know it was anything like that?"

Rostov glanced at me briefly with those damned dark, piercing eyes as he reloaded his rifle to full-up with cartridges from his bandoleer. "You wanted to in the first place. He knew you were determined, and somehow right. Therefore, he made the gift."

"You sure are jumpin' to conclusions."

"I looked at you the night Igor had to shoot his horse. Right then you were almost ready to give him your own."

"I hadn't even *thought* about anything like that."

"Yes. You had. Whether you know it or not. You couldn't even look at me, or Igor. You understood."

"Well, when you get right down to it then, Shad finally understood everything. And a whole lot better than me."

Rostov finished reloading his rifle. "That's right. He's not a bad fellow. Except for being opinionated and prejudiced."

I started to get mad, but Rostov didn't give me time. His deep eyes fixed on mine with a certain sadness in them, he shoved his rifle firmly back into its saddle holster.

"I hope not, but one day I may be forced to kill him."

That was a stopper.

Getting mad went clear out of my head, and I wanted to say a thousand things against the idea but couldn't think of any one thing to say in particular.

But it was too late anyway.

Rostov had already spurred his horse off at a gallop toward the two deer.

That night I took one of the deer back to camp tied behind the cantle of my saddle. It was dressed and bled and all ready to cut up and cook.

Every man there was really tickled at the prospect of fresh vension. Mushy and Link, who were on cooking duty, set up a Dutch oven by the fire to make two rump roasts with onions and beans, and a little bacon fat added for flavor.

Crab, who still had his arm in a sling but was feeling a lot better, said, "Hey, goddamnit, this is gonna be a goddamn feast!"

Shad said, "I heard two shots, Levi. Neither one came from your thirty-thirty."

"Rostov got two deer. Gave one to us."

"Why?"

He didn't say it loud or hard, but it made everybody silent. "It was his way a' thankin' us a little bit – for givin' Blackeye to Igor."

Dixie frowned up from where he was working on one of his stirrups near the fire. "I ain't so sure I want no goddamn cossack-shot venison."

Old Keats raised his bad arm as high as he

could in an exasperated gesture. "I imagine it tastes just about the same as if it was cowboy-shot."

"Hell." Slim grinned. "Meat's meat. I just hope *nobody* else eats it, so then I can finish it all."

The two roasts turned out really fine, and everybody did eat their share of them.

Except Shad.

After all of us others had helped ourselves, he just quietly took some beans and coffee and let it go at that.

On top of what Rostov had said before, that made me damned sad and thoughtful.

Later, after we'd eaten, Old Keats came over and sat down on the ground beside me. Sammy the Kid was idly fooling with his guitar, and a few of the others were playing showdown by the fire, laughing and passing the deal back and forth among them.

Off in the distance, from the cossack camp, we could dimly hear another string instrument, and some of the cossacks were humming a pretty, peaceful tune in a low, strong way.

"How ya' feelin'?" Old Keats said quietly, and I knew that Shad was on his mind too.

"Sad an' thoughtful," I told him accurately.

"Yeah?" He hunched forward, clasping his arms around his knees. "Well, personally I'm not feelin' too bad, m'self."

"How come?"

"Shad didn't eat any a' that venison. But on the other hand, he didn't send you packin' right over t' the cossack camp t' give it back. I think there might be some hope there for that hardheaded bastard, somewhere."

Shad had gone out to take a ride around the herd, checking it. He rode back in now and took care of Red. Then he poured a cup of coffee and came over to sit beside us.

After he'd settled down and taken a couple of sips, he said, "Somethin's botherin' you, Levi."

"I dunno exactly how ya' know, but damn right there is."

"What?"

"Rostov."

"Why?"

"He — He's got an idea that — sometime you an' him may come t' tanglin' ass. And that wouldn't be any fun at all, for anybody."

"Hell." Shad took another slow sip of coffee. "Didn't you know about that possibility up front, Levi?"

"Not the way he said it!" I kept my voice down so that it was just the three of us in the conversation, but I couldn't keep the worry out of my voice. "What he said about you, word for word, was 'I hope not, but one day I may be forced to kill him.' An' that Rostov's sure as hell one tough sonofabitch!"

Shad shrugged very slightly and drank some more of his coffee.

Old Keats frowned. "What the hell'd he say a thing like that for? He knew ya'd have t' tell Shad."

"It's pretty easy," Shad said. "He figures we're gonna come up against some tough times. And he thinks that as bosses he and me may have some strong differences of opinion on what t' do under certain circumstances."

"Well, then —" Keats hesitated. "What he told Levi wasn't so much a threat as a friendly warnin'."

I nodded. "I think maybe so. He sure looked unhappy as hell when he said it. Maybe if you just tried to cooperate with 'im —"

Shad ignored what I was suggesting. "One way or the other, I won't lose much sleep over it." He finished his coffee and stared quietly at the cup. "All I want is t' get those longhorns delivered. If there's need for any fights along the way, then they'll be fought."

"Maybe he didn't actually mean nothin'," I said hopefully, without really believing it. "Maybe he was just kinda foolin' with me a little."

"That man would never fool about fightin',

or killin'." Old Keats had the same sense of foreboding that I had, and he looked grimly at Shad. "I'd sure as hell hate t' see you two rough bastards go against each other. It'd have t' be kinda like the earth itself gettin' torn apart."

Shad wasn't all that impressed. He stood up, stretched and yawned slightly. "One thing I meant for damn sure. About not losin' any sleep."

He went over to get into his bedroll, and Old Keats turned to me. "You got an extra problem that I shoulda guessed by now."

"Which extra problem?"

"Well, Shad's like your big brother. But you've also gotten t' kinda respect an' like Rostov."

"Oh, hell!"

"Don't oh-hell me. That's as it should be, and I know Rostov earned it." He scratched his chin, frowning. "It's just — If they do get around t' getting into a scrap, don't get yourself in the middle. That'd be awful perilous ground. With them two, only one of 'em would come out alive."

Maybe what he said about not getting in the middle gave me the idea, or maybe I'd have thought of it anyway, but the next day I told Rostov what was uppermost in my mind. We'd ridden ahead and he'd paused at the top of a hill, so it gave me a chance to speak.

"Captain Rostov, sir?" I said.

"Umm?" He'd been intensely studying the far hills, and he turned to me.

"You — you said somethin' about one day maybe havin' t' kill Shad Northshield."

"Yes." He was now studying me with that same intensity, and yet as always it was mixed with that strange kind of humor that seemed to forever be lurking somewhere in his eyes.

"Well" — I took a deep breath — "I just wanted t' mention that even if ya' could kill Shad, which is unlikely, that you'll have t' kill me first."

Even though there was a tiny grin at one edge of his mouth, his gaze was still boring right through to the back of my head.

"And don't tell me nothin', please, about a puppy barkin'. I'm just tellin' you right now. But I can bite, too."

He looked at me for a long, fairly spooky moment, and then his teeth flashed in an unexpected and totally genuine smile that damnere dazzled me. "Good for you, Levi. But I expected no less."

Then he turned abruptly and rode off, and that was the end of the conversation.

"Well hell," I muttered to myself and Buck. "Is Shad still in jeopardy, or me, or both of us, or whomever the hell ever?" Buck twisted his left ear back, thinking what I was saying was a little silly.

So after all my intended bravery, I had no choice but to let the talk stop there and follow Rostov, going at a full run to try to keep up.

Rostov had said his piece, and for damn sure meant it. I'd said mine, and meant it. And Shad hadn't even bothered to put his two-cents worth into it, which in my mind made them about even.

I rode after Rostov knowing that he would never say anything more about killing Shad.

He might do it, but he wouldn't talk about it.

And that was the hell of it. Just the idea that while he'd never talk about killing him again, he might just up, sometime, and take a crack at it.

9

Rostov now started taking even more of an interest in talking to me, telling me about things as we went along, and that tended to be one hell of an education all in itself. I guess he'd decided maybe I wasn't a puppy.

I'd like to think that.

Also, he quietly saw to it that I gradually got to know the other cossacks.

Aside from Igor, the two others who spoke American, though they called it English, were Lieutenant Vassily Bruk and Sergeant Nikolai Razin. They hadn't got the language down quite as good as Igor, but they held their own pretty well.

The lieutenant, Bruk, was the oldest man among the cossacks. He was lean and taciturn, and despite his age, which was probably pushing up over fifty, was as tough as a hardened old iron bar. Actually, I think our old man, Keats, had a few years on Bruk. But as Rostov later explained to me, in better words of course, when a fella's as far advanced in years as either one of them was, and still banging around on hard, active duty, you have to figure he's pretty special in the first place, and likely has that extra inner resilience of mind and body that can push a rare man clear up over the hundred-year mark and find him still raring to go for a good fight, a few drinks, and maybe even a lady or two.

If I'd had to compare the other one, Sergeant Nikolai Razin, to anyone in our outfit, it would have been Slim. He was as heavy-set as Slim, with what looked like a fat belly, but in both their cases it was still all muscle. And while they were both quick to smile and loved to laugh, running up against either one of them would be like taking a knife and fork and trying to make a quick dinner out of a good-natured, slightly potbellied bear. You wouldn't get much to eat, but it would be your most memorable, and last, dinner.

The sergeant sure didn't actually look a lot like Slim otherwise. He had a strongly Oriental cast to his eyes, and a deep, ugly scar that ran from the top of his forehead down narrowly around his left eye and clear to the bottom of his chin. And something I'd never seen before, he only wore a beard on the right side of his face. I think he liked to keep the left side clean-shaven because he was proud of that scar and that way everyone could see the huge, ugly battle mark in all its glory.

Aside from their quickness to laughter and their big stomachs, there were two other things that made me think of them in the same way. Sergeant Nikolai Razin didn't want to be called anything by anybody except "Nick." And Slim was so much that way that most of us would have been hard put to remember his last name. Another similarity, it was Nick that I'd happened to see that one time before, giving his last drink of water to his horse.

As for the rest of the cossacks, they were kind of a mixed bunch. Not as mixed up as we were, with Shiny Joe and Link, and Natcho and Chakko, and even Purse. But you could tell they came from a lot of different people and places and times. Their eyes went from blue and green to dark brown and hazel. And tall or short, they ranged from a few sandy-haired ones to mostly jet-black hair.

Their full names were too hard to even fool around with. They had last names like Yevdokimov, Gordiyenko, Naumenko and Vishnevetski.

One night Crab Smith and some of the others got me trying to pronounce the few full names I could think of offhand. There weren't many.

"Jesus Christ!" Crab's hurt arm was nearly completely okay by now and he rubbed his head with it. "Ain't one of 'em got a good, simple, civilized name like Smith? They must be crazy?"

"How's your arm?" Old Keats was being sarcastic and Crab knew he was right, so he shut up then.

"Their first names're generally easier," I told them.

"Like what?" Mushy grunted suspiciously.

"Well —" I concentrated. "Essaul, Ilya, Ivan,

Yuri, Dmitri, Victor —"

"Victor?" Sammy the Kid asked. "You sure you ain't confused?"

"That sounds almost American," Dixie said.

Shad was rolling a cigarette. "Go ahead, Levi."

"Kirdyaga, Vody, Gerasmin, Pietre, Yakov." I frowned. "That's all, best m' memory serves."

"Talk about dumb names!" Rufe shook his head.

"Our names are just exactly as dumb t' them!" Old Keats looked at Purse, Natcho and Link, who happened to be sitting near each other. "Want some real dumb names? Percival! Ignacio! Lincoln Washington Jefferson Jackson!"

"Hell," Purse said, "no reason t' get pissed off at us."

"Shoot, no," Link added. "We didn't have nothin' t' do with gettin' them names."

"That's exactly what I'm sayin', goddamnit!" Keats told us.

"No point gettin' all excited," Dixie said. "Levi's the only one who's got t' keep track a' them dumb Russian names." He added, with a kind of a mean, troublemaking look at me, "And friendly as he's got with them, an' with that stupid name a' his, he's the perfect one t' do it."

You could never tell about Dixie. A few of the others laughed, and as tired as I was that night, I started to stand up to fight if need be. But Shad was on his feet already. "My official given name ain't Shad," he said quietly and not too easily. "It's Shadrack." He looked around with hard eyes. "Anybody want t' make a joke about that?"

Nobody wanted to, which was kind of natural under those circumstances.

He went on. "Nobody's gonna make fun of anybody's name from here on out. Not the Russian names. Not our own. And it's time t' get some sleep."

My bedroll wasn't far from his, so we wound up facing each other a little away by ourselves while we pulled off our boots.

"You sure are good at savin' me from fearful fights," I said, pulling off one boot.

"Hate t' get my messenger killed." He pulled his first boot off.

I tugged on the second boot. My left foot's always been bigger than the right one, for some reason. "I didn't know your official given name was Shadrack."

He pulled his second boot off. "It ain't."

"Well, then —"

"I didn't like the way that talk was goin' because it wasn't fair." He took off his hat and hung it over his saddle horn. "A name ain't never nothin', good or bad, until the man behind that name makes it so." And then he laid his head down in the seat of the saddle and was asleep.

I thought about what he'd said for a while, feeling real good about it, and then before I knew it, I was asleep too.

In the days that came, Rostov kept teaching me things, and maybe just in general conversation learning a little bit, too. For example, he asked me about the leather chaps that most of us cowboys wore, and I told him they were mostly for protecting your legs in rough brush country where, if you were riding hard, scrub oak and snagging low branches and such could cut you all to hell without them.

Rostov said they didn't have that kind of country over here. Mostly just grass and thick stands of trees going on forever, and sometimes willows where there were creeks or water naturally laid up for long times. But he still liked the look and the idea of chaps and thought mine were kind of artistic because of the brass studs I'd lined the edges with. I also had a hunch he thought they might be useful in protecting a man's legs in battle.

Another time, he took an interest in the hard

leather cuffs around my wrists. I told him that they were partly for fancy and partly to keep my wrists from being chewed up and rope-burned when I was working cattle and using the lariat on my saddle. He nodded politely at my answer, but there was no way for him to know exactly what I was talking about because he'd never seen anybody do any roping. I was tempted to lasso a tree branch or a rock or something, but it seemed kind of foolish so I just let it go that it was a way of throwing a rope and catching a cow, presuming you threw the rope right in the first place. Then he told me about the closest thing he knew of for that purpose. It was called an *"urga"* and it was used by herders in Mongolia and Siberia. It was a thirty-foot-long pole that was light and strong, and there was a loop hooked to the end of it. If you wanted to catch something, you just rode up near it, held out the long pole, and dropped the noose around the animal's neck.

The very idea of lugging a thirty-foot-long pole all over the place struck me as being funny as hell.

But there were other things that weren't so funny, like why the cossacks all wore those scarlet-red vests. That was so that if they got their bodies chopped up badly in a battle, the bleeding wouldn't show so much. The vest would be the same color as the flowing blood it was soaking up.

Therefore, if a bleeding cossack rode on through a battle half dead, he'd look unbloody and unbeaten. And if he was just barely strong enough to stay in the saddle and sit up straight, he'd still look like the toughest horseman who ever bore down on you.

And then one day Rostov told me about the swans.

It was late in the afternoon, and we were crossing a wide plain, riding at an easy walk for a change.

Two huge, beautiful birds flew high over us, crossing gracefully under the lowering sun and then finally dipping and turning and at last disappearing far away in the northern sky. I'd never seen a sight quite like those big, white, lovely birds. It seemed as though they were almost softly playing together, and even teasing each other a little, while they were taking their own kind of a friendly, casual stroll a thousand feet up in the clear blue air. It was just too pretty not to watch, even though I was supposed to be searching the horizon, and I felt Rostov glancing at me before they flew out of my sight.

"Swans," he said.

"Well — sure. Anybody knows that." The

only swan I'd ever seen before in my life was in picture book.

"Male and female."

"How could ya' tell, from so far?"

"They always travel in couples, rather as man and wife, if you will. Do you have many swans in Montana?"

"Well — not too many."

He looked at me briefly with those eyes of his, and I got the definite feeling that I not only couldn't ever get away with lying to him, but that I'd have a hard time even ever exaggerating to him. It was as though the back of my mind was saying loud and clear to the back of his mind, "This dumb little bastard never saw a swan before in his life."

I said out loud, "They sure are beautiful."

He said thoughtfully, "They are beautiful. In more ways than one."

He stopped for a drink, taking the water bag from his saddle. He offered it to me first, and without hardly thinking about it because by then it seemed a natural thing to do, I took it. Unplugging the top, I said, "I ain't really too up on swans. What d'ya' mean, more ways than one?"

"They choose a mate when they're very young. And they stay together for all the rest of their lives."

"Well, that is a kind of a nice, friendly thing."

"We could learn much from them in terms of loyalty, steadfastness, love."

I handed him back the water bag.

He drank just enough to wet his mouth and throat. "When I first came out east to Siberia, I was just a youngster, about your age. That's when I saw my first pair of them."

His thinking was so far away, and he was going back so quietly to some gentle memory, that it never even occurred to me to take any exception to his describing me with the word "youngster."

"We'd been out hunting, and we'd made camp near the end of the day, when two swans flew overhead. The other men were also new to the country, and one of them grabbed his gun and shot the female of the swans. It fell almost at our feet, dead." He took a long breath, hooking the water bag back onto his saddle. "All that night the male swan flew overhead, circling the camp in the dark, never landing anywhere to rest, and crying pitifully in its low, keening way for some answer from its mate. I've never heard cries more pleading, more terribly sad." He paused a moment. "The next morning, it continued to circle high over us, still in its own soft, searching way, making those tragic, weeping sounds." Rostov looked up at the sky above, but he was still really looking into the past. "Then at noon, with the sun nearly directly above us, the swan finally lost all hope. It gave up and stopped crying for an answer from her. It flew up and up, as high and as far as its weakened wings would take it into the sky. And then that great bird simply folded its wings and plummeted down like a stone to smash itself to death on the earth far below." He paused and then said huskily, "It had done the one thing it possibly could do to rejoin its mate."

We were both silent for a long moment.

As for me, I was so moved by that story, and by the way Rostov had told it and had felt it, that I couldn't have trusted myself to say anything I might have said, in any case.

He led off at an easy walk again.

We were heading across a wide plain of golden, knee-deep grass that bowed slightly as the wind touched it, and in the far distance there were some low tree-covered hills.

There were three words he'd used that stuck hard in my mind. They were "loyalty," "steadfastness" and "love."

Finally, still touched about the whole damn thing, I spurred closer abreast of Rostov and managed a small half grin. "Guess you're right, about what a fella could learn about from them swans. About loyalty an' all that."

He nodded briefly. "The story applies to many things — in many ways."

"Yeah." I couldn't really figure out what all he meant by that, at the moment. So just trying to say something, anything, I said, "It'd sure be nice if while they're at it swans could teach us how t' fly, too."

He glanced at me, his expression quiet and serious. "If you think of what I just told you enough, you'll find that that swan, and the absolute loyalty it was capable of, does indeed teach you how to fly in the most important possible way."

"Yeah?"

He could see he'd lost me, but he was patient about it. He said gently, "Don't you understand the simple thing I mean? Just the very awareness alone of one such magnificent and complete sacrifice should be an inspiration for every man's spirit to fly, and soar forever within his heart. And, so inspired, he should want to be able to hopefully emulate that life-and-death devotion."

Good God, I thought. And we call Old Keats the Poet.

"Well, yeah," I said. "But — that's kinda philosophic, for me."

"Simply thinking and speaking of action is philosophy, of course. Taking action is something else. And, as with the swan, the greatest and ultimate test of a man taking action must also be his willingness, while loving life, to give his life for something he loves."

"Yeah." He'd never talked to me like that before, and I couldn't think of much else to say.

And then there were the sounds of hoofbeats coming closer from behind. It was Nick, moving at an easy run to catch up with us. He pulled down to a walk and tried out his American in his deep, rasping voice. "In the small mountains up ahead, we have seen two wolves."

Without missing a beat, Rostov said, "There were three."

That got to me quite a bit. We'd been riding along easily and with no trouble, philosophizing and such, and for that time I hadn't been paying much attention to anything. But that Rostov, without seeming to pay any attention either, hadn't missed one goddamn thing. "There are no Tartars on the other side of those hills," he said. "The wolves crossed over without hesitation."

I decided that maybe I could learn something from swans, but that I could sure as hell learn a lot more from Rostov himself.

Two mornings later, riding far ahead of the others toward the top of a steep hill, Rostov dismounted and tied his horse to a tree. Wondering, but without question, I followed his example. He took a small spyglass from his saddlebag and we went on up to the crest of the hill on foot, going on all fours the last few feet and finally lying down at the very top. Far off and below there was a wide, slow-running river. On the near side there were a few hovels and shacks scattered along its muddy banks. There were perhaps a dozen people visible in the village, and a handful of small boats in the river.

Studying the area through his small telescope, Rostov said, "The Ussuri River."

There were also a small number of distant huts on the far bank of the river.

"What's on the other side?" I asked.

"Manchuria." He adjusted the scope for another look. "The buildings on this side are a Russian town. Uporaskaya."

"Upor — what?"

"Uporaskaya. Freely translated, it means 'the stubborn man.'" He'd seen enough, and we moved back down the slope without ever showing ourselves against the skyline. As we remounted, he said, "We're going to swing east to avoid Uporaskaya."

"Yeah?"

He nodded. "There are no Tartar warriors there or across the river. But just one Tartar sympathizer could give us away."

I frowned and grinned a little at the same time. "Considerin' we got five hundred longhorns, somebody's sure as hell bound t' notice us sooner or later."

"With luck, we'll be able to get to Khabarovsk without being seen." He shrugged slightly. "After that we certainly will be seen — sooner or later."

Something about the grim way he said it made me hope it would be later.

Rostov waved far back to the nearest cossacks behind us, signaling them to angle eastward behind us.

About the time that the main herd was safely bypassing the town, two or three miles east of it, with high hills in between, Igor came galloping up to us on Blackeye, not looking too happy.

At Shad's instructions he'd taken to calling Shad Shad, so he said, "Shad would like to known why we have taken this change of direction."

Rostov was faintly amused. "He'd 'like' to know?"

Igor wet his lips. "I am sure that he was joking." He wasn't at all sure Shad was joking. "But he said" — Igor concentrated — "that 'there better be a damn good reason, or heads will roll.'"

Rostov's faint amusement still remained in his eyes, but his jaw hardened. "Tell him if we hadn't changed directions, heads *would* have rolled."

Igor was caught dead center between those two strong men, and was getting nervous as a cat in a dog kennel. "But he very much wants some reason, Captain."

The last tiny traces of humor were gone from Rostov's eyes. "That's all, Corporal."

"But —"

"Add one more thing." Rostov's voice became deadly. "Tell him if he ever disagrees with any decision of mine in the future, I'll be only too glad to discuss it with him personally, instead of by messenger."

Rostov swung his horse around and rode off.

Igor and I looked at each other, and I could see how miserable he felt. "Just tell Shad that Rostov was busy but that I told you everything's okay. Tell him I want to explain the reason to him myself tonight."

Igor understood that this would kind of get him off the hook. He nodded, grateful and relieved. Then he rode back, and I galloped ahead to catch up with Rostov.

We rode particularly fast during the rest of that long, hard day. I knew Rostov was concerned about any people who might be out of the town, hunting or whatever, and might see us. So we scoured the mountains and forests on every side, but there wasn't a living soul in sight.

Finally, toward the end of the day, Rostov slowed down to a walk. I offered him a drink of water from my canteen, and he took it.

As he drank I said, "Funny thing about Upor — Uporaskaya meaning a stubborn man. I never knew any a' them funny Russian names for towns meant anything."

He handed the canteen back. "In any unsettled land, the names of towns come from the pioneers who settle them, from colorful incidents that happen, from legends, or sometimes from the topography."

Not knowing what that last word meant, I just said, "Yeah?"

"Translated, some Siberian towns are called Too-Far Mountain, Pancake Flats, Broken-Jaw Creek."

"Hell, sounds kinda like some names back home."

He continued, growing thoughtful. "As for

Uporaskaya, there's a legend around that name. When it was first settled, a man there was reputed to be the most stubborn man in the world. The other few people there, his friends, decided to move out. But he'd planted some pumpkins, so he wouldn't go. He was working in the pumpkin patch as the others left, and a couple of them, knowing that he would be all alone, called out that he just *had* to move with them." Rostov paused. "Since he'd been told he *had* to move, the stubborn fellow *wouldn't* move. He wouldn't move at all. He just stood there stubbornly, without ever moving one bit. And finally the pumpkin vines started to grow up around his legs. They grew until at last, in time, the vines reached his throat, and they strangled him to death where he stood."

He looked at me as he finished the legend, and I could see that he was trying to tell me two things at once. "Well, he sure was one stubborn bastard," I said. "A hell of a lot more stubborn than my Shad."

He was pleased at my jumping the gun on his story that way, but he was still serious. "For the sake of all of us, I hope you're right."

"Another thing," I said with as much innocence as I could, "if the Russians made up that legend, they musta had some pretty stubborn fellas themselves."

He gave me a quick, hard look. "Meaning?"

I kind of chickened out. "Oh, nothin'." Then I added, "But you were sayin' before about the difference between thinkin' an' talkin', an' actually doin'. He actually *did* turn the cattle."

There was another quick, iron-hard look. "His message about 'heads rolling' was arrogant and hostile."

I'd already gone about far enough, but I managed to build up enough courage to say quietly, "An' your reply, sir?"

He studied me for a long moment with those piercing eyes.

And then he spurred on ahead.

That night we camped closer to the cossacks than ever before. There was just one small spring for water, so the two fires, with the spring shared in the middle, were only about fifty feet away from each other.

"Christ!" Dixie muttered later, as we were sitting around our fire. "Every time ya' wanna git a goddamn cup a' water, ya' have t' rub elbows with some goddamn cossack!"

"Shoot," Slim snorted. "Think how worried they must be for fear a' catchin' some excruciatin' an' fatal disease from a scabrous rebel like you."

156

Sammy the Kid said, "Why don't they go camp by their own spring? I say to hell with 'em!"

Some of the others nodded and grunted in agreement.

"All of ya' just relax." Shad stood up. "Slim, let's go take a look at the herd an' night riders."

A moment later the two of them rode off.

I'd already told Shad the reason we'd made the detour earlier that day, and he knew right off that it made sense. All he'd done was to say gruffly, "Rostov shoulda sent you back t' tell me. We'd a' made an even wider circle."

All along, of course, I'd kept Shad up on most of the things that were said and that happened to me while I was with the cossacks. I'd mentioned the line about the puppy barking and the wolf biting, though I didn't include the fact that I was the butt of it. And I'd told the story of the swans, and things like that. However, that night I hadn't brought up the legend of Uporaskaya because it just didn't seem like too good of an idea right then.

Now, with Shad and Slim gone to check out the herd and the men that were on duty, the rest of us were just sitting quietly.

Then, from over at the Russian camp, there came the soft sounds of that musical instrument of theirs. For the first time, at this nearer distance, I could see that it was Ilya who was playing it. A few of the cossacks around the fire started humming with deep, quiet voices along with the tune that he was strumming gently on the strings.

"Goddamnit!" Dixie grumbled. "Now they're gonna keep us awake all night with that infernal racket!"

"I think it's kinda nice," I said.

"We can fix 'em!" Sammy the Kid reached for his guitar and hit a couple of loud chords. Then he started a fast, noisy version of "De Camptown Races," and Dixie and some of the others went to singing that peppy song with a whole lot more enthusiasm than talent.

It was clear as hell that our camp was dead set on drowning out their camp.

Disgusted, Old Keats called out, "That's stupid! Why don't ya' all just shut up!"

But he didn't have enough authority to make it stick.

And then, from the Russian camp, where damnere all of them had now joined in their song to drown us out in turn, I heard Rostov's voice giving a short command.

Their music stopped abruptly, and Sammy and our singers were suddenly left out on a musical limb that was loud and unmelodious as hell.

"De Camptown Races" sort of stumbled to a stop about where somebody was puttin' their "money on the bob-tailed nag," and Sammy gave up playing.

"Well," Dixie said, "I guess we showed them."

Shad and Slim rode back up and dismounted, and Shad walked closer in toward the fire. We could see he was mad, and Sammy put his guitar away quickly.

"If we ever do run into any Tartars," Shad said, "there'll be no need of guns. You dumb bastards can sing 'em t' death!"

Everybody went to bed pretty fast about then, but within most of them there was still a general feeling of resentment and downright hostility toward those nearby cossacks. And it wasn't too difficult to figure out that the cossacks were feeling the same way toward us.

It exploded just after breakfast the next morning.

Dixie had gone over to the spring where Shiny Joe and Link were filling their canteens, and at the same time three or four cossacks came up to their side of the spring to fill some water bags.

One of the cossacks, Yuri, looked at the two black brothers and said something to his friend Vody, and they both laughed.

It may have been an innocent remark or otherwise, but Dixie took it as being otherwise. "What the hell're you laughin' about?" he growled.

"Aww, take it easy," Link said. "They dunno what you're sayin' anyway."

"Nobody," Dixie snarled, "makes fun a' my friends just b'cause through no fault a' their own they happen t' to be niggers!"

That was kind of funny because Dixie was the most prejudiced fella who ever walked. And, in an unfortunate way, it got even funnier. Sergeant Razin, Nick, was one of the cossacks there. He looked at Dixie and said as quietly as he could in his rasping accent, "No one is making fun of you niggers."

Not even knowing what the word meant, he'd accidentally cut Dixie to the quick by calling him a nigger too, and from there on it started getting unfunny real fast.

"Nigger!" Dixie roared. "Me?" And he put one foot forward into the shallows of the spring to swing his fist across and hit Nick on the jaw. That was sort of like hitting an oak tree, and it probably hurt Dixie's fist more than Nick's jaw, but Yuri and Vody were already lunging across the spring at Dixie. He went down beneath them and Shiny Joe and Link jumped in to help Dixie. Nick and the other cossacks splashed through the spring to join in, and in about three seconds, with cossacks and cowboys hurtling in from both directions, it was a full-scale riot that was getting closer to killing with each flying second.

Some of the participants were really getting hurt, and aside from the furious, swirling mass of fistfighting and rassling, cowboys were suddenly starting to grab for their guns and cossacks for their sabers.

Yuri with his head lowered so all he could see was a pair of chaps, hit me in the stomach as I came running up, and an instant later Natcho, Big Yawn and Chakko charged by me like a three-man battering-ram, knocking him to the ground as they joined the main battle. Yuri leaped up and was the first cossack to get his saber out.

Shad appeared beside him, revolver in hand, and knocked the saber out of his hand with the gun, then swung the gun in a back-handed blow that knocked Yuri flat again. Then Shad raised his gun and fired three times into the air.

At those three roaring blasts everyone was brought up short and the fighting suddenly stopped.

Even Nick, who'd been busy strangling Dixie in the spring, now let go and stood up, soaking wet. Dixie, choking and gasping for breath, sat up half in and half out of the spring.

Rostov, who'd been out of camp a little ways, galloped up now and dismounted.

Nobody was moving, but there was still a tension and anger among all the men there that you could actually feel in your skin, like hot, stormy weather.

Rostov's blazing eyes swept over us. "Who started this?"

Shad put his gun away and said flatly, "One a' my men."

The fight was over, but if it just got left like that, with the mean and bitter feelings we all had now, there'd be scars of anger on both sides that wouldn't ever heal. And there was no possible way to say anything, or do anything, that could somehow make things right between our outfit and the cossacks.

Except for one thing.

And that's the thing that Shad did.

Yuri was just getting up, and he now stepped forward to pick up his fallen saber.

But Shad reached down and picked it up for him. With all of the men watching, he slowly put his left hand out in front of him. Then, without a word, but with all the quiet meaning in the world, he drew the razor-sharp edge of the saber across the back of his own wrist, cutting it so deeply that his blood gushed out and flowed freely.

After that, paying no attention to the bleeding, he tossed the saber slightly into the air with his right hand, caught it by the blade, and offered it back handle first to Yuri.

The saber had drawn blood.

Yuri and Shad looked at each other for a long, stony moment.

Then Yuri finally nodded, understanding, and though his outside expression didn't change much, you could see that on the inside there was a new and growing respect for our boss. He and all the other cossacks were getting an insight into the caliber of the man that Shad was.

Yuri took his saber and, silently accepting Shad's blood on the blade, slowly put it back into its scabbard.

And somehow, by a strange magic in that quiet, strong thing that Shad had done, none of us around that spring there felt much like enemies anymore.

No one had to say anything about that sudden kind of a warm feeling Shad had caused. We all just felt it.

I had a hunch Rostov felt it most. He was still sore about the fight, but he was looking at Shad in a slightly different way, his original, hard anger now tempered almost involuntarily by something else. If I'd had to name just what that something else was, I'd have made an educated guess, knowing Rostov, that it was a small, almost begrudging touch of admiration.

Shad then turned and started back to camp, and fifteen minutes later the herd was moving through the early-morning sunshine and some faint low-valley mists, on its way north again, toward Khabarovsk.

10

In a way, that fight had made us closer. During the next few days, even though we generally camped along streams that ran damnere forever on a roughly east-to-west basis, small tributaries of the Ussuri, our camps at night just somehow managed to get a little nearer, and nobody seemed to mind it a whole lot.

Old Keats used to say that the more men were really men, the more they were like little boys. And sometimes they had to just naturally knock each other down, just to sort of get a general feeling about each other.

In any case, we weren't quite so much total

foreigners, back and forth, as we'd been up until then.

One night I finally got around to telling our outfit about why the cossacks all wore those scarlet-red vests, so that if they were hurt in a rough battle their blood wouldn't show up so much. And even Dixie didn't make any fun of that idea.

On the contrary, he said, "That ain't too bad of a notion, all in all. Half a' bein' on top a' the other guy is just showin' him you ain't hurt or scared."

Shiny Joe looked at his brother, Link, with the kind of a look that would normally require a wink, but between them the understanding was already inbuilt. "You sure did that the other mornin' in that fracas, Dixie. When that big cossack sergeant was holdin' your head under the water, you didn't say one damn thing t' give him any hint that you were in trouble."

"That's very hilarious," Dixie said. "But the whole damn thing wouldn't a' happened except that I was stickin' up for you two goddamned niggers."

But that was all in fun, and nobody was in the least bit mad at anybody else.

Rufe, sitting by the fire, tossed a small piece of wood into it. "I said it before, an' I'll say it again. They're both a hasty an' a heavy-lookin' bunch, them cossacks."

Shad was chewing a small wad of tobacco. He shifted it slowly in his mouth, glancing at the cossack camp nearby. "I ain't about t' issue you fellas red vests," he said. "Hopefully you'll have enough brains not t' go around gettin' yourselves hurt in the first place." His tone of voice was just about as tough as ever.

I couldn't help but think that Shad was a strange and unusual case. He was sure as hell a kind of an all-around genius in his own ways, and yet on the other hand it wasn't too difficult for me to picture him standing for a whole long time in a pumpkin patch in Uporaskaya.

Rostov and I spent the next afternoon crossing some almost endless, low rocky hills a mile or so ahead of the herd. He was making it a point to learn every little bit I knew about longhorns, and we'd somehow gotten onto the subject of their coloring.

"There's an old Western sayin'," I told him, "that longhorns come, solid or speckled or painted, in every single color of the rainbow."

He thought about this for a moment. "Purple?"

"Well —" I hesitated. "Some of 'em, sort of — in a way."

"Green?"

"Well —" He never asked an easy question in

his life. "I guess I've seen a few of 'em that had kinda, more or less, greenish spots."

He thought about that for a moment. Then he said, "They are colorful, but I think that old saying is an exaggeration."

He let it go at that for a while, and we passed over the last, low rocky hills into a vast, level plain of high, waving grass. In the distance far before us there was a jagged range of steep, tough mountains that looked like they'd been shoved up abruptly by God's fingers on an angry morning.

And, somehow, it was an absolutely magnificent view, with ten million miles of crystal-clear blue sky above it.

Maybe it was that view that kicked me off, but whatever the reason, as we were cantering along through the high grass, I asked Rostov without thinking much about it, "Say, sir, do you believe in God?"

"I beg your pardon?" he said in that faultless English that was so good I was beginning to wonder where the hell he ever learned it. And in his case, it wasn't American, it was English.

Repeating that kind of dumb question, that I shouldn't even have asked in the first place, was sort of embarrassing, but I was stuck with it. I said once more, "Do you believe in God?"

We rode on a few strides before he finally

answered, "Yes — and no."

He was looking far ahead, across that huge plain of yellow, gently waving grass, toward the jagged brown mountains and the immensity of cool blue sky above. I didn't think he was going to say anything more about that, but after a time he said, rather factually, "I believe that people who are devoutly religious, within any specific religion, have no true respect for the ultimate vastness that is God."

That was surely some kind of an answer, and there was just no way that I could come up with any kind of a reply to it.

And the subject never came up again.

We rode on to where those steep, jagged brown mountains started to slope up, and by then it was getting along toward evening. There wasn't any water here, but we'd had plenty most every day on the trek so far and were well supplied. So Rostov decided this would be as good a place as any to camp.

The outriding cossacks, the herd-riding cowboys and the cattle were strung out on the big plain of grass about a mile behind us. By the time they got up to us on the rising slope, Rostov and I had scouted the top of the mountain and beyond.

Shad and the Slash-Diamond hands started to settle down near a large rock only about seventy feet away. Rostov's men were building their camp near where he and I were sitting our horses. That was a friendly, near distance, considering there was no water to share, or anything like that.

The day was close to over, and I was about to take off when Rostov said in a low, serious voice, "Will you do me a favor, Levi?"

"Sure." I turned Buck back a little.

He hesitated thoughtfully. "Will you tell Shad, in your own way, that the blood he shed when he cut himself with Yuri's saber seems to make excellent cement."

I looked at him for a quiet moment. "If ya' don't mind, I'll tell him in your way."

And then I walked Buck the little distance to our camp and got Shad aside to tell him privately. When I repeated Rostov's kind of poetic line about blood and cement, Shad said in a low, fairly hard voice, "So? Tell me a thing, Levi. Do you think I owe him something back, for him sayin' such a neat goddamned thing?"

"I don't think he wants anything back, Shad."

And it was just at that time that Slim and Old Keats spotted the wolves.

They'd just dismounted twenty feet or so away, where some of the others were bringing up wood for a campfire, and they were staring down at the flat plain sloping off below. "Hey!" Slim hollered over to us. "There's two wolves way off down there!"

And then Shad did the goddamnedest thing. He did to them exactly what Rostov had done to Nick back along the trail. Without seeming to have even been looking, he said, "Three."

And damned if he, and Rostov before, weren't right.

We all looked down across the plain, and there was the pack leader of the wolves that had hit us some time back, that giant black bastard with the last half of his tail chewed off. He was far enough away to feel safe. But he'd evidently been circling us ever since that first disastrous attack. He'd probably picked up a rabbit or two along the way, but what he must have been really hoping for was for one of the cows or bulls, or maybe a calf, to get separated from the main herd so he could nail it and have a big supper for the whole pack.

The whole pack, what was left of it, consisted of one slightly smaller brown bitch and an about one-fourth-grown little wolf cub.

Seeing them out there on the plain, I could understand why most people had seen two wolves, and only Shad and Rostov had seen three. That little cub, lagging timidly behind, could have hidden himself with no trouble at all behind the one-half of a remaining tail that the big black still had on his husky butt.

I don't know why he'd decided to be so bold, but he sure was, just standing there like a kind of a magnificent half-tailed nobleman among wolves, watching us wisely from a few yards beyond the range of a rifle shot.

Shad studied that tough old wolf on the plain far below for a long moment. Then he said, "You were tellin' me, one time, that Rostov never actually saw anybody do any ropin'."

"Yeah, he ain't."

"Well, hell, since he just said such a nice thing about my blood bein' cement, let's show 'im some Montana ropework."

"Like what?"

"Like catchin' that big wolf down there."

"Jesus Christ, boss!" I said. "Don't you never think a' nothin' easy t' do?"

But he was already swinging back up onto Red. "Hey, Slim!" he called. "How's your ropin' arm?"

"Well, it ain't broken."

"Then let's go snare ourselves that half-tailed lobo down there!"

"Shoot, that's a good idea!" Slim quickly got back aboard Charlie. "I ain't lassoed a wolf in a coon's age!"

"You take the left point! Levi, when we're ready you bust outta here!"

"Right!" I said with as much phony excitement as I could muster up. That kind of tricky, expert roping wasn't exactly the strongest card in my deck, and I was frankly sort of concerned about the high possibility of making an ass of myself. I was a little surprised he'd told me to join in with them instead of somebody like Natcho, who could damnere ride out blindfolded and rope a jack rabbit. I guess his decision may have had something to do with me being his more or less official representative with the cossacks.

In any case, Slim to the left and Shad to the right, they spurred out at wide angles from the camp, both of them at a dead run. They both skirted the herd that was much nearer to us on the down-sloping plain, neither one of them seeming to have any interest in the wolves far beyond at all.

This way, when they got into position, there'd be three of us coming in on the wolves from three different directions, sort of like an inside-out triangle. Shad could have had five or six of us go along, but I knew he felt that only three of us would make it more of an impressive and sporting proposition. That is, *if* we managed to catch the wolf in the first place.

There was a five-dollar bounty on wolves back in Montana, which was nearly a week's pay, so any wolf was just naturally always fair game for any cowboy. But sometimes instead of just shooting it, which was comparatively easy, we'd make a fairly rough sport out of it by trying to lasso it, and making bets on who'd be the first one, if any, to get a rope around its neck.

That big wolf was pretty smart. He was watching Shad and Slim as they galloped off on both sides of his flanks. But they were far away and not headed in his direction, so that it would seem to him that he was reasonably safe.

And we sure as hell had the attention of the cossacks. They were watching Shad and Slim, slightly puzzled, or possibly even thinking both men had suddenly gone crazy.

They reached their far-off points and turned their horses, so now it was my turn to act. I lunged Buck down the slope before me, straight toward the distant wolves, at the same time letting out a long, fierce yell. I'm not a great lassoer, but I'm a hell of a good yeller, and a lot of the cows I was now galloping by shied off nervously, thinking the end of the world was roaring past them.

The wolf started away in an easy, loping retreat, the bitch and pup following after him.

And then for the first time that big black male began to realize he was in deep trouble.

From each of their points Shad and Slim were barreling toward him too, yelling their lungs out. All that hollering was supposed to scare and confuse a wolf, to panic him so he wouldn't be quite as smart as usual, and it generally worked. But not with that tough, half-tailed big bastard. He stopped dead, seeing that he was kind of surrounded and sizing up the situation calmly.

He didn't have a whole lot of time to think about it, because we were coming in like bats out of hell. Both Shad and Slim had their lariats out, and Slim was already twirling a loop in his right hand. I got my rope off the saddle and damnere dropped it as Buck leaped over a knee-high outcropping of rocks that appeared in our path.

And then the big wolf made its decision. It seemed to instinctively know that it was him we were after. And he gave some kind of a command to the bitch and the pup in whatever kind of talk wolves talk. Apropos of that wolf talk, I have been known to be wrong, but I do believe that animals do talk, even though they may have a pretty limited choice of words. Then he turned and raced in my general direction like a streak of greased lightning.

I sure as hell had to admire that damn wolf, for two reasons. First, he'd somehow unerringly picked the weakest of the three links, me, for an escape route. Second, and most important, was the fact that the bitch and the pup, following his orders, took off as fast as they could in exactly the opposite direction. That wolf, like any really good man would have done, was pulling us enemies off after him so that the other two weaker ones would have a better chance to live.

And his plan worked perfectly. Both Shad and Slim instantly veered in that slightly new direction, and with my legs I turned Buck just a little left to match the angle that it looked like the wolf was going. I had a loop going now, but Jesus the timing was going to be tough. I rode a train once that went sixty miles per hour, and that was kind of breathtaking. But estimating by that, at the rate that wolf was going and Buck was going, we'd pass each other at roughly goddamn near one thousand miles per minute.

At the very last minute, as he was streaking past me on my left, I threw that loop as hard and fast as a rock. From the swift move of my arm, he guessed that something bad was about to maybe happen. He was going too fast to change direction too much or too quickly, but in that split second he suddenly leaped nearly six feet straight up in the air.

My throw must have been terrible, because if he hadn't leaped like that I'd have missed him by a mile. As it was, I accidentally caught his left hind leg while he was in mid-flight.

He must have weighed over a hundred pounds, and when his flying, lunging weight snapped violently tight on my right hand holding the other end of the rope, it felt like I'd lassoed a speeding mountain.

I hadn't had time or even thought of taking a dolly around the saddle horn, so the whole force hit me instead of the saddle with Buck's weight under it. Therefore, I was damnere jerked off onto the ground. I wound up with only my right knee across the saddle, clutching desperately to it with all the muscles in that leg, and for a while my head was so far down it was hitting the tall grass.

I'd have gone off altogether except that, luckily, the rope only stayed on the wolf's leg for maybe a second. Then it slipped off as the wolf somersaulted down from its six-foot leap. He must have rolled over three or four times before he got his feet back under him again, running.

But that brief time he lost turned the tables against him. Shad and Slim sped past me as I tried to slow and turn Buck. And Shad tossed the first noose over the wolf's neck while I was turning Buck. Caught, the big black struggled furiously for a moment, leaping against the rope. Then, finding he couldn't jerk free, he turned and charged defiantly at Shad to do all the damage he could to both Shad and Red.

But Slim's rope snaked out now, and this second noose snapped tight around the wolf's neck from the other side, so that he was strung out between the two of them, unable to either attack or get away.

"Boy!" Slim muttered, dollying out a little rope so that the big, thrashing wolf wouldn't strangle itself. "He surely is a monster."

We could hear the cowboys, and maybe some of the cossacks, yelling and cheering from off in the distance.

I was rolling up my rope, making loops down from my thumb and around my elbow, and Shad said, "That was some hell of a throw, Levi, leg-catching him right in mid-air that way."

I hung the lariat back on my saddle. "I was aimin' for his neck."

I guess he knew this in the first place because he just answered with one of those brief half-grins of his.

"Now we got 'im," Slim said, "what

177

we gonna do with 'im?"

"There's only one courteous thing to do. We'll give 'im to Rostov as a token of our affection."

"Aw, c'mon, Shad," I said.

"Yeah," Slim agreed. "I doubt he'd take that as bein' altogether friendly."

Shad looked at me. "He told you once about puppies barkin' and wolves bitin'."

"Yeah, but —"

"C'mon." Shad led off, Slim matching his pace so that the still-fighting wolf was dragged forcibly along between them.

As we approached the cossack camp, all of the cowboys from our camp nearby came over to get a better look at the giant wolf, and also to sort of see what was going on.

By now the sun was gone and it was only a short while until dark.

Shad and Slim came to a stop, with me just behind the wolf and a little off to one side.

Rostov stepped toward us, studying the savage-eyed but now motionless wolf.

Then he looked at Shad. "That was an interesting exhibition with your ropes. They're very effective."

"We brought this fella over t' give t' you," Shad said quietly. Then he added, "It's a Montana puppy."

There was a whole lot being said there, and Rostov understood every word of it. Shad had put him in a tough, touchy spot to get out of.

Yet the way Shad had said it, he wasn't being quite as mean as it might sound. It was more of a hard kind of a testing where the way a man responds can sometimes make a big difference in your judgment of him.

Right now it was up to Rostov to respond. But just how the hell do you respond upon being presented with a giant, killer wolf as a pet?

He looked at the big wolf and said, "I admire the way he protected the other two with him."

"Admire!" Crab grunted from where the cowboys had gathered. "I think that's the bastard that got my arm that night! Only one thing t' do with that vicious sonofabitch! An' that's put a bullet through his head before he bites somebody else's arm clean off, or tears their throat out!"

Rostov ignored Crab, and now did an amazing and downright terrifying thing, a thing that I'd never dream of doing in a hundred years.

He walked up to where the wolf was still strung out tight between the two lassos. He grabbed Slim's rope with his left hand about two feet away from those savagely bared fangs and lifted the wolf up onto its hind legs by that rope on its neck. Then, as the wolf thrashed around violently, trying to get its teeth into Rostov anyplace it could, he grabbed it firmly by the neck with his right hand, so that its slashing fangs couldn't quite get at his arm.

"Slack off your ropes," he said.

Shad and Slim both gave him slack in their lariats, and he managed somehow to get the nooses quickly off the wolf's neck with his left hand without losing it.

Then with his powerful right hand still around the wolf's neck, he lifted it completely off the ground as it snapped and thrashed violently in that iron grip.

It was a damn impressive, and frightening, sight to see.

Holding the wolf up almost at eye level, its fangs flashing only a few inches from his face, he said, "I appreciate your gift, Mr. Northshield. In return I'm going to give this Montana puppy a gift he'll appreciate too — his freedom."

With this, he threw the heavy wolf away from him. It landed about six feet from where he stood, whirled and charged away with blinding speed.

On its way out it sped by Mushy Callahan and Mushy leaped aside so fast that he damnere fell over.

Crab, whose arm still wasn't completely

cured, might just possibly have been mad about what Rostov had done, but nobody else was.

Even Shad had a kind of a good look on his face as he watched that big black wolf race off toward the darkening horizon, that one-half of a tail of his sticking straight and level out behind him at the speed he was going.

Rostov turned toward Shad. "I think both gifts that were given were rather interesting, in their own ways."

Shad nodded briefly, impassively. "They weren't too bad, Rostov."

And then, with most everyone somehow feeling sort of good, we rode back to our camp to start supper.

It was two days later that I saw my first Tartars.

Rostov and I were far ahead, as usual, and were approaching the top of a high bluff. I don't know whether it was out of instinct or because of something he'd seen or heard that I hadn't, but he pulled up before we were on the skyline.

We dismounted and went up cautiously, finally lying down at the top of the bluff. And ahead of us, maybe two miles away on the flats, were thirty or forty riders that you could just barely see in the distance. Rostov studied them through his little telescope and then, handing the scope grimly to me, he went back down the hill to signal his men behind us to stop.

Rostov hadn't told me they were Tartars, but when I looked through his spyglass I realized that he hadn't had to.

In that little round opening I was staring through, the horsemen were brought up pretty close. And they were a scary-looking bunch. A lot of them had long, braided hair hanging far down their backs, and they were dressed every which way, some of them with almost nothing on, and others with dirty and ragged but colorful voluminous shirts and pants, and even some old robes that looked like tucked-in nightgowns.

Most of their weapons weren't modern, but they sure as hell looked like they were made for killing. Among them they were carrying swords, daggers, spears, bows and arrows and a few rifles and handguns. Some of them were wearing big earrings and other kinds of jewelry. And a lot of them had painted their horses. Some of them were painted in white-and-black stripes, like zebras, and others were designed with blue or red polka dots.

But what got to me most, watching them silently riding along in much the same direction we were going, was the feeling I had deep down in my bones, even from this distance, of intense, animal savagery about them. With that black half-tailed wolf still in the back of my mind, it occurred to me that I'd seen wolf packs that seemed friendly and civilized compared to those deadly-looking Tartars up ahead.

They finally disappeared, moving north by east.

We let them get a good, long head start on us, and we never did see those particular Tartars again.

But late the next day we came upon a dreadful thing they'd left in their wake.

It was a fair-sized cart that had been carrying supplies and probably seven or eight Russians who'd been on their way to somewhere.

You couldn't tell whether it was seven or eight because of the way they'd left some of their bodies. I can't remember the scene Rostov and I came upon too well because my mind just sort of blacked out. All I can remember, and I wish I couldn't, was one little baby of about three years old. It had been nailed to a tree.

Rostov and his cossacks started to bury them, and a little while later Shad, knowing that something was wrong, came galloping up with Igor.

After a long moment Shad said in a quiet, husky voice, "I once saw what was left after a Shoshone attack. But" — it took him a minute to get his voice firmly back — "Christ, even that poor damn little kid!"

Rostov looked at him and there was almost a *camaraderie* between them because of this tragedy that would hit any man hard.

"The Tartars go by a saying they have," he said quietly. " 'Let there be no eye left open — to weep.' "

We finally left that sad place.

And three days later, from the top of a green, forest-covered mountain, we first saw Khabarovsk.

Part Two

ARMED TRUCE
AT KHABAROVSK

Diary Notes

During these parlous and often downright spooky times, the Slash-Diamond outfit discovers among other things that there are cossacks — and there are cossacks. You can't lump them all together anymore than you can lump all birds together and try to pretend that a crow and an eagle are exactly the same thing.

Shad and Rostov, for reasons that will become apparent, take our original thirty-one men and make them seem to be sixty for a while, and finally, accidentally, more than eighty. All of which ain't too easy, though it is highly interesting and sometimes even fairly amusing.

And while they're busy trying to make our bunch seem larger than life, some of us cowboys and cossacks are busy trying to cut our over-all numbers down by inflicting death or at the very least severe bodily injury upon each other. This usually takes place in the form of friendly, healthy, good-

natured competition that the cossacks jokingly refer to as war games, but not too jokingly.

And finally, under dire and very pressing circumstances, we have to suddenly and swiftly take our best shot at crossing the Amur River in the middle of a stormy night to get the hell out of Khabarovsk with all possible speed.

Sammy the Kid is still nervous about going near any water in general, and about crossing the Amur River in particular. But I try to cheer him up by telling him that, all things equal, we probably won't live long enough to even get to the goddamn river in the first place.

11

Looking far down and away from the high crest of that green mountain, Khabarovsk was, even at such a long distance, a big and impressive town.

Rostov and I, ahead of the others, had pulled up and were watching from the trees, where we could see but not be seen.

He'd already signaled the others to hold back.

Aside from the hundreds of small huts and shacks trailing and dwindling off from its center, there were fifteen or twenty main buildings, some of them two and even three stories high, that made up the inner hub of Khabarovsk. It was exciting as hell, and was surely the biggest place we'd come upon since we'd left Seattle.

Two huge rivers flowed together there, meeting and growing twice as large on the far side of the town from us. On the nearer side of the town, away from the water and stretching high up towards us, were large fields and hilly forests.

Rostov finished studying it through his telescope. He said, "No threat of Tartars." And then he handed the scope to me.

Looking through the glass, that fact about Tartars was one of the best things that struck me about the town. People were moving around free and easy down there on the streets and didn't seem to be too fearful.

I handed Rostov back his telescope, and then he gave me one of those long, dark-eyed, hard looks of his that somehow always made a fella wonder whether to smile or duck or just leave town at a full gallop. Finally he said, "Would you consider Khabarovsk a safe town, Levi?"

In my experience, it was an almost unknown occurrence for Rostov to ever ask an easy question. So I hedged it as best I could. "Sir?"

"Do you think that it's a safe town for us to go into?" The way he said it made me think that maybe he wasn't asking a question so much as he was wondering if he'd ever managed to teach me anything.

After a moment I said, "I don't know about that, sir." And then I added. "But right now it's the only town we got."

He nodded briefly, and I think there was some kind of quiet approval, and maybe even a hint of faint amusement, in that nod.

But somehow I knew that something was wrong.

And then Shad came galloping up from behind us, madder than hell. He was pushing his big Red full out, yet even in that brief, speeding time I couldn't help but notice that Shad managed to keep himself just as invisible as Rostov and I were, making sure that he and Red were always out of sight from anyone who might be watching from the town far below and off.

"What's the hang-up here?" he demanded angrily, slamming Red to a damnere skidding halt.

For a man of his own somewhat fiery temperament, Rostov did a strange thing then. First off, he didn't get in the least mad back. He didn't even bother to answer.

And second, he got off his big black stallion and hunched down among the trees, still studying the far-off town. Finally, he pulled a blade of grass and started to chew on it idly, thoughtfully.

In a funny way just then, hunched quietly down on his heels like that, Rostov reminded me of nobody else in the world quite so much as Shad.

Igor now came tearing over the hill, following behind Shad. He kept pretty well out of sight too and pulled up on Blackeye as Shad dismounted and stalked toward Rostov, his chaps slapping angrily against his legs as he walked. He stopped near Rostov and said harshly, "My herd's been held to a halt back there! *Why?*"

Rostov didn't answer for a long moment. He slowly shifted the blade of grass in his mouth and then said in a low voice, "Because I'm afraid of that town."

Those words got to Shad. And they sure as hell made Igor and me stop and think. Because if there was one thing in this world we were all damn sure of, it was that Rostov wasn't afraid of anything that either this world or even a Holy Christian Hell had to offer.

For a long time, no one said anything.

Then, finally, Shad spoke, both his frown and his voice still hard as ever. "That's one of your own goddamn *Russian* towns! What the hell *you* got t' be afraid of?"

Rostov stood up quickly, so that the two of them were now suddenly facing each other, which was a thing that always tended to make me, and anyone else who happened to be present, somewhat ill at ease.

But Rostov was still thoughtful, more than angry. "I suspect my men and I won't be overly welcome there."

Shad stared at Rostov, his frown deepening, and then Slim and Old Keats rode up to us through the trees.

Slim said, "Just wanted t' let ya' know, boss, them cows're temporarily circled an' settled." He glanced back and forth from Shad to Rostov. "Well, boss, we goin' on down there t' that town over yonder 'r not?"

Shad turned toward Slim, but before he could make an answer there were the sudden sounds of still other horsemen coming quickly through the trees. Lieutenant Bruk and the big sergeant, Nick, rode toward us, Yuri and Vody following hard behind them.

"Christ!" Shad muttered as the four oncoming cossacks sped up to join the rest of us. "This a cattle drive or a goddamn Sunday social?"

The newly arrived men dismounted, all four of them looking troubled and uneasy. Lieutenant Bruk stepped to Rostov and said, "We've placed double lookouts, Captain."

"Double lookouts!" Shad's eyes swept angrily over the cossacks. "What the hell for?"

Rostov said quietly, "Because we need them."

Shad stared at Rostov, looking about half puzzled and about half ready to erupt like a volcano.

Old Keats, seeing Shad's expression, put in quickly, "There seems t' be some kind of a confusion here, Captain. We've been led to understand all along the way that Khabarovsk was a safe place."

"That's correct," Rostov said very quietly. "And that's what my men and I had thought, too."

"What the hell d' you mean," Shad growled, "about *had* thought?"

I doubt I should have raised my voice in that edgy situation, but all of sudden there it was coming out, and it sounded just as confused and uncertain as I felt. "You just said there ain't no Tartars down there, Captain. What the hell else is there t' worry about? They got the *plague* down there or somethin'?"

"It'd take at least that." Slim grinned a little, but his words came out flat on the level. "After all this time way out in the lonely — clean all the way from Seattle — them fellas a' ours back there takin' care a' them cows ain't gonna be all too keen about passin' up this here town."

Shad's earlier anger had diminished by about one-half of a shaved inch, and he was still ready to explode, but his voice was controlled as he now spoke to Rostov. "Let's get back to that 'had thought' bullshit. What's the problem you got?"

194

Rostov's eyes matched Shad's, evenly controlled and evenly hard. "There's a reinforced contingent of cossacks down there in Khabarovsk."

This statement took a while to sink in, and I for one was vaguely aware of my mouth sort of hanging a little ajar, due to general astonishment.

And then Shad did explode. "Well what difference does *that* make? *You're* cossacks!"

Rostov still spoke quietly. "There's a difference." And somehow, from the way he said it, you could tell that whatever that difference was, it was gigantic. And you could also tell that the problem on Rostov's mind had walloped him severely. On the outside he was still as hard and tough, and his mind as keen as, say, that great steel saber hooked onto his belt. But inside him, there was an intense sorrow that went deep and couldn't be hidden because, somehow, it came out of his eyes.

Lieutenant Bruk, whose clear old eyes were now filled with the same dark sorrow, had filled and lighted the long clay pipe he carried with him. Now, he silently handed it to Rostov, who took it and said, "I honestly couldn't foresee this, Northshield." He took a puff on the pipe and passed it back to Bruk. "Otherwise, I'd have warned you."

Shad's reaction to this was both a relief and a surprise to me. Maybe it was because he too could see the hurt in these men. Or maybe it was because he was thinking on something he'd already somehow guessed about way ahead of the rest of us. In any case, instead of the anger within him growing, it now ebbed away as he reached slowly into his shirt pocket for the makings of a smoke, studying Rostov quietly. Working with the paper and tobacco, he said, "What couldn't you foresee? That you could've warned me about?"

"The garrison in Khabarovsk has been undermanned for over a year. But right now there are two new companies of cossacks down there, who must have arrived within the last three or four weeks."

Shad pulled the now rolled paper lightly across the tip of his tongue to firm his smoke together. "You'll have t' pardon my density," he said dryly, "but it sure is a strange-as-hell thing, you fellas standin' here passin' that pipe back an' forth like the end of the world happened yesterday." He struck a match with his thumbnail and lighted his smoke slowly, thoughtfully, before shaking out the flame on the match. For him, he was talking at a damnere unheard of length. And more and more, I was getting a sneaking suspicion that he was about a mile ahead of the conversation. He dropped the no-longer-lighted match and ground it into the earth with the toe of his boot. "Hell, I'd think you'd be yellin' an' dancin' an' dashin' down off there t' celebrate with them other cossacks." He inhaled on his smoke. "But then, you did mention somethin' about a — 'difference.' "

Rostov spoke in a quietly hard voice. "There's quite a bit of difference. We're not taking this herd to Blagoveshchensk, as your papers show. We're taking it farther north, to the people who bought and paid for it, in our own free town of Bakaskaya."

"Well," Shad shrugged. "The name a' your town sure as hell is a lot easier t' pronounce than that other one."

I think Rostov was as surprised as I was at Shad's calmness. But now, still quietly, he went on. "Those men down there are Imperial Cossacks. They belong to the Tzar."

Slim's face twisted into an almost painfully puzzled frown. "Well, Christ Jesus!" he finally said. "There ain't *nothin'* in all a' Russia that *don't* b'long t' the Tzar!" He glanced toward Old Keats, looking for some kind of confirmation. "Or am I *crazy?*"

Keats was still frowning, too. "That's sure as hell what we always been told."

"Captain Rostov, sir?" I asked hesitantly, partly guessing about and partly hoping for the answer I wanted to hear. "If you fellas don't belong t' the Tzar, then who *do* ya' b'long to?"

Rostov's eyes, though they were still full of deep sorrow, bored into me. "If you still have to ask me such a question, Levi, then you're not worthy of a reply."

In his own way he'd given me the answer I was hoping for, but his own way sure was a killer. Blood rushed suddenly and hotly to my face, and right then I both felt like and wished I was the tiniest little piss ant on earth so I could just shrink into practically nothing and disappear.

Whether or not he did it on purpose, Shad now saved me from dying of sheer, agonized embarrassment right there on the spot. He did it by saying a lot better what I'd meant to say myself in the first place. And something about the way he spoke made me know that there was much more, deep within him, than the words alone could say.

"I don't mind a reasonable change a' destination if the reason's right," he said quietly to Rostov. "But since it's not with the Tzar, then just where, exactly, is your outfit's allegiance?"

Rostov looked at his men gathered beside him. And then, finally, back at Shad. "Our allegiance is, Mr. Northshield, no more and certainly never less than to each other — and to our honor." He hesitated, weighing each word slowly and carefully. "And to our homes in Bakaskaya, to the people there we love. And perhaps more than anything else, our allegiance is to the beautiful, fiercely independent and free spirit of all those who have the will and the courage to be part of Bakaskaya."

He stopped then, and in the long silence no one, including Shad, had anything to say. It might just well have been, for once, that Shad had gotten a lot more of an answer back than he'd expected.

So the way it finally worked, it was Rostov who at last spoke again to Shad. "Considering the — unexpected circumstances we've found here, you and your men have no choice but to get away and go back now, while you can. You'll be safe. We're the outlaws, not you."

Except for Shad, we all frowned at each other, and then Slim said the first thought that came to his mind. "Hell, what about that damned herd?"

Rostov spoke very quietly. "You've brought it almost halfway. And by any man's judgment, that's more than far enough. Especially when there are high rivers and the Tzar's cossacks ahead." His quiet voice became even deeper now. "My men and I will take the herd from here on." He paused. "And we'll take it alone. That's as it will be." Rostov was speaking gently, but gently as he spoke, that low, quiet voice of his somehow carried, without any chance of mistake, the hollow, black echoes of approaching death.

Slim said with growing amazement, "Goddamn! You bastards're fightin' a goddamn revolution!"

Rostov shrugged slightly. "I suppose you could say that."

Old Keats leaned slowly forward on his saddle, resting his forearms on the pommel. "Tell me, Captain, is there, perhaps, some part a' that very movin' oath of allegiance you just talked about before that got left out?"

Rostov looked at him. "What do you mean?"

"Like workin' overtime t' get yourselves killed for a foolish an' hopeless reason? Like I gather your town of Bakaskaya must be."

"No attempt at a free society is ever foolish or hopeless."

"And forgettin' all about them Imperial Cossacks," Keats went, "you just for certain can't handle that herd."

Rostov's jaw hardened. "My cossacks and I can handle the herd perfectly well."

It was only then that Shad at last spoke

again. "That's very funny, Rostov," he said. "And it's always a joy to listen to a fella with a keen sense of humor." Looking far off, at Khabarovsk, he dropped his now-finished smoke and started to absently grind it down into the earth with the heel of his boot. "Well, Captain, you want t' stand around here all day bein' hilarious?" He gave one final kick against the earth with his boot heel. "Or ya' want t' try t' figure out how we can get them cattle a' ours beyond that Tzar-held town an' them flooded rivers?"

With those last few words, Shad had stated his position loud and clear. I was proud as hell about the simple, almost unsaid way he'd said the way he felt. But I didn't dare show that pride by as much as half a blink.

For his part, Rostov didn't show anything either. He took a long, deep breath. "There are probably over a hundred Imperial Cossacks down there."

Shad nodded. "And if we hang around in these trees much longer, all hundred or so of 'em will doubtless soon be up here. Let's leave a lookout." He corrected himself with a wry half-grin. "A 'double' lookout, and get back to the herd."

We left Lieutenant Bruk and Vody on guard there and, keeping out of sight, the rest of us rode back over the mountain and down the mile or so slope to where the cattle were.

And back here with the herd now, as the talk continued, it was kind of interesting to note that Shad and Rostov not only weren't right on the verge of killing each other all the time, but were actually somewhat in fairly civil agreement every once in a while.

"Hell, boss, why not cross the river t'night an' get as far the hell north as we can?" Dixie asked. But he hadn't seen the river.

Shad shook his head. "Right now it's too wide, an' too much current f'r safety's sake."

Rostov nodded. "The spring thaws are running later than usual. I'd estimate at least another week before horses and cattle will be able to get across."

"Well," Purse put in, "how about backing off and going a long way around?" But he hadn't yet seen Khabarovsk.

"Too big a town," Keats said. "Too many people. It's a miracle we haven't been discovered and attacked already."

Rostov glanced toward the horizon and the lowering sun. "Tomorrow," he said quietly, "will be the time." Then he looked back levelly at Shad. "Believe me, by this time tomorrow there will be very few survivors. You owe it to yourself and your men to go back now. This is between Russians on Russian soil, and you and your men are foreigners."

Dixie and a couple of the others looked like they were sorely tempted to follow Rostov's advice, but it never even occurred to Slim. "Who the hell you callin' foreigners, for Christ sake? We're Americans."

Shad, who'd been studying Rostov, now spoke in a quietly tough voice. "That's downright goddamn inspirin'," he said. "Tomorrow you an' fifteen rebel cossacks're gonna take on over a hundred a' the king's men. That oughtta be just one hell of a glorious battle."

Rostov's eyes hardened. "Your irony escapes me."

"You more interested in a heroic death or gettin' that herd through?"

Those words had a hard bite to them, and at any time prior to this Rostov would have flared up like a skyrocket. But right now his expression stayed as unchanging as a rock. "If you have anything worth while to say, Northshield, say it."

It was Shad, now, who hunched down on his heels. He picked up a pebble, playing with it idly. "Well, for one thing, I'm reminded of that time back in Vladivostok — when you and your handful a' men sent forty soldiers hightailin' it."

Rostov dismissed this with a shrug. "They were a scurvy lot. Hardly worth the drawing of a good saber." Then he looked at Shad thoughtfully. "Whatever else those bastards may be, the Tzar's Imperial Cossacks are fighting men."

"That so?" Shad tossed the pebble a little and caught it. "As good, man for man, as your fellas?"

"Certainly not!"

"Didn't think so." Shad dropped the pebble and stood slowly back up. "Tell me, Rostov, you ever hear of a game called showdown?"

"No."

Shad looked off, across the herd. Fat and contented, most of them were already lying down, and eight of our men were riding slowly around them. 'Dixie," Shad said, "ride out and bring those other fellas over here."

"All of them?"

"All of them." Even though it was obvious those peaceful cows weren't going anywhere, and we were near them, this was an unusual order for Shad to give. It was a pretty much ironclad rule of his to have at least three or four men flanking the herd, no matter how quiet things were.

As Dixie rode off to do as he was told, the rest of us Slash-Diamonders looked at Shad curiously, wondering what was on his mind. And by then, for that matter, Rostov and his men had just naturally figured out enough about the normal care and treatment of a herd to know that something out of the ordinary was going on.

But Shad didn't give any of us a hint. All he did, though it was rare for him to smoke so much, was to take out his Bull Durham and paper and start building another one. He worked on it very thoughtfully and carefully, building it to perfection, as though that job was the most important thing he'd ever had on his mind.

By the time it was finished, Dixie and the others now rode up and dismounted, so that the whole outfit was here. Slim, who may have had an idea what was coming, stepped to Shad and struck a match, jerking it hard and smooth across the tight hip pocket of his pants. "Light, boss?"

Shad sucked in on the smoke, and Slim blew the match out before dropping it and grinding it slowly into the ground with his foot.

Looking at Rostov, Shad finally said, "I was talkin', before, about showdown."

Rostov nodded. "That's right."

"Well, it's a game. One that any fool can play. But what makes it interestin' is that if a man's got enough pure guts, he can sometimes manage t' win even when by all the odds on God's green earth he was just plain bound t' lose."

Rostov said quietly, "I, myself, am a chess player, which is also a game any fool can play — but he won't win."

"Then I strongly suggest we stick to showdown."

Rostov's eyes were serious, but he spoke dryly. "Are we to learn it in time for the battle tomorrow?"

"No. *Now.*"

Not only Rostov but some of the rest of us were a little startled at this.

But Shad was already going on. "If you and those goddamned cossacks a' yours can drive off forty soldiers, think what could happen with these rough bastards a' mine thrown in!"

Rostov was too thoughtful to be angered at Shad's phrase "goddamned cossacks." He said, "That's still only about thirty men against well over one hundred." He looked at Shad, his dark eyes searching. "You've been paid for these cattle. They are certainly no longer your responsibility."

"The deal included deliverin' them."

"No man can hold you to a thing like that in times such as these."

"One man can."

Rostov knew Shad meant himself. He took another tack then. "Are you men ready to die, too?"

Dixie said hesitantly, "In a way he's right, boss. Ain't no way this is our fight."

"That's the reason I wanted every man here." Shad dropped his second smoke and booted it into the ground. "No bullshit about votin', or anything like that. I'm goin' on with the herd." He glanced off at the nearly setting sun. "It's gettin' late, so the rest of ya' got about three minutes t' decide which direction you're goin'."

And then he walked up the hill, away from us, to be by himself while we decided.

"Hell," Dixie complained, "I didn't mean —"

"Oh, shut up!" Rufe growled, and Crab Smith muttered something angrily beneath his breath.

"This is not your problem," Rostov said firmly. "You should all go while you can!"

"This is the way it seems t' me it is." Old Keats spoke quietly. "Sometimes Shad has a hard time sayin' what's on his mind, so right now I'll try t' say it for him. An' you, Slim, or Levi, or anybody else, can correct me if I'm wrong. Shad's goin' on ahead, with or without any or all of the rest of us, for two reasons. One of 'em is his kind of half-ass, but still admirable, sense of stubborn honor. He said he'd deliver this herd, and he'll do it, come hell or high water."

"Or," Mushy said grimly, "die tryin'."

"The second reason he's got," Keats continued, "has t' do with somethin' most of ya' don't know about, yet." He waved toward Rostov and his men, his bad hand raised about chest high. "These fellas here just lately turned out t' be nothin' but phony, goddamned rebel cossacks who bought and paid for this herd."

And now, Old Keats sort of started to get poetic, though his voice was hard. "They don't belong to the great and magnificent Tzar of All the Russias. They don't belong to anyone on earth but to themselves — and to the people they love. And perhaps even more rare than that, their greatest allegiance of all is to an invisible and priceless spirit called — called freedom. Shad knows that in their own stupid, splendid way they're ready to die tomorrow rather than change."

Rostov and his cossacks were getting embarrassed as hell at this, but it was all new to most of the Slash-Diamond men.

"There happens to be a large group of the Tzar's men in Khabarovsk right now, and there are bound to be tough times ahead. We can stick with these crazy, rebel cossacks, and maybe get ourselves killed. Or we can desert both them and the herd, and head back south as fast as we can go, and be safe." He paused. "I know how Shad feels, and I hope I've sort of said it for him. And I damn well know my own decision."

I think Old Keats might have gone on for hours, except that Shad was now heading back down toward us. Shad came to where we were and looked around at us. "Well?" he said. "Whoever wants t' go back better move out."

There was a long, silent moment, and then it was Dixie who said, "Looks like nobody's goin'."

Rostov said harshly, "I told them that they should all leave."

Shad nodded. "I figured you would. But right now, Rostov, let's talk about showdown."

12

It was early evening when the eight of us rode into the outskirts of Khabarovsk. Shad and Rostov were up front, with Lieutenant Bruk and Old Keats just behind them. Next came Sergeant Nick and Slim, with me and Igor trailing just behind.

We'd been slowed down just once in the dark outside of town. Two guards had ridden by, about a hundred feet away, and called out in Russian to find out who we were. Whatever Nick had answered, in that booming, deep voice of his, was enough to satisfy them, and they'd gone on their way with no further comment.

Even halfway into town there still wasn't much light, and we were finally approaching the center of it before people first began to take notice of us. They didn't seem to be so much scared as curious, whispering among themselves and sometimes hurrying into their small homes to peer out at us from their windows.

Compared to the dreary shacks of Vladivostok, some of these little houses were really nice, with hand-carved frames around the doors and fancy gingerbread woodwork on the roofs. There was just a natural feeling here that this town had been around a whole lot longer and was a whole lot more loved by its citizens than was Vladivostok.

And there seemed to be a large number of females of various ages, too, which was kind of pleasant. Every now and then, as we rode along, you'd hear some giggling, or some girl voices whispering off in the shadows.

But then, at last, that all tapered off, and the town suddenly got more serious. We were moving in close toward the main part, and there was a kind of a square that we were coming to. I could see that Igor wasn't too happy, and his jaw was getting set up as tight as a sprung bear trap.

Already guessing the answer, I said, "We gettin' there?"

He nodded, looking almost straight in front of us, and I followed his look. On one side of the square there was a long two-story building, with two armed and uniformed men in front of the main door. Above them, on top of the building, was a flagstaff with three flags fluttering on it, one over the other.

Those flags must have been what I hadn't seen through the telescope earlier that day when Rostov had handed it to me. The highest and biggest flag had a bear on it. The two smaller ones beneath it were triangle-shaped, with different colors.

My immediate thought was that the top one stood for the Tzar and the others stood for the two companies of Imperial Cossacks, and it seemed to me that it was unfair for Rostov to have expected me to know all that. But there wasn't much time for me to pursue that possible injustice any further because we now rode out onto the hard-packed dirt square. And for damn sure somebody had just gotten the word that some strangers were in town. As we moved straight ahead toward that building at an easy walk, Imperial Cossacks started showing up all around the square, some of them pulling on their jackets and others buckling on sabers or quietly checking their guns. As still others appeared, all of them just staying their distance and gradually surrounding us, it began to be one hell of a hairy situation.

"Boy," Slim muttered in a low voice, "right now a lot a' fellas could get hurt real serious an' sudden around here."

We got to where the two guards were standing in front of the building, their rifles now held in readiness at angles across their chests. We dismounted and tied our horses at about the same time that the door behind the guards opened and a young officer came quickly out. After a brief, stunned glance at us, he stepped toward Rostov to speak. But before he could manage to say anything, it was Rostov, instead, who gave a short, sharp order. I understood enough to know that Rostov had demanded to see the commanding officer.

And then a man spoke in reply to Rostov from the open main door. About forty, lean and tall, there was a cruel and somehow aristocratic arrogance about him, despite the fact that he was standing there casually in his shirt sleeves.

He and Rostov exchanged a few words, and then Rostov turned to us. "This is Colonel Verushki. He agrees to listen to what we have to say."

"He damned well better agree," Shad said to Rostov, "unless he wants his goddamn town torn down."

Verushki gave Shad a quick, sharp glance, and right then I knew he could understand us. A second later it dawned on me that Shad now knew too, and that that was probably why he'd said what he said in the first place.

With the Tzar's men on all sides and behind us, we went into the building and followed Colonel Verushki down a wide hallway. He even had men with ready rifles lined up on both sides of the hallway. I'd never seen so many soldiers holding so many guns in my life. "Jesus," I murmured to Old Keats, "this looks more like a thousand men than a hundred."

Keats said quietly, "He's rousted out every man in his command."

"Yeah. Like I said. All thousand of 'em."

Farther down the hall we entered what looked like a big council room of some sort. Verushki sat facing us from a large desk up front, with nine or ten armed men lined up behind him. There were some benches where our men either sat or stood, as they felt. Then at least half of the Tzar's thousand soldiers outside crowded into the rest of the room. And after about two minutes, I wasn't sure whether their guns or their sweating was their most dangerous weapon.

Verushki said something to his men in Russian, and then he glanced at Shad and me. "You both recently became aware that I speak English, so there's no need for linguistic games."

Without seeming to, he'd noticed both of our reactions outside.

And now, almost as a compliment, Shad said quietly, "I'm pleased for all of us t' see that you're a smart sonofabitch."

Verushki said two words in Russian and every rifle in the room was suddenly cocked, with deadly, dry metallic sounds.

Rostov said quickly, "The word 'sonofabitch' is colloquial, Colonel, and has nothing to do with one's ancestry."

"I'm aware of both that and the impertinence intended." Verushki looked at Rostov and at the uniform he was wearing. "I agreed to listen to you. But I presume you understand that, as of now, you and your outlaw cossacks are under arrest."

Rostov said, "And the firing squad is already waiting, undoubtedly."

There was a tight, deadly moment, and then Shad stood up and began one of the great speeches ever made. "That kind a' trouble is sort of what we're here t' talk about." He walked over to the closest Imperial Cossack and put the tip of his finger lightly on the muzzle of the rifle being held by that suddenly astonished man. Then, with his finger still on the muzzle, he gently pushed the barrel slightly to one side. It was such an audacious move that the only reaction in the room was one of stunned silence. "You know, Colonel," Shad said easily, "if he shoots right now, it'll blow off about half of my finger — and I'll kill this poor Imperial Cossack bastard dead before he even knows he's made an unfortunate mistake."

Verushki snapped an order in Russian, and the still astonished man slowly released the hammer of his rifle, uncocking it. Then, as Shad turned toward him, Verushki said, "Was there some sort of point to that idiotic flamboyance?"

That was a six-bit word to use, but Shad came back with a pretty good one too. "It's got t' do with economics." He let that word sink in, and then continued. "That finger a' mine ain't worth a whole lot because I've got nine more t' go. But like I said, I'd have killed your man. And that would have led t' all kinds of hell in this here immediate vicinity."

Verushki was frowning, but he forced the frown into a small, thin smile. "Are you trying to tell me that *we* should be afraid of *you?*"

Shad's voice took on a low, hard edge. "I'm not *tryin'* t' tell you. I'm *tellin'* you. First off, Colonel, we're all armed, and damned well armed, and we'll stay armed because no man in his right mind will be about t' try t' *disarm* us. Now second, consider my little finger against your life, Colonel. Much as I'm fond of that little finger, I seriously doubt you would agree that one's worth the other. And if a fight starts here and now, I guarantee that you will not be one of the few people who gets out of this room alive."

"And you and your men?" Verushki's eyes were hard and thoughtful.

Shad shrugged a little. "We'd all wind up dead, and I'd be one a' the first t' go. But then, Colonel, after all the bloody carnage that'd take place in this room, another bad thing would happen t'night. With you an' about half a' your men dead or wounded, fifty of the toughest, meanest, best-armed men in the world would come into town, curious t' find out what the hell happened to us." He paused briefly. "I guess, while you're at it, you could measure that little finger of mine against all of Khabarovsk."

Verushki studied Shad thoughtfully, his hands folded together before him on the desk. "If you're bluffing, it's quite impressive."

"Just try me, Colonel."

"I presume there is some alternative to these disastrous events, and I further presume that alternative is the reason you're here."

"That's exactly what I've been talkin' about. Economics. It'd be downright silly an' unfeasible for you t' be dead and dishonored and Khabarovsk burned down, all for one damned little finger."

"In my opinion," Verushki said slowly, "you must be very heavily outnumbered."

Rostov stood up then, and as he did so, several rifles were now turned toward him. He glanced at them disdainfully, as though they were wooden toys held by children. "Even in this room we are outnumbered, Colonel. But I suggest you also consider wisely the economics of the human spirit. Sometimes, because of that spirit, one man can be worth many in a battle."

Whether he thought we were bluffing or not,

Verushki was losing ground and he knew it. He said gruffly, "Fine words, from a traitor cossack!"

"From a *free* cossack," Rostov growled, glaring darkly at the colonel. "Not from one of the Tzar's whores on horseback!"

There was a deathly still, damnere fighting moment there, but then Shad broke it up with a flat, hard voice. "We ain't got all night," he said to Verushki, who was smoldering with anger. "So let's get back t' simple economics. You electin' for the previously discussed trouble t' start right here an' now? Or ya' want t' consider some other, more amicable arrangement?"

Verushki still didn't back down, even though he knew every man in that room might be dead in no time flat. With an icy calm, he said, "I agreed before to listen to what you had to say."

"Us an' some a' these free cossacks're takin' some cattle north. We'll only be here a week or so and we'll be peaceful as hell, as long as you are."

"If such a peace were established, and then broken, do you really think you could win against me?"

"Jesus *Christ!*" Shad said, "I just know that there'd be pure *hell* t' pay! That's the whole reason for my goddamned lecture on economics!"

"If you did win, Colonel," Rostov said levelly, "it would be a Pyrrhic victory." He must have guessed that he'd lost some of the rest of us there. "A victory in which the winner is hurt so badly that he, himself, also dies." He added grimly, "The word 'Pyrrhic' has a certain similarity to 'funeral pyre.' "

Verushki studied all of us for a long, quiet moment before he finally reached a decision. "Perhaps it may be possible for us to reach an honorable understanding among ourselves." He spoke a brief, low order in Russian and his men, puzzled but obedient, now uncocked and lowered their guns. Then Verushki gave Shad a hard, bitter look. "But this is in no way amicable. I'd like nothing more than to cut off that damned finger of yours and keep it as a souvenir of this meeting."

Shad said, "We ain't expectin' a parade. Just a workable agreement."

It took about an hour for the colonel and us to agree on what our agreement was. And shortly after that the eight of us walked back out onto the square. There were still a number of Imperial Cossacks standing around who stared at us with hate-filled eyes but did nothing to interfere with us.

For our part, we did our best to seem like we were casually ignoring them, but I for one still felt as tight in my chest as a stretched rawhide drum. "God*damn!*" Slim muttered so that only we could hear him. "I was sure mainly convinced we'd *never* git outta there in upright positions!"

As he untied his black, Rostov said, "In chess, Northshield, we'd call you a Grand Master."

"Huh?"

"At playing that game of yours — showdown."

Shad swung up aboard Red. "You didn't do too bad, yourself."

Slim glanced from one of them to the other, as surprised as the rest of us that they'd actually said something pleasant to each other. "Well, unless you two plan on spendin' all night congratulatin' yourselves, how 'bout us findin' the nearest saloon?"

Rostov said, "I think that's an excellent idea. Right now it would be an even further indication of how secure we feel." He glanced at Shad, not asking his opinion, but ready to hear it.

"I doubt we'll ever again agree on anything twice in a row" — Shad turned Red from the hitching rail — "so let's go drink t' that rare occurrence while we got the chance."

13

Rostov knew where to go, and he and Shad led us off at an easy walk across the square and down one of the wider, better lighted streets.

As we rode slowly, quietly along, my head was kind of divided. The part of it that belonged to my eyes was fascinated by the people on the street and on the boardwalks. There sure was every kind, and most of them were looking at us with interest and curiosity. Young and old, tall and short, they were usually on the heavy side, but not always. The thick, rough clothes most of them wore added to that feeling of heaviness, the men in rugged home-spun jackets and coats, the women in long, generally black, wool dresses. Most of the men wore fur hats, but some of them were made out of thick cloth or felt, and I even saw one top hat on a man in a black suit. Almost all of the women had white handkerchiefs on their heads, folded in the shape of a triangle and tied under their chins.

Aside from those who looked like farmers and laborers, and a few businessmen, there were some men who I judged by their worn fringed buckskins to be the equivalent of our mountain men, trappers and hunters and the like. Ranging the street, aside from the normal riding horses and pack mules, there were some dogs and pigs that looked for all the world like they owned the place, and they'd move out of the way resentfully when an occasional wagon or carriage drove by. Along the sides of the street or on the boardwalks, there were quite a few noisy vendors, fellas shouting out from near their little stands to call attention to whatever it was they had for sale.

But as I mentioned before, despite all these fascinating things, my head was divided, and the back of it wouldn't let go of a kind of throbbing fear that was sort of like a dull headache. It had a whole lot to do with what we'd agreed on with Verushki, which seemed to me to be a shaky enough agreement in the first place. But in the second place, even that shaky deal was based on there being sixty of us. And such a count was ridiculous, because no matter how hard you added us all up, there were only thirty-one of us.

Rostov pulled in to the hitching rail before a well-lighted two-story building that had a hand-printed sign on it and half a dozen big windows facing the street on the ground floor.

nside you could see people eating and drinking at large, heavy tables, and all in all seeming o be having a pretty good time. We dismounted to tie up, and Slim, studying the place, said, "It ain't exactly the Silver Slipper, but it don't look half bad either."

And then a nice thing happened. From not far away, a band struck up and started playing. We all turned to look, and about a half a block farther down the street there was a small round building that was built about six or eight feet up off the ground. It didn't have any sides at all, but just some beams holding up the roof over it. So that way, from any angle, you could see the band sitting inside and now playing away with a lot of pep and vigor as another fella waved a little stick in front of them. They were all in real fancy uniforms, blue pants and jackets with considerable strands of gold braid on their shoulders and around their waists, and ribbons and medals across their chests.

"Cossacks?" I said.

"Hell, no, Levi," Slim told me. 'What them fellas're wearin' is musicians' outfits. Anybody tried t' fight in them uniforms, he'd strangle hisself on his own gold braid."

The street widened out where the little round building was, and a lot of people were walking up in a circle around it now, just to stand there and listen to those men playing their music.

"That's a real goddamn fine thing," I said but the others were already going around the hitching rail and starting across the crowded boardwalk.

As I stepped onto the boardwalk, Igor suddenly grabbed my arm, holding me protectively back. Since the only person walking in front of me was a feeble old lady with a bucket I couldn't imagine what he was protecting me from, and gave him a puzzled look.

When she'd moved on a few slow steps, he let go of my arm. "Never pass a woman carrying an empty pail," he said. "It's bad luck."

"Oh."

I looked back at the old lady, and sure enough most of the people were giving her a wide berth as she went trudging along the boardwalk to wherever she was going with her bucket.

And then we crossed the walk to enter the building, where the others were already going in.

Igor and I were the last ones through the door, and I stood for a moment, sort of awestruck. This was only the second time I'd been indoors in Russia, not counting the Imperial Cossacks' headquarters we'd just come out of, which right then I was trying hard to forget, anyway. The other time had been that night in Vladivostok, in that lopsided, rough little place where we'd bought the vodka for the herd, with the three grubby soldiers, staring at us from off in one corner, and the fat greasy-aproned bartender.

But this big, fine place was really different.

It was just one wide, long room, with a swinging door on a far side that led to the kitchen and some stairs on the other side going up to the second floor. Everything in it was made of heavy, dark wood, the floors and walls and tables and chairs and the beamed ceiling. And, according to the smell, some of it was fresh cut and hewn. Beyond that, there was the rich, homey smell about the place of good food being cooked and eaten. And, somehow, the people themselves had that same thing about them, the warm feel and smell of fresh-cut wood and good simple cooking.

And, too, there was the deep, bubbling sound of men's laughter, which often sounds deeper and better when they're laughing only partly because of what's being said and mostly because of just having a good time with their friends and some strong liquor. But the best part of all was that the big, handsomely carved tables were being tended by six or eight girls.

And except for one, who was a tough-looking old gal, they wore those same floor-length dresses and the triangle-shaped handkerchiefs on their heads. And like the theory of long-horns, their dresses came in every color of the rainbow. One girl, carrying a trayful of drinks to some men at a nearby table, was wearing a red-and-white-checked dress, and she looked as spunky and cheerful as a brand-new tablecloth. Except for the fact that no table was ever in history built along the same sort of overwhelming lines as that young lady. She looked at our bunch near the door and gave us all a big, sunny smile as she headed back toward the door to the kitchen.

And it was a kind of interesting thing that everybody in that big room, although they seemed a little surprised, also seemed to be just about as friendly as she was. They could tell at a glance, of course, that us Slash-Diamonders were foreigners. But when they looked at Rostov and his men, sizing up their uniforms, their reactions were just the opposite of Verushki's and his Imperial Cossacks. They showed open admiration, and a couple of big men waved their glasses toward Rostov and called out something in rough, friendly voices before drinking.

The one older, tough-looking woman came

up to us now, and even her hard face became almost pleasant as she looked at Rostov. He said a few words, and she nodded and gestured to a large round table that was by itself near the rear of the room.

She led us back to the table, and Rostov spoke to her again, ordering for us as we all sat down. But instead of simply accepting his order, she shook her head and told him something quietly before leaving the table.

"Someone," Rostov explained, "has already bought us a bottle of vodka."

Slim frowned across the table at him. "Well, that surely is big-hearted. But how the hell come?"

Rostov shrugged. "We're strangers. It's a fairly common custom out here."

Nick stroked the unbearded, scarred side of his big, solid face. "There is more," he rumbled.

Bruk nodded. "A few of the people here know who we are and where we come from."

What they'd left unsaid seemed more important to me. But it was Old Keats who put words to it. "I'd venture," he said, "that many American colonists felt much the same way as these people do around the time of our Revolutionary War."

Rostov said thoughtfully, "Your point may

be well taken."

The pretty girl in the tablecloth dress came up now with a tray that had eight glasses and a bottle of vodka on it. As she beamed at us and started to place the glasses around, Shad said to Rostov, "Tell 'er that we're buyin' two bottles back for whoever bought us this one."

I half expected Rostov to go against this, but he didn't. It was almost as if the same thing had been on his mind, and he was already talking to the girl as Shad's last couple of words came out. She smiled and nodded and went away.

Bruk did the pouring, which with eight of us took a minute. Slim raised his glass and said, "Here's t' the best goddamned game a' showdown ever I seen!" He added with feeling, "Or ever *hope* to!"

Shad picked up his glass. "Let's also just hope we can make it stick."

We all drank then, and the way those cossacks drank was an awful thing for me to take note of. I took a sip of the fiery vodka and was about to put the rest of it back down in a civilized fashion. But around the edges of my glass I suddenly saw that they were all downing every drop in their glasses all at once. So, despite the furious burning in my throat, I forced myself to finish my glass too.

Everybody at the table put down an empty glass.

After that time back in Vladivostok, Shad was sort of geared to vodka, and Old Keats could drink it like water. For myself, I couldn't have managed to say one word on a large bet. But Slim, whether he was hurting or not, came through in his normal, winning way. He breathed out a long, heavy breath and said, "*Say*, that white whiskey ain't too bad at all!" He picked up the now half-empty bottle and looked at it. "Matter a' fact, it's downright jim-dandy." He began refilling our glasses, mine first. "There ya' go, Levi!" he said, pouring for the others.

Knowing Slim, I knew damn well that he knew damn well how bad I was feeling.

"Yeah," I muttered, finally just barely able to talk. "There I go."

Looking around the table, I saw one encouraging thing. As Slim leaned across to fill Igor's glass, I noticed tears, or at least a lot of very suspicious moisture, in Igor's eyes. He looked at me at the same time, and both of us, without words, knew that neither one of us was alone in his agony.

And then, as Slim finally filled his own glass, emptying the bottle, the pretty, tablecloth girl, as smiling as ever, came back carrying a tray with four brand-new bottles of vodka on it.

Igor and I gave each other a second pain-filled glance as she spoke to Rostov in a cheerful voice, placing the bottles before us.

As she left the table, Rostov turned to Shad. "We sent two bottles, so —"

"Yeah," Shad broke in. "I gathered."

Rostov said, "It's those two big men who spoke to us as we came in."

Old Keats grinned. "Shall we send 'em back eight bottles?"

It didn't take a genius at arithmetic to figure out what was going on. "Jesus *Christ,* boss!" I said. "They'll send us back *sixteen!*"

Slim turned to give the two men a short, friendly look. "Tell the truth, I can't help but kinda admire their style."

Shad said nothing, but his face was set in a hard half-angry frown.

Looking at Shad now, Slim saw deeper, beyond the frown. And when he spoke it was in a quiet, easy voice. "I know it's a sorta dumb spot t' be put in, boss. But in Montana it'd be easy. Back there we'd either invite them fellas over t' join us, or send the booze back, which'd sure be askin' for trouble."

Rostov said flatly, "It won't be sent back."

Slim nodded and spoke for all of us to Rostov, though he was speaking mostly for

Shad. "We just hate somehow t' give less than we get. T' ever be beholden t' anybody. It ain't in our nature. An' this white whiskey thing's gettin' sorta foolish an' outta hand. In some kind of a good way, how can we come out fair an' even with them fellas?"

"Very easily," Rostov said quietly, knowing our minds were all on Shad. "Simply by thanking them."

Old Keats muttered, "Hell!" Then he shook his head slightly and said, half to himself, "The easiest and yet the most difficult thing of all."

It looked to me like Rostov was about to get up and go to the far table where the two men were when Shad suddenly spoke in a low, gruff voice. "What's a good word?"

If Rostov felt as startled as the rest of us, he didn't show it. He said, "You might try *vostrovia.*"

"What's it mean?"

"To your health."

Shad grabbed his glass and stood up from the table, glaring at the two men across the room. Raising his glass high he roared, "*Vostrovia!*" so powerfully that it seemed like the whole room damnere shook.

That was probably the hardest thing he ever did in his life.

But it sure worked.

The two big men stood up with their glasses raised and shouted "*Vostrovia!*" back at him.

There was something a whole lot more than simple "good health" in the air, and whatever it was, it was so exciting and contagious that all of us at our table and most everyone else in the room suddenly started rearing up with glasses held high, yelling deafening "*Vostrovias!*" all over the place.

And then, as the thunder of voices subsided, we all drank.

Carried along, even I drank again, and the second glass wasn't as hard on my already numb throat as the first one had been.

As they finished their drinks, the two big men suddenly and swiftly threw their glasses as hard as hell to the floor, shattering each glass into maybe a million pieces. Shad's and Rostov's empty glasses were the next to slam explosively down against the floor. And then, with glassware now being shattered all over the room, I got to the end of my drink and threw it down as hard as I could.

It was strangest thing, but in the instant my glass crashed to the floor, I somehow understood with great clearness two things I hadn't known before. One of them was that all these people throwing their glasses down had a pretty good idea of what Rostov and his free cossacks stood for and this was their way of wordlessly wishing them good luck.

And the second thing I realized in that instant was that the actual reason for smashing the glasses. It had to do with the human mind and spirit, as if it were a way of showing that the idea within that last drink was so damned true and important that the glass had to be destroyed and never used again. And in never being used again, the truth and importance of the idea it held could never ever drain away like the casual drink the glass held. The drink would be forgotten soon. But the shattered glass and the idea behind it would be remembered forever.

After all that noisy breakage, there was a long, warm moment of silence as the other men in the room stood facing us, the good feeling so thick in the air that you could almost breathe it in.

Then, as if everything that needed saying had been said, everybody started sitting back down, talking and laughing once more between themselves. At the same time some of the girls working there started sweeping up the broken bits of glass all over the floor, while the others quickly began bringing out trays of new glasses to set at the tables. They not only didn't seem miffed at what had happened, but I got the idea they were actually pleased about it. For that matter a couple of them, including the tablecloth girl, had clapped their hands delightedly as we were demolishing our glasses. She came up with a trayload of new ones as we settled back into our chairs. Putting eight of them down for us, she said something to Rostov, and then she was gone.

As Old Keats and Bruk each took a bottle and started pouring refills around, Rostov said, "Her name is Irenia. She just said that in her heart she drank and broke a glass with us."

Slim, like me, was still deeply impressed with what had happened. "Does that crazy kinda thing go on all the time?"

Rostov shook his head. "No."

"Only," Bruk said slowly, "when it's something special."

Slim nodded thoughtfully. "All the same, special or not, back in Montana any barkeep I know sure'd take a dim view a' the custom." He pulled his drink toward him. "Just outta idle curiosity, in a saloon like this who gets stuck with payin' for all them glasses?"

Rostov glanced at Shad. "Traditionally, the man who proposed the toast."

I think Shad himself was still in a small state of shock, both for having forced himself to thank some Russians for something and also

234

for being moved by their magnificent reaction to it. "Good," he said, quietly studying the re-filled glass in front of him, "that's exactly as it ought t' be."

The noise in the rest of the room, though it wasn't all that loud, suddenly became lower, voices going down and laughter either stopping or easing off. It was as though somebody might have been playing one of those new Magic Talking Machines I'd heard about and a nasty neighbor had complained so they'd turned it down so far that the good time wasn't really any fun anymore. The whole place suddenly had a cold, different feeling in it.

We swung around a little in our chairs and saw the reason, which wasn't hard to figure out. A bunch of Imperial Cossacks, ten or twelve of them, were coming in. They looked around the room with hard eyes, paying particular attention to us. Then they took a couple of tables near one of the front windows, and I had the thought that they probably didn't even know, or certainly care, that they'd just ruined a fine, warm Magic Talking Machine time.

For that matter, a great many people in the room now began to quietly finish their drinks and leave. The two big men were among the first to go.

Saddened, and even more angered by all this,

though I could almost swear I wasn't feeling the vodka, I raised my glass and said to Rostov, "It's my turn! What's the opposite of *vostrovia?* How do ya' wish somebody *bad* health?"

"Nurse your drink," Shad said quietly. "I'm not all that anxious t' get you out of a riot, or carry ya' home."

Rostov spoke to Igor in almost the same voice. "You will drink everything in your glass — but gradually."

So the rest of them continued their regular drinking, while Igor and I tried to look indignant about being cut down but were secretly grateful as hell.

Shad downed his drink in the Russian one-raise-of-the-wrist fashion and then frowned at the Tzar's cossacks near the window. "Seein' us relaxin' here, they know we're either awful strong or awful stupid."

Slim swallowed his vodka neat and said, "That's one major advantage we got over 'em. They ain't yet picked up no inklin' a' how stupid we *really* are."

The others emptied their glasses and Rostov said, "Verushki has already sent night patrols out, of course." He leaned forward to speak quietly. "Let's look at it from Verushki's point of view. We camp on the broken flats two miles outside of town. We will not bother him, and he is not to bother us. No more than a few of our men are to come into town together at any time. As soon as we can cross the Amur, we'll go."

Slim put down another charge of vodka. "That's about the simple right of it."

Rostov looked at Shad, who was listening quietly, turning his now empty glass between his thumb and forefinger on the tabletop, making little circles of water on the wood. As Nick filled the empty glasses, Rostov went on. "It's supposed to be a gentlemen's agreement that he won't spy on us, but he will. He'll do everything he can to collect Shad's little finger and everything that goes with it."

"Sure he will," Shad put in. "That's why we'll be way out on those broken flats. With our men and cattle movin' in and out of those far-off breaks, they'll never be able to figure out for sure that there ain't too many of us."

Bruk put away another glass of vodka as though it was clear spring water and said grimly, "If Verushki had any idea how few of us there are, or if he finds out —"

"*If* this an' *if* that!" Shad said in a low, impatient voice. "The whole *point* a' showdown is t' out-*if* the other fella! We're sittin' here because Verushki *ain't* got no idea our last card is a deuce!"

Rostov had been studying Shad thoughtfully. "In one strange way, Northshield, showdown and chess are the same game."

"The hell you say." Shad frowned. "Plain old showdown got us this far."

"In chess one sometimes mounts a seeming show of strength where there is no intention or real ability of attacking at all. It's usually referred to as a diversionary tactic."

Genuinely puzzled, Slim said, "Huh?"

"Let's *show* Verushki our last card. But we'll make our deuce look to him like an ace."

I expected almost any reaction from Shad except the one he finally had. He said quietly, "Tell me about makin' an ace."

"Verushki would massacre the thirty of us, the deuce."

Taking another sip of vodka I muttered, "Thirty-one," wanting to keep the count as high as possible.

"But he's afraid of sixty of us." Rostov paused and then went on. "So let's show him that ace. All sixty of us."

The others at the table just looked at each other, wondering if Rostov was quite right in his head.

Except for Shad. Once again his reaction was thoughtful and quiet. "My fellas would raise a lotta hell over that."

Rostov nodded. "So would mine."

Even with the vodka not helping me much, it was then that I first started to realize that Rostov and Shad were each slowly beginning, somehow, to damnere be able to know, or at least guess, what the other one had on his mind. Maybe, even seeming so different, they were that much alike. In any case, right now they were already talking back and forth about something that hadn't even been said out loud yet.

Frowning, Bruk spoke for the rest of us. "Just what is it that we would all raise hell over?"

"Verushki's men," Rostov explained, "will be watching us from a great distance, and on broken terrain. Therefore, aside from our normal movements, from time to time we will all put on American clothes and deliberately show ourselves all at once against the skyline. At other times, we'll all wear cossack uniforms and do the same thing. That way there will sometimes seem to be thirty cowboys. And at other times, thirty cossacks."

"Rostov's chess ain't too bad," Shad said. "When Verushki's already been buffaloed up front, thirty an' thirty sure add up fast t' sixty."

Slim started pouring again, glancing off toward the Imperial Cossacks. 'Them two games do have one thing in common."

"What?" I asked.

Slim shrugged. "T' play either one like a real champion, looks like ya' got t' be slightly crazy."

14

It was a good while later before the Imperial Cossacks finally got up to leave. We'd already decided not to take off until after they did. We were bound and determined to be more relaxed than they were if it killed us.

As they gave us hard looks and started to go out, Old Keats and Nick were pouring from our last two bottles, which were both getting fairly empty by now. There weren't many people left in the place, and the girls were sort of straightening things and cleaning up in general.

The Tzar's men went through the door and Shad said, "We'll give them a couple of minutes, then bust out."

Bruk said, "They're probably waiting to follow us."

Nick nodded strongly. "Yes. They follow."

"Won't matter." Shad looked at Rostov. "It's too dark t' count anything tonight, and we'll move ourselves an' the herd out t' the flats b'fore daylight."

Again they were understanding each other's thoughts without words. Rostov just looked at Shad, silently agreeing, and then turned and called out in Russian, obviously asking for the bill.

We started to get up and the tablecloth girl, Irenia, came over and said something that was nice, in a low, happy voice, smiling all the while at Rostov. And after all that niceness of hers, she was no more prepared for Rostov's sudden anger than I was. If a man could ever speak quietly and yet carry a lion's roar at the same time, Rostov did it then. Whatever it sounded like to her, she rushed away, frightened half to death.

Appalled, I said to Rostov, "What was all that?"

Rostov was still too angry to answer, but Bruk did. "She let those two big men pay for everything."

Shad spoke to Rostov, his eyes harder than any voice could ever try to match.

"The broken glasses?"

"Yes," Rostov said angrily. "Those too."

And then the tough older lady came hurrying

up to the table to talk to Rostov. As they spoke, Bruk translated, with Old Keats nodding in agreement whenever he got the gist of it.

"She says this is a matter of honor," Bruk said, having a hard time listening and talking at the same time. "And the captain just told her the honor belonged here at this table. She says no, the honor belonged at both tables. And" — Bruk hesitated — "she says both of those men have spoken out against the Tzar already, and with no free cossacks around to help them speak out."

The tough-looking lady suddenly put her hand over her eyes as if she were holding back quick tears of her own, and then she too rushed away.

Rostov was touched by her. "Our bill seems to have been paid in full," he said quietly.

Shad had already taken a big handful of silver dollars out of his pocket. "How 'bout payin' it twice?"

"No," Rostov said. "Let's just let it go."

Shad studied Rostov and then said, "All right. Let's get back and move the herd." He put the coins back in his pocket, and we all started for the front door.

The tablecloth girl came out of the kitchen just then, and I couldn't help but notice her and slow down in following the others. She was standing there, not too far away, looking unhappy as hell, and I said to her, "Thank you, Irenia."

She only understood the word "Irenia" and my tone of voice. But that was enough. She knew the way I felt and she smiled, so there was a good feeling between us.

Then I turned and went on out through the door.

Outside, we all mounted up and followed Shad and Rostov out of the dimming lights of the town into the ink-black darkness beyond.

That big group of Imperial Cossacks followed us, which was kind of silly. About a half mile out of town we just pulled off and sat our horses quietly. They rode on by, bits and spurs jingling in the dark stillness and the leather of their saddles creaking, and pretty quick they had gone on their noisy way. If you don't happen to want to make all that racket, you simply take off your spurs, reach up and hold the bit gentle, and don't shift the weight of your butt around in the saddle. We did that until we reached the herd. And then, as the others gathered around in the pitch-black night, Shad said, "We're drivin' the herd over t' them broke-up flats. As of now, make all the noise ya' want. Matter a' fact, it'd help some if each one of ya' sounded like five or ten."

So with that encouragement there was a lot of whoopin' and hollerin' and yah-hooin' as we woke up the sleepy, resentful herd and started driving it up over the sloping mountain and down the far side.

We got the herd to the breaks two miles outside of Khabarovsk and had it bedded down long before sunrise.

There were two problems that came with sunup that morning. One was trying to explain to the Slash-Diamond outfit and to Rostov's cossacks about how it would be an advantage for one and all to wear each other's clothes once in a while. This plan met with quite a bit of disapproval.

The second, and killing, problem had to do with two fellas who'd befriended us and paid our tariff in Khabarovsk the night before.

That morning those two big men were both hanged by the neck until dead. And finding out about that hit us like a sledge hammer.

One thing came on top of another pretty fast.

Just about to a man, our fellas hated the idea of wearing any kind of cossack clothes and therefore refused.

"It — it ain't American!" Rufe said.

"Damn it," Mushy said simply.

"A nigger cossack?" Shiny demanded.

"Shit, boss!" Dixie grumbled. "Ain't there

some better way t' protect them dumb bastards?"

"I ain't gonna be no clown f'r nobody," Crab said, and Chakko grunted "Uhh!" in a way that meant something more negative than all the "no's" ever said.

Bit Yawn stood up to his full height. "I like them fellas enough t' fight for 'em! But pretend t' *be* one, never!"

I got the feeling that Rostov was having somewhat the same sort of hard time with his men, who'd camped right next to us in the dark. But his cossacks were better disciplined than our bunch, so he seemed to have the situation more in hand.

And then Lieutenant Bruk, who'd been on lookout with Old Keats, came galloping over a twenty-foot slanting bluff and rode quickly down to us.

Bruk, who'd been watching Khabarovsk through Rostov's telescope, handed it slowly back to him and said something in a choked, twisted voice.

The cossacks knew first, and then we finally learned.

The two big men, recognizable in their size and their clothes, had just been hanged from an oak tree on the outskirts of Khabarovsk. Being big and strong, they'd struggled quite a lot, and Old Keats and Bruk had watched them through those long, long moments of death.

We all knew it was because of last night, because of them taking up for us, and someone, some terrible little person there, who had told about it.

And looking at Shad, I could see that all he was thinking of was the toast he'd made.

"Vostrovia!" his powerful voice echoed in my mind.

"Vostrovia!" both big men had roared back, meaning so much more than simple good health.

And now, with all the good, strong things they'd intended, those giant-hearted, generous, free-spirited Russians were dead.

Rostov and Shad now looked at each other for a long, quiet moment, their eyes meeting and locking in silent thought. And the way their look was, even the other men who hadn't been with us the night before could see how hard and deeply both of them were hit.

Finally Shad turned a little and said in a low voice, "Purse, go up an' relieve Old Keats."

Purse said huskily, "Yes, sir, boss." And he mounted and rode off.

Rostov stepped over to stand near Shad now, though still neither of them said anything. They both looked down thoughtfully at the ground about halfway between them, as though that little patch of dirt was worth a lot of quiet study.

Igor and Bruk and some of the other cossacks came over now, sort of following behind Rostov so that we were all standing pretty close together.

It was Slim who finally spoke, his low, quiet voice just barely breaking the silence, like a pebble dropped gently into a quiet pond. And his words were as easy and soft as the ripples spreading out. "Darnest thing. None of us never ever said but that there one word t' them, an' them t' us. But somehow it's just like they was one of us. And, sort of, always was."

My voice wasn't that low or controlled, but I tried my best to at least keep it level. "Verushki did that outta pure crazy *meanness*. Just f'r *nothin'*. What're *we* gonna do *back?*" That was as far as I could make it without my voice going out on me altogether.

Shad gave me a quiet, hard look that managed to hide the pain he was feeling inside. "Not one goddamn thing."

Even though I knew he had to be right, my face must have showed something else. Anger maybe, or disappointment, or both.

Old Keats now rode back and joined us, touching Bruk's shoulder with brief warmth because of the grim sorrow they'd just shared.

Slim said grimly, "Shad's right, f'r hard-rock sure. We don't do nothin'."

Rostov looked at Old Keats and Bruk, who were still standing near each other, silently seeming to think and even look a little bit like each other. "Do you think it was meant as a lesson to us, or the people of Khabarovsk?"

Old Keats, his narrowed eyes still filled with what he'd seen, said bitterly, "Both."

Bruk nodded. "Most of the Imperial Cossacks were there, and they'd gathered many, many people to watch."

"Captain?" Igor said, and I could see he felt the same hopeless frustration that I did. "Two good men have been deliberately murdered!"

Rostov said quietly, "That's exactly right. So then, in the interest of justice, what would you suggest we do?" He glanced from Igor to me. "Or you?"

Igor and I looked at each other, and we both knew that between us we couldn't come up with a decent answer.

"Well — maybe," I said lamely, "at least if they had families, maybe we could — "

"No." Rostov cut me short. "If we helped their families, they would be the next to suffer." Off to one side, in a low voice, Sergeant Nick translated to the other cossacks what Rostov was saying. "There's nothing we can do for those two men." He paused briefly, filled with his thoughts, and then went on, speaking as movingly for the first time to all of us as he had once spoken to me alone about swans. "Nor is there anything we can do for the millions, beyond counting, who have died in Mother Russia over the years in the name of the Tzar.

"What we can do, and will do, is what we started out to do. We'll get these cattle to Bakaskaya, so that that town, and the movement toward freedom that it stands for, will have a chance to survive." It's just possible that Rostov felt even more deeply about the deaths of those two men than Shad and us others. Because in his voice and his eyes, as well as what he was saying, he was sure sending chills up a lot of spines, including mine. "There is an ancient philosophy that gives us the choice of weeping in the darkness or lighting a candle. Bakaskaya is our candle. And to keep it lighted against the day when there will no longer be a Tzar is everything." He paused, and when he went on, his voice was almost harsh. "We will survive here until we can cross the Amur. Some of us will make daily visits into Khabarovsk for supplies and relaxation, and while we're there we will not only show the Imperial Cossacks no fear, but to the contrary, rather superior and casual disdain.

"And to successfully manage these things, we must keep the military in Khabarovsk convinced that our force is much larger than it actually is."

He now stopped, but the way he'd ended his talk brought the whole thing right smack-dab back in a circle to where it had been, up front, in the first place. It was still a question of whether or not the Slash-Diamonders would put on cossack clothes every now and then.

For a time, no one moved or spoke.

And then Shad moved and spoke. He took off his old beaten-up, front-pointed black cowboy hat, which was normally an object that couldn't even be touched by anyone else without serious risk of both life and limb, and he handed it over to Rostov. *"Vostrovia,"* he said quietly.

Rostov handled the hat carefully, with the respect and dignity it deserved, and after a moment he took off his fur cossack hat and held it out to Shad.

Shad took it and looked it over curiously.

Then, finally, as if they were both wondering whether their heads could stand this radical kind of a change, they very slowly put on each other's hat.

And when they'd done this, and started

frowning around at the rest of us, trying to see some kind of a reaction, there wasn't a man among us brave enough to tell them the truth.

They both looked great!

Rostov growled something in Russian to his men, and Shad at last said, "Well, goddamnit! Can ya' *recognize* me, at least?"

Slim was the first one who got up the nerve to grin a little and say something to Shad. "Ya' look downright gorgeous, Captain Rostov."

Shad glared at Slim, and Old Keats said with some impatience, "You look exactly like Shad Northshield wearing a fur hat! What the hell did ya' expect?"

Still a little uncomfortable, Shad shrugged. "Wasn't quite sure."

Ilya now said something in Russian to Rostov which caused some laughter among the cossacks. Igor told me later that Ilya had promised to write a song about an American cowboy named Rostov.

But between the two of them, and their simple exchange of hats, the whole idea about clothes was getting easier now.

Sammy the Kid said, "That cossack stuff ain't all that bad. I'd look outstandin' as hell in one a' them black cloaks with the red linin'!"

"You wouldn't be outstandin'," Crab muttered, "in the bottom of a hole under an outhouse."

Natcho's white teeth flashed in a wide smile. "I've been wanting t' try on one of those swords!"

"Sabers," someone corrected him.

The cossacks now laughed a little bit at something else, and the whole feeling about clothes was rapidly improving.

I pulled off my leather jacket and handed it to Igor. He grinned and nodded and untied a little cord around his neck so that he could hand me his cape.

Within a few minutes, just exchanging things around in a friendly and curious way, we wound up being about as mixed-up an outfit as anybody ever saw.

But it was just that. Friendly and curious. Once in a while there'd be a little laughter here or there because some of our half-and-half outfits were downright absurd, but it still wasn't a happy time, or even anything like that.

Those two hanged men were too much on all of our minds for any of us to want to, or be able to, just haul off and get a kick out of anything.

As a matter of pure fact, there wasn't one man there who didn't know just exactly what direction Shad and Rostov were pushing us in. Even Big Yawn, who was generally as thick as a brick wall, and who had been maybe the hardest-set against cossack clothes, was examining a big, baggy pair of flaming red britches that belonged to Kirdyaga, who was about his same size. And Big Yawn had already made his mind up what he was going to do when he looked up from those red britches as Shad spoke out in a hard voice.

"In about ten minutes," he said, "I want thirty cossacks t' ride over that hill t' pay homage t' them two fellas."

And about ten minutes later, that's exactly what happened.

It wasn't all that easy for the whole bunch of us to hurry up and look like cossacks, but we managed. Boots and hats were the scarcest items because a lot of Rostov's men weren't carrying spares. But there were plenty of capes and britches to go around, and those were what would be most easily seen and recognized at a distance anyway. For most of those ten minutes, us cowboys in that camp looked too ridiculous to even try to describe. Picking out fellas about their same size, the cossacks were bringing over their spare stuff, while we were getting down to our long johns and starting, with a good deal of cussing and growling, to get into those unfamiliar things.

"My *god!*" Crab snarled. "This goddamn

shirt buttons up the *back!*"

But Ilya, who owned the silken-looking shirt, saw the problem and started to give Crab a hand with buttoning it. I lucked out, because Igor had a complete second uniform that fit me like it had been made to order. The fur hat felt funniest of all, not having any brim to take hold of, but I was soon to find out that the good feeling of the cape more than made up for that. It felt kind of good and free when you were just wearing it normally, but mounted, when you opened your horse up a little, it went whipping out behind and around you like a huge bird's wings flapping, giving you the feeling of damnere halfway flying.

Struggling into one of those blood-red vests that Nick had given him, Slim said to Shad and Rostov, "You ain't leavin' nobody at all in camp?"

"Nope." Shad swung one of Rostov's capes around his shoulders. "We ain't gonna be gone but a few minutes."

Rostov nodded. "This way, they'll see the greatest show of force we can mount."

"I still ain't sure about me an' Link," Shiny said, pulling on a pair of Yuri's britches. "Our complexions're awful dark."

"Pull your hats down," Dixie said dryly.

"We won't give 'em much time t' study on

us," Shad told them. "Let's get t' horse."

And a moment later we were mounting up and moving out.

Poor old Purse Mayhew, standing lookout, almost collapsed from sheer shock as all those cossacks came galloping up toward him, but then he saw Shad up front, and some of us others, and realized what was going on.

We rode past the still-openmouthed Purse, over the crest of the rise, and started down the far side. From here we could see Khabarovsk far off and below in the distance.

There were still a lot of people gathered around that big oak tree on the edge of town, so far away that even the huge tree itself looked small. I could just barely make out the two tiny figures hanging motionlessly from one large limb, and I swallowed hard.

"Pull up!" Shad ordered. "And line out!"

Rostov repeated the order in Russian, and within a few seconds there were thirty of us sitting our horses side by side, facing the distant crowd around the grim, terrible oak tree with its two hanging bodies.

Even from that far away we'd already been noticed by Verushki's cossacks and the rest of the people there. Verushki's men, staring off and up at us, must have had the same feeling I did. As I looked from one side to the other, at all of our fellas lined up, we sure didn't appear to be a bunch to mess around with lightly.

Shad and Rostov were next to each other in the center of the long line, and they said something back and forth.

"Take out your rifles!" Shad ordered. "We're gonna give them two fellas a three-gun salute!"

Rostov was calling out the same instructions to his men.

"Aim your rifles up!" Shad told us. "And shoot when I yell *fire!*"

We all cocked our rifles and raised them toward the sky.

Shad now called out, "Ready! — *Fire!*"

A slightly ragged, but damned impressive volley roared out and echoed across the wide, sloping meadows toward Khabarovsk.

Before the sound of the first volley had faded out of the air, Shad yelled "Fire!" again and the second thunder boomed out from our assembled guns. A few cossacks had single-shot rifles and couldn't fire again, but with all the smoke and noise it was impossible to tell the difference. Buck started to rear under me a little, thinking we were overdoing the whole thing, and a couple of other horses weren't all too happy, but by that time the third command came and the third roar of rifles rolled boomingly out across the meadow.

"Put your guns back, and let's go!" Shad called. He and Rostov led off, and we followed the two of them back up over the rise and out of sight of Khabarovsk. I doubt if all told we'd actually been in sight of the town for as much as one full minute.

"Jesus!" Purse yelled as we rode back past him. "I sure am glad I'm on *your* side!"

He might have been sort of trying to kid us a little, what with our uniforms and all, but his voice came out sounding flat dead on the level.

15

At camp we finally got our clothes situation straightened back around without too much confusion.

Rostov sent some of his cossacks out to stand guard at high, strategic points, and Shad put half a dozen of our men on the herd, which was gathered in a wide, grassy depression in the broken flats. A stream ran by near our camp, and widened out into a small lake not far beyond, so there was plenty of grass and water handy to keep the herd in good shape.

We'd got a fire going and put some water on

to boil coffee. And now, not much more than spitting distance away, some of the cossacks were starting to build their own fire.

"Say, Captain Rostov," Slim said, "we'll have a big pot a' coffee ready pretty quick."

The cossacks looked at us, and Old Keats said, "there'll be more'n enough."

Rostov didn't exactly turn the offer down, but he didn't exactly accept it either. "My men drink tea."

"It would be interesting, sir," Igor said. "I've never drank coffee."

"Never?" I asked, stunned at such an unbelievable thing.

"No." He shook his head. "Never."

"Then," Shad said, quietly making the invitation official, "maybe it's time ya' did."

Igor looked at Rostov, ready to go along with whatever he decided.

"All right," Rostov said finally. "Coffee."

As the cossacks gathered around our fire with us, Slim got out a bag of Acme Prime Grade Coffee Beans and started to grind them.

It was kind of a strange feeling just then, because after all the weeks we'd more or less been together, it was the first time we'd ever really been together in a friendly, easygoing way of everybody sitting around one fire.

The cossacks gradually settled in next to the

rest of us around the burning, crackling wood, and there was a long silence, but it wasn't a bad silence.

Taking note of our general, warm feeling, Rostov was the first to quietly speak. "Ordering those two men hanged may have been a serious mistake on Verushki's part."

In a low voice, Igor told the others what Rostov had said.

Shad was staring into the fire with a small frown, and while he'd been the first one to want to help this independent bunch, and at the same time to get his herd through, I knew the stubborn bastard would be the last one, if ever, to admit anything in terms of being friends.

"Well, after all," I said, "we did at least do one thing for the two of 'em. That three-gun salute."

"Bein' fatally dead," Shad said flatly, "I doubt they enjoyed that little show a whole lot."

"Boss!" I countered. "It was you who — "

He cut me off sharply. "What we *really* did was *this!* We showed that half-ass colonel thirty armed cossacks who were madder'n hell and who couldn't care less about him an' his — whores on horseback!" He shot a look at Rostov to acknowledge this last phrase. "That three-gun salute scared the shit outta Verushki an' he's in one hell of a lot worse shape than he was before!"

I couldn't put words to it just then, but that damned Shad could go out and risk his neck for a good reason one minute and the next minute turn right around and act like he hadn't really done a thing. Or if he had, it was for some totally impersonal and other reason that nobody had ever known about or even suspected, in the first place.

His words had sounded so hard that there was a touchy kind of uncertainness among all of us as Igor, in a low voice, put into Russian what Shad had said.

Old Keats, God bless him, now spoke in a thoughtful way. "We've all of us just been through a sad time. I saw them hang. But I was also there with those two men last night. And I don't think they'd want for it to go on too long, being a sad time."

There was no question but what he was right. The question was, what to do about it. Sure as hell, not one person there was about to try to end that sadness by going into a song or leaping up to dance.

The water was boiling real good now, and Slim started pouring the Acme Prime Grade Coffee Beans into it. Clearing his throat, he said, "The second-best cowboy coffee in the world is coffee that's strong enough t' float a horseshoe in." He poured out all of the ground beans and then dropped the empty bag into the fire to burn. "But the first best, which is the kind a' coffee I make, is strong enough t' dissolve the goddamn horseshoe." He picked up a nearby ladle to stir it with. "I just thought you Russians might be grateful f'r that little piece a' information."

Bruk translated to the Russians what Slim had just said, and in the whole group there wasn't as much as a raised eyebrow among them. Several of them nodded thoughtfully, and Ilya and Yakov both said a few quiet words.

Equally without expression, Bruk now said to us, "They are grateful for the information and they are pleased that you always tell the truth and would not exaggerate."

"Absolutely." Slim stirred the darkening coffee. "T' me, any small exaggeration's almost as heinous a crime as an outright lie. An' anybody knows that lyin' is a mortal sin."

This time Nick translated, and the cossacks nodded in thoughtful agreement as Ilya got up and walked slowly off.

A little later the coffee was getting even darker. "Good," Slim muttered. "Has t' be black as a landlord's heart." He dropped in some egg-shells to settle the grains to the bottom.

About this time Ilya walked back up and, saying a few innocent-sounding words, held out a horseshoe to Slim.

"He's asking," Bruk said, "if he can help you test your coffee."

In its own way, this whole thing was getting kind of warm and nice, and we were all equally interested to see if Slim could manage his way out of the trap he'd built for himself.

"Hell," Slim said easily, "tell 'im I took a sacred vow never t' waste another horseshoe. Cause t' waste anything is almost as mortal as sin as lyin'."

Bruk explained that in Russian.

"Reason I took that vow," Slim went on, "is one winter when I was just a green kid, I made a lot a' coffee. An' come springtime, there wasn't one horseshoe t' be found in all Montana."

After this had been translated, Ilya nodded solemnly and held out his empty other hand, saying a few more words.

"We have the greatest blacksmiths in the world in Siberia," Bruk explained. "And they do very delicate and fantastic work. What he is offering you is a very special and tiny horse-shoe that was made to be worn on the hoof of a flea. It's so small it's almost impossible to see."

It looked to our outfit like Ilya had nailed him, and though they took pains not to show it, the rest of the cossacks felt the same way as we did. But Slim rose to the occasion.

Just as solemnly as Ilya, he slowly reached out and pretended to take something from Ilya's hand and then to examine it between his thumb and forefinger very carefully. "Tell 'im that this here is surely one a' the finest examples a' blacksmithin' I ever seen," he said. "An' if this here horseshoe dissolves in there, it'll surely prove beyond any shadow a' doubt, that we all been tellin' God's absolute truth." Then he opened his fingers, seeming to drop something very tiny into the boiling coffee.

Ilya didn't need Bruk's translation. What Slim had done was clear enough, and Ilya knew there was no way to get his nonexistent horseshoe out of Slim's horseshoe-dissolving coffee. He laughed good-naturedly and slapped Slim on the shoulder, and while the rest of us were grinning and chuckling with each other, we got coffee served around.

From their reactions upon drinking, some of those cossacks must have suddenly thought there was some truth in what Slim had claimed. In all honesty he did make strongish coffee, and there was a great deal of almost gagging and almost choking among a number of them, that was just barely held back.

Rostov raised his cup toward Slim. "They compliment you on making such a drink, so quickly, out of simple water."

"Tell 'em," Slim said, "that dissolved 'r not, horseshoes ain't too easy t' swalla'."

But despite the hardship of getting used to Slim's coffee, the idea of them sitting with us, and drinking what we normally drank, was a good thing. In a still friendly, natural way, with just a hint of the possible death and destruction behind it, the conversation now veered into another direction.

A few of his men now spoke to him, and Rostov, without seeming too overjoyed about it, said, "In the time that we will be waiting here, my men who are not on duty will be practicing war games." He looked at Shad. "My men have invited your men to join with them, if they wish."

Shad tossed the last few drops of his coffee into the fire, where the wet sputtered briefly on the heat. "With 'em or against 'em?"

"Never against them. But even so, the games are competitive, and sometimes quite rough."

"Hell, boss," Sammy the Kid grinned, "we'd take it easy on 'em."

Shad said, "Okay, when you're not workin' you can join in. But don't run any far-out risks. I don't want anybody gettin' laid up."

Rostov translated to his men, adding what I guessed to be his own words of caution.

Grinning and nodding with pleased expressions, the cossacks finished their coffee and started over toward where their own gear was stacked nearby. And Shad and Rostov got into a quiet conversation between themselves.

"Heck," Mushy said, "them cossacks're as tickled as little kids about the idea a' us joinin' their games with 'em."

"Just make sure it stays on a gamin' level," Old Keats told us. "Get yourself injured in some foolish way, and I got a hunch Shad'll be just about mad enough t' finish the job, includin' a free burial service."

"Hell," Dixie said, "after all, they ain't nothin' but games."

"*War* games," Slim corrected him, "which has a different an' somewhat more serious sound to it."

That afternoon a bunch of us who weren't on any kind of duty rode over a low hill near the camp and down to a broken part of the wide meadow where a bunch of the cossacks were doing something. The camp was only a minute away, but you couldn't see it from here.

Shad and Old Keats were talking to Rostov and Bruk and didn't take much notice of our going. I had the impression that Shad had a kind of a disdain for any sort of a war game, probably based on an instinctive feeling that everybody, like he was, ought to be a first-class natural-born warrior in the first place.

Slim and me and six or seven others rode toward where Igor was sitting on Blackeye near a big rock, and he grinned and waved. Some of the other cossacks were riding far out across the broken meadow, stopping once in a while to dismount and jab tall, thin poles into the ground so they stuck up about six feet.

"What they doin'?" I asked, as we pulled up near Igor.

"Laying out a racing course," Igor said.

"Goddamn," Slim grunted, studying the men out on the meadow. "That shapes up t' be some kind of a rough track."

"Ahh!" Dixie said with an edge of contempt. "It sure ain't what *I'd* call rough."

Igor glanced at Dixie without expression, and then went on explaining to the rest of us. "Right here, at this rock, is where the course will begin and end." He pointed off, in a wide, sweeping gesture. "It goes in a rough circle of about three kilometers."

"What the hell's that?" Dixie asked, almost suspiciously.

A little annoyed at his general attitude, I said, "It's a distance, stupid."

Annoyed back at me, he gave me a hard look, and I suddenly realized I'd gotten myself out on a limb. Either Dixie or someone else was going to have to ask me the next question, which had to be, how the hell long a distance? And now, after calling Dixie stupid, I was going to be stuck with absolutely no answer. So I gave the track a swift glance and took a quick, hopeful guess before anybody could nail me down. "Three kilometers is — about two miles."

"Yeah?" Dixie frowned.

"That's right," Igor said, backing me up so neatly that it looked like I'd known what I was talking about all along. "Three kilometers is one-point-eight-six miles."

"Huh?" Link muttered.

Figuring fast as hell, I said casually, "Just a shade under two miles," thereby ending my brief but enjoyable career as a genius.

"Just watch who you're callin' stupid," Dixie muttered.

"I do, I do."

Slim said to us, "Cut it out." Then he looked off across the meadow again, where the cossacks had just finished placing what added up to twenty poles. "Goddamn," he said to Igor, "that's a mean couple a' miles. You ain't missed one rough spot in that whole busted-up field."

"In a race a rider can take any route he wants," Igor told him, "as long as he goes outside of every one of the poles."

"Sure makes it more interestin' than a regular race track," Link said.

Igor grinned. "Wars aren't fought on race tracks."

Slim snorted with faint humor. "There ain't even no good cavalry on 'em. 'Specially the horses I bet on."

The poles all set now, the cossacks were riding back toward us. And the way they'd placed the poles did make a lot of sense for a hard, broken-country run. Going down the slight slope from the big rock near us, the first obstacle was the stream in the meadow, about a hundred yards away. The pole was stuck at the widest place to jump the stream. It was about a ten-foot leap from bank to bank, with a four-foot drop to the water below. You could circle fifty feet to the left of the pole and have no trouble splashing through the shallows there. But in taking that longer way, you'd lose time. And every one of those poles had been placed in a similar, tricky fashion. Wherever there were patches of rocky ground or thick stands of trees or steep gulleys, you were always given your choice. Racing just outside the pole was the fastest and most dangerous. The safer you wanted to play it, riding farther around outside the poles, the longer it would take.

And toward the end of the course, coming back in full circle, the last obstacle was once again the stream. If you wanted to take the long, safe way around, you had to go about three or four hundred feet downstream. Again, where that last pole was placed, it was about a ten-foot leap across, but the ground was higher there, with the stream cutting deeper, so if you were trying to make the best time, and jumped and missed, it was about a twenty-foot drop to where the swift, foaming water below had a whole lot of large, unfriendly rocks jutting up out of it.

"Jesus!" Slim finally said. "T' take that run rightly, an' fast as possible, is goddamn near out-an'-out suicide!"

"Ah, damn," Dixie grumbled. "It more'n likely takes them cossacks two hours t' make a run like that."

Igor said simple, "No."

"Slim's right." Natcho shook his head grimly. And since Natcho was one of the finest horsemen ever born, even Dixie paid attention. "There are about fifteen places where a man on a good horse could go straight through at top speed without hurting either one of them. But there are about five — " He stopped and whistled low under his breath.

Igor nodded, understanding and agreeing. "Those are the ones you circle around as quickly as you can."

The other cossacks, about seven of them, now splashed through a shallow part of the stream and rode toward us. Leading them, big as a bear in the saddle, was Sergeant Nick. They pulled up, facing us, and Nick looked back at the meadow, then at Slim. "What you think?" he asked in his growling heavy accent.

"I hate t' tell ya' this, Nick," Slim said slowly, "but I think you fellas're outta your minds."

Nick chuckled deep in his throat and started to fill his long-stemmed clay pipe. "Why?"

"That goddamn thing's dangerous!" Sort of joining along with Nick, Slim took out an old plug of Red Devil Chewing Tobacco and bit off a chunk before offering it around. "Run like that's bound t' cripple 'r kill somebody ever'time."

Dixie and a couple of others took chaws off Slim's worn old plug, and then it came to me. I passed because I hate and can't stand chewing tobacco, but I could see that Igor was curious.

I held it out to him, thinking he only wanted to look at it. But he thought I was just being polite, and giving him first go. As he raised it to his mouth I quickly said, "It's awful" – but he was already forcing his teeth through the tough plug, and I finished lamely – "strong."

Nick, now lighting his pipe, looked at Igor. "You talk more good. You tell about games."

Both the responsibility and the taste of the tobacco hit Igor at about the same time. He handed me back the plug, trying to keep the stricken look off his face. "The games –" he said, unable to go further at the moment.

Old Keats had once told me, in one of his moments of rare insight, "There is no hole that goes so far, or is so forever unending, as an asshole." And though I should have known better, I fit that category right then. Because when Igor handed me back the plug, out of sheer idiocy or misguided loyalty or whatever, I went so far as to take a big goddamn chew off of it too. I guess I just couldn't stand seeing him go through all that suffering all by himself.

As bitter fire surged up through my throat and nostrils and head, and started to move sickeningly down my throat, I handed Slim back what was left of his Red Devil.

He pocketed it, him and the others who were

chewing, slowly working their jaws in easy, practiced contentment, and waiting quietly for what Igor had to say. About the same time, Nick passed his lighted pipe to Ilya, who was sitting his chestnut mare next to Nick.

Igor looked at me, his pain-filled eyes knowing that I'd tried to warn him and was now going through the same torture.

"We have never," he said in a thin voice, "had anyone killed in our games."

With the cossacks paying close attention, and Nick nodding at both the questions and the answers from time to time, Slim went on. "Well, how the hell come not? That there sure is a killin' course."

"Captain Rostov," Igor managed to say, "has taught us that it can be a matter of honor — to die for someone or something — loved." He hesitated, and I realized he was doing the same thing I always did, which can kill anybody who's chewing tobacco. I've always hated to spit and therefore didn't, and he wasn't spitting either, and when you're chewing tobacco you've got to spit or wind up turned inside out. Then, swallowing a little, he went on. "But Captain Rostov has also taught us that it's a crime for anyone to be hurt, or to die, for foolish reasons."

Slim spit expertly, hitting a small rock near

Charlie's left forehoof. "In this rough ol' race ya' got lined up here, what's foolish an' what ain't?"

"He's taught us that each rider must only do what he *knows* he can do." Igor was struggling against the same nausea that I was. "If there's *any* doubt he must not try it."

"Makes good horsemen," Nick rumbled. "Hurt your horse is even worse than hurt yourself."

"Well," I said, forcing my words one at a time through lips that were sealed against throwing up, "that explains that."

"As long as there's common sense," Slim said, shrugging, "there can't be too much damage."

"You're a goddamned spy," Mushy said to Slim indignantly. "You're here t' see Shad don't lose no hands!"

"Oh, hell, no." Slim frowned. "You fellas can fool around all ya' want, far as I'm concerned." He spit again, hitting the same rock with deadly accuracy. "I'd just feel better knowin' you're not all gonna get yourselves killed off, for some dumb damn reason here in this peaceful valley."

I looked at Igor and saw that he couldn't take it much longer. And sure as hell, I couldn't either. "Igor's explained it," I just barely managed to say. "Hell, we'll show you the first part of the ride!"

Igor, in all his torment, caught on like a shot. His fading eyes looked at me like twin suns trying to come up feebly over a dark and dismal horizon. All he said, or could say, was, "Let's go!"

He whirled Blackeye, and I spurred Buck, and we raced down toward the first pole by the creek. I guess he felt the same way I did, which was that if we happened to miss that first ten-foot jump we'd just fall in the water and hopefully drown, which right at that time would have been one hell of an improvement.

Shoulder to shoulder and at a full gallop we hit the edge of the creek and went flying into the air, and an instant later his good old Blackeye and my goddamned Buck were landing us down at full speed on the far side.

We didn't pay any attention to the dimly heard cheers behind us, but kept going on like bats out of hell until we got to that second obstacle, which was a blessed stand of thick trees. Once inside those trees, we both jerked our horses up so hard they damnere sat down, and then we both slightly quicker than instantly abandoned ship.

With our horses staring at us in some mild confusion, both Igor and I started throwing up, our stomachs and throats and every other part of us trying to get rid of that poisonous chewing tobacco.

He finished first, standing there drawing in deep breaths. And then I finally came more or less to an end of all that painful heaving and stepped over to him, with one hand clutched hard against my aching chest.

"I tried t' warn ya'," I said.

He took another deep breath. "How will we explain about disappearing in these trees?"

"Well," I said, "we'll just tell them we stopped t' take a casual piss."

Igor had learned that word some time back, so he knew what I was talking about but still wasn't too happy. He even swore for one of the first times. "All this time for a goddamn *piss?*"

Impatiently I said, "Then we'll just tell 'em we came here t' throw up! 'Cause neither one of us can take Slim's goddamned more'n-year-old Red Devil Chewing Tobacco!"

He thought about this, weighing it back and forth for a moment. "We stopped to take a long piss."

Then we got on Blackeye and Buck and rode out of the trees and back through the stream toward where the others were waiting near the rock.

"You fellas made pretty good time gettin' t'

them trees," Slim said, "but ya' were a little slow gettin' out."

"We stopped t' take a piss."

"Oh?"

"A long one."

Slim reined Charlie around and he and Nick led us off back toward camp.

"If we all ride as fast as you two," Nick said, "we have good games."

"That's f'r sure," Slim agreed. He pulled out his plug. "Either one of ya' care for a little more Red Devil?"

Igor shook his head. "No thanks."

I said, "Some other time."

"F'r me, personal, m'self," Slim said, taking another chew, "I sometimes find Red Devil downright inspirational in makin' good time."

He and Nick looked at each other and then spurred into a lope, and we followed them back up over the hill toward camp.

16

Five of us woke up at an ungodly hour that night to ride the second half of the graveyard shift, and it was around sunup that Mushy and some others came out to relieve us. We went back to camp and got a few hours sleep, so it was pushing noon when we woke up and pulled on our boots and went over to see if there was any coffee.

Some of Slim's coffee was still left over from yesterday, a little bit warmed over and added to. And tasting it on that second day, I'd guarantee no horseshoe or anything else would survive in it one way or the other.

Shad and Old Keats came riding in from checking out the herd and dismounted, Shad glancing up at the near high-noon sun. "Four of ya' are gonna go in town t'day," he said, "along with four cossacks. You're gonna buy some supplies an' have a good time. Who wants t' go?"

Remembering Irenia in her tablecloth dress, I spoke right up. But after those hangings, not many others did.

From the cossack camp next to us, Rostov called, "Northshield?" And Shad and he took about three steps toward each other so they could talk.

Old Keats went on talking for Shad. "T' kind a' keep 'em off balance in there, these visits are gonna go on regular, every day. So on this first day especially, just to break them in right, whoever the first four of ya' are, ya' gotta handle yourselves just proper."

"What the hell's just proper?" Crab wanted to know.

"T' act like ya' own the town an' yet not get anywhere's near t' gettin' in a fight. An' that ain't gonna be easy."

Like Old Keats said, it sure wouldn't be easy, but their idea shaped up to be pretty simple. We were still playing showdown or chess or whatever. And we had to put on an absolutely fearless front without accidentally causing Khabarovsk or our far-off hidden meadow to become a battle-ground. Because with or without one of Rostov's "Pyrrhic" victories, we'd sure as hell finally lose.

From off on one of the high points, there were now a couple of rifle shots. We looked in that direction, and a minute later Ilya galloped down to speak excitedly to Rostov. Rostov then sent him back where he'd been on lookout slapping his pony on the rump to speed him on his way. Turning to us he said, "Some of Verushki's men had circled and were coming in from the far south side to examine our camp. They didn't make it."

"The two shots?" Shad asked.

"They wounded one man and shot another's horse out from under him."

"That," Old Keats said dryly, "is really nifty."

Shad nodded. "It is. An' this is the time, right *now* on top a' that, t' send our men in just like we planned, big as brass an' twice as shiny."

"Yes," Rostov agreed. "But after the incident this morning, today will be an even more difficult time." He paused. "My four men will be Lieutenant Bruk, Kirdyaga, Vody and Yakov."

Rostov moved back to speak to his men and Shad thought hard for a moment. Volunteers were suddenly out, and he was considering which of us he would send.

At last Shad said, "The four of us who are goin' are Old Keats, Big Yawn, Shiny an' Link."

The other three, without a word one way or the other, started to get ready. But Shiny just stood without moving, staring down at the ground.

"Well?" Shad said.

Shiny cleared his throat slightly and looked up at Shad. "They been hangin' our friends an' we just shot one a' them. Maybe dead, maybe not." He hesitated. "An' now, with all that trouble goin' on, some a' us cowboys an' some cossacks're supposed t' ride into that town big as life."

Shad didn't answer, waiting for him to go on.

"I hate t' remind ya' about this again" — Shiny frowned — "but me an' Link ain't exactly typical."

"Nobody said ya' were," Shad told him flatly. "Get mounted."

As Shiny moved resentfully off, it occurred to me that Yawn wasn't exactly typical either. He was by far the biggest man in our outfit, like Kirdyaga was among the cossacks. And it further occurred to me that next to Sergeant Nick, Vody and Yakov were the biggest and toughest-looking men among them. So Rostov had chosen the three roughest, most spine-chilling customers in his whole outfit to go into town with Bruk on this particular day.

Shad and Rostov were both stacking their small going-into-town decks with the largest, meanest-looking, most untypical men they had. And in favor of Shad's decision making, Shiny and Link were not only Negro, but both of them topped six feet and weighed in at a long way over two hundred pounds. In addition, if you didn't know them, and therefore know how gentle they really were, they just happened to look as fierce as wet wildcats.

The four men now led up their horses, and Shiny said quietly, "Me an' Link goin' 'cause we're niggers?"

"Partly," Shad said.

"Hell, boss!" Shiny grumbled as he and the others swung up on their horses. "You're gettin' rid a' your misfits!"

"Who you callin' a misfit?" Big Yawn growled.

But right then Shad had already grabbed the bit on Shiny's mare Ginger, so that she wasn't about to move without getting her jaw broken. And the funny thing was that as he did this he wasn't even mad so much as he was kind of saddened. Holding Ginger motionless he said quietly, "Ya' feel that way, get off. I'll send somebody else."

But Shiny wasn't yet quite ready to get down. He sat in the saddle, frowning vaguely, as though he had a feeling he'd done something wrong but didn't know exactly what.

Keats, who had mounted to lead the others off, turned and spoke with more anger than I'd ever heard in his voice before. *"Shiny!"*

Every eye there jerked around to him, and he went on as hard as before, every word slamming against Shiny like a clenched fist. "You think Shad'd send you 'cause you're a *nigger?* Who went night b'fore last?"

Shiny's gaze winced and narrowed under those battering words.

"You're goin' 'cause you're a good man an' thank *God* black! You an' Link'll be outstandin' as *hell!* Like Big Yawn here, who'll stand about a foot an' a half taller than anybody there!" Keats took a quick, angry breath. "Shad's sendin' you three with me 'cause he thinks you're the most all-round impressive bastards t' go along on this first, hard day!"

Shiny's low voice just barely hung on. "Won't do nothin'," he muttered, "made t' feel like a dumb, black nigger sonofabitch."

For some reason, Shiny was really hurting, and we all looked at him, puzzled.

As one of the chosen three, uncomfortable, and with nothing better to say just then, Big Yawn rumbled, "Me neither."

Slim was quiet but about equally as sore as Old Keats. They both felt that Shad's fairness was in question. "Civil War's finished these fifteen years, Shiny. Slavery abolished an' all. An' you still think, either way, whether you're *picked* or *not* picked, you're bein' picked *on!*"

282

Rostov's four cossacks were mounted and waiting, and it was easy for them to see that we had some kind of problem, so Shad cut it short. He twisted the bit in his hand just slightly, so that Shiny's mare was damned ready and willing to back away and sit down. "I told ya' t' get off, Shiny, and I'll send somebody else."

"Easy, boss, ya' might hurt her."

"I won't hurt her. I'll just get on the saddle when you finally get off."

And then, with Shiny's mare Ginger about to be forced down on her haunches, Shiny said the damnedest thing to Shad. "Did you ever say I was a dumb, black nigger sonofabitch?"

"No! But I'll say it right now, you dumb, nigger sonofabitch!"

Somehow that suddenly turned things around. Shiny said "Okay" in such an easy way that Shad damnere let go of Ginger's bit, and she reared back up to a full standing position.

Knowing Shad the way I did, I couldn't see any reason for it, but Shiny repeated the question. "You never said that?"

"I just now *did!*" Shad told him flatly, still holding the bit and controlling the mare.

I looked at Shiny, who knew that Shad couldn't tell him anything but the truth. And for maybe the first and the last time I had a brief, fleeting look then into Shiny's mind, which was both at once so smart and yet so innocent, and even more, so terribly hardened, that it would be the first to collapse under a gentle pressure of kindness.

And Shad, not trying to be kind, was so. "If you an' me don't know what the hell we're talkin' about," he said gruffly, "then there ain't no goddamn sense in the whole world. So what are you talkin' about a dumb, nigger sonofabitch for?"

Shiny had a hard time asking. "Am I goin' into that town as a nigger or as a man?"

"That's up t' you." Shad's quiet voice still cut hard as an ax. "And don't never question me on that again. Because if ya' have t' ask about bein' a man, then you already said the answer."

Shiny took this in, and understood. "Boss," he said, "if you don't let go a' that bit, it'll be harder'n hell for me t' ever make it t' town with them fellas."

Our other three men now moved off to join the cossacks, who were starting up over the hill toward Khabarovsk.

Shad released the bit and stepped back.

Shiny fingered the reins briefly, gently regaining control of Ginger, and calming her. He said, "I'll tell ya' one thing, boss. Bein' picked as a man sure does make a difference." And then he spurred off at a dead run.

284

We watched as he raced his pony to catch up to the other seven men, and then together they mounted the hills between us and Khabarovsk. Finally they disappeared, topping the last high crest and going out of our sight down those far, sloping meadows stretching toward the town.

"That can turn out t' be a kind of a rough detail," I said, feeling a lot, but not talking to anybody in particular.

"They'll be okay," Slim said in the same general way, "if they just remember t' handle themselves like they ought."

"Eight good men there." Shad stepped over and swung up aboard his big Red. "They'll bluff that town out, like we did an' be back in good shape."

He put his spurs to Red and loped on over to the meadow to take stock of the herd and the men riding it. About the same time, Slim went off to do something or other, and the rest of us were free for a little while to do whatever we wanted.

For myself, I got some neat's-foot oil and sat by my bedroll to put some of it on my bridle. The leather had been hardening up, and that oil would sink right into it, making it softer and stronger, so it wouldn't brittle up and crack. Neat's-foot oil was the best cure in the world for bad-off leather. And the funny thing about that sticky yellow stuff was that like the very leather it was saving, it came from a cow, too. It was made from the crushed bones of cattle, and along with being a cure-all for leather, it was also a first-class medicine for saddlesores or for cuts or tick infections or whatever cattle might get. Old Keats had first brought that fact to my attention a few years back. "It's as though, in a strange way, everything in the world starts an' stops with one ol 'cow." We'd been fixing a beaten-up harness with neat's-foot. "Yep," Keats had gone on thoughtfully. "As though God never gave us a problem without the answer being right next to it."

Maybe what's made me go on like this was the problem of Shiny Jackson. And I was about to find out that the answer was sitting right next to me.

A small card game had started up nearby, and I wound up both working with the bridle and at the same time sort of halfway listening to Crab and Rufe and Dixie playing blackjack for beans and arguing quietly among themselves about the game.

Dixie spoke a word that somehow jarred my ear. He said "misfit," which sure as hell didn't seem to me to be a word that's used all that much. And also, sure as hell, I'd heard that unoften word used not long before.

I looked over at their game at about the same time that the ace of spades came up in front of Dixie. It was his first card faceup and it gave him blackjack, and he said to that ace of spades in a real pleased way, "You black nigger sonofabitch!" as he started to gather his beans in from the pot.

I put down the bridle and stood up and faced him, just looking at him without saying anything.

He glanced at me once or twice, just standing there before him. Then he finally glared at me and said, "What are you starin' at?"

"It was you," I said.

He'd gone over twenty-one in this hand anyway, so he tossed his cards back in with a violent, angry gesture. "Yeah? – *What* was me?"

I still couldn't think of any better words, so I said simply, once again, "It was you."

He reared halfway up, onto one knee, madder than one of them Indian cobras coming up out of a basket, and damned if his tongue wasn't flicking around in that same kind of a spooky way. "I told Shiny the way it would be!" He reared even higher, the tongue still going, with the threat of fangs somewhere behind it. "Them two niggers'll be the first t' go!"

"Maybe." I was too filled up with feeling to say any more.

"Then what are ya' starin' at?"

Crab and Rufe didn't know quite what was going on, but they knew Dixie was ignoring the cards he'd just been dealt. And they knew there was somethng rough in the air. "Levi," Crab said to my silence, "you ain't bein' your normal quick an' witty self."

That broke me loose enough to finally at least say more than a couple of words at a time. "Just who told Shiny that Shad said that he was a dumb, black nigger sonofabitch?"

"Anybody *knows* that he is!" Dixie stood full up, ready to fight.

But, oh, God, was he going to lose, judging from the hard power and fury raging up inside me.

And he did lose.

But I got slightly whacked around in the process.

The way that now came about was that Dixie said, "Just buzz off, nigger lover!"

I replied to that, "Shiny Jackson is worth ten thousand of you, lined up side by side."

And then we went into the battle, which I had the advantage of because I was so mad that while he was swinging at me, I'd already knocked him ass over teakettle in the first place.

It happened to, actually in truth, be an ass over a teakettle.

We were so close to the cossacks that Dixie's butt, with him attached to it, went sailing across the small fire with some tea boiling on it.

He leaped up out of that overturned boiling tea and scattered fire with a great deal of alacrity and charged back upon me, and with the cowboys and cossacks not interfering on either side, we went to it. Since it was between two Slash-Diamonders, even Rostov stayed out of it.

I won, as I sort of hinted before.

But I wasn't too proud of it. Every time he hit me, it hurt. But it was almost like it didn't really matter. Because he could have hit me with a goddamned ax and I'd have still gone back at him. And every time I hit him, I felt sorry for the whole way he was. Maybe it was because I knew that in the final, final judgment of whatever gods there are, I was right and he was wrong. In any case, I knew I'd whip him. And I also knew that then I'd have to take care of him.

And that's what happened.

When Shad came back to camp a little later, packing his saddle on his shoulder, he looked at me swabbing down Dixie's beaten-up face and asked, which was kind of natural, "What happened?"

"He fell down," I said.

"And you?"

I couldn't see Rostov, but I had a feeling there was a faint grin on his face as he and some of his men now mounted up and rode away. It was plain that he'd just stayed long enough to make sure nobody got killed.

Dixie was awake enough to know what was going on. And he was damn well aware that he'd caused what could have been an ugly time between Shiny and Shad. I squeezed some more water from the cloth into his black left eye and said, "I fell down tryin' t' hold him up."

"That ain't too funny," Shad said.

I'd done as much as I could for Dixie medically, so I stood up. "I know. Shad. We had a fight."

"What over?"

I could see Dixie getting ready to die then, for what he'd done, and he deserved it. "I just don't like 'im," I said.

We walked back over toward Shad's bunk, where he dropped his saddle to the ground, quietly looking around. "Camp got torn up a little."

"Yeah," I said, "a little."

He laid down, his head resting in the seat of

his saddle and his hat shading his eyes. "You just don't like Dixie?"

"That's right."

Shad shifted his hat better against the sun. "Levi," he said, so tired and yet so patient, "I know that fight was because of Shiny." He took a deep, long breath. "And I appreciate your point of view."

"That leads up to a 'but,' " I said, "where a boss tells a dumb roustabout like me what t' do."

"Right," Shad moved his hat a little bit again. "And ya 'ought t' be more peaceful." He relaxed now like a cougar I'd seen napping one time, relaxed but ready and powerful all in the same instant. "Don't waste your time on little fights" – he yawned – "when at any minute there're so many big ones all ready an' waitin' to bust out."

"Would you have had me do other?"

I'm pretty sure he almost said something like, "I guess not," but that sort of backing-away statement went against his nature. Instead he said, "Just don't do it again."

"Okay, boss."

And then he was into his first brief sleep in about twenty-four hours.

Looking down at him, still reminded of that cougar who'd been asleep yet ready to move instantly, I had a brief, sudden insight into the meaning of the term "cat nap."

With both the cougar and Shad there was so much easy, quick power there that either one of them could tear an enemy in half while their eyes were still flicking open.

Spooky if they were against you.

Reassuring if they were on your side.

17

When I turned to move off, I almost bumped into Slim, who'd come back into camp and was quietly sizing things up. And he'd heard enough of what Shad and I were saying to take it from there.

"You an' Dixie been playin' Civil War?"

"Sort of."

"Hmm. Looks like the South lost again."

"It was close t' bein' Pyrrhic." It hadn't been at all close, but that seemed like kind of the right thing to say.

Slim nodded. "While Shad's gettin' his forty winks, let's wander over t' the cossacks' playgrounds. Rostov's over there."

"Okay. I'll toss a saddle on Buck." In turning, Dixie came into my line of sight. His eye and a couple of big bruises were starting to lump up something fierce. I hesitated. "Hey, Dixie?"

"Yeah?"

"Want t' come along, over t' the meadow?"

"Sure." He shrugged. "Why not?"

A couple of minutes later about half a dozen of us rode off over the hill and down into the big meadow where the cossacks were already doing some interesting things. Rostov was on his big black near the rock, and except for two of his men in camp and six on lookout, the rest of them were out galloping around in the meadow, but they weren't racing.

We all pulled up near him and took a better look at what was going on. All of the men in the meadow had their sabers out. About half of them were going at full speed to where the creek flowed quietly, leaping it, and slashing the water with their sabers as they flew over. The others were near the center of the meadow, and what they were doing seemed even sillier, if possible. They'd put up six more slender poles in a fairly straight line about fifty feet apart from each other, and on the top of each pole they'd mounted a giant pine cone. The men down there were charging along the line swinging at each pine cone, but never hitting it hard enough to cut it really deep or topple it to the ground.

Slim was watching carefully and not making any quick judgments, but Dixie did, and for once I was inclined to agree with him. "What the hell they doin', Captain?" He frowned, his tone indicating a kind of puzzled disbelief.

"Practicing and improving their use of the saber."

"Well, hell," Crab said, "it sure don't look like much t' hit some water an' a pine cone."

"Remember," Slim said easily, "the way they hit them wolves that night?"

His point was damn well taken, and none of us had a quick answer to it.

"Notice the way they slash the water," Rostov explained. "Of course anyone can hit it. But try doing it in mid-leap with the cutting edge of the blade entering so perfectly that the water is not disturbed."

"My God!" Natcho said, watching more closely. "That's impossible!"

And that sure as hell was right. Between the next three cossacks leaping the stream I doubt if their blades caused more than two drops of water. And Natcho was the best one of us to remark on it, too. I remembered one time when some of us had gone for a kind of a halfway bath and halfway swim in a pond on the Slash-

D Ranch. When most of us had leaped in, we'd damnere splashed the pond dry. But when Natcho had jumped in, his hands were held out together in front of him and his legs were straight out behind him, so that altogether he was shaped like an arrow, and he hadn't made hardly more than a ripple.

"What about them big pine cones?" Slim asked.

"They're the best natural duplication, with a similar resilience, that we have on hand to represent a man's head, which is the best place to hit him with a saber."

Rufe spoke for a number of us when he said, *"Yuck."*

Rostov glanced at him, then looked at me and saw that I felt the same way. There was a tiny flicker of dark but somehow warm humor deep within his eyes. "It requires a powerful cut or thrust to make a body wound fatal, and it takes a moment to get your saber back into use. The neck and the throat are the most vulnerable to a relatively light, fatal slash." Rostov gave me and Rufe another brief look. "It's not difficult to decapitate a man, but in a battle it takes too much time and effort."

"So them fellas out there," Slim said, "are just cuttin' deep enough into their pine cones, without loppin' 'em off."

Rostov nodded. "These are just a small part of *Dzhigitovkas,* our war games on horseback."

"Of Diggy – " Crab started, but then gave up on the word. "Well, anyhow, when ya' explain it like that, it's kind of interestin'."

Rostov put his thumb and little finger in his mouth and gave a sharp, blasting whistle that brought his cossacks up short. Their sabers held out at an angle before them, they all rode back to where we were sitting our horses near the big rock.

When they'd pulled up near us, Ilya asked Rostov something in a respectful, quiet voice. It was so respectful and quiet that both Slim and I knew right off what he'd said.

"Captain," Slim said, "is that expert on various-sized horseshoes askin' whether or not we'd care t' try?"

"Yes," Rostov said.

"Well" – Slim rubbed his jaw – "tell 'im when he can lasso a flea at full gallop, we'll take up with them Mexican toothpicks."

While Rostov was translating, as best as anyone could, what Slim had said, the rest of us looked around at each other and wordlessly agreed to go against Slim.

"Damn that!" Rufe said.

"Right!" Crab agreed, and Dixie added, "*Damn* right!"

Natcho and Purse were nodding, and Chakko hadn't silently ridden away, which was as close to his saying "Yes" as we needed.

"You're outvoted," I told Slim, but he'd known that was going to happen all along.

"I was afraid of that," he grumbled. "Just don't break them pigstickers, especially on yourselves."

At a word from Rostov, the cossacks offered us their sabers, handle first.

I took Igor's, and he almost winced as he let it out of his hand.

Rostov said in a quiet voice, "This is a challenge. But it's a compliment too."

We understood how it was about their letting us use their blades, and in case we didn't, Slim had already just told us.

There were five of us now holding those unfamiliar weapons, getting the feel and balance of them. Chakko, though his presence showed he agreed in principle with what we were doing, hadn't accepted a saber. As for Slim, the question never even came up, anymore than it would have with Shad or Old Keats if they'd been there. Sort of realizing that this meant they were smarter, I said, "Well, it's just us fearless dumbbells against all that water an' all them pine cones."

Two cossacks still held their sabers, and they

now cut their wrists slightly before putting them back in their scabbards.

"Just exactly what the hell we gonna do?" Crab asked.

"Leap the stream and slash the water without disturbing it," Rostov said. "Then, both going and coming back, strike each pine cone so that you cut it without taking it off. To cut it off is the worst thing you can do on the ride. Then cross the stream one more time and come back here."

"Wait!" Rufe said. "Shouldn't we be racin' some a' these cossacks?"

"I suspect you'll have your hands full," Slim said, "racin' yourselves. Get ready!"

The five of us put our horses into a rough line.

"Go!" Slim yelled, and we charged toward the quiet part of the stream.

When I jumped it and slashed, my saber sent up enough water for an average-sized man to take a bath in. Out of the corner of my eye it looked like Natcho and Dixie both did a lot better than me. But Crab and Rufe, it turned out in later conversation, both fell upon evil times. Crab went so deep he brought up some mud. And Rufe swung wild and missed altogether. The only thing he did hit, toward the end of his swing, was Bobtail's ear. Luckily, he just nicked the tip of it, though Bobtail didn't consider it particularly lucky, and shied off to one side, breaking his stride and obviously wondering who the hell, and for what possible reason, was attacking his ear.

Natcho went into the lead with Dixie a little behind him and me and Crab neck and neck for third and fourth. By the time Rufe got Bobtail straightened out he was about three lengths to the rear.

We didn't do as bad as I thought we would on the pine cones. That had to do with a little bit of instinctive skill and a whole lot of instinctive cheating. After using the sabers on the water, it was clearly true that they weren't all that simple to handle at a full gallop. So, for myself, I took what I hoped seemed to be genuine swings at the first three pine cones, but I was trying my level damnedest to just tap them as lightly as Queen Victoria might do upon knighting some old fella.

If there was one honest rider among us, it was Natcho. From fairly close range, I could see that he was sending chips out of the pine cones without even coming close to knocking them off the poles they were stuck on. Right then I'd have bet Buck and myself both against a plugged nickel that that smooth Mexican bastard had handled sabers before, while in my whole life I'd never had anything but a pocketknife.

He was already halfway back along the pine cones on Diablo, while Buck and me, stretched full out, were halfway into them.

"Cuidado!" he yelled, which was sometimes his way of saying "Look out!" as he almost ran me and Buck down. And before I had a chance to yell anything fitting back at him, he was long gone.

Then Dixie, who was about a hundred feet ahead of me, made an unforgivable mistake that I cherished a lot. He got carried away and cut the last pine cone and slashed right through it, sending the pine cone itself flying three or four feet into the air. A little later, looking madder than thunder, he sped back past me.

I felt much better. Rufe and Crab were a little behind me, and Dixie'd just chopped off a head, which kind of disqualified him. Things were looking up.

So, continuing at full speed, I knighted the last standing pine cone as gently as possible and whirled Buck to charge back the way we'd come.

I roared back past Rufe and Crab and could see that except for Natcho I would win. And Buck was just as fast as Diablo, so if Natcho made a mistake, I could even beat him too.

Also going as fast as I was, I was picking up time on both Dixie and Natcho.

I really did saber the next pine cone neatly, sending a few chips flying, and then there was only one more pine cone between me and Buck and the stream, and we were going like greased lightning.

Old Keats told me about a Greek word called *"hubris,"* which he said meant false pride. Or a sort of stupid confidence that gets turned inside out and comes out arrogance.

Anyway, I really whacked at that last pine cone and damnere got jerked out of the saddle as I realized how tough a two- or three-pound pine cone can be. My blade had gone about halfway through the cone, and between the sudden pressures being exerted, my arm almost came out of its socket, and would have except that the goddamn pole came out of the ground instead.

I guess that was better than me being ripped off old Buck, but not much better. He went into a circle, and I was left learning about parallel to the ground, with my arm stretched out, and the saber after that, and then the pine cone, and then the trailing pole. I grabbed for the saber with my other hand too and cut it trying to get free.

Then, about the time I struggled back to a sitting-up position, Rufe and Crab hurtled by me on their way back, but I still had that awful problem.

Finally, with both hands, I pulled the saber loose from that heavy, sticky pine cone.

Humiliated as hell, I still made the best ride I could on the way back.

The others were there before I jumped Buck over the stream, but I didn't pick up too much water with the saber this time and I at least got back in while everybody else was still breathing heavy.

I gave Igor his saber, handle first. As he took it, I said, "You can put it back. It's not only drawn blood, but pine-cone sap." As I started to hold my other hand to stop the bleeding, Igor grinned slightly and put his saber in its scabbard. Then he handed me a handkerchief to hold against the flowing blood.

At an order from Rostov, two of the cossacks rode down to the meadow to undo the damage Dixie and I had caused to their poles and pine cones. Dixie watched after them, still with a hint of that same dark thunder in his eyes.

"Well, Rostov," Slim said, "what was the order a' winnin' among these fellas?"

Rostov said, "Natcho, Crab and Rufe were first, second and third. Then Dixie and Levi."

302

I was surprised at Slim asking such a question, and his next line made me wonder even more. "Umm," he nodded. "Kinda' thought maybe ol' Levi'd won."

"Levi?" Crab said as we all frowned at Slim.

"Yeah. Downright spectacular."

I began to sense Slim's devious mind at work, so I didn't say anything, but Rufe now got sucked in along with Crab. "What d'ya mean?"

"I doubt if in the history a' them war games nobody ever b'fore took both a pine cone an' a pole prisoner simultaneous like Levi just did."

I looked at Slim and pretended to be mad, but I wasn't. I couldn't be because I suddenly knew that bighearted bastard was putting pressure on me to make it easier on Dixie, who'd not only lopped a pine cone clean off, but also lost a fairly rough scrap just before.

"You think you're jokin', you dumb sonofabitch," I told Slim. "But it takes years a' hard practice t' perfect a saber blow like that."

Rostov, who somehow understood everything that was going on, said, "How long do you think it would take you, Levi, to teach my men that fantastic saber thrust?"

"A lot more'n the week or so we'll be here, sir."

"A pity," Rostov said. "Not knowing the

Levi Dougherty thrust will probably set back cossackdom a hundred years."

All the others were grinning now, at my expense, and it was cheap at twice the price because Dixie was now grinning too.

"This is all very goddamn funny," I said. "But in the meantime I'm sittin' here bleedin' t' death."

Slim looked at my cut hand. "Ya' got some sap in the cut, along with the blood."

"No foolin'?" I said dryly. "An' it just happens t' sting like hell."

"Go back t' camp an' wash it out," he told me. "Put a little Jack Daniel's on it, but don't waste any, an' wrap a piece a' tape around it. An' chances are you'll survive."

"Thanks a lot, doctor," I said. And then we both knew what the other one was going to say. "Ya' think I can manage t' do all that by m'self?"

"Frankly, I doubt it." Slim turned to Dixie. "Think ya' can help this poor wounded fella long enough t' see he gets patched up?"

Everything was working fine and Dixie even started to go along with the fun.

"I'll try 'm best, if he don't bleed t' death on the way back."

So Dixie and I rode off, with him helping me.

And it was hard to tell, right then, whether or not Dixie knew or didn't know, that it was really him who was being helped.

But be that as it may, you had to chalk a good thing up for Slim. And for Rostov. And if it can be construed to my credit, I whined and grumbled a whole lot more than necessary while Dixie washed out the cut, put a dash of Jack Daniel's in it for health, and taped it to stop the bleeding.

One thing that kind of interested me. Chakko rode into camp just behind the two of us. He went over to where his bedroll and his gear was and got out something that was long and slender and wrapped in canvas. He took it and rode off again toward the meadow, without a word to anyone.

Even in his sleep, it seemed like Shad was aware of everything that was going on. He sat up now and tipped his hat up away from shading his eyes. "What did y'a do t' your hand?"

"Cut it."

Maybe it was the fact that of all people Dixie was taping it, and maybe it had to do with an instinct that went far beyond that, but I swear to God that Shad read my mind just then, and pretty much knew everything that had happened. He stood up and stretched his shoulder muscles. "If Levi's gonna go through life bein' s' goddamn clumsy, Dixie, maybe ya' oughtta just amputate while you're at it an' have done with it."

Somehow, just like Slim had done, he was making it seem like I was the biggest jackass in the world, who was lucky as hell to have a good friend like Dixie.

And also, somehow, that's exactly the way they made it work. While Dixie was bandaging my hand, I can guarantee he was just about ready to adopt me. Funniest damn thing that way, about two men fighting each other and helping each other, because if those two men are worth anything at all, both the fighting and the helping, in about equal measure, can make them closer.

Feeling kind of good about the way Dixie felt, I said, "Amputate 'em both, Dixie. Always wanted t' go through life bein' spoon-fed."

Shad came over and said quietly, "How'd ya' cut it?"

All of a sudden it wasn't quite so funny, and I wet my lips a little. "Saber."

"Kinda' thought so."

"It was an accident, boss." Dixie finished the bandage and stood back. "Coulda' happened t' anybody."

Shad gave Dixie a look. "Like you?"

"Well" — Dixie hesitated — "yeah. Five of us

made a run with sabers. You wouldn't want us t' back down, boss, in some kind of a coward's way?"

Like Slim, Shad rarely chewed tobacco but he nearly always carried an ancient plug. He took it out now and bit off a chew. Then he handed it toward Dixie and me. I shook my head and Dixie took a chew before passing it back.

Pocketing the plug, Shad said, "Let's take a ride over there."

A little later the three of us arrived at where the others were by the big rock. The two cossacks had finished fixing the poles and pine cones down in the meadow and were on their way back.

Shad pulled up near Rostov and spent a moment studying the many poles that made up the race-track layout and the six pine-cone-topped poles in the middle of the meadow. I wish he'd said almost anything else for starters, but he chose to say, as a flat statement of fact, "These games a' yours, Rostov, got one a' my men hurt."

The hard way he said it, and further the simple fact that it was true, left a kind of a hole in the conversation because there wasn't much for Rostov to say by way of an answer. Shad turned from studying the meadow and faced

Rostov, and again there was that feeling of two earthquakes about to happen all at once.

"It was my own damn fault, Shad," I said. "An' I ain't hurt hardly at all."

"Coulda' been worse, just as easy."

Rostov finally spoke, his voice quiet and flat. "Getting hurt, as Levi did, makes a man stronger and wiser."

"I'd hope my men are both strong and wise already."

Neither one of them was about to back off, and since it was my fault, right or wrong, I had to throw the rest of my two-bits worth in. "Not me, Shad. Maybe them others are, but I ain't nowhere near neither strong or wise enough. Igor did me the honor a' lendin' me his saber, an' I plain fucked up by gettin' carried away and not usin' it right." I added lamely, "You know I ain't goin' against ya', boss, but —"

Instead of getting mad, which I fully expected and probably deserved, Shad gave me a look of such quiet patience that I knew that somewhere, and somehow, he was righter than I was. Then he turned back to Rostov, more thoughtful now than angry. "My men will compete too hard."

Rostov nodded, and the brief, dark feeling that had been between them was gone now. "Perhaps you should forbid your men from taking part."

None of us said anything about that, but our expressions showed how we felt.

Looking around at us, Slim said dryly, "Seems ya' got your choice of a bunch a' cripples here, boss. Broken bones on one hand, an' broken hearts on the other."

With similar, grim humor, Rostov said, "Perhaps we should adopt the Tartar method."

"What's that?" Shad asked.

"The Tartars divide their warriors into groups of ten. And if any one man in that group of ten is hurt or killed, the other nine are hurt in exactly the same way, or killed in the same way."

"Jesus!" Rufe muttered.

"Seems a little drastic," Shad said. And then, "I guess the best we can do, all things equal, is try t' at least keep these games down to a god-damned dull roar."

Rostov nodded.

"Well," Slim said, "by any standard a' measurin', the cossacks sure came out on top t'day."

"That's hardly fair," Igor said. "We've used sabers all our lives."

Chakko was now unwrapping his long, slen-der piece of canvas, and within it there was an unstrung bow and a quiver of arrows.

"Pine cones," he muttered, quickly stringing his bow. "Fuck 'em."

When Chakko said four words, he meant exactly four words, and with those particular four words he galloped to the meadow at a full dead run. And shooting from impossible positions all over his horse, even shooting from beneath its neck, and managing always to keep his body partially or completely hidden from the "enemy" by his own mount, he in blindingly swift succession put six arrows through the six pine cones. And he'd already spun his pony and was racing back as his last arrow pierced the last pine cone.

Every deadly, lightning move Chakko had made from beginning to end was a thing of pure beauty, and so in his own unique way, he rode out of the meadow as the undisputed champion of the day.

In the awed silence, Slim finally muttered, "Well, that goddamned simple Sioux bastard!"

And right then, nobody else there had anything else to add.

18

Shortly after sundown, with our eight men still not back from Khabarovsk, Rostov sent out replacements for his guards, and after a while those who'd been on lookout rode back into camp. Sergeant Nick was among them, and he spoke briefly with Rostov. Then they left their fire and approached ours, where Sammy the Kid and Mushy, taking their turn at cooking duty, were starting beans and biscuits and coffee for supper.

Rostov said to Shad, "Verushki still has several small patrols spotted around us."

"That ain't hardly a surprise."

"At least," Rostov said, "they've been staying far away, well out of shooting distance, simply trying to discover what they can about us."

"Which ain't much in this broke-up country," Slim said. "They can't make a halfway educated guess how many we are. F'r that matter, even how many cows we got."

"Tonight," Nick rumbled, "they maybe come in closer, in dark."

Along with some others, Rufe was listening.

"They do," he volunteered, "they'll git their asses shot off."

Nick nodded his big head heavily. "Right. But makes trouble."

"What the hell." Slim shrugged. "Even in the dark they won't be able t' come in near 'nough t' see a whole lot."

For a moment no one spoke, and then Shad changed the subject abruptly, almost angrily. "I wish t' Christ those fellas'd get back."

To use Shad's words from a minute before, what he'd just now said wasn't hardly a surprise, either. We were all feeling that same way, especially since the going of the sun, with the quick Siberian darkness moving like a sudden black wave rolling across the sky to sweep out all the light in the world.

"Well, boss," Slim ventured to say, "ya' told 'em t' be sure t' have a good time."

"Not *that* good!" Shad tried to make his anger hide his deep concern, but we all could see it was there. He growled, "They oughtta be back here *right now!*"

And at that very instant Rostov's guard on the point overlooking Khabarovsk called out in Russian, his voice dimly reaching us. Rostov looked at Shad and laughed one of his rare laughs. "Our eight men are on their way into camp."

There couldn't have been more than a millionth of a second between Shad's growl and the yell from the hill, and it was somehow so funny we were all torn about halfway between sheer relief, and laughing our relieved heads off.

"By God!" Slim said with a broad grin. "When you say somethin' boss, fellas really do jump!"

The sound of hoofbeats came closer, and the eight men rode into the light of our two fires and dismounted. The only sign of a problem I could see was that Shiny's right hand was bandaged just about the same as my left one was.

Old Keats nodded at Shad and said, "It's a nice place to visit, but I wouldn't want to live there."

Then, as Bruk told the cossacks what had happened in Russian, Keats went on to us. "First thing we did was pay Colonel Verushki a social visit, big as life an' twice as brassy, Shad, like you said. He was madder'n hell about his man gettin' shot this mornin' — in the leg incidentally. And we reminded him of the terms previously arranged, whereby we'll soon go on our way in peace as long as he and his men don't bother us."

Sammy and Mushy brought up some cups and a pot of coffee.

"For our conquerin' heroes," Sammy said.

When Mushy poured into the cup Shiny was holding, I saw for the first time by the unsteady way the cup moved that Shiny was in worse shape than a simple bandaged hand would cause. All of a sudden, at ten feet away, I could sense that he'd had as much white whiskey as I'd had and couldn't hold it any better.

"Verushki's still worried about us," Keats went on, "but only just barely. He still thinks that somehow we're bluffin', but he ain't quite prepared to move against us upon that hopeful concept."

"Go on," Shad said.

"So then, actin' like we owned the town, we bought some supplies. An' then went back to that same place for a few drinks." He hesitated, a little sadly. "Maybe it had t' do with the two big fellas who got hanged, but the place was pretty filled up with hostile Imperial Cossacks and they were lookin' for trouble." Keats shook his head in a brief, rueful way. "Right now, in that one place, I've seen glasses broken for the most beautiful and the most ugly reasons ya' could imagine."

Already Shad was glancing at Shiny's bandaged hand. "Yeah?"

"They challenged us t' some 'friendly' armrassling, for drinks. But they smashed off the top of two glasses an' put them on the table where each man's hand'd be forced down if he lost." Old Keats gave Shiny a warm look. "He took on the biggest bastard they had."

"And lost!" Shiny said cheerfully, holding up his bandaged and slightly weaving hand.

"Between you and Levi," Shad told Shiny, "I now have two hands."

Shiny misunderstood. "We're not just *two* hands, boss! We're your *best* two hands!"

"With two men I normally hope for four hands," Shad said quietly, but Keats was already going on with growing excitement.

"And then we put in Kirdyaga and Big Yawn! And honest t' God, I guarantee that there are at least ten Imperial Cossacks who don't have full use of both of their hands right now."

Rostov and Bruk had come up, and Bruk said, "This is true. We impressed them first with our boldness. Secondly the two blacks impressed them very much. Finally our strength impressed them. They are as respectful and afraid of us as we are of them. And that is the final measure of our day."

That sounded like a pretty good measure to all of us. But, a little wobbly himself, Big Yawn now lifted his nearly empty coffee cup.

"An' here's t' Levi!"

None of us could see any point in that, and I said, "Why?"

"That sweet-lookin' girl there asked for ya'."

It had to be Irenia, and my heart gave a kind of a little jump in my throat. "Yeah? How did she happen t' remember me?" I knew it had to be something like because I was so handsome or charming, or both at once, but all of that ought to come from her, so I manfully held off. "Just how?"

Bruk took over, since he was the one who had talked to her. "She asked about you as the youngest American, the one who couldn't drink."

"– Oh."

That was a hard blow. I remembered her because of her pretty face and tablecloth dress, and she remembered me because I was a drunk. I tried to act like I didn't care in the first place, but it didn't matter in the second place, because nobody was paying any attention to me anyway, back in the first place.

Supper was about ready in both camps, and the group was starting to break up, even though it was only a few steps back and forth.

But before my brokenhearted supper, that nobody took note of, two things happened.

First, Dixie came over and said in a low

voice, but straight out to Shiny, "I lied to you. Nobody never called you nothin' this mornin'."

Shiny looked at him with those big, friendly, slightly bleary eyes of his.

"You're wrong," Shiny told him. "A man called me a man this mornin'."

That got to Dixie, and I don't think Dixie could have taken much more of anything just then. All in all, it hadn't been too great of a day for him. So what he said was short and to the point. "I just told ya' I lied to ya'." He hesitated a moment. "That's by way a' sayin' I'm sorry for the way I felt."

Shiny did a strange and nice thing then. It reminded me, somehow, of me with the pine cones before, when I'd tried to tap each one like Queen Victoria gently knighting some old fellow. Shiny reached out and touched Dixie just that gently on the shoulder, as if he were forgiving him, or knighting him. And he said, "I'm sorry for the way I felt, too."

Then they both turned and walked away. But they always seemed close after that, before the first one died. So close that you could almost feel it between them, invisible and warm as a summer breeze in the air.

And then that second thing before supper happened.

Shad said to Rostov, "Are your lookouts

good enough to let one a' them patrols out there get through for a little while t'night?"

"Yes." Rostov nodded. "Why?"

"Build a couple more fires. And have every man lay out an extra bedroll. From a distance, in the dark, it'll shape up t' be a sixty-man camp."

But Rostov had already started nodding before Shad finished talking. "We'll let them through just far enough and long enough to give them that impression, and then drive them away."

Shad said, "Just for the hell of it, think I'll ride lookout with your men me'self t'night."

"You take the first half of the watch and I'll relieve you for the second."

Shad didn't disagree with Rostov, which for him was a quiet agreement.

"For Christ's sake," Old Keats said, "let's try t' not shoot any more of Verushki's men. He's all set t' blow sky-high any minute."

"We want 'em t' ride out in one piece," Shad said, "so they can report what they think they've seen."

Rostov doubled his guard right after supper, and Shad was getting ready to ride off, when Slim said, "Mind if I come along, boss?"

A little later they left camp together, and the rest of us built the extra fires and laid out the added bedrolls. Most of us had only two blankets, so it was kind of cold sleeping in just one, with the other one made up off to one side with an imaginary fella in it. I'd stuffed a few clothes and a couple of rocks into my other blanket to make a sort of a dummy. But that dummy was sure sleeping a hell of a lot better than I was. It was not only cold, but my cut hand was throbbing, so I finally gave up and pulled on my boots and went over to the nearest fire, where four men were gathered.

Natcho and Old Keats were watching Rostov and Igor, who were seated and playing some kind of a game on a checkerboard by the light of the fire.

In the silence, Natcho was the only one who glanced at me as I came up. "Chess," he said.

It seemed like both he and Old Keats had a fair idea what was going on, and I didn't want to appear too dumb. "Yeah." I nodded as though this came as no news to me at all. "Quite a lot like checkers."

Rostov gave me one of those expressionless looks, which still somehow managed to hold brief, silent laughter deep in his eyes. "You understand the game?"

I'd done it again. "Well, t' be perfectly honest, Captain, there's a whole lot I don't know about it — hardly at all."

Igor now made a funny kind of a zigzag move with a piece shaped like a horse's head, and then Rostov made an even funnier move clear across the board at an angle and wound up taking one of Igor's pieces.

"T' be real perfectly honest," I said, sort of hinting for a clue about these strange moves, "I guess I've just about forgotten every damn thing I ever did know about it."

"The word 'chess' is a derivation of the Persian word '*shah*,' meaning 'king,' " Rostov said, waiting for Igor's next move. "It's a game of war that's probably more than four thousand years old." Then, as they continued playing, he patiently named all the pieces and the different ways they could move, which I immediately forgot.

But then Rostov said something none of us forgot. "It's not only a game of war. There's a great deal of philosophy in it. And it represents the way the world has been for thousands of years. Even since the beginning of time.

"The king and the queen, each in its own way, have and wield the ultimate power. In approximately equal proportion, they use religion and their military, the bishops and the knights, to defend whatever positions they may choose to take and to attack the enemies of those positions. The castles at each corner of the board represent their crucial power of wealth in terms of land and possessions."

He paused, frowning inwardly at the comparison he was making, and moved by it. Then, finally, he continued. "But always and forever, it's the pawns, the simple people themselves, who are the first to be sacrificed ruthlessly, for whatever reasons seem at the moment to be an advantage to any of the others."

None of us had ever heard any game defined like that, and it was plain to see that Rostov was thinking of a lot more than just chess.

After a silence, I said, "Sure beats the hell outta checkers."

Studying Rostov, Old Keats added quietly, "You like the game of 'king.' But you sure don't like livin' it in real life, here in Russia."

"Yeah," I said. "Poor damned pawns."

"It's almost impossible," Rostov said, "but if a pawn can manage to get to the far end of the board, while he'll be under the heaviest possible attack, he'll also have a chance of becoming the most important piece there." He glanced at Igor and at some of his sleeping cossacks. "We are the pawns. And Siberia is our far end of the board."

Igor nodded at these words, as thoughtful as the rest of us. And then, concentrating, he slowly made his next move.

It was also his last move.

Without hesitation Rostov shifted a piece to another square and said, "Checkmate."

Under his breath, Igor grumbled a couple of words in Russian that must have translated something like "Sonofabitch!" Then he grinned and shrugged and knocked one of his pieces down in a gesture of defeat.

They turned the board over then and I saw that it was actually a small box that they could put the pieces back in and then snap shut. Putting them away, Rostov said, "Checkmate is from the Persian *shah mat,* which means 'the king is dead.'"

"And no king was ever more dead than mine," Igor said. Then he added quietly, "I'd never thought of the philosophy of chess that way, sir. It's almost as though —" He hesitated, uncertain of which words to use.

But Rostov understood. "As though each game contains its own complete life-and-death drama."

Igor nodded, and now snapped the filled chess box shut.

Rostov stood up and stretched his shoulders, and then we heard the shots. There were about seven of them, in quick, broken order, and the roaring guns were close enough out there in the dark to make my ears ring a little.

By the second or third shot, Rostov had already swung into the saddle of his nearby black and was racing off into the night toward where they were coming from. All over the camp sleepy men were reaching in different ways, some of them leaping out of their bedrolls, others just raising up slightly, still partly asleep and groggy.

Now there were three more shots, farther away, and then silence. I doubt if the whole thing, from first to last shot, took more than a minute or so. For myself, I'd figured it best to make it back to my bedroll and get out my old Remington .44 and cock it, just in case. And then the shooting stopped.

Everybody in camp had a gun at hand by then. But already, even while a couple of fellas were still swearing and jerking on their boots, there was the sound of distant, galloping hoofbeats returning.

"Four horses," Natcho said.

It was Shad, Rostov, Slim and Nick who rode out of the night and up to the light of the fires. Nick had a grin so wide that it ran from the bearded half of his face clear over to crinkle up the scar running down the other side. He and Rostov rode on a few paces to tell the cossacks what had happened, as Shad and Slim dismounted near us.

Slim looked just about as pleased as Nick did, and Shad himself didn't seem exactly displeased.

"Well?" Old Keats demanded. "What happened?"

Slim stepped to the fire to warm his hands over it. "It was so goddamned purely perfect! An' then funny as hell on top a' that!"

"Funny?" Keats frowned from Slim to Shad.

"It was fairly amusin'," Shad admitted, starting to unsaddle and take care of Red.

"First, we spotted this three-man patrol," Slim went on. "We held back an' let 'em sneak in just close 'nough t' take a quick peek. An' they *damn* well figure we're twice as many as what we are."

"Christ," I said, "they coulda been standin' right here b'side me for a minute an' got that same idea from all these bedrolls."

"Then we cut loose an' shot all 'round 'em," Slim continued, "an' they beat a retreat that'd make greased lightnin' look lackadaisical. An' about that time two more lookouts spotted 'em an' blasted away. They musta thought they was surrounded by all the hounds a' hell!" Slim laughed and rubbed his chin. "What's funny," he chuckled, "is one of 'em plain damn fell right smack off his horse! An' them other two

324

lookouts a' ours *captured* it! By pure accident, we got ourselves one a' the Tzar's most outstandin' subjects!"

Keats was the only one by now who wasn't grinning along with Slim.

"How d'ya' know ya' didn't *shoot* 'im?"

Still chuckling, Slim said, "Nobody who's just got shot c'n git up an' damnere outdistance his fella horsemen on foot!"

But Old Keats still wasn't too happy. "Goddamnit, Shad," he said, "we just might *embarrass* Verushki into a fight!"

"Hell," Shad said with quiet innocence, "we can't hardly help it if his men can't stay put aboard their own damn ponies."

'Well," Keats said firmly, "I think we oughtta take 'im back."

"Oh, we will," Shad agreed, still innocently. "First thing t'morrow."

Somehow, Keats didn't quite like the sound of that, and somehow I couldn't blame him. But then Ilya rode into camp at a trot, leading the captured horse, a good-sized gray with an unusually fancy silver-inlaid saddle on its back.

We and the cossacks, all of us still looking pretty pleased, gathered around to take a look at the gray.

"Damn shame t' return 'im," Slim said. "If there's anything I purely hate, it's givin' up

325

well-earned spoils a' war."

I got a few hours' sleep before it was my turn with the herd, and it was well into morning when Mushy rode up to take over for me. On the way back to camp, I circled around a little to see what was going on at the war-games meadow. And I was glad I hadn't gotten there before, in time to join the activities going on.

Lieutenant Bruk and Slim and a few others were standing near their horses by the big rock, watching seven men who were going like bats out of hell out there on the meadow, finishing that wicked race course.

Three of them were Slash-Diamonders — Natcho, Sammy and Purse. And except for Natcho, they weren't faring too well. Sammy and Purse trailing behind, both elected to go too close to the next-to-last pole, which was in some thick trees, and they both had to pull up at the last minute and pick their way through or they'd have likely had their heads torn off by the stout low branches. Most of the others were strung out and approaching the last obstacle, the creek, where the quickest way involved that suicidal ten-foot jump over the twenty-foot drop. Most of them chose to take a wide berth around that last pole, some of them even splashing through the shallows about three hundred feet off to the far side of the high, dangerous leap. Natcho took the stream closest in, where it was about an eight-foot drop, but he did it so easily that you could see there was no risk for either him or his Diablo. That put him neck to neck with Gregorio, who'd had a slight lead before, and that's the way they finished, flashing past the finish line near the rock in a dead heat. The other cossacks now came roaring by, and Purse and Sammy finished a faraway last and next to last, looking like they might melt in their own anger.

Even after they'd slowed their mounts and come back, they were both still too mad to say anything. Bruk said flatly, not talking down to them, "You both did well."

"Bullshit," Sammy said.

"He's right." Slim's voice was quietly hard. "Idea is t' git there fast as ya' can, but *git* there. If you'd tried t' bust through them thick trees at a run, you'd both still be back there lookin' around f'r your heads."

Bruk said something to his men, and five of them went galloping out toward the center of the meadow. Then he told us, "This is a cossack way of making a rider and horse one and the same. I imagine you'd call it trick riding."

"Hell." Slim frowned. "Ridin' a horse ain't no trick; it's a way a' makin' a livin'."

But when those cossacks got out in the meadow, they started doing things that are in total honesty almost impossible to relate.

They were up and over and under their full galloping horses. They dropped little handkerchiefs out there in the meadow, and charged back by and picked them up with their teeth, nine-tenths out of the saddle. Two of them even raced in together, and one fella, Pietre, leaped full speed onto the back of the other fella's horse. The other fella happened to be Dmitri. I'd actually never gotten to know them too well, and therefore never had a really great opinion of either one of them, and I was a lot more than a little startled at how graceful they were when Pietre now somehow got his feet on Dmitri's shoulders and stood full up.

There is just no way to ride a horse like that, with one man standing on top of another man's shoulders.

But they did it, for about three or four agonizing, long seconds, and then Pietre lost his balance, though he pretended not to, and did a neat flip off of Dmitri's shoulders and landed, kind of skidding, but still on his feet.

Without my even thinking about it, an enthusiastic yell of approval busted out of me, but it was just part of the general whooping from all of us. About the only one who didn't yell was Slim, who simply muttered, "Well I'll be *goddamned*."

Around that time, Crab rode up and said, "Hey, Levi, Shad wants ya'. An' you too, Natcho."

"Now?" Natcho asked.

"Well what d'ya' think?"

"Damn," Natcho said, seeming disappointed. "I wanted to show them what we can do in trick riding."

"*We?*" Sammy said incredulously.

"Sure," I told him casually. "Damn pity Natcho an' me can't stay an' put them fellas in their places, due t' the boss's orders."

"Come off it," Purse said. "The only trick riding I've seen you do is when you fell off your horse with your foot caught in the stirrup."

"He's also our local expert," Slim said, "at harpoonin' pine cones."

'Well," I turned Buck to go, "Natcho an' me'll just have t' leave the honor a' the Slash-Diamond in you fellas' hands. Let us know how ya' do."

Nobody ever mentioned just what happened after that, so I have my doubts if things went too well, if at all.

On the way back to camp I asked Natcho, "Can you *really* do trick ridin'?"

"Of course." He was surprised at the question. "It's part of the curriculum at the Military Academy in Mexico City."

"Oh." That part of Natcho's past had simply never before come up, but then another thought struck me. "That's where you learned to use a saber."

He nodded, but his mind was still dwelling thoughtfully on the first subject. "The pyramid would impress our cossack friends. Two riders stand on horses galloping side by side, and a third rider then stands on their shoulders. But we'd need a third rider."

He was smarter than all hell, and loved life and laughter as much or maybe more than anyone. But sometimes, as indicated by the lines he'd just missed back at the big rock, he had to be pounded rather severely on the head to get his sense of humor jarred loose.

"Natcho?"

"Yes?"

"I was exaggeratin' a little bit back there." I grinned. "If you're plannin' on tryin' one a' them pyramids, I wouldn't count too much on me f'r any one a' them three crucial positions."

"Oh. Too bad." He was sincerely disappointed again. "But then," he shrugged, "we'd have still had to get a third man."

I let it go at that and we rode on up over the hill.

Back in camp, we dismounted and went over to see Shad. He was discussing something quietly with Old Keats, so we stood a little away and a moment later Dixie joined us. Then Keats walked away and Shad turned around. "You three're comin' into town with me," he said.

All three of us felt a kind of a good, chilly excitement about going with him, but on top of that I was curious. "How come me again, boss? I already been."

I could see in his eyes it was a stupid question, but he wasn't too hard on me. "We ain't got sixty faces t' show off. So dependin' on how long that river stays high, we're gonna be stuck with some repeat performances."

By the same token, Rostov brought Igor along again, plus Ilya and Yuri. Two known cossack faces and two unknown, same as us.

Just before we mounted up, Shiny came over and said to Dixie, "Looks like t'day's the day f'r gettin' rid a' our no-good misfits."

"Hell." Dixie snorted. "You dumb black nigger sonofabitch. We'll bring ya' that whole goddamned town back on a big silver platter."

But even if they'd really tried to ignore it, or go against it, that quiet, good feeling between them was still there.

And then the eight of us for this day

rode out of camp.

Ilya had that triangular Russian guitar of his, the balalaika, strung over one shoulder, and I somehow wound up leading our captured cossack gray, his saddle still on him, as we went over the hill past the cossack lookout and started down that long, open meadow toward Khabarovsk.

It came almost like a violent physical slap against my face as I saw that they hadn't yet cut those two big men down. Maybe I hadn't heard, maybe it hadn't been mentioned, or maybe I'd just somehow made myself not hear it. But seeing them even at this distance, the sudden, unexpected sight of them still hanging motionless from that faraway oak tree gagged me.

Some of the others weren't prepared for it either, but Shad and Rostov knew.

All three of the cossacks behind Rostov reacted, and Dixie, his voice way down in his gut, said, "Oh, *God.*"

Rostov and Shad both glanced around at us, and Shad said, "There's one last thing we can do for 'em."

That cleared up one small mystery. I knew then, for the first time, why Shad and Rostov had both strapped two shovels onto their saddle gear.

No point in going into how grotesquely long a human neck gets stretched, or how hideous a faint blue against pale, empty white can make a face, or how terribly and unforgivingly stiff and unyielding a man's body can get. As though he's suddenly mad about every injustice ever done to him in his life, and even madder and more unbending because he can no longer do or say one damn final thing about it.

All that matters of that time is that we got there and we cut them down and we buried them at the foot of the oak.

Rostov said a short, husky-voiced prayer over them in Russian, and then we went on into town, so that finally somewhere around mid-afternoon, we pulled up in front of that same bar.

After those grim burials, it had taken me all this time before I could now finally speak. "Igor," I said, "what's this place called?"

He was having pretty much the same problem, and he wet his lips. "The Far East."

"Thanks," I managed to say.

He swallowed and said, "You're welcome."

"Come on, Levi," Shad called.

"You others," Rostov said, "go in and wait for us."

Leading the mare, I followed the two of them until we came to the square where the Imperial

Cossacks' headquarters was, and we crossed again toward the main building.

As we came into sight, the guards there held their rifles in a tense, ready manner, and some fella went rushing into the building. By the time we got there, Colonel Verushki, in a fine uniform, came out of the door with about a dozen armed cossacks following him.

His angry men were burning up inside as they faced us, so much so that there was almost an acrid smell in the air. They wanted nothing more than to start shooting at us right then and there. Verushki must have felt the same way, but he didn't show it. Instead, he looked at us in kind of a haughty, superior way and said flatly, "You men are beginning to tax my patience."

Rostov shrugged slightly, as easy and relaxed as a cat on a warm wooden roof. "We must insist, Colonel, that you request your men to keep away from our camp. Particularly when we're inconvenienced by having to go out of our way to return their horses."

That last line got under Verushki's skin, and his eyes and voice both suddenly became harder. "I understand you buried two criminals I recently had executed. I was leaving them where they were as an object lesson."

Shad said, "Tie up the gray, Levi." And as I

got off and did so, he turned back to Colonel Verushki. "Consider well what I'm sayin'. We're tradin' you this one riderless horse f'r the privilege a' diggin' them two graves." He paused. "If you want t' try for a whole lot more riderless horses an' a whole lot more graves, then just keep fuckin' around."

That was a deadly hammer-hard statement, and I could now see why Shad and Rostov had looked forward to bringing the gray back. Whether he showed it or not it was embarrassing as hell to Verushki, and they were both taking grim pleasure in pushing him on it.

Verushki was squinting slightly at Shad's last few words, and Rostov said quietly, "By 'fucking around,' Colonel, he means meddling, or interfering."

Verushki got the basic idea of the word, and finally said curtly, "I will not fuck about with you if you do not fuck about with me!" Then he added, "It's unavoidable that some of my patrols may occasionally approach your camp. Should this happen in the future and you do not use more restraint, you will regret it."

With this he spoke one harsh word to his cossacks, then turned abruptly and stalked back into the building. The dozen or so men stayed where they were, and one of them yelled something toward a big stable at the end of the square.

As I stepped back to Buck to remount, there were shouted orders from inside the stable, and almost immediately a huge bunch of Imperial Cossacks came galloping out of the wide double doors. For a spooky minute I thought we were about to be massacred, but from the way they were riding, in order, Shad seemed to know that something else was going on, and Rostov's face was a little sad underneath its outside hardness.

As I swung aboard Buck there were other shouted commands and the Imperial Cossacks lined up around the square, all of them facing in toward the center. Then one last rider came barreling through the door with a rope stretched tightly out behind him. At the end of the rope, dragging and bouncing along the ground like a damnere shapeless bundle of bloody, torn old rags, was a man. He was conscious but could just barely move. Judging from the hideously ripped skin on his back he must have been whipped half to death.

"Let's go," Rostov said quietly.

We went across the square at an angle, walking our horses.

Neither Shad nor Rostov did, but I couldn't help glancing back. Despite the blood already caked on his face, I could see that that shapeless bundle of a man was the young officer who'd first spoken to Rostov on the first night we'd come into town. In the center of the square, four men now lifted him face up under the gray mare. Then, with the same rope they'd been dragging him with, they started lashing him into place underneath the horse.

As we finally rode out of the square, one of the four men let go of the gray's reins and whacked it on the butt, giving a loud yell so that it galloped away, frightened by all that had happened, and even more terrified by the strange load it was carrying under its stomach.

It got to me. Just now, especially right on top of burying those two men, the whole damn world suddenly seemed to be nothing but plain downright horrible.

From Shad's and Rostov's expressions when I spurred ahead to catch up with them, they both knew what had happened.

"Jesus!" I muttered, hardly believing what I'd seen. "All *that* f'r fallin' off a goddamned horse?"

"Evidently," Rostov said dryly, "Verushki is an unusually strict disciplinarian." Then, seeing the way I looked, he added, "The gray will finally come back to the stable, and they'll cut him down. He'll probably survive. Don't let what happened disturb you too much, Levi.

In his own warped way, that's certainly one o
the things Verushki was hoping for."

Shad looked at me, knowing that the bruta
punishment had gotten to me. He grinned
slightly and said, "Every damn thing that poor
bastard does t' show us how rough he is some
how backfires an' winds up makin' us rougher
instead. Right, Levi?"

They were both kind of coddling me and]
resented it and appreciated it, but damn wel
had to make myself be worth a lot more. So
forced that bloody bundle of human agony
back in my thoughts and worked up my own
grin. "I'll drink t' that, boss."

"Drink all ya' want, but just watch out f'
that girl."

I knew he was pulling me up even farther by
getting on to something breezy and light
"Why?" I asked him.

"Because you're a goddamn virgin."

"The hell I am! And besides, that can't las
forever!"

Rostov now grinned faintly too. "With tha
girl, in this town, Levi may lose his virginity o
his life. Or perhaps both at the same time
which would be interesting."

19

The three of us dismounted and tied up in front of The Far East next to the other five horses belonging to our men. A step or so behind, I clumped across the wooden walk after Shad and Rostov and we went into the place.

There was almost no one in the whole big room. Our five men were at that same big table toward the rear where we'd sat before. They were just waiting, with no drinks before them yet. As they saw us, Ilya stopped playing a soft little tune on his Russian guitar. There were three or four men sitting quietly around closer to the door and the front windows. Other than that, the only person in the room was that older woman who looked tough but really wasn't. As we started back toward our group I couldn't help but feel a pang of disappointment somewhere inside. I hadn't realized how much I'd hoped Irenia would be here, just so I could maybe at least look at her once in a while.

The woman, her eyes becoming friendly and warm within her deep-creased, hardened old face, came over to take our order from Rostov as we sat down. Then she talked to him in a low, urgent voice for a moment before leaving. Igor was nodding gravely during this, as though he already knew what was going on.

When she left, Dixie said, "There ain't been not one single Tzar cossack show 'is nose around here! They must be scared shitless of us, Shad!"

But Shad was watching Rostov and Igor, who were now speaking in low, intense voices in Russian. Ilya and Yuri were listening, quiet and thoughtful.

Natcho smiled. "Were they grateful to get that gray mare of theirs back?"

Shad still didn't answer, and I began to get the same feeling I guess he had, that something that mattered was being talked about.

Then Rostov turned to us. "The old woman, Anna, is a friend. From what she's been telling us, we may be in luck."

"That'd sure be a welcome change," Shad said.

"The crest of the Amur went down nearly fourteen centimeters last night."

"What's that in American?" Dixie frowned.

"Over five inches," Rostov told him.

"Keeps goin' down like that," Shad said, "we oughtta be able t' cross 'er in three, four days."

At this point Natcho looked off and smiled

appreciatively, his perfect teeth gleaming in his deeply tanned face. I turned and reacted as I saw Irenia coming through the door toward us carrying a tray with glasses and vodka on it.

"Hey, Levi," Dixie said, "better shut y'r mouth b'fore somebody comes along an' steps on your jaw."

I almost snarled a fitting reply back at Dixie, but she was getting too close, and I didn't want her to get the wrong impression of me. So I just gave Dixie a murderous glance and closed my mouth.

Then she was at the table, smiling that beautiful dimpled smile of hers as she placed glasses for us. She was still wearing her same red-checkered tablecloth dress, and it still looked as fresh and clean as it had before. It occurred to me that she probably washed and dried it every night.

She smiled at me and nodded and Dixie said, "By God, Levi's blushin'!"

I wasn't, but when he said I was, it got me started, and despite trying desperately to control that terrible reaction, I could feel my face getting fiercely hot and flushed. Powerless to say even one word just then, I clenched my teeth and managed to nod back at Irenia.

And then, with or without meaning to, Ilya saved me from dying of sheer mortification right on the spot. He struck up a quick, lively tune and sang a very short, happy song to Irenia. It was only a few lines, but it must have also been kind of funny because as he stopped she giggled, putting her hand over her mouth, and hurried back out of the room.

As Natcho and Igor poured drinks around, Dixie said, "That song on that there Russian guitar wasn't half bad."

Finally daring to try my voice again I said, "It's a balalaika, *stupid*. And you'll never guess how goddamned lucky you are to've lived long enough t' hear that song!"

"Hell," Dixie protested innocently. "Who coulda ever imagined that you was s' awful girl shy?"

"I *ain't!*"

"All right," Shad said with firm easiness, and Dixie and I let it go at that, but it seemed to me I could still detect the shadow of a self-satisfied smirk on that bastard's face.

Rostov glanced at the two of us with faint amusement and raised his glass. "There is some further good luck we can drink to. *Vostrovia!*"

I knew damn well that he and Shad, like me, were thinking of the last time we'd made that toast in this room, and thinking back to that good time I couldn't just take a sip but downed the whole glass.

Neither Dixie nor Natcho had tangled with a glass of vodka before. Natcho winced a little, but Dixie was almost strangling, his eyes watering.

He blinked his eyes rapidly against the wetness in them, and I said sympathetically, "You just remember a sad story, Dixie?" He couldn't yet reply, so apropos of my earlier blushing I added, "A little healthy red in a fella's colorin' sure does beat a bilious green."

Shad said to Rostov, "What more luck?"

"Genghis Kharlagawl and his Tartars have been seen heading north toward the Stanovoi mountains. On our route, skirting the Kamchatka Territory, we should miss them by more than two hundred and fifty miles."

"Unless they change direction."

"That's always possible, of course. But at least they're not aware of us yet or they'd be out there laying in wait for us now."

Dixie was finally getting almost back to normal, so I immediately started to pour another round, generously filling his glass first and right up to the brim, at the same time giving him a nice, friendly smile, which he seemed to somehow mistake for gloating, and to which he therefore responded with a still slightly damp glare.

Yuri was pouring at the other side of the table, and Igor was speaking to Ilya and him in a low voice, probably telling them what Shad and Rostov were saying.

"Any idea of how many Tartars with him?" Shad asked.

"Evidently fewer than usual. Between two and three hundred." Rostov shrugged. "But whoever actually saw them probably left rather hurriedly, instead of taking the time to make an accurate count. Then too, Kharlagawl usually has a number of raiding parties ranging out from his main force, which makes any estimate of his total strength questionable."

"Well," I said, "however many there are, thank God they're headin' off north." Giving Dixie a pleasant look, I raised my glass. "I pr'pose we all drink t' that!"

"Why not?" Dixie managed to say in a slightly strange voice, and we all drank.

I had to give Dixie credit for seconding that or any other toast, and he did down his glass this time with a little more style, but he still couldn't completely hide his relief when Shad told him he didn't necessarily have to drink the whole thing every time.

Old Keats and the others, the day before, had picked up all the supplies the Slash-Diamond needed, but there were still a couple of things

Rostov wanted, so a little later he and Yuri left the rest of us for a while to go get them.

And then, as Ilya started quietly strumming his balalaika, Irenia came to the table again with two more bottles of vodka and said something to Igor. This time I could talk at least, so I took the bull by the horns and said right out, "Hello, Irenia." My timing was kind of off, saying "hello" that way, like I hadn't happened to notice her up until now. But I figured better late than never, and anyway there was nothing much else I could say to her. She gave me the kind of a look and smile that I guess is what tends to turn bachelors into married men. Then, timidly and cautiously, she said, "Hay-loh, Lay-vee." And with that she turned quickly and fled back through the door.

I was so overwhelmed I almost fell out of my chair. "My *God!* Did y'a hear *that?* She *spoke* t' me!"

"Way I got it," Dixie said, "she was tryin' t' ask ya' t' please not get s' goddamn drunk this time."

"No." Natcho shook his head and stretched his sense of humor to the breaking point. "They have just become engaged."

"Now *c'mon!* She said plain as day, '*Hello, Levi!*' " I turned to Shad for support. "*Boss?*"

He nodded. "That's the way I heard it, more 'r less."

Working hard at holding back his laughter, Igor now said, "She asked Lieutenant Bruk how to say that yesterday."

Still pretty much in a delightful state of shock I muttered, "Well, *ain't* that *nice!*"

Before Dixie or Natcho could give me any more hard times, Shad now turned dead serious. "Igor? Did you or Rostov order those two bottles?"

"No. They're from Anna and Irenia and the other people who work here at The Far East."

Shad said quietly, "Givin' us presents ain't too healthy a practice around here."

Igor understood Shad's concern. "Believe me, it's not the same as with those two men. No one will know. And in a small way, like those two men, they want to pay honor to Bakaskaya, and to Captain Rostov and his father."

"Rostov's father?" Dixie's speech was beginning to sound slurred. "I didn't even know he had one."

"The captain's father was one of the first high-ranking Kuban Cossacks in European Russia to defy the Tzar. He gave up everything, great wealth and power, and moved far east into the wilderness to try to establish a free, independent state. With a few loyal followers, he founded Bakaskaya many years ago, when his son, our captain, was still a very young man."

"Just what the hell," Dixie wanted to know, "has all a' that got t' do with these here bottles a' vodka?"

"Since his father's death, our captain has gone on to become even more of" – Igor frowned, searching his mind for the right word – "of a legend. Many people have much respect for him, his name, and what they stand for." As he looked around at us, his eyes began to grow impatient and even angry. "You just don't know, and *can't* know! The false papers that had to be drawn up to make the officials in Moscow think that the cattle were going to the good Tzar city of Irkutsk! The fact that less than three thousand of us in Bakaskaya, men, women and children, have been starving for over five years to put every kopek we could gather together into this purchase! I honestly do not know what the herd means to you, except that delivering it is a matter of pride. To us it is a matter of life and death! And the principle of what the term 'cossacks,' long ago and originally, stood for – 'a society of free people'!" He took a deep, long breath. "Some of the people here in Khabarovsk understand what I speak of." He hesitated again and then said, "That is the reason for these two bottles."

Right about then I think Igor was ready to fight all of us at once if we'd gone against him or anything he'd told us. And I, for one, was too much on his side to do anything like that.

Shad looked at the bottles thoughtfully and then finally said, "All right."

Dixie and the vodka were getting used to each other. He started to open a bottle. "No point lettin' it git spoilt fr'm ol' age."

Natcho said, "Where did the captain learn such perfect English, Igor?"

"As the son of a wealthy landowner, he was educated in many schools in Europe and England. He speaks seven languages."

"Jesus Christ!" Dixie muttered, making some headway at opening the bottle. "I didn't know there *was* seven languages!"

Some more customers had been drifting into the big room, two or three at a time, every now and then. And now, for whatever reasons, the Imperial Cossacks suddenly started swarming into The Far East.

"My God," Dixie mumbled. "They're showin' up faster an' thicker than flies around a fat ol' hog gittin' slaughtered."

Within a couple of minutes the big room was packed with those loud-talking, boisterous bastards, and half a dozen girls, including Irenia, were running all over the place to serve them.

And once again my nostrils could almost sense that acrid smell of intense hostility. Those Imperials weren't going to come right out and declare war on us, but they sure as hell weren't about to go out of their way to avoid it. And if they could maybe push it a little, they wouldn't mind that either. One of them, a gigantic moose of a fella with a voice like a cannon, was sitting at the table right behind me, and he kept leaning back hard in his chair, deliberately slamming into the back of my chair.

"Shad," I said, "ya' think we oughtta bust outta here?"

"We'll wait."

Then Rostov and Yuri entered and made their way through the crowded room to sit back down with us.

Pouring them both drinks, Shad said quietly, "What the hell is all this?"

"That gray mare just brought back the man Verushki had punished this morning — dead." Rostov downed his drink calmly. "The ropes came partly loose while the gray was running, and with his head dragging on the ground the man's neck was broken."

"Then why don't they go out an' hang Verushki?"

"They consider us responsible."

Looking around with an easy, level gaze,

Shad said, "Tell ya' the truth, Rostov, that ain't too staggerin' a surprise."

Gradually realizing the spot we were in, even Dixie's head was starting to clear up, and Natcho said, "Perhaps it would be wise to leave, now."

Rostov said, "We will when, without hurrying, we've finished all the vodka on the table."

But we were doomed to a different kind of time schedule than that. And it was my fault, but I couldn't help it.

Irenia, carrying a tray of drinks raised high over her head so that she could squeeze through the crowd, hurried to the table behind me, where the cannon-voiced moose was thundering harsh words at her and leaning backward against me and my chair hard enough to damnere crush both it and me.

I'd spent a lot of my spare time in there trying to watch Irenia without seeming to. And it ain't easy to somehow look at a girl yet not look at her at exactly the same time. But now, moving the tilt of my head just enough to cheat a little, I saw out of the corner of my eye what happened.

As she was leaning over to serve the drinks, that big bastard reached out behind her and actually grabbed her with his oversized hand, right on the butt. I never was sure whether I was more mad or more stunned at such an un-speakable action, but things happened so fast afterward that it really didn't matter.

She let out a little, breathless "Eek!" and jumped in surprise, accidentally tipped a few of the drinks on the moose. He reared up furi-ously, his cannon voice roaring, and shoved her away so hard that both she and her tray went flying to the floor.

And boy, that was that.

I was up while Irenia's tray was still clatter-ing, and I pushed that giant sonofabitch on his mammoth chest with a strength that nobody, including me, ever dreamed I had. Even so, as a matter of fact, it's a good thing he was stand-ing up. Because I could never have budged him if all that monstrous weight had been sitting down.

But as it happened to work out, he went sail-ing across the table, scattering drinks right and left, and finally, taking two friends on the far side down with him, he crashed thunderously to the floor.

About that time, both Shad and Rostov were beside me, each taking one of my elbows and almost lifting me off the ground. Right then I felt like a picture hanging on the wall. There wasn't one goddamned move I had any chance to make, except possibly to fall down.

The moose came bellowing up to his feet, totally prepared and ready, and even anxious, to tear me in half, with absolutely no sportsmanlike regard for the fact that I was being held helpless.

He was about to walk right through that massive table at me when five or six of his men got ahold of him and managed to slow him down.

Rostov roared something in Russian, and the angry noise and confusion stopped as though somebody had pulled some kind of a magic cord. But the ominous silence wasn't too cheerful, either. Later on I found out that Rostov had simply asked, a little harshly, how many of them wanted to die for the moose, though he evidently didn't use that exact phrase of mine.

Old Anna did us some good at this moment. Helping Irenia to her feet, she shattered that grim silence with a few no doubt well-chosen screams directed furiously at the moose. Whatever she yelled made some of the men recognize their shame in siding with the man who had mistreated Irenia.

Rostov growled a few more words, and for a touchy, short while, it began to feel like the time of outright killing was beginning to ease off. The giant snorted angrily, and then looked around and saw that he wasn't the most popular man in the house. In a deep, rumbling voice he said something to Rostov.

Rostov now let go of my elbow. "That big one just agreed not to kill you, Levi."

Shad released my other elbow and said flatly, "Damn nice of 'im."

"But he challenged you. And you may get your right hand cut up."

I didn't yet understand, and I sure as hell didn't mean it to be funny, but I guess it sort of was, as I raised my already cut and bandaged left hand and said, "I ain't sure I can afford it."

Dixie chuckled, but nobody else did.

And then, as a couple of Tzar cossacks brought over a smaller, regular-sized table, I remembered about the armrassling and the broken glasses. "Oh — that." It was easy to see I was in trouble.

Rostov said, "I might persuade him to accept a substitute, in your place."

I just looked at him and didn't say anything, and I think he kind of liked that answer. "This is for blood, not drinks," he went on. "It's only over when the loser finally cries out or when the winner decides to be merciful and let go."

With the moose laughing and saying loud, patently dumb things in Russian, they brought up two chairs and put two full glasses of vodka on the table.

"Drink it and then break the glass," Rostov said.

The moose and I, still standing, downed the vodka and then smashed the tops of our glasses on the table. Trouble was, I hit mine too hard and the whole damn glass broke in my hand, cutting one finger slightly. This struck the moose and his friends crowded around as being hilarious as hell. They did everything but double up with laughter. And as Rostov handed me another glass, it seemed to me that this was turning out to be the pattern of my life. Not only forever getting somewhat mangled, but forever being highly embarrassed in the goddamned painful process.

My second glass broke all right and we placed the two jagged, vicious-looking broken glasses on the table. Then we sat down facing each other, our elbows on the table, and when we clasped hands mine went damnere out of sight, lost inside the moose's huge grip.

The minute we started putting pressure against each other, his ugly grin got as wide as a barn door and I began to wish even more than before that I was someplace, anyplace, else.

With every damn bit of strength I had, and even with the added inspiration of that jagged glass waiting for the back of my hand to be forced down on it, I just couldn't hold him back. Very slowly, with salty sweat now starting to come down into my eyes from the immense effort I was making, I could see my hand, as though it belonged to someone else, going gradually over and down.

From what seemed a mile or so off, I heard Shad's low voice. "Levi ain't gonna yell, an' that mean bastard's out t' go through bones an' everything else an' cripple 'im."

From equally far away Rostov said grimly, "We'll soon know."

"I ain't about t' let that happen."

"Nor am I, Northshield."

And then the back of my hand went slowly down onto the jagged glass, and though I didn't feel anything, blood began to appear on the table and within the glass.

Some kind of extra strength came from somewhere within me, and I forced the giant's hand back up two or three inches. But I could see, hazily, that he was still wearing that barn-door smile, and he started crushing my bleeding hand back down once more.

Suddenly a hand swept that jagged, red-stained glass onto the floor and the moose glared furiously up, releasing his grip on me.

It was Rostov who had done it. And he now downed his own glass of vodka, smashed the top of it, and put the broken remainder down in the widening pool of blood where mine had been.

I didn't know if that was a standard rule, and I suspected he'd just made it up on the spur of the moment, but it sure as hell didn't need any clarification.

And now seeing that it was Rostov, the giant moose didn't stay mad. Instead, he seemed happier than ever.

I was the only one who complained. "Goddamn it, Rostov. I was just about t' take 'im."

"Get out of the way, Levi."

I stood up, holding my left hand against the right hand's bleeding, and Rostov sat down in my place. And whereas the Tzar's cossacks had been yelling and laughing before, it suddenly became as still and quiet as an empty church.

Shad was standing just behind Rostov, and though there was no way for it to mean that much to Verushki's men, his right thumb was hooked casually in his belt, just a few short inches away from the worn walnut handle of his revolver.

In the silence, Dixie leaned close to my ear and whispered, "Igor says that big one's a ringer." I frowned, not understanding, and he added, still in a whisper, "He ain't never ever been beat. He wasn't even here that night Big

Yawn an' Kirdyaga was puttin' fellas down."

Igor guessed what Dixie was whispering and nodded grimly at me. And all of our other fellas were looking just as grim as Igor.

But Rostov and the moose were now locking hands, their elbows on the table, and as they started putting pressure against each other, it look like all the brute strength in the world was being centered right there on that table. Finally, the moose slowly closed the doors of that barn-door grin of his, and still neither man's hand had budged a fraction of an inch. I half expected the thick oak table itself to split in half under the sheer power of our big man and the giant.

From where I was, behind Rostov, I could tell more what was happening from the moose's face than from their hands. Rostov's hand must have given way so slightly that it was impossible to see, and could only be felt by his opponent, because the moose's barn-door grin opened just a crack. But then it slammed shut again as Rostov evidently got him back to even, or maybe a little more.

About then, my head finally clearing after the rough time I'd just had at that table, I began to realize more fully why Shad's hand wasn't too far from his gun. Any idea of Rostov crying out in defeat or pain was too absurd to even think about. But we sure as hell wouldn't stand by and let the moose make minced meat out of Rostov's hand. And by the same token, those phony goddamned Tzar cossacks probably felt the same way about the moose. The single and only possible way not to have an all-out war on our hands was for Rostov to win and for the moose to give a quick yell, so that this stupid, cruel game would be finished for once and for all.

Then, for the first time, their hands moved enough to be seen. And they moved in Rostov's favor.

"Damn, damn, damn," I whispered, dumbfounded, knowing it had to be raw will power Rostov was using more than strength.

The giant leaned his head forward and down, as though to gather even more force, and for a backbreaking moment he held Rostov's hand motionless. But then, as though he were a silently roaring, irresistibly powerful storm bending a huge tree before him, Rostov again moved the massive hand and arm back and back and down.

The giant's hand went down onto the ugly, broken circle of sharp glass until it had been cut about the same as mine had been, and then Rostov let his bleeding hand back up and away from the glass.

And that damned stubborn moose did not yell. His teeth were tightly clenched against any sound at all.

To one side, Natcho muttered an odd thing in a low voice, "The moment of truth."

All of a sudden now, it was easy to see that Verushki's men felt exactly the same way that we did. They weren't about to stand by and let the moose get his hand maimed, either, and there was a change of feeling in the air, a very slight, but damned ominous shifting of weight and position among them.

There was one rule we'd forgotten, since it hadn't even come close to showing up between the moose and me. The one about mercy. Rostov now let go of the moose's big, bleeding hand and said a few easy words that had to mean he was being merciful, and their game was done.

But with a swift, furious move, the giant again slapped his hand against Rostov's, grabbing it to start all over.

As Rostov bent into it again, Shad said to him quietly, "This dumb bastard's dead set on either cuttin' your hand off or losin' his. An' no matter which way it is, it'll sure cause a bloody mix-up around here."

Rostov was too hard put with the giant's massive hand and arm at that time to make any kind of an answer. And now, for the second time, he started making headway, very slowly moving that great mass of muscle back and down.

"When ya' cut 'im again," Shad said, still quietly, "be pr'pared that same instant t' take on the rest of 'em with us, 'cause that's sure as hell what's gonna happen."

And then, for no reason, Shad did such a strange thing that I could have sworn on a stack of Bibles that those two were reading each other's minds again. He touched Rostov's mightily straining shoulder briefly and gently, almost the same way Shiny had touched Dixie's shoulder before, and said mostly to himself, "yeah."

It was a mystery to me, but it was soon solved.

The moose, his lowering hand getting closer and closer to being cut, was putting all the desperate last strength he had within him against Rostov.

And then, just short of those final jagged edges of blood-red glass, Rostov instantly switched every bit of power in his arm full backward into the opposite direction, which was the same direction that the giant's total strength was aimed at.

The combined result was an extraordinary

sight to witness.

The moose, with Rostov's help, went flying in what would have been a complete somersault except that he hit the floor too fast, primarily on his head. And as he raised his head, shaking it a little, Rostov was already standing over him with the point of his drawn saber pressing against his throat. Rostov said a quiet word or two, and the moose said one strangled word, which was "*Dah.*"

The point of Rostov's saber now moved in a blindingly swift, short arc that drew what seemed to be exactly one drop of blood from the giant's throat. In another swift move, his saber flashing almost invisibly, Rostov returned his blade to its sheath.

And then, maybe best of all, he reached down and helped the moose back to his feet.

Old Keats had once remarked to me, "It's generally hard t' lose. But if ya' lose t' a certain kind of a man, who ya' know t' be one hell of a man, then ya' can take a certain kind a' proud joy in the pure pleasure a' havin' done your best against 'im."

It seemed to me that maybe that was the way the moose felt about Rostov just then. After having had that saber at his throat, he knew as well as, or better than, the rest of us that he was a dead man who'd been given a second chance at life. He looked at Rostov for a long, silent moment, and then finally moved off, most of the Imperial Cossacks following him out of The Far East.

Igor came up and said, "Come with me," and I did, as the others sat down to finish their vodka the way Rostov had said, without hurrying.

With Igor leading, we went through the door to the kitchen, which I wouldn't ever have done without him, because, it looked to me like it was being kind of pushy.

But just behind the door, standing there beside a basin of water and some clean pieces of cloth, with tears running down her cheeks, was Irenia.

"She wants to take care of your hand," Igor said.

He was feeling more than he let his voice show, and so was I. "Ah, heck," I said, somehow switching to softer words in her presence, even though she couldn't understand them. "Tell 'er I'm just fine."

He told her what I'd said, but she only shook her head in an impatient way that meant absolutely not. So he just kind of pushed me toward her and went back out the door, and there we stood.

She reached toward my hurt right hand and I

didn't move it fast enough to suit her so she took it and raised it toward the basin of water and started to bathe it.

Her hands were so gentle that it was hard to be equally gentle back. But it seemed to me there was something that had to be done, and with that damned bandaged, roughed-up and weather-beaten left hand of mine, I reached out as soft as I could and brushed those tears of hers away.

She stopped bathing my hand and looked up at me.

And I swear sincerely, by all the gods that ever may be, past, present or future, that our eyes said more to each other in that fleeting little moment than most two people can ever say to each other in their whole, entire lifetimes.

And then she lowered her eyes, but that shouldn't have been the end of the conversation, because we still felt each other so much.

She was tying the bandage when Igor came back in. "We're going now."

"Igor," I said, "will you tell her —"

"What?"

How can you say a lifetime of words, especially through another fella, in the time it takes to walk from a basin of water to a door? So I just gave up and looked at her and said, "Nothin'."

But she understood.

And then we were gone.

20

The next day three of our fellas and three cossacks, with Sergeant Nick in charge of them, went into town. None of our men, Mushy, Sammy the Kid and Chakko, had been in before, and it was the same with the cossacks, so except for Nick they were all new faces.

Before they left, Shad told the Slash-Diamonders not to mess around with the Imperials in any way, shape or form, and particularly not to do any arm-rassling. But after that bout between Rostov and the Imperial moose, it just never came up again anyway, as though everybody on both sides realized that any further contest would just have to be plain silly by comparison.

Later that afternoon, a bunch of mounted Imperials were doing some sort of a toy-soldier drill just outside of Khabarovsk on that huge meadow, so Rostov and Shad decided it was time to show them a reversal of our first all-cossack performance, just for the hell of it. Us cowboys outfitted the cossacks as best we could. Shad and me gave Rostov and Igor each spare jackets and pants and boots and bandannas. The thing we were shyest of was hats, because most of us had only one. But Big Yawn was a help there. He always wore a kind of a hunting cap with a visor in front of it and ear flaps on the sides that you could pull down if you wanted to against the cold. And for some reason he was packing half a dozen spares that he passed out among the cossacks.

So it came to pass that over twenty cowboys rode up against the skyline, just briefly, to watch the Imperials drilling far off on the meadow. And then, as though we were almost immediately bored by what we were watching, we soon drifted back away and out of sight again.

Our men came back from Khabarovsk just after nightfall, and the most exciting thing they had to report was that Mushy had caused a mild sensation by finishing his last drink at The Far East, and then eating the glass. Mushy did that every now and then, especially after a few too many. Damnedest thing, he'd chomp down and bite off a chunk from the rim, chew it slowly and thoughtfully, and then swallow it. And he'd just keep that up until the whole goddamn glass was gone, except that he usually left the bottom of the glass because it was thicker there, and he also claimed it didn't taste as good.

I kept waiting for one of them to pass on some word to me from Irenia, but nobody said anything.

I did let my pride go down a peg by saying offhandedly to Mushy and Sammy, "Ya' talk t' anybody in town?"

"How the hell could we?" Sammy said. "Ain't nobody in there can talk American."

"That's right." Mushy nodded. "Nick did all our talkin' for us."

At supper, Slim and I wound up sitting beside Nick, and I finally couldn't stand it any longer. "Did ya' see that girl, Irenia?" I asked Nick casually.

He nodded, and kept on eating.

After a long time, I said, "She — say anything?"

Between mouthfuls he said, "She ask how your hand. I say fine."

"Well, goddamnit, why didn't ya' say so?"

He finished eating and turned his massive face toward me with a hurt expression. "I *say* so. Just now." And then he got up and walked away.

"Stupid goddamn cossack," I muttered.

"You been slightly an' subtly had by that stupid goddamn cossack." Slim grinned. "He told me all about that more'n an hour ago."

"Oh."

The following day I rode the morning stretch on the herd, and the sun was a little past high noon when Crab relieved me. I swung around by the big rock on the war-games meadow to see if anything might be going on, and on this day my timing wasn't too good because I got stuck in a race that was about to begin around that tough damn course.

The good part was that it was a relay, with four men on each team, so we'd each have only about half a mile to go, instead of the whole rugged two miles.

The bad part was that instead of each racer passing on a baton, or something light like that, to the next fella, what we were supposed to carry and pass on was a large, rounded rock weighing over twenty pounds. And if anybody dropped it, that would probably lose the race for his team because he'd have to go back to get it. And it was easy to drop because just standing there on the ground holding that rounded rock in one hand wasn't all that simple.

"Jesus," Dixie said, "whoever invented this idea musta been mad as hell at somebody."

"Well, Dixie, you can see how it'd help train ya' for warfare," I said dryly. "If you ain't got a cannon, you just ride up carryin' the cannon ball and throw it."

"This is child's play compared to some of the games," Rostov told us. "Such as racing the entire course with a sharp saber clenched between your teeth."

"Yuck," I said.

"However," he continued, "this race will do. Particularly in deference to Northshield's common sense, and also the fact that right now we can't afford to have anyone get his head cut off."

This sounded pretty grim, but Purse managed to take it lightly. "Put a saber in Mushy's mouth," he said, "and he'd probably eat it."

Aside from Rostov, Slim and Nick, there were eight of us there, me being the lucky number eight who made the cowboy team complete. Dixie, Purse, Mushy and I made up our bunch, and Igor, Ilya, Pietre and Kirdyaga were the cossacks.

It was decided that Pietre and I were to ride the final heat for our teams, and we rode at an easy gait out to the fourth pole about half a mile off at an angle to the right.

We got there and pulled up to wait, giving each other a grin. I couldn't help but remember some of that fancy riding I'd seen Pietre do and felt pretty outclassed. But then I shrugged mentally, thinking what the hell, at least old Buck was every bit the horse that Pietre's fine skewbald mare was.

Looking back I studied the three final poles we had to race outside of on our way back to the finish line. The first was at a tricky out-cropping of rocks, and the second was in a thick grove of trees. The third, and last, was that one next to that murderous ten-foot jump over the swift, rock-studded stream twenty feet below, which I had absolutely no intention of even trying to make. I figured I'd swing about a hundred feet down to the left of that pole. It would be safe to jump there, and I'd still be making pretty good time.

Everybody was in place by then, and at about that time I saw Shad ride up to join the others over near the big rock.

Igor and Mushy, the starters for the teams, were mounted, each holding a heavy rock in one hand and ready to go. Nick raised his arm and then quickly dropped it, signaling the two of them to bust out.

They took off like demons, and both of them made that first low jump over the stream all right, each of them holding their rock kind of up against their chests so they could hang on to it better. But by the time they approached the first relay point far across the meadow, where Dixie and Ilya were waiting and raring to go, Igor, on that fast Blackeye, had now pulled about two or three lengths ahead of Mushy. He handed his rock to Ilya, who in turn took off at full tilt. And then Mushy was there, passing his big rock over to Dixie. It looked like they damnere dropped it, but then Dixie was also on his way, galloping furiously to try to narrow the cossack lead.

Dixie was on his handsome Appaloosa, Shiloh, who could outrun damnere any living thing on four legs, and taking that second part of the course in almost exactly the same route as Ilya used, Dixie picked up a couple of lengths.

The race was getting exciting as hell, and was now suddenly half over as Ilya and Dixie barreled up to Purse and Kirdyaga with at the very most one second difference in their running time. With growing, eager excitement, Pietre leaned over and whacked me powerfully on the back, letting out a wild whoop that may have been Russian, but sure sounded like a pure cowboy yell.

And then Ilya, who was handier with balalaikas than rocks, dropped his as he was handing it over to Kirdyaga. The giant Kirdyaga didn't even dismount to get the heavy rock. He spun his horse around and, leaning far down, did an almost impossible thing by simply picking it back up in one huge hand.

But just that brief time still lost them three or four lengths because Dixie had passed his rock to Purse and Purse was on his way. It would have been a shoo-in for us then except that Purse tried to gain even more time by cutting too close to a pole in some thick trees and he got slowed down for a long, maddening moment, so that when he and Kirdyaga came charging out of that grove of trees and onto the open meadow, they were as close together as the two sides of a silver dollar.

Pietre was going crazy, and I guess I was too, because all of a sudden I realized I was hollering at Purse, and urging him on, as loud as Pietre was yelling at Kirdyaga.

The two of us each got handed our rock at about the same time, and I damnere lost myself along with the rock as Buck, feeling all the intense excitement, roared away so fast he almost left me sitting there in mid-air.

Getting my seat back, I took the rough outcropping of rock closer to the first pole than Pietre did and for a few seconds had to slow down or Buck could have hurt himself. Pietre took a way that was farther around but faster, so we both galloped out of the rocks about even.

We exactly reversed that process going through the thick stand of trees farther on. Pietre elected this time for the shorter, more tangled route, and a grasping branch almost tore the rock out of his hand, slowing him briefly as he went ducking and weaving through. Playing it safer this time, I spotted a wide path forty feet to the left of the pole where I could charge through at a dead run, and I chose that way.

And again, goddamned if we weren't still flying along neck and neck on the far side of the trees.

And now, in these last seconds, the whole, entire race boiled down to whatever the two of us made up our minds to do.

It was a flat-out straightaway toward that final, deadly obstacle, and we were going so fast I don't think any one of those combined eight hooves were hardly even touching the ground.

It was going to be awful damn tight.

Maybe Pietre suddenly got the same idea about me that I suddenly got about him. But I for sure suddenly got the idea that he wasn't going to play it in the least bit safe, but was going right smack at that last pole to take that killer of a jump there. So no matter who was reading whose mind, before there was any time to think it over, that's exactly where we were both headed, like blistered bats out of burning hell.

I knew as sure as I knew my own name that I shouldn't try to make that jump. But in those last feverish, speeding moments, I'd have probably needed three guesses to come up with my own name anyway. Winning that race had crowded out everything else in the world. And yet I did somehow know that the jump was wrong.

All things equal, I suddenly decided on what seemed to me to be a brilliant way out of my dilemma.

Cradling my rock against my chest, I leaned forward over Buck's ears and said, "I've decided t' leave this up t' you. If ya' can make that jump, then make it. An' if ya' can't, then forget it. As f'r me, I'm just gonna sit here with this rock."

Even at the blinding speed that we were traveling, Buck's ears were twitching back every now and then as I spoke, as though he wanted to be sure not to miss anything.

And that dumb buckskin sonofabitch decided to make it. If possible, he opened up even a little more, his neck and nose stretched out ahead as straight and graceful as the prow of a speeding ship.

All this time, Pietre and his skewbald were staying so close alongside us that he and I could've shook hands without leaning over.

Right now there was just time for one quick breath before we'd be at that brutal, empty space looming swiftly up ahead, so I sucked in a half breath of air as I leaned forward, balancing myself into the killing jump.

And at that precise moment, Buck changed his mind and stopped. When I say he stopped, I don't mean he just slowed down or anything like that, because there wasn't enough time to fool around. I mean he slammed on every goddamn brake he had as he sat right down and dragged his butt holding both forelegs stretched stiffly out before him so that he dug up enough dirt to start a small farm with, and skidded to a halt that was just slightly less abrupt than running straight into a brick wall.

Both me and my rock came awful close to sailing on all by ourselves and completing the remainder of that jump, or at least a portion of it, without benefit of Buck. It was so close, that gripping onto Buck's ribs and then his flanks with every bit of foot and leg power I had, I swear it was only my toenails finally holding firm that just barely kept me from going on.

But Pietre did take that awesome leap. As me and Buck were skidding, he and his mare were flying, and that skewbald of his was one hell of a jumper. They just made it, but the ground on the far side wasn't firm enough for all that flying weight, and as they came down, some of the dirt at that far edge broke away under her hind hooves and, slipping, she almost went over and down backward.

But superb horseman that he was, Pietre's right hand instinctively flashed back and whacked her on the rear as his left hand swiftly hauled her head around so that she was jerked into one of the quickest half-turns ever seen, and her struggling hind hooves were now on secure ground farther from the edge.

This had all happened with such split-second timing that it was just about now that the rock he'd had to drop in order to save his mare splashed into the stream below.

After a deep sigh of relief that Pietre and his mare weren't hurt, I spurred Buck down to where the stream was easy to cross and rode unhurriedly up to the big rock, and the finish line, where the others were gathering.

Pietre was sitting his mare quietly, just past the finish line, looking miserable as hell. He'd crossed over it, but crossing without his rock didn't count. And as if that didn't add up to enough misery for him already, it wasn't hard to guess that Nick had given him hell for ever trying the dangerous jump in the first place.

I pulled up just short of the finish line, and Nick rumbled, "Well, cross over, so to win!"

I almost did what he said, both him and his voice being so big and tough, but some kind of an invisible string, somehow, was pulling me back the other way.

Just letting the string tug on me, I didn't go over the finish line. But instead I rode Buck the short distance back to the stream and threw my team's rock down into its waters too.

There was silence as I rode back from the creek, and now I finally spurred Buck a little so that we also crossed empty-handed over the finish line to where Pietre was sitting his mare.

I didn't have any idea that doing that simple thing would touch those cossacks so much. It was almost too much, as though what I'd done was so damned right that they wanted to be silent about it so it'd remain in their memories for sure. But I couldn't let it stay that quiet and serious, because no matter how you looked at it, Pietre had rode the best race.

So I looked at Pietre and held both hands up just to start all over again with the simple fact that they were as empty as his. Then I grinned and shrugged my shoulders broadly, which meant in any language, "What the hell!" With a whole lot of "Who cares anyway?" thrown in.

He grinned back, and it was a damned good grin. And then everybody, cowboys and cossacks, were grinning and talking and laughing all at once, and the whole feeling among us was warm and fine.

Shad had already dismounted and when I got off my horse he came over. After a quiet moment, and in a voice he made sure no one else could hear, he paid me one of those rare, generous compliments of his. "You didn't make too much of an ass a' yourself, Levi."

I hated to admit it, but I had to. "Boss, I wasn't the brains behind not takin' that jump. Buck was."

"I know that!" he said impatiently. "I ain't blind." After a moment, he went on. "I meant about tossin' your goddamn rock in the creek."

Then he frowned a little, at nothing in particular, as though he might be secretly mad at himself for having talked too much.

"Thanks, boss."

"Well," he said, still quietly, "you're mostly such a screwup, it's refreshin' t' see ya' do somethin' partway right once in a while."

Then he walked away.

If there is anything on earth more sensitive than a sensitive man who tries to act like he ain't, I'd sure like to know what it is.

Later that afternoon, there was still a long time left before sundown when Bruk and Old Keats hurried unexpectedly back toward camp with the four men they'd taken into town that day.

There was something wrong for them to be riding back to camp so early, and the looks on their faces didn't help. On top of that a cold, mean wind was rising quickly, while angry black clouds were suddenly starting to fill the sky in the west, and there was occasional dim rumbles of distant thunder.

Slim was standing next to me and was sharing my thoughts. "Kinda feels like the devil just now stretched an' woke up," he said, "an' is out t' cause some mischief."

Old Keats and Bruk dismounted near the fire, where Shad and Rostov and some of us others were gathered. Link, who'd been one of the men with them, sat his horse a few feet away, his eyes cast down.

"It's just possible," Keats said grimly, "that we got us a small problem on our hands."

"If we have," Link muttered, "then it's my doin'."

Keats frowned at Link, but his expression was more thoughtful than angry.

"Well, ya gonna tell us about it," Shad said flatly, "or are we supposed t' guess?"

Link got off his horse and forced himself to look directly at Shad. "I made a toast t' Rostov an' his men." He hesitated. "Way it come out, I said, 'Here's t' the best fifteen cossacks in Russia.'"

Link dropped his gaze toward the ground again, and Keats took over. "Some Imperials who'd been sittin' close by got up an' took off like they'd all of a sudden been whistled for. We think that maybe one of 'em understood enough t' get the drift of what Link said."

"There's no way of knowing for certain," Bruk said. "But if any of Verushki's men do speak some English, he'd have them listening to us in town as much as possible."

There was a moment of grim, thoughtful silence, and then Slim said, "What ya' think we oughtta do, Shad?"

Shad looked off toward the black storm clouds that were now blotting out the lowering sun and surging across the sky closer toward us. "I think them clouds've made up our minds what t' do."

Knowing what he meant, Rostov said to Bruk, "What's the level of the river?"

"It's down another twelve centimeters."

Shad and Rostov studied each other, and

Rostov said, "It's still higher than we'd intended."

"With heavy rain hittin' upstream, that river's gonna rise a lot b'fore goin' down again, an' we ain't got all summer."

Rostov nodded. "Then it's tonight. The storm will help cover our movements." He paused. "One more thing. Some of us should go into town for a while."

Now it was Shad's turn to agree. "And make it look like that rain's got us stuck here."

Rostov started giving orders to his men as Slim said, "Shad, our pack animals' gonna be overloaded f'r much swimmin'."

"Lash some of the stuff onto some a' the cows."

"They ain't gonna like that too much," Crab said.

"Then convince 'em!"

Link hadn't moved since he'd gotten off his horse, but now he stepped to Shad, his eyes still as pained as ever. "Boss, it was *stupid* a' me, mentionin' fifteen cossacks!"

Shad looked at him. "You ain't s' stupid as I thought. I didn't think ya' could count t' fifteen."

Like Shad knew it would, this somehow made things better for Link, and most of the pain eased out of his eyes.

"All right!" Slim called out. "Time f'r you third-rate wranglers t' start earnin' y'r wages agin! Everybody git ready t' bust outta here!"

We moved off, and Sammy the Kid was putting his possibles together near where I was wrapping up my own bedroll when the first advance drops of rain started to hit us. He looked up at the darkening, cloud-swept sky and rubbed those first light splashes of rain from his face, but I could see he was thinking a whole lot more about that river we had yet to cross.

"I don't like it," he muttered.

"One thing, Sammy," I said, trying to be encouraging, "this'll be a cinch compared t' that swim off the *Great Eastern Queen*."

"I never could stand bein' in more water at once than takin' a bath in a washtub. An' I ain't too keen about that."

"We'll be wadin' most a' the way across."

"Don't like wadin' neither. An' there's damn deep spots in that river."

"Hell, cheer up!" I said. "Maybe Verushki's onto us an' we'll be dead b'fore we get t' the river anyhow."

The edges of his mouth curled up a little, but the grin didn't make it all the way to his eyes. "You sure do always manage t' see the bright side."

About then Old Keats came up and said to me, "Don't tie your travelin' gear on Buck. Slim'll take care of it."

"How come?"

"You're goin' t' town with Shad an' me, an' a full pack on our horses'd be a dead giveaway."

A few minutes later everybody was mounted and ready to move out. The rain was now pouring down like one huge waterfall and it was as dark as the middle of a black cat turned inside out, except for flashes of lightning roaring across the sky every now and then.

Gathering his rain-covered, dripping slicker a little closer around his neck, Dixie rode up near me. "Saw you an' Sammy talkin'. He scairt a' the river?"

I remembered the mean way Dixie had been with Sammy on the beach near Vladivostok that long-ago night, but I couldn't see one mean thing at all in his face right now, so I just nodded.

Shad and Keats rode off then and I followed after them. We joined Igor, Nick and Kirdyaga, and the six of us rode toward Khabarovsk.

We were still playing showdown, with elements of chess mixed into the game. While the others, under Rostov and Slim, got the herd moving and swung in a wide circle around Khabarovsk to the river, it was up to us to give the Imperials the idea that the rain would keep us right where we were indefinitely.

On our way down the huge, sloping meadow toward the faraway lights of Khabarovsk showing faintly through the storm, and thinking of Irenia, I said to Shad, "Thanks, boss."

He didn't answer.

There was almost no one on the flooded, muddy streets where the rain water was rushing and swirling within its own mad foam in whichever way happened to be mostly downhill.

We tied up and went into The Far East, our slickers leaving puddles of water on the floor near the door. Seeing Irenia toward the rear of the room, I nodded toward her and made another small puddle as water spilled down off the brim of my hat.

It wasn't too crowded, but there were a few Imperials seated here and there around the place.

The big table on the far side where we normally sat wasn't being used, and so we moved toward it. Right then I had the damnedest feeling that no matter what happened this night, win, lose or draw, I'd never sit at this table again in my life. And while I wasn't all that crazy about the table, the same thought came to mind about Irenia, that same feeling that whatever happened I would also never see her again, forever more in my life.

She'd already gone away, and I guess it was a good thing, because she couldn't see my face just then, with those sad thoughts stamped all over it. That would have been a lot more of a dead giveaway than if our horses outside had been carrying full packs.

The older woman, Anna, came to the table and spoke in a low voice to Igor and Nick before starting away to get what they'd ordered.

Nick now called something after her in a good-natured roar loud enough to carry all over the room. She turned and called something back to him that made him slap his leg and laugh.

Then Nick got up, muttering and still chuckling at what had been said, and went to another door I'd never noticed before at the back of the room.

I think Old Keats had understood some of all this, but it was a mystery to Shad and me. Irenia now came in carrying some vodka and glasses on a tray and put them down for us, smiling and happy as can be. I was managing to smile too, now, and when our smiles came together hers got so strong her nose crinkled for an instant.

Grinning, Igor asked her something in a

carrying, clear voice.

She didn't reply to his question, but she smiled from him to me and gave me a quick little wink that was so innocent and unpracticed it almost came out as a tiny, smiling blink instead. Then she hurried happily away from the table.

And now, whether it meant anything or not, two of the Imperials got up and went out the front door.

As Kirdyaga began filling our glasses, Igor leaned forward and spoke in a low, easy voice, as if quietly discussing the rotten weather. "Anna wanted to, but couldn't, speak in here. The sergeant called after her that if this rain kept up he might have to buy a house and marry her. She said she doubted if he could afford the small house in back — the toilet. He said he just happened to feel like inspecting it anyway."

"So they can talk out back," Shad said.

Igor nodded. "Those two Imperial Cossacks just left to report to headquarters. So far, I think we have them fooled."

"What did you say to Irenia about me?" I asked him.

"I asked her if she could tolerate having you around for a longer time than we'd planned on."

A moment later Nick came back in, brushing rain from his uniform and sitting down at the table. He swallowed the vodka before him with great, noisy pleasure and then said a few quiet words to Igor. They both laughed at whatever it was, and Nick started refilling the glasses that had been emptied.

In a low voice Igor said, "Verushki has had a man here who speaks some English. But not well enough to be certain whether Link said 'fifteen' cossacks or 'fifty' cossacks. And either figure must be bewildering."

"Good God," Old Keats muttered. "He may think we been *hidin'* men from 'im! Just t' surprise 'im in case of a fight!"

"Either way," Shad said, "he's got to be too curious for comfort right now. We're leavin' pretty quick."

Even though part of me felt like a damn fool, the other part just wouldn't shut up. "Shad," I asked, "is it okay if —"

"Go ahead," he said, understanding before I could even get it all out. "But don't take all night."

So I gathered all my nerve and got up and went through that door into the back room where Irenia had fixed my hand, just hoping that she'd be back there.

And she was.

She and old Anna looked up from washing some dishes, and she just sort of stopped in mid-motion, with that smile of hers slowly starting and then growing, like a sunrise starts slowly and then grows until the whole world becomes bright.

Anna now disappeared someplace, and I walked over to Irenia with everything in the world to say and not one word to say it with, like some kind of a dumb ox.

As I approached her, she quickly dried her hands on a cloth, still smiling, and reached down to take my hand that she'd bandaged. I knew as sure as if we'd somehow both just had a long conversation about it, that she was going to check the hand out and maybe soak it a little, and rebandage it, but there wasn't anywhere near that kind of time.

So as she took it I pulled the hand back away from her, and probably my movement was more abrupt than I knew. Because when she looked up at me, her smile suddenly fading, she knew for absolute sure that I was in a hurry and that I was going away, for good.

To see a smile like hers fade away is hard enough, but then to see the eyes above it take on a far-off, not-quite-clear look, and fall away filled with wordless sorrow, is something that's just about to not be endured.

I wished, right then, that I had something, anything, to give her.

In all the old stories I'd ever heard about, and the few I'd read, it seemed like a decent sort of a fella always had something special and meaningful to give a girl when he was going away. Or at least he was off to do something that'd make her real proud. But I didn't have one solitary thing in the world to give her, and delivering a bunch of cows someplace sure as hell wasn't exactly searching for that Holy goddamned Grail.

Looking at Irenia's downcast eyes as they clouded over sadder and sadder, I took a desperate inventory of everything I had on me and it still added up to nothing. I couldn't give her my ugly, beaten-up old Stetson or my hand-tooled boots that'd looked pretty good a few years back. And the idea of my pocketknife or gun was even more foolish, if possible.

The only thing left to do was plain give up.

But then one final thought at last came to me. I was wearing my deer-hide jacket under that slicker, and it had two big matching buttons that held the front of it together. They were flat jet-black stones that had been made into buttons, and buffed and polished to a high gloss, so that they were really kind of pretty to look at in their own way.

Old Keats had given me those two buttons when I was just a kid, and I'd outworn a dozen jackets with them since then, wearing the buttons so much that they were simply a part of me. And you never normally think of that kind of a close part of you, anymore than you normally think of your left or right foot while you're walking.

Keats had also told me that there was some kind of an ancient and sad story about black stones like these, and about an Indian warrior and maiden who never had any luck getting together. So that the stones had finally become known as Apache Tears.

Anyway, I opened my slicker and pulled the top Apache Tear off my jacket and handed it to Irenia.

She saw that there were just two buttons and that each of us had one of them now.

She knew somehow, that I'd been trying to think of something of myself to leave with her. And she could also tell that my time was getting short.

So she looked at me and said softly and gently the only two words she knew to say, "Hello, Levi."

In all my life, and I know it will be so until I die, I have never heard a more beautiful way of one person saying to another — goodbye.

And then something made a sudden slamming noise behind me and I spun around to see an Imperial Cossack who'd just burst through the door. Now he swung on his heels just as quickly and went back out. He may have been drunk or he may have been checking up on me, but either way it was time to go.

Irenia had turned slightly away from me, her head bent down a little, so I didn't try to touch her or to say any of the things I couldn't have said anyway. All I could do was back quietly, softly out of the room, and then go quickly to where Shad and the others were getting ready to leave.

A few minutes later we were out of town and gathering speed through the almost blinding rain toward the point on the Amur River where the herd, hopefully, would just about be in position to cross by now.

In the lead, Shad had suddenly put up his hand and pulled his big Red to a sudden stop. We all jerked up behind him. And then, in a crash of thunder and lightning, I saw what he'd already seen. On a hilltop before us, and facing down in the other direction toward where the cattle should now be, Colonal Verushki was ordering the forty or so Imperial Cossacks with him to move on, waving one arm and shouting something we couldn't hear. His men galloped ahead and out of sight down the far side of the hill, and he waited on his horse there, peering off and evidently trying to make out what was happening below in the dark.

"Levi, stay with me!" Shad said. "You others circle 'round this hill t' the right an' ya' oughtta come up drag on the herd!"

"An' start 'em?" Old Keats called over the pounding rain.

"Damn right!"

"What about those Imperials?" Igor called.

"If they're in the way, get 'em *outta* the way, *however!*"

They galloped off in the dark and the rain.

I'd thought the two of us were going to circle to the left and come up point on the herd, and that was what Shad had in mind, but not just yet. He spurred Red straight up the hill toward Verushki, with me sticking right on Red's tail so that Buck and I wouldn't lose them in the dark.

A few times, on that swift run up the hill, I could get a brief glimpse of what was happening in front of me, either by bursts of deafening, flashing lightning or sometimes, though it was harder to make out, just in the half-seen stormy shifting of darknesses ahead.

About a hundred feet from Verushki, Shad took his lasso off his saddle, but he didn't uncoil it to make any kind of a throw. And then, as Shad sped on toward him, the colonel either heard the hoofbeats or sensed some danger, for he spun his horse around, jerking swiftly at his saber. But the blade never cleared its scabbard as Red raced that last short distance and Shad hit Verushki a slamming, powerful blow on the side of the head with his lariat. There was just enough give in that tough coil of rope not to kill Verushki where he sat in the saddle. Otherwise, it might just as well have been a club. The colonel's hat went flying off into space, and he himself flew off his horse and went rolling across the muddy ground.

And when the colonel started to raise himself, still stunned, the first thing he saw was Shad sitting quietly there in the saddle, just above him, with a cocked revolver aimed right down at his head.

Verushki stood up slowly in the rain, instinctively reaching over to take hold of his horse's reins. Maybe it was his cossack training or maybe some kind of a pride in what was an obvious aristocratic sort of a background, but he showed absolutely no fear.

"Are you going to shoot?" he asked Shad, in about the same way he might have asked what time it was.

"Hand me your saber," Shad told him flatly.

Verushki frowned and hesitated, as curious as I was about this demand. Because sure as hell, Shad had no particular use for a saber. But he slowly took it out and handed it to Shad, handle first. Then, for the first and only time that I ever saw, he smiled. Or at least he showed most of his front teeth all at once. "Are you planning on killing me with my own blade?"

"Now your gun," Shad's voice stayed deadly flat, with nothing showing in it.

When Verushki handed his revolver up, Shad's hands were getting kind of full, so he handed the gun over to me and said, "Levi, throw that as far as you can."

I gave it a good heave, way out into the rain and the dark, wondering even more just what the hell Shad was up to.

And Verushki, with a whole lot more at stake, must have been wondering the same thing. "Either kill me or let me ride out," he demanded.

"Two things I want ya' t' remember," Shad said.

"I have an excellent memory."

"One, fifteen free cossacks made fools outta you and your whole goddamned garrison."

"I was aware of that possibility."

"More important, number two. Remember

that poor little bastard cossack a' yours who got bounced off his horse, an' what you did to 'im." Shad paused. "Remember that when you explain t' your men how come you lost your gun an' your saber *and* your horse all at once."

I would never have thought that anything could get to Verushki as much as those words, but they did. Even though he'd been unafraid of outright death, he took a step back, his hand tightening on the reins he was holding. "There is honor!"

"That makes ya' break a kid's neck?"

"Then *kill* me!" Verushki screamed, suddenly hysterical with fear.

"No such luck." Shad swung the saber and cut the reins so that Verushki was left holding two pieces of empty leather. Then Shad whacked the horse on the butt with the saber so that it went lunging off into the stormy night. And now, finished with the blade, Shad broke it over the pommel of his saddle and threw the handle half of it down into the muddy ground so that it stuck there.

Then he galloped away and I raced after him.

We got to the point of the herd, where Old Fooler and some of the braver head following close on his heels were already brisket-deep out into the rivers.

"Move 'em out!" Shad yelled, galloping full speed into the shallows of the Amur. There were a few shots from behind us that didn't sound too unfriendly, but who can tell, and there was a great, loud whooping and hollering that made itself heard against the crashing rain and the thunder. And pretty quick, with Old Fooler trailing Shad and Red, his nose just above the water, man and beast in one massive group were headed toward the far side.

It was a funny river to cross. Right in the middle of it we were suddenly on top of a high, firm sand bar so that every man, horse and cow there sort of reminded me of Christ walking on the water. And then we were back in the deeps, and not too much later we were straggling out onto the far side.

But this time, unlike Vladivostok, there was no fire to warm and dry ourselves by, and there was no time to get any sleep or even to sit around and grumble for a little while about all those damned hardships already faced and yet to be faced.

Shad and Rostov had determined that we were going to push on past the river as far north of Khabarovsk as we could get without falling flat on our tired faces.

On a small rise, I turned to take one last look at the tiny, flickering handful of lights that was

Khabarovsk, wrapped in that immensity of darkness.

It was such a small handful of lights that even my own hand, held up before me, was bigger.

And yet, somewhere within those pitiful few dim and fading lights trying to hold out against the great darkness filling all the rest of the world as far as my eyes could see, was Irenia. And somehow I could still feel and see there the spirit of those two big men who had been hanged.

Suddenly, I was afraid. Irenia had been friendly to all of us, and especially to me. And I'd given her that Apache Tear. If that pretty, black stone should somehow cause her any trouble or pain, it could really become a tear. — It could cause her to be hanged!

And that one Imperial Cossack had seen us together tonight!

With those silent words that aren't actually spoken but are so thunderous in the mind, I lowered my head and said to myself, "Oh, God, God, *God!*"

Shad rode up and sat his big Red beside me for just a moment. I knew he was looking where I'd been looking, and I'm pretty sure he was thinking what I'd been thinking.

Finally he said, "It's all right. The way she

is, Levi, makes it so."

Then he tured his big Red and rode away into the blackness that was north.

I was only half sure that what he'd said was right. But I was double sure that what he wanted most was just to make me feel easier.

I took one final look at those faint pinpoint lights trembling bravely against the dark in the distance across that wide river.

And then, knowing it was the only thing to do, I turned Buck and spurred him north, catching up with the men and the cows moving that same way.

None of us yet knew in that night of swift black movement and grinding rain that we had already lost our first man.

A good one.

Part Three

THE BATTLE OF BAKASKAYA

Diary Notes

The majority of incidents that befall us on our hazardous trek toward Bakaskaya tend to be too grim to contemplate, briefly or easily.

Aside from these harrowing times, there are a couple of pretty amusing things mixed in among them I guess, like when Shad is given a fairly large Siberian kitten. Or when me and a Tartar warrior manage to sneak up on each other one night and damnere give each other heart attacks upon the mutual surprise.

But otherwise, to be perfectly truthful, it's just too damned heartfelt and too hard for me to simply take pen in hand and make any short or casual notes.

The only thing to do, or at least the only thing I can do, is try to tell, as faithfully as possible, what happened before those of us who survived finally managed at last to come to that place called Bakaskaya.

21

We drove straight through the black night and the driving rain until late in the following morning, when the blackness above was at last slowly and angrily giving way to strips of bleak gray so that the sky looked like a never-ending ceiling of lead mixed with streaks of muddy milk.

The hard rain was easing off just a little as Shad signaled for a halt near a scattering of maple trees in the center of a broad plain that was surrounded in the distance by low hills. We didn't have to do much convincing to get the exhausted cows to stop. We'd been hollering ourselves hoarse all that black night over the noise of the rain and whopping them with our lariats to keep them moving at a good clip. All we had to do was stop yelling and leave them alone, and with the forward momentum gone, most of them sank down into the mud and grass of the plain like wiped-out drunks hitting their bedrolls after a heavy Saturday night. And strong as he was, Old Fooler was one of the first to sag down.

Rostov put a few men on watch, and then he and his cossacks joined the rest of us as Shad broke out two or three bottles of Jack Daniel's from a pack animal and started them around.

We were all drenched and half frozen, and I for one was so tired I didn't trust myself to dismount for fear of my legs buckling under me.

Old Keats took a healthy slug of the Daniel's and handed it to Slim who was standing next to him and Shad. "We must a' come over fifteen miles."

Slim took a drink and then held it up to me in the saddle. "I'd guess right close t' twenty."

Shiny Joe was drinking from another bottle. "One more night goin' north like that an' we oughtta damnere be at the goddamned North Pole."

I passed my bottle of Daniel's to Igor, who was next to me, still mounted.

And as I did so, I noticed a funny thing. Rostov had taken out some bottles of vodka, which were making the rounds. And with all of us kind of mingled there around Shad and Rostov, not one of us, cowboy or cossack, was paying a hell of a lot of attention to whether he was drinking bourbon or vodka. On second thought, I guess it wasn't so funny after all, but just a kind of a good and natural thing.

Shad started to frown, glancing around at us

through the still dim light and heavy rain. "Where's Dixie?"

Rufe looked off to one side. "His 'paloosa's over there, under the same tree as mine."

I followed Rufe's look, and Dixie's Appaloosa, Shiloh, was standing next to Rufe's Bobtail, but I got a hard, cold feeling inside me when I saw that Shiloh wasn't tied or even ground-reined. His reins were still strung up around the back of his neck.

"Who saw Dixie last?" Shad said, his voice now quiet and flat.

"I saw 'im when he went ahead a' me into the river," Crab said. "But Christ! In that dark ya' couldn't see more'n a few feet. An' that's the last I know."

"Oh my God!" Sammy murmured.

And I suddenly knew that I knew the answer.

"Your God what?" Shad demanded.

"I — I come of my horse in the river." Even in that downpour, Sammny now wet his lips. "I was drownin', went under. An' then all of a sudden he was right down there beside me in the water. An' he got me up an' got my hands gripped on m' horse's tail — an' I made it." He took a deep breath. "I thought he was right b'hind me!"

Natcho said quietly, "No. I was near you

403

when you came out. You were alone."

Sammy suddenly just slumped down over the pommel of his saddle, his face buried in his arms so that we wouldn't be able to see that he was crying.

After a second or so I said to Shad, "I'm goin' back t' look for 'im."

"You can't hardly sit up, you're s' tired," Slim said.

"I ain't tired. I'm the one to go."

"You?" Old Keats asked.

"Me." It was a dumb answer, but it was all I had.

Sammy raised his head and just barely managed to say, "I'll go with ya', Levi."

"No."

And Shad understood. "Take Shiloh."

Igor and Rostov spoke a few words in quiet Russian as I rode over to Shiloh and took his reins to lead him.

I'd only gotten a hundred yards or so back along the way toward the river when Igor rode up on his Blackeye and pulled alongside me.

"What're you doin'?" I said.

"I'm going with you."

"I don't need ya'."

"I know."

It's hard to argue with a statement like that, and I sure didn't feel much like arguing anyway. I didn't think there was one chance in hell of finding Dixie. Christ! If worst hadn't come to worst, in or out of the river, he could have grabbed onto Shiloh or yelled a rebel yell to get somebody's attention, or maybe even somehow got himself aboard a longhorn just to keep up with the night's drive. I tried thinking maybe he'd broken a leg or knocked himself out on a tree branch, but those ideas just didn't ring true.

There were a thousand other thoughts that didn't work any better. He could have been swept downstream and then swam out. Hell, the river wasn't moving all that quick. Or maybe he could have simply been thrown by Shiloh, though we hadn't been moving all that swift and fast.

He just had to be dead.

And he was.

I saw Dixie just one more and last time.

When we pulled up beside the Amur River, we hadn't yet seen a thing in all that immensity of gray, pelting rain. And then, on one of those sand bars pretty far out in the river, I saw a tree branch that was caught against it. And caught against the tree branch was a piece of cloth. It took a moment for me to see that that piece of cloth was Dixie's plaid shirt, and it took a little longer to see that Dixie was still in it, sort of floating part up and part down, like a dead fish.

I ran Buck down to the river's edge, to go and get him. But then, as though God felt like playing a simple, mean trick on me and on the whole world, the tree branch shifted in the tide and Dixie was tugged away by the ebbing, muddy water and disappeared beneath its surface.

And he just never showed up again.

Far up and across the river you could just barely see a little of Khabarovsk — gray buildings with the gray rain against a gray sky.

Last night I'd thought I'd never see Khabarovsk again, and I'd never dreamed that I wouldn't see Dixie alive again.

Funny as hell, the way the world works.

I must have been looking at the river for a long time, because Igor finally put his hand on my shoulder, gently reminding me that we couldn't stay there forever.

And we went away.

On the way back Igor rode ahead, leading Shiloh.

Buck just followed behind because I wasn't pushing him much in the way of instructions or encouragement. The pain and sorrow in my mind kept slamming home the fact that in my own dumb way I'd done a whole lot too much pushing already. I'd pushed Dixie real hard, to the point of knocking him ass over teakettle, to try to show him that men ought to have a certain kind of nobility and a sense of duty toward others.

Somewhere along the line, Dixie had picked up real good on that nobility and that sense of duty toward others.

And it had killed him.

And it was my fault.

Finally, toward the end of that dark, bitter day, Igor and I caught back up to the herd that was now being driven in a north-by-westerly direction.

I was grateful that not much explaining had to be done. Shiloh's still empty saddle pretty much told the story all by itself.

Purse, Big Yawn and Sammy were with the pack animals and the remuda, behind the herd. Igor went on ahead to join Shad as I led Shiloh over to the remuda and pulled up. I was about to get off and unsaddle the Appaloosa, but Purse spurred back and took a look at me. He swung down before I could. "I'll do it."

Sammy rode up silently, the skin under his eyes black from worry and grief.

Big Yawn rode back too, his huge, craggy face hard and thoughtful, and it seemed like about ten minutes between each time that any-body said anything.

Purse pulled slowly at the cinch strap to loosen it. "See 'im?"

I nodded just once. "River got 'im."

Finally, Sammy said in a whisper, "I shoulda gone back with ya', Levi."

I shook my head. "No need."

"Hadn't been f'r me —" His voice choked and stopped.

I couldn't tell him, or ever let him know, Dixie had deliberately followed behind him in the river. "Hell, Sammy, he'd a' helped me 'r you 'r anybody else who was in a fix back there."

Sammy glanced at me with a fleeting look of relief in his sorrow-filled eyes. What I'd said helped a little. But right then nothing could help enough, and he rode away again to be by himself.

Big Yawn now reached over and untied the bedroll on Shiloh, then took off the saddlebags. "I'll put these here possibles a' his on one a' the packs."

Big Yawn could have simply left those things on the saddle, but in his own way he was just trying to be helpful. And then he said, "Too damn bad, Levi."

"Yeah." Purse nodded.

"Well, hell," I said quietly, "he was a friend t' both a' you too."

"Yeah, but —" Big Yawn ran out of words and rode off with the bedroll and saddlebags.

Buck was as ready to fall down as I was, but I spurred him off now as Purse sent Shiloh toward the remuda with a slap on the rump.

I headed on around the herd to catch up with Rostov and take over my normal duties as messenger boy. And all along the way every puncher I passed had something quiet and sympathetic to say, as though Dixie'd been my goddamned brother or something.

Finally I caught up with Rostov, riding far point about a mile ahead of the herd.

He glanced at me. Then, with no mention of Dixie, he said flatly, "Did you see any sign of a pursuit?"

With everyone else feeling so bad about Dixie, this came as kind of a shock. I hesitated and then said harshly, "No! All we saw was a dead man in a muddy river!"

And then he said another thing that threw me also. "I liked that fight you had with him, with fists."

"Well I'm glad you did, because neither one of us did, because bein' pounded on ain't all that much fun!"

And then he really got to me.

"His death was not your responsibility," he said quietly, his eyes searching the far rainswept distances ahead.

The best answer I could come up with was "Who said it was?"

"When he helped that young Sammy, he did so of his own free will and volition."

I had to guess what "volition" meant but it wasn't too hard, and the talk was reaching down into me where it made my voice unsteady. "He asked me if Sammy was scared. He was watchin' him all the way in that water."

Rostov's eyes were still searching far ahead. "Anyone who could see, knew that Dixie was following in your footsteps."

My voice had been unsteady before, but it was ready to crack now. "There ain't no footsteps t' follow in a goddamn big bunch a' water."

And then Rostov hit me hardest of all. "As you are following in Shad's."

That voice of mine just wasn't working at all by then, so I didn't, and couldn't, say a thing.

Rostov's eyes never left the far distances ahead. "Shad has made you know that you are responsible for others. And in turn, you gave that gift to Dixie." He paused. "Would you or Shad have ignored Sammy or done anything other than Dixie did last night?"

I couldn't talk, but neither could I help but think of how Rostov and his cossacks were ready to die for the people, and for the spirit, of Bakaskaya.

And then he went on. "The gift Shad has given you and you gave Dixie, of caring for others, is sometimes hard to live with and always hard to die with." He paused again. "But it is, and forever will be, the most treasured gift in the world."

We rode on in silence, and a little later the night's black darkness started to close in, seeming to squeeze away the now slowing rain, until finally the night was full upon us and the rain had stopped.

There was a broad meadow before us, and we camped there, our fires close to each other. I must have been starved, but I didn't feel like eating, so I just took off my boots and climbed into my bedroll.

Before I'd passed out completely, Slim kneeled beside me. "Hey, Levi?"

"Yeah?"

"Shad an' Old Keats're out on the herd now, an' I'm workin' out a schedule. You feel up t' takin' the late graveyard?"

"Sure."

And it seemed like I'd just leaned my head back when Slim was pushing me again and it was dead black night and time to go.

I pulled on my boots and saddled Buck, who felt about the same as I did, and rode out to relieve Natcho.

But even through all my exhaustion, the hammering, relentless sorrow I felt about Dixie just wouldn't go away. That damned lifeless plaid shirt, and the lifeless body inside it, and that terribly gray, muddy water.

In a way, then, it reminded me of that poor, sad cow when we went off the boat at Vladivostok. And I couldn't help but wonder how many lives are taken mercilessly by the cold, unfeeling waters of the world.

With all those grim thoughts, the wrong I'd done seemed more and more unforgivable. If I'd just minded my own goddamned business. If I just hadn't told Dixie that Sammy was scared of the river. And the craziest part of it all was that I didn't know whether to feel worse about the Dixie who was or the Dixie who was starting to be.

Given time, instead of death, that simple sonofabitch could have been great.

About then, while I was blaming myself all over again for Dixie, Rostov's words came to mind. And I knew that anything that brilliant bastard had ever said was undoubtedly right.

But just being right, even having all the

rightness there is on earth, couldn't do much to make me feel any better. Life and death isn't right and wrong. They're both part of a giant, natural right, but that doesn't make death any easier to take.

I was surely grateful to Rostov for having given me at least some kind of an edge against the terrible way I felt. But out here in the black night, and by myself, I suddenly felt as lonely and broken as I guess Dixie must have felt in those dark waters, being pulled and twisted, lifelessly and endlessly.

It was then that a strange, wordless and wonderful thing happened.

There were hoofbeats from behind and off to one side, and a moment later Shad reined his big Red up beside me, pulling to a stop.

He didn't do or say anything, and I wasn't in any great shape to talk. He just sat there beside me quietly, looking out over the shadowed, sleeping herd. He'd already been up most of this second sleepless night in a row, and should have been in his bedroll and out like a rock by now. But he knew the rough feelings I'd be having, so he'd put off sleep to ride out this one last time. And somehow, just by his silent presence, he was sharing the pain of those deep feelings within me, and wordlessly giving me part of his own inner strength.

It was a sad, rich, warm time.

And then, finally, he rode away into the dark.

Being a man, I sure as hell could never let on to Shad how deeply I was moved. So at last I told it softly to Buck instead. "I'll tell you somethin'." I looked off, where Shad was safely gone, and Buck twisted one ear back wondering who I was talking to. "I love you most, Shad, for the things you never said to me."

22

Along toward morning the rain started to come down heavy again, and it lasted six more days and six nights without stopping for one minute or even slowing down enough for us to get at least slightly dried out. And in its own cruel way, there is nothing that is finally more brutally depressing than a forever hostile sky flooding down constant, battering waves of chilling raindrops that go on and on without end.

We must have made about seventy miles through that everlasting sea of shallow water and mud, but every drenched, exhausting mile was damn hard won. The mud was like glue, and often as not the horses and cattle were plowing along nearly knee-deep in it. On the fourth day one speckled, lop-horned cow and her yearling calf came within an eyelash of being buried altogether in the thick oozing stuff. Rufe happened to spot her as she was bawling helplessly, stuck more than shoulder-deep in the soft, shifting, deep muck at the bottom of an arroyo. Her calf was in worse shape, with only its small muzzle sticking desperately up out of the rain-driven mire. Four men slid down there with ropes to tie around them and managed to finally haul them out to firmer ground. But by the time they'd rescued the cow and calf, every inch of the men, from head to toe, was covered with a thick layer of sticky mud, which didn't add much to their general cheerfulness.

Most of us were beginning to figure that hell wasn't made out of fire and brimstone after all, but was made out of mud and rain.

On the sixth morning, as pitch-black night and gray-black dawn fought against each other vaguely and dimly in the east, all us Slash-Diamonders except for Shad and the men on herd were hunched miserably down in our slickers around a campfire that had its own special little fight going, spitting and hissing angrily as it struggled to survive against the rain. And most of us grouped silently around it felt pretty much the same bitter way the fire sounded, like plain furiously spitting back at the blinding, unending torrent.

Mushy was pouring himself some coffee and Crab, next to him, held out his cup. "I'll take some too."

"Git it y'rself!" Mushy put the pot right back past Crab's outstretched cup and onto the fire.

"Well fuck you!" Crab reached out and poured his own.

Acting like that wasn't usually Mushy's style, but almost everybody there was in a short-tempered, mean mood that was just shy of being downright savage.

It seemed to me that Slim and Old Keats gave each other a brief, expressionless glance, and then Slim said easily, "By God, I swear we coulda made it this far, in all this water, without ever gittin' offa that goddamned big boat we was on."

Old Keats took a sip of coffee. "I'm reminded of forty days and forty nights of rain. All of you remember that, of course, being conscientious students of the Bible."

Several of the man gave him darkly annoyed glances, and Rufe said gruffly, "I ain't no con-scientious student a' nothin'!"

416

"Anybody brought out a Bible right now," Mushy snarled, "and I'd shove it up his ass!"

"Now hold on, you fellas," Slim said very quietly and seriously. "A man c'n learn from damnere anythin', if he just puts 'is mind to it. Even the Bible. An' I just got me a hunch that Ol' Keats is thinkin' on the very same notion as me." He paused. "An' it just well might be goddamned important t' all of us."

"Thinkin' on what?" Big Yawn had been one of the rescuers of the speckled cow and her calf, and he still had small bits of hard-caked mud on him here and there to prove it. He was so fed up with everything that I don't think he knew how harsh and tough his voice was coming out. *Well?*"

Deadly serious and thoughtful, Slim said, "It just might be the answer t' all our problems. An' it sure beats the hell outta all a' you sittin' around here, gradually workin' yourselves up t'ward tearin' each other limb from limb. What d' you think, Keats?"

Keats frowned in deep concentration. "I think you're right, Slim. It'd take a little work, but at least it would get us and the cows comfortable and dry and out of all this rain and misery."

"Us *and* the cows?" Rufe frowned. *"Nothin'* can keep us an' all them dumb beasts outta the rain!"

"Frankly, Keats," Slim said, a little muffed, "I ain't sure it's even worth tellin' these dumb bastards what we can do."

"What in *hell can* we do?" Crab demanded. And by now the rest of us were all staring at them, curious and hopeful as we waited.

"*Well?*" Mushy half shouted. "F'r *Christ's* sakes, *what?*"

"It's just as simple as hell," Keats explained. "All we have t' do is build us an ark."

While everyone else slowly reacted, staring with vacant disbelief at Keats, Slim now plunged ahead. "By *God*, Keats, ya' got right t' their simple hearts. Just look at all them grateful, water-soaked eyes."

Big Yawn finally almost yelled, "*Goddamn, sonofabitch!*"

"See?" Slim said to Keats. "Big Yawn's already gettin' excited about it!"

"You dirty *bastards!*" Crab snarled, but for the first time in days he was holding back a grin rather than a inner anger.

"I take it that that's our first negative vote," Keats said to Slim.

"Hell, Crab," Slim argued, "try t' be reasonable f'r once. Ol' Noah got two a' every livin' animal on his ark, so us gittin' that Slash-D herd aboard ours ain't gonna pose no problem at all."

Rufe was shaking his head slowly. "You misleadin' *pricks!*" he grumbled. But like everybody else, his whole outlook was changing for the better.

"Misleading?" Keats looked wounded. "We said right up front it'd be a little work."

"That's right." Slim nodded gravely. "All we need for starts is one a' you fellas t' volunteer t' run out an' chop down a couple thousand trees."

Crab stood up and poured the last drops of his coffee into the fire. "Just one nice thing 'bout you two bastards," he muttered. "Y'r sense a' humor's the only dry thing f'r miles around."

"Watch it," Mushy told Crab. "Wouldn't want t' dampen their spirits."

"Well, hell, Slim." Old Keats shrugged his shoulders. "Small-minded men have always made fun of us geniuses."

"Well, screw 'em." Slim grunted. "I wouldn't build 'em no ark now if they begged me."

"One blessin' about all this goddamned rain," Rufe put in. "Every one of us gits t' have a wet dream every night."

And that's the good, relaxed way it now started to be.

A little later, when Shad rode up and said, "Time t' move out," there was a little easy horseplay among some of the men as they walked off. And Purse, looking at the untended fire quickly dying in the rain, called after them, "Hey! Somebody bring me some water t' put this out!"

It wasn't exactly that our whole greasy-sack outfit was miraculously and instantly overjoyed about everything in life. But the sullen resentment and anger that had been silently building up just wasn't there anymore.

Keats and Slim were near me, and as I tossed away what was left of my coffee, Keats said, "Slim, we ought t' go into that new thing they're startin' up, vaudeville."

"Huh?" Slim said as he and I both frowned, not knowing the word.

"All ya' do is make jokes that make people feel better, an' damn if ya' don't get paid for it."

"Christ," Slim said as they started away, "I'm ready right now."

A minute later, swinging up into Buck's saddle, I was thinking that if anybody ever got paid for making somebody else feel better, Slim and Old Keats sure as hell deserved an extra month's bonus salary. The men mounting around me were no longer grimly silent, but were just naturally cussing out their horses, the rain or each other, and sometimes all three at once. And now and then you could hear some equally natural, low laughter among them.

As I reined Buck out and away from the others, Shad rode up beside me. He spoke quietly, glancing keenly at the others. "Encouragin', them gettin' t' like the rain s' much."

"With much more of it, boss, we figure we c'n build an ark." He looked at me and I added, "Slim an' Keats' idea."

"Sounds like." Shad squinted briefly up against the rain and the sky. "If this was Montana, it'd quit t'day. In five, six hours."

He rode away, and before spurring on to join Rostov I looked up where he'd been looking. The sky was a million ugly miles of gray-streaked, rain-swept blackness, and it hadn't changed one damn little bit since yesterday or any of the days before.

Five or six hours later, the rain stopped.

Rostov and I had been mounting a low rise about two miles ahead of the herd, which was still out of our sight beyond some rounded hills behind us.

And then, as though an invisible giant had suddenly put a protective hand over us, the torrent of falling rain was instantly gone. It happened so fast I didn't quite believe it, especially with water still dripping off the front of my hat, and tending to fool me.

But the noise and the darkness were gone. The abrupt silence was so complete that I thought for a moment I'd gone deaf. And the sudden light of the sun was blinding in its brightness. Rostov pointed off, and I turned, blinking, to see the damnedest sight. There was an immense, solid wall of dark, almost impenetrable rain that stretched and roared as far as the eye could see, and it was rushing away from us more swiftly than any horse could ever gallop. One instant an entire plain would be drenched and nearly invisible and in the next moment, as that final, black curtain of rain swept over and beyond it, the plain would be a soggy, muddy field of grass that was now, suddenly, basking in the sun.

"An interesting phenomenon," Rostov said.

All I could think of to add was *"Jesus."*

And by then the great black wall of rain, with occasional bolts of lightning flashing briefly within it, was already a mile or so away as it receded swiftly in the distance.

The huge, burning sun went to work quickly in the now clear blue sky, and by nightfall most of the world around us was just about dry again. At supper our spirits were way up, and Old Keats and Slim had to take a lot of criticism about the idea they'd had that morning.

Crab pretty much summed it up over a serving of beans that had stayed steaming hot in the plate for the first time in a week. "All right, you dumb bastards. If we'd gone ahead an' built us that goddamned ark this mornin', what the hell'd we do with it now?"

"Christ, that's simple," Slim said. "We'd make the world's biggest outhouse outta it. At least a thousand-seater."

Old Keats nodded. "Of course if we put in different levels, it'd be better to be sittin' t'ward the top than t'ward the bottom."

I turned in early, my bedroll warm and comfortable around me. For about two seconds I considered the beautiful difference between wet and dry, and then I was out.

Slim woke me for my turn on the herd, the late graveyard. I rode out to relieve Purse, and an hour or so later Shad suddenly appeared alongside me.

Out there in the wide, dark meadow stretching below us, even the cattle were now feeling a hundred per cent better, and a few of them were grunting and lowing back and forth in quiet, contented cow talk.

"Couldn't be more peaceful," I said to Shad. "Why don't you go back an' grab forty winks?"

He was silent for a long moment. Then, leaning forward and rubbing Red between the ears, he said, "No — not yet."

From the far side of the herd Big Yawn softly sang a couple of choruses of "I'm Leaving Ohio," which would normally be enough to make anybody leave if they were free to.

But still Shad remained, watching and listening, and seeming to almost be damnere smelling at the clear, unmoving air.

And then, very quietly and without saying anything, Rostov rode his big black out of the night and up to us.

Both of them just sitting there silently was getting kind of spooky. After a long moment I said, "Much as I'm enjoyin' all this cheerful company, you fellas know somethin' that I don't?"

They both ignored me, and Shad spoke in a low voice to Rostov. "I c'n feel somethin' out there, but it ain't nothin' I know about."

Rostov nodded. "I believe I do. But we'll both know soon."

This was getting downright scary. In my mind's eye I could see an entire army of Tartars sneaking up on us through the dark so stealthily that they made absolutely no sound, but moved along like ghosts.

And then the peaceful silence was suddenly shattered by the fiercest, most horrifying and earth-shaking noise I'd ever heard. It sounded like a thousand cougars lined up side by side and roaring furiously in perfect unison.

Buck reared nervously out of his half sleep, and you could sense the startled herd starting to mill around, instantly spooked.

Holding Buck down as the noise abruptly stopped I said, "What the *Christ* was *that?*"

As I was speaking, the early full moon appeared quickly from behind scudding clouds, filling the meadow and surrounding hills with sudden, silvery light. Beyond the herd, on the crest of a hill, I had a brief glimpse of some kind of a huge beast before it streaked out of sight over the far side of the crest, moving with incredible speed.

Rostov said to Shad, "Once you gave me a Montana puppy." He nodded toward where the beast had disappeared. "In return, I'd like to present you with a Siberian kitten."

"Thanks," Shad said dryly. "Who's gonna put the pink ribbon around its neck?"

"What the hell *is* it?" I asked.

"A Siberian tiger. They're larger than Bengals or any other species." Rostov was studying the far moonlit hills keenly. "That one over there will weigh approximately a thousand pounds."

Shad rubbed his chin thoughtfully. "All these strange smells, an' then the moon comin' out bright, maybe scared 'im off."

Rostov shrugged slightly. "He's probably hungry from not hunting during the rains. Also, at this time of year he has a mate and possibly some youngsters to take care of." He hesitated. "And these snow tigers are very brave."

"Then let's go check 'im out."

Shad rode down the moonlit slope with Rostov at his side, and figuring I was somehow included, I spurred after them.

The three of us were pushing our way through the now close-packed, defensively grouped cattle when the tiger hit the herd. Moving silently, but with the speed and impact of a cannon ball, he appeared from nowhere and charged a big bull longhorn standing a few feet out and away from the others. And that particular bull, for whatever personal reasons, felt like standing its ground instead of running, so it whirled swiftly toward the big onrushing cat.

And longhorns, if they feel like fighting, are among the toughest creatures that the Good Lord ever created. With their powerful hooves and sharp, raking horns, they've been known to battle grizzly bears to a standoff. And one of them, in a belligerent mood, actually routed and damnere demolished an entire regiment of

General Winfield Scott's army on its way to Mexico.

So that unsuspecting cat was running up against a whole lot more than a simple Guernsey milk cow.

But by the same token, that bull longhorn sure as hell didn't know what it was facing either.

The whole fight, including everything, lasted maybe as long as one second. The longhorn swung at empty air with its great horns and the flying cat whacked him on the side of his massive head with one huge paw. The longhorn may have been dead, its neck broken, as it hit the ground. But one way or the other it was surely dead an instant later as the tiger whirled and crunched his teeth down into the back of its neck. And then, though it was hard to believe, that big, powerful cat actually started trotting away, half carrying and half dragging the huge, lifeless carcass of the bull.

It had all happened so fast that Big Yawn, even at a full gallop around the edge of the herd, was still a distance away. He fired a wild shot toward the tiger, and at the unfamiliar sound of the gun, the big cat dropped the longhorn, hesitated briefly, and then dashed away.

A few moments later six of us, including Sergeant Nick and Igor, who'd been on lookout, rode up to the dead bull. Behind us, the herd was uneasy but not panicked. The tiger's earlier roar had scared them more than the quick, silent death of one of them. They were settling back down, and it looked to me, all in all, like we'd gotten off pretty easy.

But Shad, mortally hating to ever lose one of his herd, was quietly furious. His eyes hard, he glared from the dead bull to where the tiger had disappeared. Then, jerking his rifle from its scabbard, he rode swiftly off in that direction. And the rest of us followed him.

Just naturally, we fanned out behind Shad in the moonlight so that pretty soon, between all six of us, we were covering a pretty wide swath. And about a mile from the herd we rousted out the tiger. He'd been holed up in some rocks at the beginning of a wide plateau that narrowed down to a point farther on. Big Yawn, riding not far from Sergeant Nick, accidentally busted him out as he approached the rocks.

Not yet knowing it was in a trap, the tiger bounded away from the rocks to the triangular plateau beyond, making a good thirty feet with that first effortless leap of his, and then speeding on across the moon-drenched earth.

We followed as fast as we could, riding closer in together as the slice of land grew narrower.

And finally, slowing down, the big cat got as far as he could go and saw that there were only two things he could do. He could charge right back through us or take what was roughly a two-hundred-foot sheer jump off that final small piece of plateau where he was.

At the edge he turned back, snarling, and we pulled up in a ragged line about a hundred yards away from him.

He was dead, and somehow he realized it.

But he wasn't afraid.

That big, beautiful bastard was going to go down fighting. His eyes were alive and glowing, even in the cold moonlight, as he slowly shifted his majestic head to size us up, taking in a thousand small details that would make him determine any possible chance of escaping through us.

And God, how beautiful and brave he was, roaring defiance and majesty toward us in what I swear he knew to be his final dark moments of danger and death.

Near Shad, Rostov said, "There is your Siberian kitten, Northshield."

Shad raised his rifle. The rest of us were silent, and I was busy getting a lump in my throat.

Then, sighting in on the magnificent tiger, he called to Big Yawn, who was off to the far left. "Yawn! Come 'ere!"

And as Big Yawn was riding over toward us, Shad fired. His bullet slammed into and whined off a rock near the rear end of the tiger, and that made the giant cat's mind up. My guess was that flying pieces of rock stung the tiger's butt and tail, but however that may be, he took off like striped lightning on greased wheels at the empty space that Big Yawn had just vacated.

And he was gone so fast that the human eye could hardly keep up with him and watch him go.

Shad slowly returned his rifle to its saddle scabbard. "Goddamn," he said quietly. "Missed."

No one said anything, but I couldn't help but think of the long ago time when Rostov had given the Montana puppy its freedom.

And after that, there was nothing left to do but ride back to the herd, which was settled down as though nothing had ever happened.

It was almost breaking daylight by then, and we were ready to move out within the hour.

There was only one problem, and that was the dead longhorn. I'd already joined up with Rostov, and we rode over to where it was lying after being dragged halfway up the hill by the huge tiger.

Shad got there at about the same time, and the two men studied each other for a moment.

It was Shad who first spoke. "Your kitten will be back."

That was a lot of beef, a lot of meat and life lying there, and Rostov knew it. "He will be back. But that kitten is not mine. He's yours."

Shad shrugged. "I got a strong hunch he thinks he's his own boss." And then he swung down from Red and glanced at the dead bull. "We'll leave this carcass for 'im. It'll keep him an' his family in groceries for a week or two — plenty a' time for us t' be long gone from here."

"Sure." I nodded. "An' I guess, boss, that's the only reason for leavin' it then?"

He gave me a hard look. "That's right."

Rostov said quietly, "That's an excellent way for a man to handle the situation we have here."

Shad remounted. "It's just a natural man's way, anywhere in the world." He rode down to the herd, and the cattle now started moving out with whoops and hollers from the cowboys encouraging and pushing them along their way.

As Rostov and I galloped to our point position far ahead, four of the words that Shad had used kept ringing in my mind. Those were the words "anywhere in the world."

Shad had somehow come to be anywhere,

and everywhere, in the world.

After riding in silence for a long time, Rostov finally said, "Northshield gave a full bull to the people of Vladivostok, and now to the tiger. In both cases, he was right."

"He mostly tends t' be right," I said. And then I couldn't help adding, "But he's also kinda partial t' that tiger."

Rostov looked at me with those dark, penetrating eyes of his. And then he said quietly, "He's not just partial to that tiger, Levi — he is that tiger."

And then, in silence, we continued to ride on.

23

The next few weeks were about as peaceful and easygoing as any bunch of fellas could ask for. The weather stayed sunny and warm, and the nights were balmy and clear. The Siberian moon looming hugely over us was often so silvery bright you could read a book by it at midnight, if you had a book to read. Matter of fact, Old Keats proved the above fact by doing just the opposite. He went to doing a little writing while he was on the relaxed, contented herd at night and there was nothing much better to do.

I caught him at it in the middle of one brightly moonlit graveyard shift. Near camp I saddled Buck and rode out to relieve Keats, taking my time. From the top of a low hill, he could be seen easily, sitting his horse by the sleeping herd, his back to me. He was doing something with both hands, and I realized a minute later he'd been whittling with his pocketknife to sharpen the short stub of a pencil he sometimes carried on him. As I walked Buck on down the hill, his hooves nearly soundless in the soft earth, Old Keats stuck the fresh-sharpened pencil into his mouth to wet the lead. And then he started, or maybe continued, to put down something slowly and laboriously in a small writing tablet.

As I got closer to Keats, I heard him whisper two words to himself. "Beautiful. – Beautiful."

He was so wrapped up in whatever he was doing that I was just about near enough to reach out and touch him before he knew I was here. And when he finally did see me, his reaction was so sudden and startled that he damnere jumped out of his saddle.

"God*damn* it, Levi!" he grumbled, quickly putting away his pencil and writing tablet.

"What's the idea a' sneakin' up on me that way?"

"Well, hell," I said, a little taken aback. "It just never occurred t' me t' fire some warnin' shots."

And then I suddenly understood, or at least was pretty sure that I did. Ever since I could remember as a kid, there'd been vague rumors that Old Keats, on very rare occasions when he was really deeply moved by something or other, actually did turn his hand to poetry. But if that was partly the reason for his nickname "The Poet," he was awful secretive and touchy as hell about it. Nobody had ever been allowed to read one word of anything he'd ever written down, so that's why after all those years the talk about him writing poetry had remained only a rumor.

But still, especially after that uncalled-for and strange reaction of his, I couldn't help but ask him innocently, "What ya' been writin'?"

"None a' your goddamn business!"

For some reason, as grouchy and unreasonable as he was being, I couldn't bring myself to be mad back at him. "I guess you're right. It ain't."

Still frowning, he muttered, "Just don't care t' be snuck up on."

"I really am sorry, Keats."

His anger eased off gradually now, and he started filling his pipe. "Didn't mean t' jump on ya' that way."

"Well I guess I coulda said hello or cleared m' throat 'r somethin'."

"Oh, hell," he said, lighting a match. "Truth is, I'm just gettin' old an' crotchety." He puffed on the pipestem until the tobacco was glowing, then blew out the match, broke it and threw it away. "It was me who was in the wrong, Levi. An' I'm sorry."

Before I could reply, he abruptly turned his horse and rode off back toward camp. And watching him go, I knew as plain as could be that neither one of us had been in the wrong. I'd just happened to catch him writing down something that was, somehow, so dear to him that he simply couldn't bring himself to admit it, or even talk about it.

As he rode over the hill and out of sight, I murmured a thought to myself without even thinking about the fact I was repeating the word he'd used earlier, "You beautiful old sonofabitch."

Buck ignored what I said. I guess, by then, he was getting used to me talking to myself.

And then I shook the reins a little and began to walk Buck slowly around the edge of the drowsing herd.

During those easygoing weeks, Mushy, who was a sometime shoemaker, started using his spare time to fix our boots, most of which were getting pretty beat-up. To help in this worthy cause, Shad let him off night duty, so whenever we'd make camp Mushy would get out his trusy old dollar-fifty Economic Cobbler outfit, with its one upside-down iron foot sticking up, and hammer away at some needy person's soles and heels.

The cossacks were impressed as hell with Mushy's cobbling artistry, so he offered to repair any of their boots that needed work. He must have had requests for nearly thirty pairs to be fixed, all in all.

We were eating on a first-class basis during those good days, too. The cossacks were riding guard far enough out on the flanks to manage to spot and bring down plenty of fresh game. One time they even came in with an impossible animal that they claimed was so rare they had to cook it in their own special way for all of us. The mysterious animal was an antelope, but the damn thing's thick coat was as pure wool as any sheep who ever walked.

It tasted so good that over supper there was only a halfhearted argument between some of us Slash-Diamonders about whether the strange beast actually was an antelope or a sheep.

Chakko finally settled the question by saying flatly, "Eat antelope. Make coat from sheepskin."

Slim nodded. "That kind a' common sense sure cuts through all the bullshit."

"Wish I had that much logic in my chess," Old Keats said, moving off to where Lieutenant Bruk was now setting up the chess set that he'd hand-carved by himself. The two of them had gotten more and more into the habit of playing really hard at that game whenever they had a chance, and despite his claims to the contrary, Keats was evidently holding his own pretty well.

And then, a few nights later, Mushy finally finished the last pair of boots he had to fix, which belonged to Slim.

"Christ," Slim said, pulling on the roughouts that Mushy had made like new. "Fine times an' good boots is about all anybody c'n ever hope t' want. This here drive's turnin' out t' be a regular goddamn picnic."

And that just about summed up all of our good, easy feelings.

At least it did until late the next day, when we first saw that big way-off pile of rocks.

Rostov and I were in our normal position ahead of the others, riding far point. For the last few hours the land had been getting rougher, and we were moving into high, rugged hills that stretched brokenly up toward distant mountain peaks.

As he approached the crest of the ridge, Rostov suddenly pulled up and dismounted in one swift, flowing motion. A little behind him, I did the same thing as fast as I could. And then crouching out of sight in the gently waving waist-high grass, we went quickly to the top, Rostov taking out his telescope.

There wasn't one damn thing moving up ahead of us. And before I'd figured out what we were supposed to be looking at, or even looking for, Rostov lowered his telescope from his eye, then handed it to me.

"The top of the next ridge," he said grimly.

The ridge was over two miles away, but squinting through the scope I finally made something out. What had looked to my naked eye like one huge, unusually square but natural rock was actually hundreds or maybe thousands of smaller rocks that had been stacked up in the shape of a massive, solid square that was about twenty feet high. And somehow, the fact that the vast, senseless thing was man-made gave it an ugly, spooky feeling.

With a puzzled look, I handed Rostov back his telescope. He raised it once more to silently study the faraway ridge a moment longer, and then he at last stood up, slowly pushing the scope back down into itself to its shortest length. As I stood up too, he spoke again, his voice still grim. "There is no one over there. At least no one living."

At that distance, even with the telescope, how he could be so sure of himself about no one being over there beat the hell out of me.

We went quickly back down the slope and re-mounted as Lieutenant Bruk and Sergeant Nick, who must have been wondering what was going on, came galloping swiftly up to us.

The three men spoke briefly in Russian and then Nick spurred back to spread the news, whatever the news was, which nobody had seen fit to bother telling me.

Rostov and Bruk, with me close behind them, now rode up over the nearby crest and moved at a walk out onto the plain leading toward the bunch of piled rocks on the far ridge. Both of them were searching the distance ahead keenly, but there didn't seem to be any immediate danger. So after a while I couldn't resist pushing Buck up almost abreast of Rostov and saying with quiet, intense curiosity, "What is it, sir?"

Equally quietly, as though his two words were explaining everything, he said, "An *obo*."

That sure was one hell of an answer, and I

was sorely tempted to mention how grateful I was to him for letting me in on all that priceless information. But he suddenly waved the two of us to a stop. Then he lunged his black ahead fifty yards or so through the deep grass to lean down and pick up something that was stuck on a brambly kind of a bush. Finally he raised his arm, signaling that it was all right for us to come on.

When we pulled up near Rostov, he held out his hand for Bruk to see what he'd found. It was nothing but a few long red threads that looked like they'd been torn from a piece of red cloth on the brambles, hardly enough of it all together to sew a button on a shirt.

Bruk nodded thoughtfully, studying the ground around us, and Rostov said, "They were here before the rains, at least a month ago."

For some reason or other they both were relieved at finding those threads of cloth, but I was getting more curious and puzzled every minute. So finally I blurted out the first of a number of questions bothering me. "What the goddamn hell, sir, is an *obo?*"

Rostov glanced at me with a brief, impatient frown, as though I should have somehow known or guessed the answer. "It's a Tartar religious symbol." And then he rode on ahead a short distance, still looking carefully at both the nearby ground and the far distances on each side of us and before us.

More relaxed now, as we walked our horses on across the wide plain, Bruk reached for his long-stemmed clay pipe and started to fill it.

"Damn it," I muttered, my pride unaccountably hurt bacause of my ignorance, "how the hell am I supposed t' know what a goddamned *obo* is?"

Lighting his pipe, Bruk gave me a quick, keen look. "What would you have guessed it to be?"

"Hell, just t' look at − a landmark?"

He nodded quietly, as though agreeing with me, but when he spoke he said, "No. If you really look, Levi, every ridge and mountain in our sight can serve as its own landmark. That *obo* was built as a sacred offering from the Tartars to whatever gods there may be in this area."

Funny, Bruk talking that way about "really looking." It reminded me, somehow, of Old Keats telling me way back there on the boat that a man had to see with more than just his eyes. The similar way those two old fellas were in a lot of ways sort of forced a fella to stop and think sometimes.

By now we were halfway across the wide plain. The sun was sinking lower in the west.

And the *obo* ahead of us seemed to grow larger and spookier at about the same slow rate of speed that the sun was sinking.

"How can you an' the captain be so sure there ain't no Tartars waitin' for us up there?" I asked uneasily.

"The birds, even the most timid ones, are flying and landing over there without fear."

That answer was so simple that I didn't even dare ask how the threads on that thorny bush meant the Tartars had gone through here a month ago, before the rain. Probably, when it was raining, the goddamned bush sank clear into the ground, or something.

As we got still closer to the ridge with that great pile of rocks on top of it, I just hoped I didn't sound too much on edge and said, "Dumb bastards! All that work t' git in good with a bunch a' gods that ain't even there!"

Bruk pulled slowly on his pipe. "The Tartars see spirits and gods in every tree and rock, in the sky and earth, even in the stars and the wind. There's a certain beauty in such a belief."

The quiet and surprisingly respectful way he said that kind thing about his deadly enemies reminded me so much again of how Old Keats might feel that it almost made me forget about being nervous for a minute. "You damnere

442

sound like ya' *like* 'em."

"No. But I certainly respect them." He shrugged. "How can you not respect men whose very name means 'brave'? Or who claim, as a race, to be the descendants of a great mythical blue wolf?" He paused. "A Tartar warrior pierces his horse's hind hoof at night for a few drops of blood and mixes that blood with a handful of rice for his day's food."

"Ugh," I said.

"And with only that handful of rice and blood, he can outlast, outride and outfight any other mounted warrior in the world." Bruk turned his weather-beaten old face toward me, and a faint hint of humor came into his eyes. "Except a cossack, of course."

Before I had time to defend us cowboys with some kind of a witty response, we heard hoofbeats coming up fast. Shad and Old Keats, with Igor right on their tails, were barreling toward us across the wide plain.

Rostov trotted his black over as the other three galloped to us and pulled up.

Shad squinted at the huge, square pile of rocks looming darkly above and said, "Puttin' that thing up took a lot a' men."

Rostov nodded. "From the size of the structure, it had to be Genghis Kharlagawl."

"Scary bastard, ain't it?" I said with what I

hoped was a fearless grin.

Bruk said, "I've seen many of them." And then I realized that he'd been sticking with me, trying to bolster me up, as he added, "But that one — it's the biggest I've ever seen, and it becomes more and more frightening when you approach it. As though it's been dedicated to the gods of death."

Shad turned his big Red slightly. "Rocks're rocks. It's what lies behind 'em that counts."

With Shad and Rostov leading off, the six of us rode up the slanting incline toward the crest of the ridge high above and the *obo*, which by now looked almost as gigantic as the darkening sky behind it.

And damned soon it seemed to me that whatever local gods the magic of that Tartar *obo* had drawn about it had to be the meanest, blackest, ungodly demons to ever get a leave of absence out of hell.

Struggling up that incline, which was suddenly a whole lot steeper than it had looked from below, the ground shifted and slipped beneath our horses' hooves. And it started to get darker than any normal, mortal day ought to get dark. On top of that, a cold blasting wind came screeching out of nowhere with enough slamming force to almost tear a man out of the saddle or even knock both a horse and rider down.

When we finally managed to scramble to the top and rode over to the twenty-foot-high monster, Shad reached out from the saddle into the shrieking wind and touched one of the boulders in the *obo*. And being this close up to it, I was so spooked by now that I swear to God when he touched it I fully expected the entire mountain of rock to come avalanching down and bury all six of us.

But it was as though that simple touch of Shad's hand had instantly chased away the whole gathering of fierce demons. That snarling banshee wind suddenly broke and faded and then disappeared, for all the world like a crying, spoiled kid who's been whacked on the butt and sent running home.

Within a moment, the demons of darkness and cold followed as fast as they could, leaving a sun that was not too far from setting, but was at least a regular sun putting out normal late-afternoon warmth and light.

Even the rocks must have had bad spirits in them because with the appearance of the sun their ugly darkness changed to a lighter, warmer tone that was as cheerful as the front of the First Baptist Church at Butte.

"You frightened the spirits off!" Igor said to Shad, only half joking in his own nervous fear.

Catching my breath and not even half joking,

445

I muttered, "Sure as *hell!*"

Shad glanced at us and then squinted briefly up at the sky. "You two dumb bastards sure would make easy converts. That ugly weather was nothin' but a fast north wind carryin' some clouds on it."

"Well, damnit, Shad," I said defensively, "ya gotta admit that you just reachin' out an' touchin' that goddamn thing, an' then the whole world changin' like that was sure as hell downright spooky timin'!"

Igor nodded. "Yes!"

That rare, dusty-dry humor of Bruk's came into his eyes once more. "Perhaps we should do something to placate these fearful gods."

Reading Bruk's mind, Old Keats picked up instantly on his friend's words and said wryly. "Maybe, Levi, you an' Igor'd like t' offer up a human sacrifice 'r somethin'."

Igor and I exchanged frowning, slightly embarrassed looks before I grumbled, "That's very hilarious, Keats. You sure as hell ought t' consider vaudeville."

Then Shad and Rostov led off again, and we rode on over to the far edge of the top of the hill.

From here we first saw the grim meadow below. And we also saw that more than enough human sacrifices had already been made.

24

Less than half a mile from us, down in a richly fertile, green meadow, there was a large, beautiful stand of white birch, and within the surrounding trees four small cabins had been built around a small clearing.

It must have been a kind of pretty sight at one time. But no longer. Two of the cabins had been burned completely to the ground, leaving only their two stone fireplaces standing like tall, blackened tombstones over the ashes. The other two had been gutted by fire, but there were parts of the walls still remaining.

From where we were, I could make out several small grayish-white outlines scattered on the ground near the cabins. A moment later, a sudden wave of sickness came over me as I realized that those scattered outlines were skeletons of the people who had once lived there.

Slowly, and with no word spoken, the six of us rode down the far side of the hill and across the grassy meadow toward the trees and what was left of the homes within them.

As we entered the small, tragic circle of ruined cabins, Buck almost stepped on the bones of a single torn-off human arm that was lying all by itself, half-buried in the ground. I just happened to see what the grisly thing was at the last minute, and I jerked the reins so hard that the bit hurt Buck's mouth and he reared slightly, snorting resentment at my unexpected roughness.

Then I walked him on, looking the hideous place over with stunned, maybe even partly glazed eyes. For the unbelievable horror all around was just about too damn much to take.

Before I finally gave it up, I silently counted to myself nineteen skeletons. Two of them had been tied to charred stakes and were almost part of the fallen ashes where they must have been burned. Some of them were mingled together, forming jumbled, ghastly jigsaw puzzles of decaying bones. Others were sprawled singly in such grotesque shapes that their backs and other bones must have been broken before they were dead. A few, but not many, had strips of cloth on or near them that might have been strips of clothing. But boots and belts, and any weapons they might have had, were gone.

I'd counted to nineteen because I was right on the edge of plain cracking up, and I had an idea that the counting might help me keep some kind of a grip on myself. But then I realized numbly that I was starting to go crazy anyway, so I quit.

Near the center of the clearing between the cabins was a well, which was about the only thing there that hadn't been destroyed. A small protective wall of rocks was still around it, and the rope and bucket had been left intact.

After a while, the six of us joined each other, still in complete silence, and dismounted near the well, though to tell the truth my mind was still so wobbly I don't recall riding over to the well or even getting off Buck.

It was Rostov's low, strong voice that finally brought me back to myself a little, his quiet words starting to nail my staggered, loosened-up mind more firmly in place once again.

"They were a brave group," he said. "They fought well."

His eyes grim, Bruk nodded. "At least eight dead Tartars are there among them."

Old Keats looked at Bruk thoughtfully. "They don't even bury their own dead?"

"They have a saying," Bruk said quietly, "that the vultures are their flying grave-diggers."

"One of the Tartars who died here was relatively important," Rostov said.

449

Igor, who'd been having his own problems hanging on to himself, now at last managed to say in a husky, strained voice, "How do you know that, sir?"

That was a pretty good question, because sure as hell none of those pathetic piles of bones was wearing any insignia.

"Come." Rostov stepped toward the partly remaining wall of the nearest cabin.

Igor, Shad and I followed him while Old Keats and Bruk stayed near the horses. And as we moved off, the two older men started to lower the bucket to get some water from the well.

Near the base of the cabin wall there was one skeleton all by itself, but as we approached it I noticed for the first time that there were two skulls there.

Finally finding my own voice, and sounding a lot like Igor had just before, I said, "Tartar leaders'r two-headed?"

I'd said it innocently, hardly even paying attention to my words, but it came out funny, and this wasn't a time or place for fun. The other three looked at me, and I had to grit my teeth hard against laughing. Because I knew if I started to laugh, I wouldn't be able to stop.

Rostov leaned down and picked up the skull that wasn't attached to the skeleton's backbone.

Handing it to Shad he said, "This man was a high-ranking warrior or they wouldn't have left this with him."

Igor and I both stared at the ugly object, and I now saw that this skull was much older than the other bones. The top of it had been neatly cut off and in its place a flat sheet of rawhide had been tightly stretched.

"It's a damaru," Rostov said.

We glanced at him questioningly and he added, "A small ritualistic drum."

Shad handed it toward Igor and me to examine, but neither one of us wanted to hold it, so he dropped it back on the ground where it had been. "Nice t' know," he said grimly, "that they're music lovers."

We turned and started back toward Old Keats and Bruk at the well. Bruk, his back to us, had finished drinking from the first bucket. Quite a bit of the water must have spilled, for Keats had leaned over to lower the bucket for a refill, and now he was hauling it up again.

Then, as Keats almost had the bucket, Bruk did an incredible thing. His back still to us, he whipped his saber out and swung the razor-sharp edge swiftly in Keats's direction. But the deadly blade didn't touch Keats. It slashed instead through the rope and a few inches below where Keats was holding it, severing the thick rope as though it were a thread. As Old Keats looked up in amazement there was the sound of the falling bucket hitting the water below. And then the saber dropped from Bruk's hand.

"Oh, God, the *water!*" Rostov said, breaking into a run toward them.

In the brief moment it took us to get there, Old Keats already had Bruk's shoulders in his hands and was shaking him as hard as he could, calling desperately, "Bruk! *Bruk!*"

The old cossack's face was turning black, and he was paralyzed inside, unable to speak or breathe.

Rostov, with Shad instinctively knowing what to do and helping, laid Bruk down on the ground on his face. Rostov knelt over him, pushing down powerfully on his back with both hands. And at the same time, Shad turned the blackening face to one side, forcing Bruk's mouth open and quickly putting his forefinger in his mouth both to hold the tongue down and to keep the stricken man from swallowing it.

Pushing down on Bruk's back with all his strength, Rostov muttered, "Watch that he doesn't bite it off."

But Old Keats had already foreseen this, and he now hurried back from a nearby birch with a slender branch about eight inches long. He knelt beside Shad and put the branch in to hold down the tongue before Shad withdrew his finger. But Shad continued to hold Bruk's jaws from the outside, forcing the mouth to stay open.

All of this had happened so quickly that Igor and I were still standing there in helpless shock. But now I stepped to Buck and with slightly trembling fingers untied a blanket. A blanket might not do much good, but it was all I could think of. Igor lent a hand, and we doubled the blanket and put it on the ground next to where they were working on Bruk.

"Maybe keep 'im warm, later," I mumbled.

But the way it was going, there might not be any "later." Bruk still hadn't breathed yet, and the last remaining awareness in his eyes was beginning to fade into unseeing glassiness.

In desperation, Rostov raised both of his open hands up and then slammed them down in a mighty blow on Bruk's back that must have come close to breaking most of his ribs. And under that crushing impact, Bruk did gasp, seeming to take in one last terribly hard-won bit of air.

But then, as Rostov pushed down fiercely hard on his back again, Bruk's eyes closed.

And he was dead.

We all knew it within the same instant. Whatever tiny bit of life he had been clinging to somewhere within himself a moment before was now finally and forever gone.

His hands still on Bruk's back, Rostov let the surging, pushing strength go out of his arms and looked at Shad with hard, level eyes.

Returning Rostov's look, Shad very slowly released his iron grip on Bruk's jaw and mouth.

"Igor," Rostov finally said in a quiet voice, "go back and tell them what's happened here." He looked at Shad. "Tell them to make a wide circle around this area."

Shad nodded, and Igor said in a broken whisper, "Yes, sir."

As Shad and Rostov now stood up, Igor turned quickly away from us, then mounted Blackeye and rode off swiftly.

Old Keats had remained kneeling beside Bruk, still holding his tongue down with the birch branch as though hopelessly willing some last invisible spark of life to show up in Bruk. And then, in an involuntary movement, the dead man's teeth clenched powerfully together, biting almost completely through the piece of wood.

"Oh, *Christ,*" Keats murmured, and I guess it was then that he at last accepted Bruk's death. But still not ready to dwell on that death, or face the brutal fact of it head on, he decided to pay more attention to the birch branch instead.

"Goddamn stick!" he muttered, trying to pull it free.

"Might as well break it off," Shad said quietly.

"And leave 'im with part of a goddamn stick in 'is mouth?"

For the first time, I was just beginning to realize how close those two older fellas had come to be. And Shad could see it too, for he spoke to Keats even more gently now. "You know as well as I do that you've either got t' break off the stick or break his jaw."

"Well," Keats said, close to tears, "that's just one hell of a goddamn note!" But he knew Shad was right and holding Bruk's forehead in place with his left hand, he bent the branch back and forth as easily as possible until the branch broke off. And as it did, Bruk's teeth at last sprang tightly against each other with a sharp snapping sound.

Keats now stood slowly up, still holding what was left of the broken branch. "He was too paralyzed t' be able t' talk an' warn me." He hesitated a moment to get his voice under control. "God*damn*, what it must a' taken t' pull that saber an' cut that rope." He hesitated again, looking at the piece of birch in his hand as though he wondered what it was doing there. Then, finally, he opened his hand and dropped it. And then he said very quietly, "If he hadn't cut that rope, I'd be layin' right alongside 'im."

Keats turned now and walked a little distance away by himself, into the nearby birches.

As I finally kneeled to spread my blanket over Bruk, Rostov said, "They probably poisoned the well because of losing that leader over there, whoever he was." He took a long, slow breath. "All the people who were here. Just wasn't enough killing for the Tartars."

Shad looked off toward Old Keats. "Poisonin' a well f'r whoever in the world might happen t' come along next —" His words trailed off. And then he added in a dangerously quiet voice. "If it should ever come t' pass that we go among 'em, that time, then an' there, will be an interestin' time."

Neither Shad nor Rostov went any further in showing their deep feelings than those few words they had each spoken.

But soon after, Sergeant Nick came thundering at a full gallop down the hill and across the meadow toward us, and he damn well showed the way he felt. Tears streaming down his huge half-bearded and half-shaven face, he leaped from his horse and kneeled silently down to lift the blanket and look at Bruk, whose face had grown even blacker in death.

Then he stood, and Rostov spoke to him quietly and briefly in Russian.

Rostov must have mentioned the "important" Tartar who had died here, for when he finished speaking, Nick turned and strode to the wall where the one skeleton and two skulls were. He stood there a moment, his giant body almost shaking in outraged grief, and then he raised his right foot and stomped it down twice, his big, heavy boot crushing both skulls and grinding the gray-white powder into the ground.

Then, with the back of one sleeve, he wiped his tearstained face and slowly returned toward us.

For myself, I'd been holding a lot back, just trying to keep up with Shad and Rostov. But now after what Nick had done, I turned to Shad, my voice partly breaking up, and said, "We got some black powder on the pack animals! Let's get it an' blow that goddamn sacred *obo* a' theirs all t' *hell!*"

Shad shook his head. "No."

"Why *not?*"

His voice tightened. "Because ya' *can't* kill a *rock*, Levi."

Nick got to us and took a shovel and heavy hammer from his saddle. Then, methodically, he started to break down the well and fill it in upon itself, so that no one else would happen along and taste its deadly waters.

And finally Rostov said the last words spoken in that grim clearing among the white birch trees. "We'll take Lieutenant Bruk far from here, and bury him in a high place."

The next evening, at sunset, they laid Bruk to rest at the top of a high, gently sloping green hill. It was a simple, moving service, with Rostov saying only a few quiet words in Russian over the open grave. When a man is as loved as Bruk was, you don't have to say a lot. And as Rostov spoke in Russian, us cowboys, without understanding, understood.

They laid Bruk's saber at an angle across his chest. And then, before filling the grave in, there was one more thing to do. Bruk, like all the other cossacks, wore a thong around his neck that held a small leather pouch. Rostov had taken it off and he now opened the pouch and poured the handful of earth within it into his right hand. Holding his hand over the grave, he let the dirt fall slowly from it, so that the first earth was from Bruk's home, Bakaskaya.

Then, silently, we began filling the grave.

On the walk back down to camp, bad as all of us Slash-Diamonders felt, I could still see that

Old Keats was the hardest hit. And when we got there he just sat down by the fire, staring into it. Finally, I brought him a plate of beans, but he silently shook his head.

"Gotta eat," I murmured. "Nothin' more c'n be done."

At last Keats wet his lips and whispered, "I just hate the idea a' him spendin' the rest of his life with that goddamn stick in his mouth."

That was a hard line to answer, so all I did was silently nod a little.

And then Rostov came over carrying a box in his hands. It was Bruk's handmade chess set. "He intended to give you this when the trip was over," he told Keats in a quiet voice, "so —" He let his sentence end there, handed the chess set to Keats, and walked away.

Later that night, a few yards away from us, Ilya got out his balalaika and started to play it slowly and softly. Whatever the tune was, it was a little sad but very pretty.

And within a minute or two, another musical instrument joined quietly in, following Ilya's lead on the balalaika. Sammy the Kid, on the far side of our campfire had gotten his guitar and was playing just as softly as Ilya, the two of them speaking a beautiful common language that said everything with no words.

I couldn't help but think back to the time

we'd tried to drown the cossacks out with "De Camptown Races." We'd come a long way, in a lot of ways, since then.

As the two of them continued playing, Old Keats moved closer to the fire. Where he was, he was sort of by himself, and he took out that little writing tablet of his, slowly thumbing through the worn pages and reading by the light of the fire, as though there was something special in the tablet that he wanted to find.

And in the middle of the night, when I got up to take my turn riding herd, Keats was still there by the fire. He had a piece of leather about eight inches square and he was working on it with a hot needle, slowly and patiently burning something into it. He was so intent on what he was doing that I didn't bother him, but quietly saddled up Buck and rode out.

In the early light just before sunup, Mushy relieved me and I started toward camp.

Up in the distance, on the hill where we'd buried Bruk, there was one solitary man sitting motionless on his horse. I realized it was Old Keats, and hoping it wasn't too forward of a thing to do, I turned Buck and rode up the hill to join him.

I came up slowly, and Keats wasn't aware of me, so this time I gave him plenty of warning. From about twenty feet away I said in a low voice, "Keats?"

He turned and saw that it was me. And then, after a moment, he said, "It's all right, Levi."

I rode on over with the idea of just sitting near him for a minute and kind of sharing his feelings in some little way. So it wasn't until I pulled up beside him that I realized he was doing a whole lot more for me than I was for him. For the first and only time I ever knew about, he was quietly letting someone else read a thing he had written. The words that he'd spent the night burning into that leather, which he'd nailed onto Lt. Bruk's small cross.

The words Old Keats had written were

> *i am i*
> *and you are you*
> *and we are both*
> *each other too*

Finally, after a long, silent time, we turned and rode slowly back down the hill.

25

For eight long days we moved on higher into the rising broken country ahead, approaching the tall, ragged line of peaks that capped the range of mountains before us.

But even with the land growing hard and mean to climb we weren't ever blocked or trapped along the way. Riding far point and scouting our route, Rostov led us wisely, so that the herd was never hung up in terrain too rough to get up and over. Somehow there was always a high meadow that joined up with an easy, gently sloping valley or a wide canyon bottom where we could gain higher ground ahead, even though we might be surrounded on both sides by sheer cliffs or by wicked, impassable levels of jagged, leg-breaking rocks.

At last, on the ninth day, near the top of the mountain range, we came upon some really tricky ground to cover. There was a dangerous pass that was actually only a ledge about forty feet wide, with a three- or four-hundred-foot drop off one side and a straight-up wall of rock on the other side. It ran for about two miles, sometimes narrowing down to around twenty feet, and if for any reason the herd had gotten spooked or panicked, we could have lost the whole bunch in about half a minute.

But we took it real slow and easy, and that beautiful Old Fooler led the cattle like they were philosophers taking a thoughtful stroll down main street. So we not only made it easily across that hellish pass, but went on to make a good seven or eight more miles through a slowly rising green valley surrounded by pine trees before quitting for the night. And when we did finally stop, the ground was level, with high peaks to each side.

That night, with our campfires right next to each other, Rostov stepped over and said in a very quiet voice, "That pass was the last hard ground we had to cover."

After a moment Shad said, "Now that we've topped these mountains, your home shouldn't be more than two or three weeks away."

"It's mostly downhill — and less than two hundred miles."

The cossacks were quietly mingling in with us now, a lot of them with bottles of vodka that they were offering around. It was a silent, easy time. Not a time for getting drunk, but more of a time to simply celebrate being glad and thankful about something important.

Even Shad now said in a kind of relaxed way, "It ain't exactly time f'r rejoicin' yet, but a couple a' you fellas break out some Jack Daniel's. Hittin' the top of a mountain pass is always worth a good drink."

We broke out the bourbon and shared the bottles back and forth.

And that's the way that ninth quiet day and night was.

And the next of those good days, the tenth since we'd left Bruk buried on the top of that lonely hillside, went just as well. Once or twice I even had the strange, haunting thought that his death had somehow given each and all of us safe passage.

I know for sure he would have wished it that way.

But I should have also known that no man's death can ever give safe passage to any other man's life.

At the end of that tenth day, when the sun was gone, yet there was still light in the sky, I could see that Rostov was suddenly disturbed about something. He signaled abruptly for a halt, and we rode quickly back to where the others were now starting to set up camp.

Mushy and Crab had gathered some wood together for a fire, and all it needed now was a match. Rostov dismounted near them and said,

'Don't light that until after dark. And then keep the fire low."

Mushy and Crab gave each other brief, puzzled glances and Crab said, "Sonofabitch. Shad just tol' us the same damn thing."

Mushy shrugged. "That's how come we ain't yet lit it."

Shad walked into camp now, from where he'd tied up Red. He got there in time to hear the last words Mushy had said, and the two big men looked at each other for a silent moment, their eyes level.

Then Rostov said, "You saw it, too."

Shad nodded. " 'Bout thirty minutes ago. Maybe ten, twelve miles b'hind us."

Some of the other cowboys and cossacks were gathering around, and in Russian Rostov asked a question of Kirdyaga and Yakov, who'd just come in from patrolling far behind the herd. From their short, uncertain answers, they didn't have any more idea what was going on than I did.

Slim, who almost always saw everything there was to see, said, "Jus' what'd you two fellas happen t' spot all that distance b'hind us?"

"A small, unusual wisp of cloud," Rostov said. "It faded so quickly in the rays of the setting sun that it might possibly have been an optical illusion."

"Or hell, at that time a' day," Slim said agreeably, "maybe y'r eyes was just playin' tricks on ya'."

"It was smoke," Shad said quietly. "From a fire that hadn't been built long, an' was then put out fast."

Rostov nodded. "That's what I believe it was."

There was a brief, grim silence among us in the now swiftly darkening camp. Smoke in the distance behind us meant humans were there, but after that it was anyone's guess.

"Hell," Purse muttered nervously, putting words to what we were all thinking, "it might just be a couple of trappers — or all the bloody Tartars in the world!"

Rostov swung up onto his black. "I intend to go back and find out."

"Not by yourself," Shad said. "I'm as curious as you are."

Rostov turned toward him in the saddle. "Say three of each of us?"

Shad nodded.

So a few minutes later, in the now complete dark, six of us were riding silently and swiftly back along the route we'd come that day.

The number six had been just about right on Rostov's part, which Shad had immediately understood and agreed to. We made up a small but pretty fair striking force if some kind of a fight should come to pass. And at the same time, all things equal, there were enough men left back with the herd to move it and, if need be, protect it.

Sergeant Nick and the giant Kirdyaga were riding just behind Rostov. And Slim and I were pacing the two of them right behind Shad. In both cases Rostov and Shad had left damned good men in charge of the herd, men who also spoke the other outfit's language — Old Keats and Igor.

Just thinking on that subject, and the way both bosses had arranged everything back at camp pretty neatly, almost like leaving a will, sort of tended to add to the uneasiness I was already feeling.

Leaning forward a little, I said in a low voice that I tried to fill with good-natured, devil-may-care humor, "Say, boss, ya' think we'll make it back alive?"

Slim was the only one who bothered to answer me. In an equally low voice he said, "Hell, Levi, the only reason we come along at all is t' make sure these dumb cossacks don't get lost in the dark."

And though they didn't help all that much, those were the last words spoken in a long time.

After another hour or so, the huge three-quarter Siberian moon appeared slowly over the horizon, seeming to nearly fill that part of the sky and spilling its bleak, cool light all over the world around us.

A mile or two later, moving at an easy, soundless lope in the soft ground, Shad and Rostov suddenly both pulled up almost as though they were one single rider.

At the exact and same moment the two of them had heard or sensed something that none of the rest of us had. But then, in the absolutely total, almost deafening silence, there was a tiny, dry click of sound far ahead. It must have been a mile away, but it was the unmistakable sound of an unshod pony's hoof hitting a small rock.

And the way it turned out, that slight sound was a terribly costly mistake.

Shad and Rostov instantly turned to the right, up toward a nearby mile-long line of thick pines, each of them walking their horses as gently as if each hoof was coming down on an eggshell that mustn't be broken. And the other four of us followed as quietly as possible. Buck's left forehoof struck lightly against a clump of earth with a faint whisper of a thud, and I would have rebuked him with a slight hit between his ears, except that I suddenly realized that even that gentle touch would make more noise than Buck had made in our deathly silent ride up the hill.

It still might be peaceful hunters or trappers ahead of us up there. But I had one nifty thought as we moved into the hidden protection of the pines and sat silently on our horses. We hadn't made one damn sound louder than hands barely rubbing together might make, so if those bastards were Tartars, and moved like ghosts, they were up against some vastly superior ghosts.

Because we knew about them and they didn't know about us.

And they were Tartars.

Thirteen of them.

They first appeared as silent black specks moving slowly over a hill in that cold, crystal moonlight more than a mile away. I couldn't understand why they were moving so slowly, because you could follow that vast, trampled trail of our cows at a full gallop in jet-black hell. And it even occurred to me that you could follow it pretty damn fast if you were blind as a bat just by following the plain old smell of cowshit leading you along the way.

But still they came on slow.

They were so slow that there was plenty of time to watch them.

In utter silence, Rostov took out his telescope and studied them. Then he handed it to Shad, who looked briefly and passed it in turn to Slim. I was the last one to look through it, and by the time it finally got to me, the Tartars were less than a quarter of a mile away.

Still keeping one hand on Buck's nose, so he wouldn't snort or come up with a foolish whinny, I raised the glass and stared at the oncoming Tartars. It took a minute to get them in view, but when I did it was as though they were about spitting distance away in the silvery light.

And Christ! Like the ones I'd seen a long time ago, before Khabarovsk, that half-dressed, long-haired bunch gave me that same feeling again of wolves on horseback. What Bruk had told me came strongly back to mind. About them being descendants of a great blue wolf. And about that handful of rice and blood for their daily ration. And about him respecting them.

I sure as hell agreed with the respect he felt, but not having his wisdom, I was feeling that respect out of pure fear. Yet I'd have rather died than show that fear to Shad or Rostov or any of the others. So I just looked, and tried to keep down any slight noise that my hard-pressed gut might start to make.

They were, like the earlier ones I'd seen, armed with every kind of a mean weapon that had ever been invented. Some of them had spears or lances, or whatever makes the difference between them, and all of them had bows and arrows and viciously curved and jagged daggers and swords of one kind or another. And with their strangely painted horses, and the feeling of deadliness and death about them, that was about all I wanted to know. But for just a second longer my eye stayed to see that some had guns, others what I took to be crossbows and wicked-looking wide-bladed hatchets. And with all those images of tools made just for the one purpose of killing, I handed Rostov back his telescope. If there had been one thing I could mention just then, it would have been the fact that a riderless horse was being led down below. I was convinced that that was the horse who'd kicked the rock a while back, and those other Tartars had killed the dumb rider who was on him when he did it.

But everything was still too silent to hardly even breathe easy, let alone say anything.

Taking the scope, Rostov gestured with his hand so that I could figure out what he meant. I was at the far end of our line of horsemen, on Rostov's right. And a few yards still farther to the right was an eight-foot-high steep rise of ground. I was supposed to get off Buck and go up on that rise to see what was beyond it, for whatever reason.

So I nodded and got off Buck without using the stirrups. Not wanting to cause a creaking of saddle leather, I pulled my feet out of the stirrups, put my arms around his neck and lowered myself in complete silence to the soft ground.

The moonlight and my eyes were working so well together that I even saw a small leafy branch along the way and stepped well beyond it so there wouldn't even be the soft murmur of a dry leaf being crushed underfoot.

And with that kind of careful silence, still not knowing what the hell I was supposed to be doing, I at last raised my face over that eight-foot-high rise. The rise was only about two feet across the top before it sloped down again on the other side.

And exactly two feet away from me, raising his face at the same time, was a fourteenth Tartar warrior who'd come up to his side of the rise just as quiet as I had.

I don't know how ugly he thought I was, but I can triple guarantee how ugly I thought he was. For one thing, the bastard's astonished lips suddenly drew back and he had no teeth. In one of those dumb things that sometimes flash through your mind, my first thought was that maybe that was why he only ate rice mixed with blood. There was no goddamn way he could eat much else. And on top of that, he was scarred all to hell and was missing one eye. His right eye was just a hollow place with the lids of it sucked back into the hollow and a narrow line of sightless black between them.

But he surely could see good with that other eye. And seeing me, he ducked back down as fast as I did, though our sudden movements even in that soft earth must have made a little noise.

And then, for whatever reasons make scared men the quickest to fight, we both bounded right back up over the two-foot ledge and smack at each other.

When we crashed into each other, he was reaching for a curved knife and I was trying to haul out my Navy Remington. But our head-on collision wasn't too fair because I must have outweighed him by forty pounds, and he went flying far backward down his side of the rise.

He was littler than me, but quick as a wildcat. Landing on his back about five yards down and away, he flipped around and up onto his feet in one swift motion, a strung bow and an arrow instantly ready to go. He let fly as I dropped to one knee and heard the arrow go whooshing by near my right ear.

Then, as I finally hauled my heavy old .44 out and cocked it, he screamed a warning to the others below. And then the dumb bastard came charging up at me with only his bow in his hands. At the rate he was coming, I guessed it would take him about one and a half seconds to get to me. But a whole lot went in and out of my mind just then. First of all, I'd never ever pulled that old gun in anger, and secondly I'd sure as hell never shot anybody. And at the same instant I couldn't help but feel sorry for that poor crazy idiot racing up toward me. How can you aim your gun and shoot some poor bastard who's only got one eye, no teeth at all, and is also underweight? Furthermore, what could he do with that dumb bow he was waving fiercely toward my chest and neck? Tickle me to death?

All of those jumbled thoughts of mine couldn't have taken more than one second of his swift charge. For in the last half second Rostov leaped over the rise and landed in front of me, his revolver drawn. As the Tartar lunged forward, jabbing out toward him with his bow, Rostov's gun roared and the Tartar went flying down the sloping earth for the last time.

And it was only then I saw that the Tartar's bow was also fashioned as a deadly spear at one end. And that sharp spear point was sticking through Rostov's right arm.

The bow was still strung, so the expanding tension of the rawhide was tearing Rostov's flesh. "Get this thing out of me!" he snarled.

I was too damn slow to shoot before, but I was fast now. As he took his revolver from his nerveless right fingers with his left hand and jabbed it back into its holster I already had a knife out and had cut the bowstring. Then, though it was a tough sonofabitch, I broke the bow itself, snapping it between hands that had never been so strong before. And finally, I grabbed the wickedly flanged spearhead sticking through Rostov's arm and jerked on it fiercely, pulling it and what was left of the shaft cleanly out.

This had all happened within seconds. And now instead of sitting, or even falling down, as I expected him to, Rostov rushed back to our horses with me following him.

But even in that short run I more or less sized up what was happening. Rostov, being closer to where I was than Shad, had come over to take care of me. The others were already galloping down to attack the Tartars below. And I suddenly realized that all of them had to be killed or they'd spread the word about us being there to every other Tartar warrior in Siberia.

And two other things I knew. One, that toothless, one-eyed killer I'd run into had been scouting far flank to make sure that the men in the valley wouldn't be trapped. Two, that the men in the valley sure didn't think they were trapped, with only four men bearing down upon them and only two more of us charging along behind to back them up.

It had to be less than one fast minute between the time that Tartar and I first scared the hell out of each other to the time the general battle was engaged in the valley below.

For whatever reasons, the Tartars were certain they had us whipped. They shied away a bit at first, and then seeing there were only six of us, with one kind of sloping in his saddle, they changed direction and charged back at us outnumbering us more than two to one.

And that's when the costly mistake before mentioned really came to pass. Without the click of the hoof before, or without this charge, they might have hung around the edges and killed a few of us and then gotten away in the night, moonlit or not.

As it was, it was a brief, swift massacre. Four of them had single shots and fired along the way toward us. One man made his shot, and the giant Kirdyaga was knocked half out of his saddle. And then we all cut loose with our repeaters and five of them were down before we were a hundred feet from each other. It's harder than hell to make a shot from a moving horse, and I don't know if I hit any of them or not, but just thinking of the damage they'd already done us, I sure as hell was aiming as best I could.

And then we slammed together, still out-numbered, and were in a swirling, close-up fight. My damned Winchester was suddenly out of bullets, and there was no time to try to get that Navy Remington out of its holster, so I reversed the rifle and slammed a Tartar alongside the head as he went by and ripped a hole in my jacket with his lance.

In almost that same instant Kirdyaga galloped up and leaped from his horse taking that Tartar down with him, and there was a cracking sound as they hit the ground that meant the Tartar's back was gone.

It seemed, all of a sudden, that everybody was out of bullets. And that last Tartar swung his horse at Shad, slashing toward him with a curved sword.

He didn't make it because Rostov was suddenly there and cut the man damnere in half, his saber held in his still strong left hand.

And that was the end of the fight.

Shad had never learned how to say thanks, and still couldn't say it, so instead he frowned and started to reload his Colt revolver.

"There's this difference between a gun and a saber," Rostov said.

Shad glanced at him. "Yeah?"

"A gun has a limited number of deaths within it. A saber has a thousand, and then still more."

And having made his point with quiet dignity, Rostov swayed far out of the saddle and, still with that same dignity, fell off of his horse.

26

Shad and I both swung down quickly and knelt beside the unconscious Rostov, raising him to a sitting position. His right sleeve was soaked with fresh blood from his wound, and Shad swiftly cut the sleeve to get a look at the arm.

"He was run through with a kind of spear. I broke it off an' pulled it on out." And then I added huskily, "Oughtta've been me."

Shad glanced at me briefly. "That so?"

Slim and Sergeant Nick had dismounted and

gotten Kirdyaga off of the dead Tartar beneath him. He was lying on his back as they unbuttoned his vest to see how bad he was hit. They were close enough that I could see Kirdyaga was still breathing, but just barely, each breath shallow and labored.

"How is Captain Rostov?" Nick called over anxiously.

"He'll be all right," Shad said, examining the two holes where the blood was almost coagulated now. "Just lost too much blood. — Kirdyaga?"

"We'll know better in a minute," Slim muttered.

Shad got a flask of bourbon and a clean red bandanna from his saddlebags, then knelt back down where I was holding Rostov up in a sitting position.

Shad deliberately squeezed the hurt arm hard, making blood start to flow from the two open wounds once more. Then he poured bourbon over them freely.

The pain of Shad's rough squeeze, plus the added fiery shock of alcohol, forced Rostov's eyes open. He looked down at his hurt arm and then said darkly, "Goddamnit, you ruined my shirt."

Shad held the flask to Rostov's lips and the captain took a long drink. Then Shad started to bandage his arm with the clean bandanna. "Lucky you're not one a' Verushki's Imperial Cossacks, fallin' off your horse that way."

The bourbon was getting to Rostov, and he was feeling a little stronger already. "I did not fall off my horse." With his free hand he took another drink of the Jack Daniel's. "That was just an original way of dismounting."

Shad was nearly finished with the bandage. "Guess it would save time," he now knotted the ends of the bandanna tightly, "if a fella was in a real hurry t' git off 'is horse an' go t' sleep."

If the average man had lost as much blood as Rostov, he'd still have been flat on his back. But Rostov, suddenly frowning over toward where the two men were kneeling near Kirdyaga, now shrugged away from my supporting grip and lurched weakly up onto his feet. And though he almost tipped over a couple of times on his way to the giant wounded cossack, we knew better than to try to help him.

Slim and Nick had bared Kirdyaga's huge chest and stomach, and there was a wicked bluish hole about six inches below and to the right of his belly button. Nick was dabbing at the ugly wound gently with a wet cloth.

Looking up at us grimly, Slim said, "Can't locate the bullet by touch. Just ain't no way t' figure where it's got to inside 'im or t' try git it out."

Rostov, though still weaving very slightly, said with finality, "We will make no attempt to remove it."

"No?" That spook me up because I'd heard somewhere or other that you always had to take the bullet out of a shot man.

"He's right," Shad said flatly.

Rostov now felt he had enough strength to kneel down without falling down, and he did so, resting his weight on one knee and gently exploring Kirdyaga's abdomen with the finger of his better hand.

And with Rostov there, Nick now stood slowly up and pulled out the enormous revolver he carried, which somehow managed to look both clumsy and lethal as hell as the same time. He checked to see that it was fully loaded and then walked off in the moonlight. I knew instinctively that he was going to make sure there was no more possible threat to us from any of the Tartars.

I hunched down on my heels near Kirdyaga and finally said helplessly, "Well, will the big sonofabitch live with that goddamned bullet in 'im?"

Rostov glanced at me, seeing how deeply I cared. Then, as he started to bandage Kir-dyaga, already beginning to use his hurt arm and that hand a little, he said, "I have one inside me that's been there about fifteen years."

"Oh."

"As to whether he'll live, that will depend on the location of the bullet, his constitution, and God."

Rostov now had the damp bandage folded and in place over the wound, but he needed some way to hold it there securely. Shad took off the wide, strong cotton mesh belt he wore and kneeled down, handing it to Rostov. "God's already done his part. Gave this big bastard the strength of an ox."

One on each side, Shad and Slim lifted Kirdyaga's huge torso gently so that Rostov could slip the belt underneath and around him. Then Rostov tightened the belt, which locked automatically in place at any point, until the bandage was held very firmly over the wound.

"Now," Slim said dryly, still looking at Kirdyaga with grim concern, "how ya' gonna hold y'r britches up?"

Those worn old Levi's fit him like a glove, so Shad wasn't in any trouble. "Hell," he shrugged, "got another belt back t' camp."

About then, Kirdyaga started to come around. His face and neck muscles moved, twitching slightly, and then his eyes blinked open and started to clear. Shad brought his flask of Jack Daniel's, and Rostov raised the big cossack's head enough to give him one or two small sips. Kirdyaga gagged briefly, but the bourbon warmed him and brought some color back to his face.

Then, finally, he murmured a few broken words in Russian to Rostov. I was pretty sure he was asking if he was going to live.

And I was damn sure about it when Rostov now grinned easily down at the hurt man and answered him with a quiet, rough humor in his voice that made his reply cheerful and encouraging. And speaking in those easy, almost joshing terms, he pointed to Kirdyaga's freshly bandaged wound and then at his own stomach.

Kirdyaga wasn't strong enough to take any more, but he did manage a small grin as he realized that he and Rostov were now both packing a bullet somewhere in their gut.

There was the sound of someone approaching and we stood up, looking off.

It was Nick, who was striding toward us through the moonlight, effortlessly dragging behind him the body of a Tartar that he was holding by one foot.

When he got near us, he let go of the roughly sandaled foot, dropping the Tartar sprawled on his back behind him. "This one's still alive, Captain."

We stepped over to look down at the wounded man. Even unconscious, his lips were curled back in a silent half snarl. He was wearing a crudely made wolfskin jacket with the fur outside, which made his shoulders seem broader than they were. And after that, except for some leather knee-length pantaloons and those beat-up old sandals, he was as naked as the wolf he'd gotten the jacket from. There was a kind of a scabbard sewed into the waist of his leather pantaloons, and in that scabbard was a curved dagger with a handle that was inlaid with some fancy stones and what I guessed to be strips of ivory.

He had been shot high up on the left side of his chest. That part of his body, and some of his long, dark hair, was covered with hardening blood that looked black in the moonlight.

Nick leaned down and took the dagger from the nearly dead Tartar, and as he stood back up Kirdyaga suddenly went into convulsions behind us.

Lying a few feet away, every muscle in the giant cossack's body began to jerk and throb so fast and hard that he was almost rolling around on the ground.

All five of us were with him in an instant, trying from both sides to hold his powerful, twisting body down. And even though his eyes were getting glassy and he was only barely conscious, it still took all five of us to do it. There was just no doubt that the huge cossack was dying, his body thrusting and surging for life violently and senselessly.

Once we got him halfway nailed down on his back, Rostov gave a command to Nick and the sergeant leaped over toward his horse. The rest of us fought like hell to keep Kirdyaga down, and a moment later Nick hurried back with what Rostov had told him to get.

All he'd brought was a little tin cup and a small bottle of vodka, which in those deadly circumstances sure didn't look like any great help to me.

But Nick took over Kirdyaga's thrashing left arm that Rostov had been holding down, and Rostov went swiftly to work. He took a rifle cartridge out of his belt and bit fiercely down on the lead slug. Then, with his teeth and his good left hand, he pulled and twisted fiercely, jerking the lead bullet out of the brass cartridge.

Doing the best I could to hold Kirdyaga's massive, kicking right leg down, and watching Rostov working feverishly, I thought for sure he'd gone crazy. But glancing at Shad's grim eyes, I could see that he had a strong hunch that something right, whatever it was, was happening.

485

Rostov poured a huge slug of vodka into the tin cup. Then he poured all of the black powder from the brass rifle cartridge into the vodka, stirring the awful mess up swiftly with the cartridge case that was still in his hand.

Then Rostov leaned forward over Kirdyaga, who was twisting and wrenching at our holding hands with all his might. His face only inches from Kirdyaga's, Rostov roared a command in Russian with such explosive fury that for one brief instant Kirdyaga just barely managed to force himself to hold still and open his mouth. And in that instant Rostov didn't pour but damnere threw the mixed vodka and gunpowder down his throat.

Kirdyaga strangled, gasping frantically for breath, and in that desperate gasping he accidentally swallowed the whole goddamned ghastly drink.

A few seconds later he went out like a small lamp in high wind, and every powerful, straining muscle in him suddenly was as limp as an old wet piece of cloth. For one awful minute, I was sure he'd died of a heart attack from that horrible mixture he'd drank. But he was staying warm and breathing a little, even though his heart was beating like the wings of a moth trapped inside his enormous chest.

There was no longer any point in our holding him against somehow hurting himself. So we all released our grips on his arms and legs and quietly stood up, and Slim and Nick went to get some blankets to tuck around him.

"Jesus," I finally whispered, "I'd think that cure'd kill 'im quicker than the bullet."

Rostov said grimly, "Vodka and gunpowder is an ancient cossack remedy for internal wounds when a man is next to death. Kirdyaga will not go into shock again and there will be no infection internally. But right now —" Rostov left the rest unsaid.

Shad finished those unsaid words. "Right now it's a matter a' whether his heart c'n keep goin'."

Rostov nodded.

As we stared quietly down at the giant Kirdyaga, silently holding on to what small edge he still had on life, there was a faint sound from nearby.

The Tartar, still unconscious, had moved slightly.

"Try to wake him," Rostov told Nick.

Nick stood up and strode the few feet to the Tartar. He leaned down and slapped the man damnere hard enough to break his jaw, but the only reaction he got was a low murmur. He slapped him twice more, even harder, and it looked to me like he was going to kill him instead of revive him. But he was a better judge of how tough the Tartar was, and at the third mighty slap the man started to come around. He gasped slightly, shaking his head, and a moment later his eyes blinked open. His first move was to reach feebly for the knife Nick had taken. Then, with tremendous effort, he raised himself slightly. But even weak as he was, his slightly shifting head and darting tongue reminded me of a big diamondback about to strike.

Rostov stepped to him and asked him a question in a strange-sounding language. The Tartar thought about it for a glaring moment, and a blind man could see there'd be no way on earth to force an answer out of him.

But then, in a hissing voice that made him seem even more like a rattlesnake, he whispered a few words.

"He asks," Rostov said, "to die by his own hand, and knife."

Shad frowned at Rostov. "Your judgment, Captain."

Rostov and the Tartar spoke in that language a little more, and I somehow had a feeling that the dying man was enjoying whatever he was saying. Then, choking feebly, the Tartar laid back flat on the ground.

Rostov took the fancy knife from Nick. Then, pulling his revolver with his right hand, he leaned down to hand the Tartar the knife. This was evidently Rostov's part of the bargain. But the Tartar was so far gone he could barely hold the knife, let alone use it on himself.

Either way, I didn't feel up to watching, so I started to turn back to Kirdyaga.

And in that instant a whole lot happened. A gun roared and I jerked around to see an impossible sight. The Tartar had lunged to his feet and toward Rostov with his knife. Rostov's bullet caught him dead center and nearly point blank, and the Tartar was thrown back to the ground, the knife flying from his hand. In that same instant Shad had his gun out too, but he didn't have to use it.

Finally, as the two men slowly put their guns back, I muttered in a stunned voice, "Jesus Christ! He was *dead!*"

"Not quite," Rostov said.

And that closed the subject. But since a rattler has been known to kill a man with its head completely cut off, that snake comparison sure came unforgettably back to mind.

Slim had stayed near Kirdyaga, and as we now gathered back around him, Slim asked, "What'd that hardcase have t' say, Captain?"

Rostov knelt beside Kirdyaga. "First he congratulated us on killing all of his group."

Kirdyaga was breathing better by now, and Slim said, "Hell maybe we ain't in too bad shape then. Nobody t' carry no tales."

Studying Rostov, Shad said, "There's more."

Rostov nodded grimly. "The Tartar knew he was dead. And he spoke to us as one dead man to other dead men. Riders are already on their way north to Genghis Karlagawl." He paused. "Within two weeks his army will be upon us."

That hit hard, an we were silent for a long moment.

Finally Shad said quietly, "How many?"

"Over six hundred."

Shad had kneeled down beside Kirdyaga and near Rostov. The giant cossack's breathing was becoming deeper and more regular. "Glad this big bastard's shapin' up," he said. "With them kinda odds, we'll need all the help we c'n git."

As Shad helped Rostov wrap the blankets closer around Kirdyaga, the two big men's broad shoulders touched and you could almost see and feel a kind of invisible power between them.

We got Kirdyaga, still wrapped warmly, up onto his horse. When he was in the saddle he slumped weakly forward over his mount's neck, clutching the mane in one feeble hand.

Then, with Slim and Nick each riding on one side to hold him aboard, we started at a fast clip back to camp.

27

When we were about half a mile from where the herd was bedded down, Old Keats and Igor rode swiftly out of the dark to meet us in the moonlit valley.

The sound of our gunfire had carried for miles through that cool, silent night and they'd heard the distant shots.

But from right up front not one word was said. They saw that we were all present and accounted for and that Kirdyaga was in a bad way. So without wasting time or slowing us down they edged out Slim and Nick to take over at holding Kirdyaga upright in the saddle, and we rode on silently past the sleeping herd to the two low-burning fires, where all the men except those on guard and on the herd were gathered. Every man here was geared for trouble too, guns and horses at hand, and ready to move out at any second to wherever fighting might start.

They all stood up as we rode in, silently taking stock of the situation. And some of them helped lift Kirdyaga from the saddle and lay him down near a fire for warmth.

Then, finally, Shad said, "There's no immediate trouble b'hind us. But a lot of it's on the way."

A short distance from us, Rostov now started speaking in quiet Russian to his cossacks.

And Shad, building a smoke, told the Slash-Diamonders what had happened. He ended with the news of the oncoming Tartar army, and in the dead silence that followed he lit his smoke from the glowing coals of a half-burned branch in the fire.

After a while Crab said, *"Six hundred?"* Then he added with quiet sincerity, "That's just too *many*, boss."

"Hell," Rufe grunted. "Might's well be six thousand!"

"One thing," I said, "from what we saw, they ain't got one good gun among 'em."

"Explain that t' poor ol' Kirdyaga," Mushy growled.

Slim now spoke up. " 'Nother thing. That there Tartar back yonder mighta been exaggeratin'. Or he mighta been plain lyin' in his teeth t' scare us."

"Well as far as I'm concerned," Crab grumbled, "he *damn* well succeeded."

"Crab's right," Rufe said. "A fight's one thing, but suicide's another. It's sure worth consideration t' just haul ass out a' here an' leave 'em the herd."

Shad stiffened very slightly at that suggestion and Old Keats noticed it. "If we all of us, cowboys an' cossacks alike, felt that same way, it'd wind up with just Shad an' Rostov drivin' them five hundred cows all by themselves. Now wouldn't leaving them all that work make you kind of ashamed of yourself, Rufe?"

But Rufe hung on. "I said it's worth our considerin'! If there's that many, they'll git the herd no matter what! So why not at least think about gettin' out an' savin' our goddamned necks?"

"I'll tell you somethin', Rufe." Slim took a bite off his plug and chewed slowly as he spoke. "Some of us tangled with them fellas t'night. An' I c'n tell ya' this about 'em. If we leave 'em the herd, they'll come after us an' kill us f'r our weapons. Leave 'em our weapons, an' they'll come after us an' kill us f'r our horses. Leave 'em our horses, an' they'll come after us an' kill us f'r our clothes." He'd worked enough on the chew now to spit a charge into the fire, where it hissed briefly on the coals. "An' if we fin'ly leave 'em our clothes, they'll come after us an' kill us f'r the pure damn sport of it."

After a moment Old Keats said quietly, "We were all given our chance to pull out before Khabarovsk. But we're too deep in now, and that chance just isn't there anymore."

Shiny nodded. "This ain't the U.S.A., an' there ain't no safe train t' Denver."

"Hell," Big Yawn grunted. "I'd ruther fight 'em doin' m' job than fight 'em runnin' away."

We all thought on that, and then Sammy the Kid ventured quietly, "B'sides, I'd hate t' think a' them cossacks havin' t' go it by themselves."

Though it hadn't come up until now, we all felt the same way, and that seemed to sum it up, for no one else said anything.

After a moment, Shad took one last drag on his smoke and tossed it into the fire. "I'm sure glad you fellas ironed our problem out all by yourselves." He tried to make it sort of sound like he was kidding, but he wasn't. And then he turned, kind of abruptly, and walked over to where Rostov had been talking to his men.

After a while the two of them came back over to us and Shad said, "Two things. One, Rostov's sending a rider on ahead to Baka-skaya. By going like a bat out a' hell, he can get help to us by about the same time that Kharla-gawl catches up."

"How much help?" Purse asked.

"Probably about five hundred men," Rostov said. "They should be able to afford that many without leaving the town itself dangerously unprotected."

"Christ," Slim said, "that's the only good news we've ever got in Russia."

"They should join us about halfway between here and Bakaskaya," Rostov continued. "Eight, perhaps nine days from now."

"Which leads t' point two," Shad said. "We're gonna drive that herd like a sonofabitch. Once we're out a' these mountains, it'll be pretty clear goin', so we'll be pushin' them hard as hell, night an' day."

We were all starting to feel a lot better about everything, and Natcho flashed that brilliant smile of his. "Excellent," he said. "The herd has been getting fat and lazy anyway."

"We'll move out at first light," Shad said, "so turn in while ya' can, now. Nobody'll be gettin' much sleep later on."

Fifteen minutes before, I doubt if anybody could have slept. But with help coming sooner or later up front and with a concrete plan of action, that Siberian night had suddenly become a whole lot more cheerful place, and Slash-Diamonders started turning in right and left.

Igor came over to where one of us were still standing by the fire, and he had Pietre with him. "Pietre is the one going on to Bakaskaya," he said. "He wants you to know that he will go very fast."

"Good man f'r the ride." Slim nodded. "You tell him t' make that skewbald mare a' his git out an' stretch 'er legs."

And he sure as hell was a good man for the ride. As Igor told Pietre what Slim had said I remembered so clearly that blindingly swift race with him on the meadow outside Khabarovsk. And the fantastic leap he'd made high over the stream with that goddamned rock in his hands.

And Pietre was remembering it too. He smiled at what Slim had said, and then he looked at me. Leaning down, he picked up a small rock at his feet, held it out before him, and dropped it.

Christ, you can say a lot with no words.

I was so damned touched by his gesture that I was sorely tempted to give him one of those big bear hugs that the cossacks sometimes give each other. But, especially with those other fellas standing around, that might have seemed kind of much. So instead I put my hand on top of his shoulder and squeezed real hard.

He grinned, and about then they brought up his saddled mare and a fine deep-chested bay gelding on a lead. He leaped up into the saddle, sitting light as a feather and strong as steel. Then, with a small wave and one parting word, and leading his second mount, he raced out of camp fast enough to pass up any and every bat who ever came out of hell.

As the swift hoofbeats faded and then disappeared, far away in the darkness, those of us around the coals of the fire started to drift away to our bedrolls.

Shad's bedroll was near mine, and as I got my head settled into the saddle, he came up silently and started to pull off his boots.

I was feeling so goddamned close to those cossacks right then. There was just no doubt that Pietre was prepared to ride two good horses, and maybe himself, to death to get to Bakaskaya. And he wasn't just doing it for the cossacks or for the herd. He was doing it for all of us. And Kirdyaga, using his last ounce of giant strength to take that Tartar lancer off me, even with a bullet inside him. I reached up to my shoulder and touched the gash in my leather jacket that the lance had left.

As for that bastard Rostov, in one night he'd taken a spear thrust meant for me and, half bleeding to death, had cut down a mounted Tartar who was on the verge of killing Shad.

With all those mingled thoughts, what Rostov had once said about Shad came to mind again. And Shad "being" that big tiger. I'd never mentioned it to Shad for a number of reasons. Mostly, I guess, because it was said as such a damned huge compliment that it was kind of embarrassing to pass on. Rostov could say it to me. But I'd sound silly repeating it.

So, right then, I did a kind of a chicken thing. Shad was pulling off his second boot as I said in a low voice, "Hey, Shad?"

"Ummm?"

"What would you think if one fella referred to another fella as a tiger?"

His boot half off, he hesitated, frowned at me and said in a quiet voice, "Huh?"

I was in too far to back off, but I could at least still keep it vague. "I said, just in general, what would ya' think of one fella referrin' to another fella as a tiger?"

"Oh, f'r Christ sake!" He shook his head in annoyance and pulled the boot off.

But having asked the question, I couldn't just let it hang there. "Well?"

Pulling his blankets up over him, he finally answered me. "Just offhand, I'd say it'd take one t' know one." He settled down. "Now get some sleep."

That was a hell of an answer.

And I got some sleep.

For the next six days we pushed the cattle and ourselves at a grinding, damnere killing pace. By the end of the second day we were already pretty much clear of the mountain range, moving quickly through lowering foothills to endless, broken flats stretching before us. And in the next four of those six days we averaged nearly twenty miles a day, if you count a day as twenty-four hours.

So by the end of the sixth day we'd made well over one hundred miles, and that high mountain range where we'd been was almost out of sight on the low horizon far behind us.

Rostov and I were still riding far-point guard, usually about a mile ahead of the herd. And the cossacks were guarding the flanks, while the Slash-Diamonders yelled and whooped their lariats and busted the herd along at a fast sort of shufflng trot that the overworked cattle resented like hell. Even Old Fooler, who was usually the most reliable and cooperative lead steer ever born, was starting to get both tired and grouchy as hell, trudging quickly along with his head down in a hostile way as though he was mad enough to be plotting some kind of a cow revolution.

There had been one change made in our traveling setup. Instead of riding with the herd, Shad and Igor went to riding far drag, about the same distance behind the cattle as Rostov and I were before them. Back there was where riders catching up with us would be spotted first. So that's where Shad elected to be.

That night, except for general exhaustion, we were all feeling pretty good. There still hadn't been one sign of one Tartar overtaking us. We were due to join up with the men from Bakaskaya within no more than two or three days. And even Kirdyaga was in miraculously good shape, sitting up and eating and joking. Igor had already told me that Kirdyaga wanted to start an exclusive club, limited to men who were packing bullets in their guts. And naturally, Kirdyaga and Rostov were in on it as the charter members.

While we were eating beans around the low fire, Slim frowned at his now empty tin plate and said, "Goddamnit t' hell, anyway."

He was fishing, so I up and took the bait. "Goddamnit what t' hell, Slim?"

"We jus' might not even *see* that big bunch a' Tartars."

"Heartbreakin' thought," Crab muttered.

"An' in that case, what'll I tell m' grandkids?"

"What grandkids?" Mushy asked.

"Ain't you fellas got no feelin's?" Slim demanded. "I was lookin' forward t' tellin' 'em some real excitin' stories in m' old age."

"Do what ya' usually do," Crab suggested. "Lie."

And Rufe added, "you're already in y'r old age, Slim."

Old Keats finished his coffee. "We're movin' out in four hours. You fellas c'n sit around regalin' each other all ya' want. But I'm gettin' some sleep."

And the next day was the seventh day.

By sunup we'd already made four or five miles, and we made even better time on level plans of knee-high waving grass through the morning and most of the afternoon.

In the late afternoon Rostov and I crossed a wide meadow and rode to the top of a high, sloping hill where he pulled his black to a halt, suddenly frowning.

The land ahead of us was a little rougher, broken up here and there by ravines and outcropping of rocks. Two or three miles beyond, there were some steep pine-covered ridges.

But the terrain wasn't rugged enough to explain Rostov's hard, thoughtful frown. He took out his telescope and studied the land ahead for a long moment. Then he turned his back and raised the telescope again to scan the horizon far to each side of us and behind us.

"Somethin' the matter?" I asked.

"Yes," he said quietly, his voice as hard as his granite expression.

Not sure that I really wanted to hear the answer, I said in a low voice, "What, sir?"

"Kharlagawl's army will not catch up with us from behind." He closed his telescope slowly. "It's up ahead, there. — Waiting for us."

28

Rostov stayed on the high hill to act as a lookout for us, and I galloped back to the herd. Seeing me headed back at full speed, the Slash-Diamonders eased off on the cattle, letting them slow down to a stop. By the time I hauled Buck to a skidding halt, my heart pounding deafeningly in my ears, most of them and some of the cossacks were already gathered to find out what was going on.

"Them Tartars!" I half shouted, trying to catch my breath. "They're up ahead!"

"Where?" Slim asked.

"Didn't see 'em! But Rostov says so!"

"Then they're there," Old Keats said grimly. But Crab, trying to cling to some kind of hope, said, "Maybe they *ain't!* Maybe Rostov —"

"Oh shut up," Slim groaned. "That bastard c'n spot a gnat from three miles off, an' then read its mind."

Shad and Igor galloped up now, and the only question Shad asked was, "What's Rostov say t' do?"

I was still having trouble breathing. "T' git the cattle into a big hollow about half a mile ahead an' off t' the left!"

"Slim, git the herd up there fast," Shad said. "You cossacks give 'em a hand. C'mon, Levi."

Then he galloped on toward the high hill where Rostov was. I spurred after him as Slim and Nick began bawling orders to the cowboys and cossacks, and they quickly got the herd moving at an angle toward the hollow ahead.

At the top of the hill Shad and I pulled up beside Rostov. They exchanged brief looks, and all of a sudden I knew both of them had had the foresight to be prepared for this possibility from the very first. Rostov silently handed Shad his telescope.

Raising the scope, Shad looked out over the broken land ahead and the pine-covered ridges beyond. Lowering it after a moment, he said, "Ridges."

Rostov nodded. "They were planning to attack us from there when we were strung out in the open meadows just below."

Shad passed me the telescope. "That sure woulda been a mess."

Squinting at the far-off land through the lens, I couldn't see a damn thing that was out of the way.

"Farther to the right, Levi," Rostov said. "The last meadow."

And Shad added, "Either they did that 'r there's a herd a' elephants up ahead — can't miss the sign."

Finally I vaguely made out in the far distance one shadowed hairline of high grass that had been beaten down by many hooves, though even with the help of the powerful lens it was still almost impossible to see.

"Yeah, Shad." I handed the telescope back to Rostov. "That's really hard t' miss."

They were both sitting there so quietly now that it kind of threw me. Scared, nervous and excited as I was, I'd somehow expected that by now each and every one of us would be galloping off in every direction at once. But Shad even took out his Bull Durham and started to build a leisurely smoke, though neither he nor Rostov took their eyes from the growingly ominous flats and ridges.

After a moment Slim rode up and said,

"Herd's just about inta' that holla', boss. How much time ya' reckon we got?"

" 'Bout two hours," Shad told him. "They ain't gonna tire their horses runnin' 'em all this distance at us."

Slim studied the land ahead. "That there Kharlagawl sure ain't nobody's dumbbell. 'Stead a' pickin' up our trail an' followin', he figures out where we're most likely headin' an' plain damn simple cuts us off."

Shad finished building his smoke as Rostov said to him quietly, "The hollow seems to me to be our best defensive position."

Shad lit up and blew the match out. "Seems that way t' me, too." He broke the matchstick and dropped it.

Then, though neither of them said anything, by common accord they turned their horses and rode easily toward the hollow, and Slim and I followed them.

I'd just glanced at the place as Rostov and I were riding past it on point, but studying it more carefully as we now got there and rode down into it, I could see what they liked about it. It was a roughly rounded-out depression, sort of like a big, natural bowl in the ground, about three hundred yards across. It was sunk down over a hundred feet, and on both sides high, jagged rocks made it hard as hell to get to. For that matter it wasn't easy to get to from the rear end, where they'd now driven the cattle in, for that was also a rocky, pitching decline that would make any four-hooved animal slow down and go careful. The front part, a wide, gradual slope leading up toward the flats, was the only clear entrance. A hell of a charge could be made from there, despite a few low outcroppings of rock. But at least it was the only direction from which the Tartars could attack in force. And there was one more thing, which turned out to be important as hell later on. There was an arroyo off to the side up front that led from somewhere up in the flats down into the hollow. It was about forty feet wide, and its steep sides were anywhere from twenty to thirty feet high.

Otherwise, the spacious hollow was filled with sweet grass that some of the cattle were already munching, while others were just lying down or standing motionless, spraddle-legged with fatigue. On the far side of the hollow there was a large spring in the center of a shady clump of maple trees.

We circled around the herd and dismounted at the front of the hollow where most of the others had gathered. The arroyo was to our left. The slope itself fanned out as it slanted easily upward, so that it was maybe a thousand feet wide up at the top. Here and there along the way it was broken by low outcroppings of rock. And where we stood, at the point that the slope dropped the last little bit down to join the hollow, most of the two-hundred-foot width there was a long, low ledge of rock about five or six feet high. It formed a perfect breastwork to help us defend ourselves against any attackers who might charge down the slope. To our left, next to the entrance to the arroyo, there was a nearby higher wall of rock where our horses could be protected and yet still be close at hand.

Igor said to Rostov, "We've placed guards in the rocks on both sides and at the rear."

"Good." Rostov scanned the gently rising slope before us carefully, finally studying the crest of it half a mile away. "But right up there is where they'll come from."

"Hell," Slim said, looking around. "All in all, this here situation ain't too damn bad a'tall."

But Rufe, who clearly represented the majority, was of a gloomier frame of mind. "Wish t' Christ you'd stop bein' so fuckin' cheerful," he muttered. "Tends t' git nauseatin'."

"Well hell," Slim countered, "this place is just as good a natural fortress as God ever built, with water an' grass t' spare. All we gotta do is settle in an' hold out till them fellas from

Bakaskaya git here."

Shad and Rostov looked at each other for a thoughtful moment, and then Shad said, "We'll camp b'hind those high rocks. Mushy, Rufe, git a fire goin'."

"A fire?" Mushy questioned.

"That's right. Might's well make it a big one."

"Hot beans're better'n cold," Slim said.

"And," Old Keats added, understanding Shad's reasoning, "if our friends are within seeing distance by now, we might as well let them know exactly where we are by the smoke."

With that encouragement, Rufe and Mushy got what looked like a ton of wood from one of the maples that was long dead. They built such a big fire it was hard to get close enough to it to cook, and Kirdyaga, lying near it, had to move his blanket away.

"Christ," Slim said, looking up at the smoke billowing into the sky, "they oughtta be able t' see that clear back t' Seattle."

We ate in shifts, with most of us staying at the natural rock breastwork, rifles in hand. At first we talked and joked a little, but it was just too spooky for much of that, and the talk slowly eased off. After that all there was for one long, nerve-racking hour, and then finally two, was dead silence and nothing. It was still so quiet after those two endless hours that the loudest things I could hear were my own breathing and a fly buzzing a few feet away near Crab, who was sweating slightly as he frowned up the long slope before us, blinking into the nearly setting sun.

Crab must have been thinking about the same thing I was, for the fly flew away and a moment later he said tightly, "Only noise f'r miles around here is my sweat droppin' off!"

Igor grinned and translated Crab's line in a low voice. The other cossacks grinned back, and a few of them chuckled.

"Goddamnit," Crab complained "Wasn't trying t' be funny."

"Only time ya' ever are," I told him, "is by accident."

"Very amusin'," he muttered. "Y'r a real scream, Levi."

Then, from farther down the line, Purse said what was on a lot of our minds. "I don't think there' s one damn bloody thing up there!"

"Maybe," I said, looking over toward Shad, "a couple of us ought t' ride up an' take a look."

Chakko spoke for the first time in two days. "Fuck it."

Shad glanced at Chakko and then at me. "Maybe after nightfall, on foot. Not now."

Chakko nodded gravely at Shad's words, and Rostov said quietly, "I believe we'll see them before then. I think they're just waiting for the most dramatic moment to show themselves."

"Dramatic?" Old Keats said.

Nick nodded his massive head. "To frighten."

A few minutes later the sun, now directly in our eyes, began to set behind the far top of the slope.

And as it did, there was a sudden hollow, haunting sound that seemed to grow slowly out from everywhere at once, and as it grew in volume it seemed to start pounding on the inside of my brain, trying to jar it loose.

"Show time," Old Keats said above the strange, booming noise.

Slim cocked his rifle. "Nice t' have ringside seats."

From down the line Sammy called, "What 'n God's name is *that?*"

In an easy, calming voice Rostov called back, "It's a Tartar war horn. If that's all they have to offer, we're in no trouble."

But as Rostov knew, that sure as hell wasn't all they had to offer.

As the hideous, long blast of noise at last stopped, and its echoes began to fade away, somebody started beating very slowly on what must have been the biggest goddamn drum ever made on earth. The very ground beneath us seemed to shake with each measured, thunderous beat.

By now the sun was about halfway down, making it a blinding proposition to try to keep your eyes on the faraway top of the slope.

And then, as slow and measured as the giant thunder of the huge drum itself, riders started to appear up there, lining themselves out and facing us, the murderous sunlight behind them making them seem to shimmer and shift like motionless, yet moving, phantoms.

There were already tears in my eyes from squinting so hard into the sun, but I'd guess that at first there were about fifty of them. And then there was maybe a hundred, and then more, and more, and still more.

Finally, as unmoving and silent as death, they covered the entire thousand feet at the top of the slope, and though my eyes weren't working too good, the thought kept slamming at me that they were *crowded* against each other up there.

From a few feet away Crab whispered hoarsely, "Now I know how it feels t' be scared shitless."

Just as quiet as Crab, and dead level, Slim whispered back, "Does sorta cut every string in y'r gut."

And the rest of us sure as hell knew how they felt.

"If I had t' make a quick move right now," Rufe managed to mutter between gritted teeth, "it'd take a whole Sears Roebuck catalogue t' erase the evidence."

Then, at some unheard command, the immense line of riders suddenly whirled and vanished soundlessly, and in that same instant the huge drum was struck for the last time, its earth-shaking echoes fading slowly away into the distance.

A moment later, the last rays of the sun now disappeared, along with the Tartar army and the thunder of the drum.

For a long time afterward no one spoke, and not many of us even moved much. Except for Shad and Rostov, who walked off a little way to talk quietly to each other about something.

At last some of the cossacks murmured a few quiet words back and forth, and then Shiny took a long breath and said quietly, "Thank Jesus we ain't playin' no hand a' solitaire all by our lonesome out here."

Not understanding Shiny's words, Igor looked at me with a question in his eyes. My throat was still too tight and dry to come up with an immediate answer, and Old Keats spoke instead. "He means he's glad there's help coming."

Igor was just about as bad off as I was, but he swallowed a little and said, "That is what our men have been saying."

"Main question is," Slim put in, "how long they'll be at gittin' here."

"Yes," Nick nodded. "It must be soon."

It was darkening fast now as Shad and Rostov came back and Rostov spoke. And in a low voice Igor told the cossacks what Rostov was saying. "It seems that time is the one thing that we have in our favor. Kharlagawl does not intend to attack us tonight. Or he would have attacked before, out of the sun." He hesitated and looked at Shad before continuing. "He hopes to leave us with our thoughts and paralyze us with terror. In his mind, after this long night, we will have either run away or be too sick with fear to fight well tomorrow."

"When d'ya think he'll hit us?" Slim asked.

"In the late morning, when the sun is high enough to be out of his men's eyes."

"Perhaps by then," Natcho said thoughtfully, "the reinforcements from Bakaskaya will be here. They shouldn't be too far away by now."

And then Shad broke in. "However that may be, we gotta hit that bunch as hard as we can all by ourselves. F'r example, we're gonna put three kegs a' gunpowder up on the slope.

That'll do notable damage if we c'n blow 'em at the right time."

"Why not all four kegs?" Big Yawn rumbled.

Shad frowned, searching for his own answer. And then he said, "Dunno, Yawn. Just feel like savin' one."

An hour or so later there was a half-moon throwing dim black-gray shadows on the earth. And in those shadows, I went with Shad and Slim to take three of our four kegs of gunpowder a hundred yards or so up the slope.

At three of the widest, easiest possible places for galloping horsemen to come down on us, we half buried the kegs in the ground, packing dirt up around their far sides so they couldn't be seen from the top of the long slope. But at the same time, about half of each keg was left visible downhill so that those of us who would be at the bottom of the slope could put a bullet into it to blow it sky-high.

When we at last slid back down and over the rocky breastwork after that spooky detail, I felt kind of like a hero, half thinking somebody might have a good word for our work.

But maybe by then my pounding heart was beating too loud in my ears to hear what everybody else was listening to.

Eager hands helped us down, but we sure weren't the center of attention. I looked at

Shad, and for one grim moment his face seemed dark and old as night. "One horse up there," he said.

And I suddenly knew what he and Rostov had been quietly talking about before, that had made them walk away from the rest of us.

The hoofbeats became louder, and a little later that one horse came galloping down through the shadows on the slope.

It was a frightened skewbald mare, and she raced down and jumped half over us into the hollow, where some of the men grabbed her and held her and brought her back.

It was Pietre's mare, and his body was tied over his saddle.

At that moment the one overwhelming thought in my numb mind was so simple. I just wished to God I had given him that last big bear hug, like I almost did.

Because after what they'd done to Pietre, there wasn't enough left of him to hug.

29

Working by the dim light of the moon, a few of us buried Pietre near the edge of the grassy hollow, while the others stayed on guard. Then, in groups of two and three, everybody had finally gone over to the grave to pay their last, silent respects.

By then it was as dark as it was going to get, and Rostov sent two more cossacks, Dmitri and Yakov, to try to get to Bakaskaya. They were to go back through the rocky rear entrance to the hollow and then keep going back for another mile or so. Then they were to split up, one going far north and the other far south, to make a several-mile-wide circle around the Tartars ahead of us.

After looking down at Pietre's grave for a long, silent time, Igor had volunteered to go, but Rostov had said no because we needed him.

As the other two cossacks rode silently away in the dark I said to Igor quietly, "Well, that's what ya' get for knowin' both languages. Miss out on all the nice, pleasant rides."

He knew I was just trying to be helpful, and he forced a small, tight grin. But the truth was that none of us held out much hope for those two fellas. Or for ourselves either, for that matter.

So that long, dark night wasn't altogether too cheerful of a time.

Some of the cossacks bedded down fairly early, but around midnight the only Slash-Diamonder who was sleeping was Chakko. Shad left the breastwork and the men on guard there to come over to the rest of us sitting silently around the low-burning fire. "Anybody here got a ribbon?" he said in a quiet, easy way.

This was an unlikely request, and Big Yawn muttered, "Huh?"

"If y'r gonna give Kharlagawl a present, ya' might as well tie it up proper."

Slim nodded, understanding. "Rate we're goin' we'll be too damn tired t'morra t' even see straight, let alone shoot straight." He stood up. "I'm gonna git me some sleep if it kills me."

Embarrassed into turning in, like all of the others, I crawled into my bedroll, but I was absolutely certain I wouldn't get ten minutes' sleep.

And on top of everything else, as though somebody up off there on the flats was reading our minds, that huge goddamned drum began its slow, measured booming again. "Dirty bastards!" I mumbled to no one in particular. And Rufe grumbled, "They're tryin' t' drive us crazy!"

A few feet away Chakko raised his head slighly and yawned. Then he said, "Fuck it," turned onto his other side, and went back to sleep. That sonofagun sure got a lot of good mileage out of that one expression.

I decided that about the best thing I could do was close my eyes and pretend to sleep.

So it came as something of a shock when I blinked my eyes back open to see the clear light of dawn around me. Some of the others were waking up now, too.

The drum was still booming out its slow thunder, and from near the fire, where he was pouring coffee, Slim grinned toward us and said, "That poor damn drummer's gotta be the tiredest bastard in Siberia."

Going to sleep on Chakko's words and then waking up to Slim's line was just about the best thing that could ever happen to a fella. Being faced with fear is a funny thing. It's like walking a tightrope inside your own head. On the one hand, if you fall, you can become a bawling, panicky coward or just a helpless, soggy bowl of cold mush. But if, somehow, you can stay balanced on that rope, then things aren't too bad. And both Chakko and Slim had been real helpful as balancers. Matter of fact, that morning's cool air seemed to taste sweeter than any I'd ever breathed, and even Slim's coffee was downright delicious. Looking around at the others, I had a strong hunch they were feeling the same sort of way.

From where they had been watching the slope above, Shad and Rostov now left the men who were there on guard at the breastwork and started over toward the fire.

"After all that good advice t' us," I said, "I doubt either one a' them closed their eyes all night."

Old Keats nodded quietly. "I'm beginning to believe those two men aren't made of muscle and bone. Something more like leather and iron."

A little later, sipping his cup of coffee, Shad glanced around at us. "Well, you fellas seem t' be fairly bright-eyed an' bushy-tailed this mornin'."

"Goddamn drum put me right off t' sleep," Mushy said.

"As f'r me," Big Yawn rumbled, "it pissed me off s' much I swore t' git m' rest just t' spite it."

"Exactly," Natcho agreed. "I can understand perfectly their wanting to kill us, but trying to disturb our sleep is going too far."

That was one of Natcho's better shots at humor, and we were all proud of him for it.

For his part, Rostov now said quietly, "Kharlagawl's tactics of terror weaken most men." He looked back toward the tip of the rising sun and added thoughtfully, "But they strengthen strong men."

By the time the sun was gaining a little toward breaking loose from the far horizon on its way up into the sky, we were all ready and waiting there at the breastwork. The way the mathematics figured out, there were just exactly twenty of us, including Kirdyaga, who was propped up with his shoulder against a rock, sitting there with his rifle in hand, ready to fire against whatever might come down upon us.

Of our original thirty-one men, three were dead, six were on guard around the hollow behind us, and two were, hopefully, on their way to Bakaskaya.

As the sun got nearly halfway to high noon, the monstrous drum stopped, and when its echoes were gone, there was a moment or two of complete, dead stillness.

Then we heard the damnedest last noise on earth anybody could ever have expected. From just beyond the top of the slope there was suddenly the vast tinkling sound of a thousand sleigh bells. Then, along with the jingling, there was a long, booming blast from the war horn.

"Show time again," Slim said.

Rostov, understanding the meaning of the bells, called out, "This will be a small exploratory attack, some of their best men testing our strength."

"In that case," Shad said, "don't nobody blow up those kegs a' gunpowder on the slope. We'll leave them f'r when they throw every damn thing they got at us."

Now, as if by magic, about a hundred Tartar riders instantly appeared all at once on the far top of the slope. Many of their horses were painted in strange colors and designs, from zebra stripes to red and yellow polka dots. Countless bells were jangling, hanging from the stirrups and other horse furniture.

Those men were probably the best-armed fighters Kharlagawl had. About half of them carried old singleshot rifles of some sort or another. One real puzzle. In addition to the weapons they were packing, every man up there, regardless of what else he might be wearing underneath, was wearing a white kind of long, lacy shawl draped down around his shoulders, with little bells on it.

"What the hell," Yawn mumbled, " 'r them white things?"

Instinctively, somehow, I knew that might be a good question not to know the answer to, but it had already been asked. "They're symbolic wedding dresses," Rostov said quietly. "Those men up there are prepared to be wedded — to death."

That was a grabber. And we were all silent with our own grim thoughts until Crab finally wet his lips and said harshly, "Them bastards c'n do however they feel like! But *I'm* too *young* t' git married!"

A big, heavy-set Tartar now rode into sight at the left end of the long line of riders. It was too far away to make out his face, but he looked very strong. He was wearing a sort of cloak that looked like bearskin, and he had some kind of a strange, round metal hat on.

"Kharlagawl," Rostov said.

Shad raised his rifle, but before he could line up on the distant, almost impossible shot, Kharlagawl rode back out of sight. Then the thunderous war horn boomed out again, and in its booming, the mass of Tartars, bells jangling shrilly in what was now one high-pitched scream of sound, lunged their horses at full speed down the slope toward us.

"Well," Slim shrugged, spitting some tobacco onto the ground, "like the man says, ya' can only die one time."

"Trouble is," I muttered, "that one time ya' die is often fatal." Which was about the best I could come up with, considering how shaky that tightrope of courage in my head was getting. Watching those warriors come at us hell-bent for election, that hideous screaming racket of theirs getting louder, the thought briefly crossed my mind to throw down my gun, turn around real fast, and outrun everything that ever lived.

"Forget it," I muttered angrily to myself. "You ain't fast enough, Levi."

Shad heard my low mutter and glanced at me, seeming to look right into my mind. And he did, for he then gave me a wooden sliver of a grin and said quietly, "Nobody is."

The charging Tartars were halfway down the slope toward us now, about a quarter mile away.

"Any man waits t' see the whites a' their eyes," Slim said, "will more'n likely wind up bein' dead."

"Each man be his own judge," Shad said. "And start shootin' when ya' won't be wastin' bullets."

With that, he raised his rifle, fired and brought down a distant Tartar who'd taken a slight lead over the others.

Before that first far-off warrior had hit the ground, Rostov's gun roared and a second warrior was sent spinning wildly off his horse.

Within a few seconds we were all blasting away. Not being the world's greatest shot, I held off longer than most. But with my first five rounds I brought three Tartars down, hitting either them or their ponies, or in one case maybe even both at once. It was still too far away to know for sure.

But the distance was closing awfully fast.

Twice I ran out of bullets and swiftly reloaded. The rifle breech and barrel were now so hot that the metal was burning blisters on my fingers, but I didn't notice.

When I raised my rifle to start firing again, that bunch of Tartars looked damnere close enough to spit at. But we just naturally started shooting faster, and at that closer range hitting our mark more often, so our bullets were tearing them to pieces.

Finally those still in the charge were close enough to start shooting back, and they handled their weapons in first-class syle. A bullet whanged against the rock in front of me and flying bits of stone cut the hell out of one side of my face, but I didn't notice the pain anymore than the heat of the rifle barrel.

Funny, but the two things I remember most right then were an ant walking across the back of my thumb and the overwhelmingly bitter smell and blinding smoke of burnt gunpowder. I saw the ant, a little red one, marching across my left thumb as I was gripping the rifle barrel with that hand and about to aim. And all of a sudden, I looked at the whole goddam roaring mess from that poor little ant's point of view. Fantastic, monstrous giants all around him, trying to blow apart the entire world. And all he wanted in that entire world, most likely, was to get back home in one piece, sit down with his ant friends, and hopefully take one huge, long sigh of relief.

So I gently brushed the ant off my thumb.

And then very quickly, to make up for that lost moment of time, I shot my next Tartar, who was less than a hundred yards away and coming on at full speed.

So many things happened so fast then that it's hard to keep them in order. But brave as they were, the Tartars in that charge had been slashed to ribbons. I doubt that more than thirty of them were still asaddle when they were within a hundred yards of us. And most of those survivors just couldn't face our deadly, withering fire any longer. So a lot of them at last spun their horses, and in all that din and confusion and heavy smoke managed to get away and back up the hill.

But not all of them went back.

Seven Tartars galloped to and over the breastwork, and there was some brief, wicked close-hand fighting.

I'd run out of bullets in my rifle for the third or fourth time, and there sure as hell wasn't time to reload now. So I jerked out my revolver, and that old Navy Remington .44 sounded like a cannon as I shot a Tartar dead center through the chest. It wasn't all that great marksmanship on my part. His chest was only about a foot from the muzzle, and at the time, he was about to hit me with one of those razor-sharp, long-bladed battle-axes that some of them carried.

In almost the same instant, two of them leaped toward Rostov. He ran one through with his saber, but the other was already swinging at him with a viciously curved, two-handed sword.

Before Rostov could jerk his saber out, and even before I could aim the Remington again and pull the trigger, Shad was there using his now-unloaded rifle as a club. Holding it by the barrel, he hit that Tartar so hard that it not only broke his head but sent him rolling wildly far out into the hollow behind us.

And by then the other men had finished the other Tartars who'd made it to the breastwork.

In the sudden, deafening silence, Rostov and Shad looked at each other, and I knew that they were both remembering the time before, when Rostov and his saber had stopped another Tartar from killing Shad. And thinking back to that, Shad finally said, "Maybe a rifle only has a few deaths in it. But a rifle butt goes on forever."

Slim stepped to them and said, "Lost three men, an' Igor's hurt." Then Slim looked at my face. "An' Jesus Christ, you're bleedin' t' death."

Gregorio had got an arrow right through his head, a mean-looking thing with ugly kind of fishhook barbs cut into the stone arrowhead itself, so it would tear the living hell out of anything it went into or came out of. And poor old Essaul had been shot in the throat. It was a terrible wound that left a gaping hole where it had come out. Looking down at him Slim said with a quiet sadness, "Goddamn bullet musta been big's a doorknob."

And the third dead man, at the end of the line, was Mushy. One of the seven Tartars who got to the breastwork had driven a lance through Mushy as his pony was leaping over.

Taking the lance out wasn't easy. Finally

some of us held his body down and Shad started to pull it out, but at first it made a couple of snapping sounds, like some little bones were breaking inside there.

"Can't ya' be a little easier, Shad?" Rufe asked, his low voice kind of uneven.

"No, Rufe, nobody can." My throat was dry. "An' we can't leave the goddamn thing stickin' out of 'im."

"Wanna pull it out yourself?" Old Keats asked him.

Rufe didn't answer.

Shad pulled very quickly and hard now so that the lance came out.

"Goddamn it all t' hell anyway," Rufe said, his voice getting more uneven than before. "Who the hell's gonna fix our goddamn boots now he's gone?" And then he couldn't speak anymore.

Right then there wasn't enough safe time to bury anybody, so we just wrapped our three lost ones in blankets, and as we were finishing that grim job, one of the cossacks on guard at the rear of the hollow came galloping up to us. It was Gerasmin, and without dismounting he spoke to Rostov briefly, then galloped back again.

"A small band of Tartars attacked from the rear," Rostov said. "Our men killed three of hem, and two others broke their horses' legs rying to go too quickly through the rocks. They won't try that area of attack again."

Old Keats looked up at the wide, half-mile lope and the bodies of men and horses that were now scattered on it. Somewhere far up, one man was still alive, crying out in dim, deirious pain. As the man's cries died away Keats said, "They came to bring death and destruction upon us. But so far, they've brought heir own death and destruction mostly upon hemselves."

"Well," Slim said quietly, "we best pr'pare ourselves f'r the next go-around."

Igor's leg had been badly cut by a sword hrust, though he could still walk. And I had a dozen or so chunks of rock in the right side of my face. So a little later, around the low fire, Rostov and Nick were bandaging Igor's leg while Shad was digging rocks out of my blood-covered face with the tip of his bone-handled hunting knife. Slim had gone into the hollow for more water and brought it back now.

Where Shad was probing hurt quite a bit, so I finally said, "Them Tartars'll never have t' lay a hand on me. I'll be dead a' sheer pain long b'fore they show up again."

As Shad kept digging, Slim washed some blood off my cheek with a wet rag and said,

"You oughtta be grateful f'r one thing, Levi
Considerin' that face a' yours, anythin' Shad
does is a big improvement."

Before going back to work on my skin, Shad
glanced at Rostov. "We hit those fellas pretty
hard. I think they'll hold back now until
around sundown."

Rostov nodded. "Then Kharlagawl will send
every man he has. And the sun will be in
our eyes."

"If I was a prayerful man," Slim said, "I'd
sure be prayin' t' God f'r clouds." He squinted
up at the clear blue sky. "Baptist clouds, Mormon clouds, Methodist clouds, any goddamn
clouds."

Shad pried the last piece of rock out of a high
part of my cheek. Then he poured some Jack
Daniels into his hand and with it he rinsed the
cut-up part of my face.

"*Jesus!*" I said as the bourbon sank in, burning and cleansing.

Shad handed me the Daniel's and I took a
drink, the warming heat on the inside kind of
pleasantly easing off the fiery burning on the
outside.

"Rostov," Shad said, "ya' think Kharlagawl
will lead the main charge comin' up?"

"I doubt it. He's too important."

Shad nodded thoughtfully. "That case, if we

do manage t' hang on until t'night, a couple of us oughtta try t' git up among 'em an' shoot 'im."

Rostov studied Shad for a moment. "Cutting off the head of the serpent might help."

"Sure wouldn't hurt," Slim said. "Could tend t' maybe bust 'em up an' confuse 'em."

Rostov's words about the serpent reminded me of the thoughts I'd had back in the mountains about our nearly dead but still dangerous Tartar prisoner. "A diamond-back," I said, "can sometimes kill a man even with his head cut off."

Shad shrugged. "Only one man, Levi. An' there's more'n one of us." Then he took a swallow of the Daniel's and passed it on around.

A little later the huge drum began its slow, earthshaking thunder again.

It was almost as though the regular, mighty sound booming down toward us was trying to let us know that not one damn thing at all had changed. That the earlier battle had been a lazy morning in the sun compared to the pure hell that was coming.

And for once, that drum was telling the truth.

A few minutes before sundown the massive war horn blasted powerfully and Kharlagawl's entire army appeared on the top of the slope with the sun at their backs, shimmering again in the distant, blinding light like faraway phantoms.

There wasn't time to make any count of them, but even with the men they'd lost that morning they were still jammed against each other shoulder to shoulder on that far thousand-foot-wide top of the slope.

I thought I had one squinting glimpse of Kharlagawl, and a moment later, the shrill noise of the giant war horn still bursting out against the sky, they roared down the slope toward us.

Some of them still had bells, some of them were blowing piercing, strange-sounding whistles, and most of them were screaming wild war cries, but the overriding, battering sound was the pounding thunder of countless horses' hooves crushing the earth.

"When it comes time," Shad called out to us, his voice calming and steady, "you take the middle keg, Slim and you take the one on the right, Levi. I'll go for the one on the left. If any of us have been hit, the man closest t' their immediate right who c'n still shoot should take over. Rest of ya' just keep poundin' the hell outta them fellas."

My first natural thought of maybe missing altogether was bad enough, but another horrifying thought occurred to me just then, too. What if I shot into my keg of black powder and the heat and friction of the bullet wasn't enough to set it off? I could just picture myself shooting into the goddamn keg that was now my responsibility and simply scattering the whole kegful of gunpowder harmlessly all over the slope, with a thousand Tartars charged right on through that place that I was supposed to blow up.

But there wasn't much time to pursue that line of worry. We all started firing sooner and faster this time. There were so damn many of them covering the slope that you could just about close both eyes and shoot and figure on somehow hitting something or other that mattered.

Yet with every one of us trying his level best to imitate a Gatling gun with his rifle, there was no way for our bullets to slow down or stop that massive charge of horsemen. Every time we'd knock down an entire front row of them, it looked like three more speeding front rows took their place. They were no longer in the direct glare of the sun now, but they were closing down on us with raging swiftness.

For a split second the thought came to my mind that that little red ant probably had the best of it after all. He ought, by now, to be safe at home somewhere in the ground, all things equal, unless some dumb bastard had stepped on him without knowing it.

Then Shad roared, "Hit the gunpowder!" and I shifted my gun sights peering through the thick, swirling gunsmoke before us. I saw the keg and fired as a swarm of Tartars started to gallop over it, and my bullet slamming into it surely did create more than enough heat and friction.

All three kegs exploded within a moment of each other, their tremendous explosions almost combining into one gigantic thunderburst that made a swelling wall of roaring flame and death.

I don't know how many Tartars were killed in those three terrible blasts, but none of the leaders got through. And there was total chaos behind them, with panicky ponies lunging and screaming, some of them rearing completely over backwards in terror.

Before the smoke of that dreadful carnage had cleared, the booming war horn sounded once more from beyond the top of the rise. And then, as the mass of acrid smoke cleared slowly away, we could see the army of Tartar warriors retreating swiftly back up the slope, going away from us as fast as they'd come.

As the last of them disappeared over the distant rise, the sun was a little time gone and the sky was beginning to darken. But a moon that seemed to have grown a lot since the night before was already looming bleak and cool in another part of the clear evening sky.

With those three kegs of gunpowder blowing the hell out of that last charge, I didn't think the Tartars had gotten close enough for any of us to be hurt.

I was wrong.

A bullet had smashed into Link's right shoulder and passed on through, shattering the bone inside. He was in so much shock he couldn't feel hardly anything, which was just as well. Shiny and Shad got the bleeding stopped and took what care of it they could. Then we put Link's arm in a firm sling and bound it tightly against his body so that it wouldn't move around too much and do more damage to the bone. Before the job was finished, Link had mercifully passed out cold, without ever saying one word.

By then it was full night. But it was one of those damned clear nights where you could read by the bright, silvery light flooding down upon the earth from the huge Siberian moon.

The measured, booming roar of the Tartar war drum started to slowly roll out again as Rostov turned quietly to Shad. "Their next charge will be the last."

Shad nodded. "We was talkin' b'fore about cuttin' the head off a serpent."

"The moonlight is against us. But Nick and I are going to make that attempt."

"Let's say the two best-suited men from each outfit."

"All right," Rostov agreed.

"Shad," I told him, "I'm goin'."

"Like hell you are," he said. "I'm takin' Chakko."

30

When the four men were about to go up the moonlit slope I spoke once more to Shad, just between the two of us. In a low voice I said, "I never went against you before, Shad, but this time I am."

He looked at me for a quiet moment, and then he said, "Okay, Levi. You c'n come, but only partway."

So it was that the four of them, Shad, Rostov, Nick and Chakko, started up the slope as silent as death, and I followed right behind, making as little sound as possible. Luck was with us, for some clouds began to drift across the face of the moon, giving us more dark to move within.

At the far top of the slope the five of us lay flattened out against the ground and looked over on to the flats beyond. There were a few mounted Tartars scattered out on guard not far away, but it's doubtful they really expected any visits from our small group in the hollow. And a distance beyond the guards, strung far out on the flats, were fifty or sixty small fires, each one with a handful of men bunched around it. Toward the center of all those fires was a bigger fire near a large kind of round and flattish-topped tent. Several men were gathered around that fire, but it was too far away to be sure in the dark if Kharlagawl was among them. Next to that fire was the big hanging drum that was twice as tall as the fella who was slowly pounding on it.

Shad whispered. "This is as far as you go, Levi. Try t' keep 'em off us durin' the retreat. But don't hang around forever."

I readied my rifle and the other four moved as soundlessly and hard to see as shadows out onto the flats and toward the Tartar camp.

In no time at all, no matter how hard I strained my eyes, they were invisible off there in the dark. I found out later that they'd split up just outside the camp. They figured that way, sooner or later, somebody would get a shot at Kharlagawl.

Then, after what seemed a hundred years or so, I saw a big man stand up by that central fire and tent. Just from his size I guessed it might be Kharlagawl. Then there was the sound of a distant rifle shot and the big man fell down.

All hell broke loose instantly down there, and at that moment a large dark cloud completely blotted out the moon, making the night as dark as a bat's wing. From out there on the flats there were the mingled sounds of men screaming, guns going off, and running hooves thudding against the ground. The only sound that stopped was the beating of the drum.

Finally I saw a deeper shadow materialize on the dark flats and realized it was a man running swiftly toward me. When he was about fifty feet away I knew from his size and shape that it was Nick, and racing after him was a Tartar on horseback. Just guessing more than aiming, I pointed my rifle and fired and the Tartar disappeared off the suddenly rearing horse. A moment later I stood up as Nick got to me.

There were some other dim, running figures farther along at the top of the slope and then the sounds of many horses galloping toward us.

"Back!" Nick said.

I hesitated, straining to see in the dark, but as the charging horses came nearer, Nick grabbed my elbow and spun me back and down on the slope.

"Now!"

And we ran like hell.

Going downhill, especially in the dark, my speed tended to get out of control. I almost went sprawling down half a dozen times, and then the cloud passed away from the bright moon, which helped a little. From below, now able to see, our men started shooting to discourage the Tartars behind us on the slope.

My lungs bursting, I sped down to the edge of the breastwork, and I was going so fast there was no way in the world to put on any brakes. So I just lunged on over and went rolling down into the hollow.

Nick landed right-side up, but the jar of it damnere broke both of his legs. When I got up and we stepped back to the breastwork Chakko was just leaping down, and even that tireless Indian was out of breath.

Looking up the moonlit slope, Slim said, "Cover 'im!"

Another shadowy figure was running down towards us, a bunch of Tartar horsemen behind him. Slim and the others put some rounds into the Tartars. Two of them went down and the others backed off.

The man racing down the hill was almost to us, and from his size and build, and that flowing, cougar grace, I knew it was Shad.

But for just that minute, I'd forgotten how much alike Shad and Rostov were.

And it was the captain.

Rostov leaped down beside us and I said, "Where's Shad?"

He frowned at me, and then we all looked back up the slope, but there was nothing moving on it.

"Likely," Slim said, "he's just layin' low out there somewheres."

"No." Chakko said finally and quietly. "He shot Kharlagawl." Chakko was having real trouble going on. "The sound a' his gun brought 'em to 'im."

"You saw?" I said.

Chakko nodded.

"An' ya' didn't go t' *help* 'im?"

Chakko shook his head. There was no fear in his face, or guilt. Just common sense and sorrow. Then, slowly, he turned and walked away.

That left the rest of us just standing there silently, looking off at nothing, or maybe looking at the ground. Looking at anything but each other.

And then the drum started again.

Finally Rostov said, "Levi?"

I just looked at him. I didn't yet feel quite up to saying "What?"

"Would you like every man here to mount up and charge that Tartar camp, on the possibility that we may still be able to help Shad?"

He meant it, and it was the hardest question anybody ever asked me. But after a long time I managed to say. "No."

And Slim said in a low, gruff voice, "If them Tartars didn't kill us, Shad would."

Looking far up the slope now, Nick muttered something in Russian to Rostov.

At the distant top of the slope some Tartars were doing something, but even with the bright moonlight it was too far away to tell what.

Watching them, and listening to the boom of the Tartar drum, Slim muttered, "One thing. Losin' their boss don't seem to've slowed 'em down much."

Rostov's face became very hard, and he started to do a strange thing. He took two cartridges out of his belt, and for the second time that I knew of, he bit on a lead slug and pulled it out of its brass cartridge case. And then, similarly, he took the slug out of the other one.

Either he knew damn well, or he'd guessed

damn well what the Tartars at the top of the slope were up to. For now a fire was lighted up there. The fire was all around a big post stuck in the ground, and Shad was tied onto the post.

Without even thinking about it, I started charging up over the breastwork to get to him. And then, for the only time in his life, Slim hit me. His big fist caught me alongside the head, and *damn* he could hit. I was flat on my back and still groggy as Slim leaned down to give me a hand back up again.

"You can't help 'im, Levi," he said in a toneless voice. "He'd be burned b'fore ya' could get up there to 'im."

And then, as my head got itself more together, I realized what Rostov was doing.

He was overloading one cartridge case, putting additional powder into it from the second one. That's one way of making a real long shot, if you know what you're doing.

Then, as the flames grew rapidly around Shad, the distant drum stopped and there was complete silence.

Nick said flatly, "They are quiet. So we hear his screams."

In a low voice that was almost a whisper Old Keats said, "That'll be the day."

God knows what they'd already done to him by then, but Shad was still awake and aware enough to know everything that was going on. And from where he was, on that high post, he could pretty much see all around. Then, as the flames were halfway up around his body, he didn't scream, but he sure as hell yelled, his roaring voice carrying all the way down the slope and to our ears.

"The *arroyo!*" His thundering far-off voice was dim but clear. "Use the *herd!*"

And then, as the fire raged higher around his body, Rostov took careful, steady aim and fired.

It was an impossible, and perfect, shot. It went right through Shad's heart and stopped the searing pain of the fire.

And in the silence that followed, a far-distant, low rumble began.

"They're chargin' upon us down through the arroyo," Slim said. "They'll be down on us in a couple a' minutes."

Rostov slowly, so very slowly, now lowered his rifle. And it was as if he was now both a cowboy and a cossack, for he'd surely read Shad's thoughts more clearly than any man ever could without having witnessed first hand the power of a longhorn stampede.

Almost softly, he said, "They're going to be faced with more than five hundred enemies. Slim, Levi, get out that last keg of powder!"

So in about one minute, under Rostov's directions, it came to pass that we were ready. Natcho and Crab goaded Old Fooler part way into the arroyo, and a few of the other head sort of followed along, wondering where everybody was going. And Slim and I had spilled that final keg of gunpowder out in a long, thick little mound that stretched like an explosive string along the flat land behind the herd.

We were all asaddle. Nick was looking after Kirdyaga, and Shiny was helping to hold Link aboard, and nobody else needed any help.

From the front part of the hollow Rostov yelled, "Light it!" and I struck a match and tossed it down at the end of that long string of powder.

I never saw such a damn thing. That powder roared like something living and, without actually hurting anything, sent rolling sheets of booming flame blasting high into the air.

Buck and I were the closest ones to it and Buck, in terror, almost reared over sideways to escape the horrifying thing.

And the cattle felt the same instant terror that Buck did. All they needed was some place to go.

Old Fooler had been madder than hell for days anyway. And all the recent fighting hadn't helped his temper. So since it was the easiest escape route there was, he took off up that arroyo like a speeding one-ton cannon ball, and every bull and cow in the whole outfit elected instantly to follow his lead.

Within the few seconds it took me to get Buck back to normal, that herd was spilling into that arroyo like a tidal wave.

I raced Buck to where Rostov was, and we galloped on up the right side of the arroyo, speeding along its rim.

Our riders were strung out at dead runs on both ridges of the arroyo, with the herd thundering at full speed below us and between us.

The Tartars were expecting to get right to us by charging down the arroyo. That way, instead of having that long, deadly run down the slope, they'd be able to burst right out upon us.

And their own massive charge must have been making so much noise that they didn't hear the answering thunder coming back at them until it was too late.

From above, it was some kind of an encounter to watch. The leading Tartars galloped around a bend in the arroyo and saw Old Fooler and his gang shaking the earth as they came at them.

Those leading Tartars had very few choices. With all the close riders behind them they couldn't stop or go back, so the best they could do was immediately try to climb the steep walls of the arroyo, which didn't work.

Old Fooler and the longhorns behind him stampeded into them like a huge iron locomotive slamming full speed through the front parlor of a house of cards, smashing the small ponies and their riders to pieces.

The crushing, thunderous disaster lasted maybe five minutes, and then Old Fooler and the herd busted wildly out of the arroyo and up onto the far flats, not quite realizing, or giving a damn, that the battle was over and that they'd won a hands-down victory. So they just kept on running for about ten miles.

Frankly, I don't know how any of those Tartars in the arroyo survived, but some of them did. And on the flats beyond there were a few small, sporadic fights.

Three Tartars came upon Slim and Sammy, and Sammy put his arm in the way of a sword being swung at Slim. They killed one of the Tartars, or maybe two, and that was the end of that. But Slim told him something as we were quickly tying off the bleeding in Sammy's arm. "Ya' know Sammy," he said, "the way ya' stretched your arm out, it was kinda — like a fella swimmin'."

Sammy liked that. And I did too.

Next morning we caught up with Old Fooler

and most of the herd. They were standing around munching grass and staring off into space with bored expressions, as though nothing exciting ever happened in their lives, and they were getting a little fed up with it all.

It took most of the rest of that day to round up the scattered wandering cows, and then, rather than retrace our steps, we headed straight on toward Bakaskaya.

It was the second day that we ran into the five hundred men from Bakaskaya. One of the two cossacks, Dmitri, had gotten through, and they were headed back toward us as fast as they could make it.

Seeing them come toward us in the distance, Old Keats said very quietly, "Three days too late. A thousand years too late."

Somehow I found myself saying, "No, Keats. They're on time. Just tryin' t' be makes it so."

Old Keats looked at me for a long, quiet moment. "Yes. Sometimes your heart can get someplace b'fore the rest of ya' can."

Then, with a few of the hands to help them, that big bunch of fellas took the herd on the last little ways to Bakaskaya, for it was surely safe now.

And the rest of us rode back.

I'd expected a hell of a mess back there around the flats and the hollow. But it's funny how fast the world takes care of things. From a mile away, your eyes couldn't tell you for sure that anything had ever happened there.

The Tartars who had lived through it had stripped the place of everything in the way of weapons or clothes they could use.

The only things that were left were bodies, too many bodies to bury. And it sure hit hard how little use a body really is. Without life and breath and spirit in it, it's worth no more than the ground it's lying on. We left them for their flying gravediggers, the vultures.

The only thing they hadn't touched was what was left of Shad. When we cut him down, I was reminded, like Rufe had been, of Mushy fixing all our boots. He'd done a real good job on Shad's, and I hated to see those good boots scorched and burned into nearly nothing but blackened ashes.

It was the damnedest thing how nobody had to say one word, in the silence of all that earth and all that sky.

We knew that he should be buried right there, and some of us dug a good, deep grave with straight sides. Then, still silently, we wrapped him gently in a warm blanket and lowered him down.

There was one more small thing that had to be done. So I got down beside him and pulled the blanket a little away from his eyes and his face. He just had to be able to see.

And there was one more thing I didn't know about, that was even more important, that had yet to be done.

Looking down at Shad, Rostov slowly took out his great saber. He drew the blade's sharp edge across his arm so that the last blood on it would be his own.

Then he put the saber back in its scabbard, and I thought there would be nothing more.

But there was.

Rostov now unbuckled the belt that held his saber. Then slowly and very gently, he put both the belt and saber down beside Shad.

Then we started slowly to fill the grave, and still not one word had been spoken.

But much has been said.

Final Notes

FROM THE DIARY
OF
LEVI DOUGHERTY

Looking back at the way we finally got home to Montana, I guess the most unusual thing about it is that we did it sort of backwards.

We spent a week or so in Bakaskaya, and the two or three thousand men, women and children who made up that small fortress of free cossacks took us in and treated us as their own.

But when it came to go, they were afraid for us to head back by way of Khabarovsk and Vladivostok. Both Tartars and the Tzar's men might be laying for us back there. And even if we weren't killed or thrown in jail, but just delayed, winter was coming on and the port of Vladivostok was often froze up solid for months.

So, all in all, it was agreed that we'd just keep heading more or less west. Thinking about it for the first time, that struck me as a funny kind of a thing. A fella leaves home and he doesn't necessarily ever have to turn around and retrace his steps to go back. If he goes in one straight line far enough, why there he'll be one day right smack back home.

If a man anyplace in the world holds up two fingers, then they're as close together as, say, two fingers. But if you move outward from one finger and keep going that way, then the most far away thing in the world, finally, is that other finger that's been right next to it all the time.

A second thing that should have surprised me, but somehow didn't, was the fact that Old Keats decided not to go with us, but to stay. They'd told us all that Bakaskaya was our home, and they'd meant it. They'd put Keats up in Lieutenant Bruk's room, and that room was a lot like Bruk himself, open and spacious, yet somehow warm and comfortable at the same time, with a fireplace and a couple of big chairs and one whole wall full of books that Keats was just starting to be able to read.

When Old Keats told Slim and me and the others about his decision to stay, his voice was low and a little gruff. And then he said, "Hell, what'd I do back there anyway, except waste away m' last years associatin' with the likes a' you. Here I c'n spend some time teachin'. An' I c'n help them look after the herd an' gradually build it up." He hesitated. "So don't argue."

Finally, just as quietly, Slim said a thing that

was already fairly apparent by our silence. "Nobody's arguin', Keats." And then, even more quietly, he added, "But that sure don't mean that ya' won't be sorely missed."

When it came time to go, and Old Keats and I faced each other alone for the last time, we were both hard put for words.

Finally, choosing from among a thousand hours of things I wanted to tell him, I said, "I like your poem."

After a moment he said, "Each man is his own poem, Levi. Keep yours a good one."

And that's about all we could manage, except for a hard hug, and then I went away.

But in leaving Bakaskaya, there was one argument we flat out lost. Rostov said that he, Igor, Nick and every other cossack who'd been with us before were going to take us safe out of Russia. We were going clear to Odessa, on the Black Sea, and on the map it looked like about a million miles. And also, being outlaws from the Tzar, they would be in real danger.

We tried to stop them from coming with us, but we had about as much chance as the night stopping the sun from coming up.

Being free, well-mounted horsemen, with spare mounts and nothing to hold us up, we made good, fast time every day and every week and finally every month. But that was one long haul. Somebody later figured out that from Bakaskaya to Odessa was hell of a lot farther than a trip clear across the whole United States.

Early in the trip, about two weeks out, we passed the biggest lake I'd ever seen, called Baykal. It could have been an ocean as far as I was concerned. And camping along the shore, Rostov told us a staggering thing about it. "They've estimated," he said, "that with its size and depth, when a drop of water enters Lake Baykal at the north, it takes four hundred years before it comes out at the south."

"Christ," Crab muttered, "I never even thought of a drop a' water *lastin'* that long."

But still, somehow, that one drop of water surely was something to think on.

A couple of months later, the Siberian winter started to thunder down out of the north like a white, cold enemy as big as the whole sky. But by then we were starting to move south and west out of the toughest winter weather. Farther up north and east, Rostov told us, it often hit seventy below, and the sap freezing inside a tree would sometimes break that tree in half with a cracking roar like a cannon going off.

The weather was bad enough where we were though, and if your forehead started to sweat a little from hard riding, it wouldn't be long before you had icicles on your eyebrows. One time when I was complaining about that very thing, and rubbing ice from around my eyes, Igor shrugged and said, "There is a saying, Levi, that one Siberian summer is worth ten Siberian winters."

And miserably cold as I was just then, thinking of all the beautiful land and weather we'd gone through with the herd, whoever made up that saying had a point.

Finally we crossed the southern tip of the Ural Mountain range, which is really nothing much more than foothills that somehow got called mountains, and we headed more southernly than before.

In the next little while the weather changed a whole lot for the better, and within two or three weeks we came into sight of the Black Sea. I don't know who named it, because it wasn't black or even dark at all, but was as blue as some kind of a sky that God had accidentally made out of water.

Our Sea Papers were still in order, and we got aboard a boat at Odessa. We had to change boats four or five times to get to Philadelphia finally, going through strange-sounding seas like the Marmara and Aegean, and then the Mediterranean, which took us out beyond the Rock of Gibraltar and into the Atlantic. From

Philadelphia, we took a train, and that was the end of the trip.

Nobody got killed along that long way, but we still lost some men.

Natcho got enamored of a Spanish lady while we were laying over in Málaga. He decided, with that gleaming smile of his, that he was more Spanish than Mexican anyway, and that's the last we saw of him.

We lost three more in Philadelphia. Link, whose arm still didn't work and maybe never would, went to Georgia to see some family. He told Shiny he'd show up later at the Slash-Diamond, but he never did. And Sammy the Kid and Rufus just decided they liked the town and were going to stay on for a while. Though what they ever saw in Philadelphia, I don't know.

The last one we lost, which came as a shock, was Chakko. We had a layover in Denver, and a couple of promoters got him drunk and signed him up to be part of a traveling show. He was billed as "The Only Living Ogallala Sioux to Ever Completely Encompass the Globe." For ten dollars a week he was supposed to do some trick shooting with his bow and arrows and say a few lines to the people. From what we later heard, Chakko did fine with the bow and arrows but had a habit of forgetting his lines in front of the audience and filling in with "Fuck it!" instead, which must have been kind of disconcerting.

So the way it was, six of the original fifteen in our greasy-sack outfit got back to the Slash-Diamond Ranch after a good more than a year of being gone. There was Big Yawn, Purse, Crab, Shiny, Slim and me.

But all that long trip back, the part I remember best is on the hills looking down at Odessa and the Black Sea, where the cossacks finally took their leave. It was too risky for them to come right down into town with us.

We were all kind of shook up about this final parting, knowing that in those vast distances that would lie between us, none of us would likely ever see or hear about any of the others again. It was one of those times when not one word you say is right, and yet somehow, every word is.

After we'd had a few drinks and made a few quiet toasts, Slim said to the cossacks, "One more thing. We all talked it over, an' we're gonna be jugglin' around on different boats an' God knows what all." He paused. "So no matter whether ya' like it or not, we're stickin' you fellas with our string a' horses."

There was a dead silence.

That string included Shad's big Red, my

Buck, Slim's Charlie, Natcho's Diablo, Purse's Vixen, even Dixie's Shiloh, and a bunch more of the best horses that ever put hoof to ground.

Finally, in that silence, I said. "They're f'r Bakaskaya. Just two horses're nailed down. Shad's Red is Rostov's. An' my Buck is yours, Igor."

Igor could hardly talk, but he managed to say, "You gave me a fine horse already."

Feeling the same way that Igor was, I said, "Can't ya' give a good man somethin' twice?"

Rostov stepped to Red and rubbed his forehead and muzzle gently. Then he came back to us. Reaching down into his shirt, he took off the leather thong he wore there, with the small leather pouch that held a handful of earth from Bakaskaya.

And he handed it to me.

Then the others slowly did the same. Nick gave his to Slim, and Igor handed his to Crab. There were eleven cossacks and eleven cowboys left, so it worked out exactly right. And, sometimes, a handful of earth can be worth more than a good horse.

One last thing that Rostov said to me before we went away. "I spoke to you of chess, and of life, one time before, Levi."

"Yes, sir?"

"In chess, every piece can be killed and taken

from the board except the king." He put his hand on my shoulder. "And it is so in life. A man who is truly a king never dies."

We looked at each other for a long moment.

He was thinking of Shad.

And I was thinking of both of them.